JEWEL E. DEARMAN

Unyielding Bronze

TO: KEMP

Blessings are always upon as.

God Is Good

Jewel E Dearman

DARKLOVE PUBLISHING
Dallas, Texas

This is a work of fiction.

ATTENTION ORGANIZATIONS:
Quantity discounts available on bulk purchases of this book for fundraising. For information, please write:

DARKLOVE PUBLISHING
P.O. Box 1662
Dallas, TX 75221

or call 214-421-1167 or 800-943-4615 PIN 65.

Library of Congress Catalog Card Number: 97-094584

Dearman, Jewel E.
Unyielding Bronze by Jewel E. Dearman

ISBN 0-9661361-9-5

Printed in the United States of America

Front Cover Artist:
Tommie Smith Lintz

ACKNOWLEDGEMENTS

To my God and Saviour, my number one hero, whom I give all my credit.

To my lovely wife Gerri for coping with all my litter on the dining room table; truly grateful for sharing each others love.

To my editor, Ella Spigner who elegantly gives her opinion and certainly receives my deepest appreciation.

To Phyllis Otto, goes many, many thanks for converting my bad writing into type.

To a special and wonderful group of beautiful women in the DW Mind Travelers Reading Group; Praise the Lord for these lovely ladies who currently tolerate me as their lone male member. Namely, they are: Yolanda Adams, Venita Allen, Sandra Barber, Marilyn Calhoun, Wanda Kay Davis, Gerri Dearman, Geraldene Dews, Paula Watkins Morgan, Phyllis Otto, Juanita M. Simmons, Cynthia Sorey, Ella Spigner, Sharon Warren, Marion Willard, Debbie Williams, Virginia Williams, Vivica Wilson.

To Nancy Albert Brembry who sends prayers on top of more prayers.

To Denise McCarthy and Debbie Borke at Madame X Typography. Thanks for putting your heart into it!

To the other Unyielding Bronze women, who sometimes seek to, but most notably, arbitrarily make a positive difference in the lives of people by their mere presence.

To the brothers in this predicament; compromising an unyielding position with patience.

DEDICATION

To mother and father who are smiling on me from above; Alma Gossett Dearman and Ceasar Bradford Dearman.

Unyielding Bronze

PREFACE

Nowhere else but this Texas-Mexican town could so many bronze figures interwine, within an urban setting, so satiated with passion. Lives enraptured with self; yet glowing beyond the darkened shadows in their path. It was the same as the sun blazed its warmth, regardless of season, through a mighty bough to touch a sapling underneath its fledging branches. Melting and blending that gives way to the sprouting of new life, without a great deal of sacrifice. If you will, sort of a live and let live, waving of the banner. Native soil, we find, grows transplants, either blown—wind-aided or flown—bird-aided; the same as it would its own. Seeds sank in and take advantage of the newly but rich cultivation. Here, they thrive and mingle; work and play; wander and seduce. San Antonio has its share of migrants, all seeking to improve their lot in life; looking for a warm and friendly habitat to sink in. Looking for a warm and caring heart to welcome them aboard.

Victor and Samantha and, well, baby Stacy were three of those sailing into town in their red shiny 1954 Studebaker-Champion. The ideal young family, with new careers and an eagerness to make an impact upon their comfortable setting. The caliber of people you want to live next door to. Neighbors, welcomed to your community, even if little Stacy made a bike trail across your yard. Small feet trampling on grass is never the same as the mailman. Afterall, she is as cute as your broken flower, in her jar, to accommodate the orange and black butterfly. Yes, there is something about newness that adds vibrancy to the heart. This happy couple had success written across their brows; though their laughter formed those independent victory lines. Nevertheless, a new age was materializing and the new woman had a right to assert herself.

If newness add vibrancy, then age add creativity; and nowhere was that to be found more succinctly, than with Grandma—Hattie Lincoln. Creativity in the sense that we are talking about society - nouveau riche - which is simply different from the uppity-make believe - bourgeois—wannabe's, we are accustomed to. Grandma

transformed the city when she arrived because, not one residence
was used to a brazen bronze figure with so much wealth. Grandma
had her mansion and all the trimmings, though it mattered only to
the degree of Angela. Angela, the heart and darling of our story,
was a beautiful black-eyed, offspring. If the sun rose at all—it
rose because of Angela—as far as grandma was concerned (beauty
often captivates others); it had nothing to do with being selfish—
it was called taking care of your own. And Angela was truly
something special to take care of; she grew into the finest cultured
young lady this side of the Magnolia orchards. Thanks, in part to
grandma and....well....we shall see. Angela, of couse, was a dream
come true. Without Angela, the story would have been a dull happening—an incidence of no significant importance. She was
mature in an era of older counterparts. If there is one thing
respected in youth—it is maturity—especially beautiful youth.
Angela was naive enough to know that everyone—should have
their space—and be treated right in the chivalrous human sense
of the word. She obviously, as Victor thought, certainly had some
southern hospitality in her breeding.

And speaking of hospitality, Carolyn was welcomed to the city
by her corporation; the same one that welcomed Victor, years earlier. Every love story, I suppose, needs a Carolyn for one purpose or
the other. For love, she was tough and assertive and a fascinating
piece of flesh. Fine was the word—real fine—especially looking
through the eyes of Victor. A bronze statue indeed—she stood tall.
Carolyn is what one would refer to as flavor—spice, a dot of this—
a dash of that. If a place functioned well before Carolyn's arrival,
it operated better afterward. She was smart, but it had more to do
with what she physically brought to the table. Women like Carolyn
generally opens up a man's thought process and simultaneously
shut down his mental capacity to perceive the obvious. Therefore,
his brain curvet to a higher plane, indicative more so by the body's
blood flow. Carolyn's migration to the city added zest for sure. You
knew Carolyn was there and if she wanted you; there was no
escaping the eroticism generated from her seductive fangs.
Characterized rightly so, as a sweet and gentle spider which could

devour you; and leave you loving her; because in the end, she was still your best friend. Love meant a lot to her, but it was out of convenience and only convenience that mattered most.

In every city, there is, or should be a native to welcome all. For this story, Helen is that caring individual. A nurse and later a doctor by profession; Helen abundantly gives her all, because she cares. Without Helen, this book would never have existed. We are talking about the backbone of humanitarianism. Helen touched ones heart the way Carolyn touched ones body. Helen knew how to love, but she showed her love more by caring. As we shall see, Helen touched the lives of all those, fortunate enough to grace her presence. A Texan by birth whose parentage origin was not exactly known; but it mattered not to Helen, because she knew the direction in which she was headed. Helen found love, rather late in childhood, in a "mama and papa" that really cared (two elderly sisters). If predestination is real—Helen is real. Her reason for being exemplify the greatest in the worse of us visitors to this planet. Helen was not a doormat, she simply embraced you.

This story primarily evolves and revolves around Victor, whose life was truly affected. He found that, loving was caring; and as always, when time goes by, things change, and so do people as they grow and mature. And Tiffani was there to help nurture him with needed consultation. She had her own thing going on, seemingly a secret thing, all to herself, but she was Victor's daytime arm to lean on, most of the time. Victor was the story's life blood, and without him, these events never happens for your reading pleasure.

CHAPTER ONE

SEPARATE WAYS

After a splendid dinner entreé, there is no finer way to cap it off, than sipping a superb cup of hot coffee; good conversation with a true friend; and an enticing delicious dessert; be it occasionally sentimental. Samantha and Victor find themselves, interestingly enough, into the middle of their second cup. Samantha's hand-ground Brazilian coffee-beans, which so often reminds her of Victor's smooth dark skin, were brewed skillfully into an ebony hue; poured lovingly as a golden cappuccino roast; was a cup certainly worth the devoted attention its maker had laboriously given it.

Their stomachs were rounded into conformation with a main course via braised leg of lamb. Two tender portions graced the tongue of Victor; a good hearty eater when it came to such succulent nourishment. Samantha, an excellent cook had graciously prepared her true friend an evening meal appropriately fitting. She was fully aware of Victor's gigantic appetite, approving of the manner he happily devoured what was before him, with watchful eyes upon his dining techniques. The use of his fingers combined with his mouth and tongue synchronization let Samantha know, Victor's fondness for her food. Samantha loved watching Victor eat her pleasantries. Now, however, Samantha and Victor simply sat at the candle lit dining room table having a wholesome conversation and sipping that wonderful café au lait.

"I feel funny saying this, and excuse me Victor if I sound awful; but I feel good now that we have decided on a divorce." Taking a sip of coffee, staring straight ahead across the table.

"I understand Samantha, good is not exactly my description though, mine is more like–burdenless." Showing an open palm to Samantha.

"Well that too Victor!" And they both laughed.

"What are you going to do with all that free time Samantha? A little more sugar in my cup please."

"Oh, I decided on that the other day, write another book, which has been on my mind for sometime now. What about you Victor?"

"Well, you know I got this new position and it involves more traveling. Incidentally I got a big promotion and some megabucks, of which a great portion will be sent your way, Samantha."

"That is not necessary, Victor, of course I will not turn it down. Are you trying to make me feel guilty Victor, you have already agreed to take care of Stacy, pay for her college and all."

"Yeah, if she ever decides to stay in one." Both laughed.

"That is the God's truth, Victor. Can you imagine who she got that laziness from? Remember, we jokingly talked about that a while back, I believe there may be some truth to what I told you."

"Yeah, the family thing might have some merit, but there is probably more to it than that. You are the psyche doctor Samantha, I thought you would have psyched Stacy into some-thing by now."

"The girl is a tough case Victor. My latest theory has to do with Stacy's instability relating to the fact of being an only child."

"Now, that is one for the books Samantha. Look at us, we were "the only child", and we did not hop from college to college."

"True Victor, but we had each other, we grew up with each other all of our lives. There was never a time you and I were not together; fussing and fighting; pushing and shoving; hugging and kissing. We were sister and brother. So you see it was not the same. Stacy had no other children in her life, only adults. You and me and all those grandparents, not to mention the godparents."

"Samantha, are you saying adults gave our child, Stacy, her

instability! That is the most ridiculous thing I have heard to date."
Laughing hard. "That one is worse than the family theory."

"Laugh if you want to Victor, but psychologically, anything is possible."

"Yes, I know, but that seems to be stretching it to me. Do you realize, you are blaming yourself, or you and me really, for not having a bunch of babies running around the house. There was a discussion, it seems, like a hundred years ago now, when Stacy was born, whether we would have more children. Our decision, I thought, as I do now was a good one. The way to get ahead in life, we both agreed Samantha, was not to have a house full of children."

"That was then Victor, this is now. We did not know up from down in those days; and you must admit, we were controlled by old folks and their thinking. They told us not to have a bunch of brats hanging onto our skirt tails; that cotton picking times and farming was a day gone bye-bye; and we just did not need all those members in a family to do hard work, which would no longer be there."

"What are you talking about Samantha; those old folks you are talking about were our parents."

"What I am talking about Victor is they were looking at what was good for us–you and me–in terms of getting ahead in life. And that was fine, but no one, not even you and me thought of what was good for the child–our child–Stacy. Do you follow me man!"

"Don't get an attitude Samantha, I follow your logic, but it is still a bit fuzzy to me."

"Oh everything is fuzzy to you Victor!" Both laughing. "Age has deposited a few cobwebs on your brain."

"Maybe! Anyway, look at the money I am not throwing away if Stacy does not stay in college Samantha."

"Is that why you freely agreed to support her Victor? Thinking about saving a buck or two. My, my, talking about a skinflint."

"No, I am sincere Samantha. Even if Stacy does not stay in college, I will not save any money, because I have decided to give it to you. Let us be thankful Stacy is at least in school for now."

"Victor, you are really a good man, it is too bad we cannot be anything but friends."

"What do you mean, anything but friends?"

"I did not mean it like friends are suppose to be a weak link Victor. We will be friends forever, I am sure; the part of lovers accidentally crept into my brain. I guess, what I am saying is, the next woman that gets you is going to be one lucky or fortunate person, whoever she is. By the way, have you had any more of those dreams lately? And before you say anything, Victor, dream girl or not, she will still not be as fortunate as myself; because we are true friends, and that runs deep." A tear falls from Samantha's hazel eyes and whimpering begins.

Victor immediately set his cup of coffee on the mahogany table, moving over swiftly to embrace and console his greatest friend. His true friend. Could it be that Samantha is having some regrets about their long and fruitful marriage ending. Yes, their marriage of twenty three years, by agreement, was coming to an end. Samantha Lundenberry Previtt, a tall beautiful, tan complexioned woman and Victor Previtt; a tall handsome, masculine figure, sporting a gray moustache to match the streaking silver over his ears; had known each other all of their lives, counting forties for each of them. So we can see why it is difficult to sit and have a simple cup of coffee, without getting sentimental. Their lives are interwoven, they are reflections of the other. And as Samantha said, "their friendship runs deep." You can separate their residence, as Victor had already moved, you can separate their minds, but there would never be a way of separating their friendship, which ran deep inside their hearts. It almost seems a shame to see it happen. Whose brilliant idea was it anyway? Samantha and Victor had agreed to never before leave the other unhappy at any time, even if it meant staying together overnight. This was just one of their cozy-intimate survival pacts; there are more. This couple realized that life is about happiness, and a divorce is not suppose to change that.

It is late in the evening, the wintry degrees of the now hidden sun has it a bit cool, so Samantha and Victor elect to spend the night together. Samantha's emotionalism perhaps. Their customary bedtime whirlpool bath together found them laughing and reminiscing as they soaked. Facing each other in the warm soapy water was more than soothing as they seriously massaged each other's toes and thighs before sitting behind each other to massage the other's shoulders and body. Victor's strong arms relaxed Samantha when she pulled them around her, falling tightly backward into his chest, letting her cheeks gently touch his. Samantha lay still, thinking how she was going to miss this nightly treatment. Her body always felt the better after emerging and tonight was no different.

"Victor, while you are holding me so securely tonight–whatever you're doing or whomever, dream girl or what–don't forget, you promised to be with me and celebrate my fiftieth birthday."

"That's a ways off, but, I'll keep the promise Samantha, don't worry about it."

"I just want to keep it fresh on your mind, Victor."

"Yeah Samantha, I gathered that much, worried about me going senile I suppose. Oops, hand me that soap!"

How well did Samantha know, her fiftieth birthday was a ways off, and that too, was part of her problem. A feeling of anxiety and apprehension tugged and pulled, rolling the number fifty, deep within her twisted insides. She wanted so much to discuss this with Victor, now that they were going their separate ways, the importance of that birthday celebration. The timing however, somehow did not seem right. Troubling as it was, Samantha thought, "she would have to wait," and on the verge of another tear, she inaudibly suppressed her natural feelings, handing Victor the floating bar of soap.

"No, not at all Victor, not as long as you can soothe my body like this."

They dried each other off and afterwards, Victor lotioned her entire body. Talking about feeling good; Victor's hands felt as though they were made of velvet. Whatever else generally took place after the massaging and lotioning, always led to a restful dessert–connoisseur–delight night, and tonight was no exception, as their nude bodies formed one; for whatever. A restful night. Morning's light still found them clenched together like a tight fist, which had been in a bare knuckles fight. There were a few noticeable bruises and intimate raw spots, not necessarily observeable. Samantha's eyes, of course, no longer were filled with moisture, but glowed with a cheery brightness. Victor completed his stay, serving Samantha breakfast in bed, later throwing her a kiss from hand to lips, upon leaving for home, pleasantly exhausted. Mindfully now, we are talking about friendship that "was deep".

Samantha, a Ph.D. and owner of her own psychological consulting firm, decided prior to Victor's leaving, today was too good for a work day. Victor's financial reassurance support, she thought, made this a perfect day for leisure. After all, her appointment book had a rare blank page, and the new corporate contract was more than a month away. And Victor's statement, "I am too full for breakfast, after last night", reminded Samantha of an electrifying explosion, not the words per sé, but, last night. So, for the first time ever in her life, today's date would carry no planned agenda, things would just happen. Samantha ease the lap-tray to the floor and slide her gorgeous nakedness between Victor's favorite satin sheets. Performance in her opinion was so much better on this smooth gliding surface. Samantha thought, "the sheets results alone was almost enough to ensure one's security within themselves." Victor's masculine scent was still there filtering through Samantha's nostrils, and into her sensitive body, especially her tender breasts, now held in place with her left wrist and maneuvering fingers, and the tingling sensation vibrating under her right hand at the thighs juncture. There was a wetness present, evident from last night, which guided Samantha's manipulative fingers easily into and on her intended targets. There would be no relaxation now, until a new sensational wetness appeared.

For some reason, since their decision to vacate matrimony, Samantha's nature rose and flowed freer. She was not ashamed and had told Victor about her recently self-serving actions following his visits. Of course, Victor's response had been a large smile with a comment, "explain it to yourself, you're the doctor." He was secure enough to know, it had nothing to do with his performance. Samantha was reminded of his words, "your delicious sweetness always has me full when I leave here." Samantha and Victor had discussed being together for a week on a non-stop basis to solve Samantha's puzzling problem. A barrage of love making on a constant level, they felt might just be the answer. The funniest thing about this to Victor was, "the psychological doctor has a problem that a poor layman can cure; if you need me for a week, honey, just holler." This brings us to another one of their cozy–intimate

survival pacts; spending unlimited time with the other, if loneliness, all inclusive becomes overbearing. Samantha felt a week or
more might be unnecessary, but told Victor she loved this pact
because it meant she would never be totally without. Plus, she
said "a smart person never closes extraordinary options."

Samantha was now thinking about how nice Victor was as a
human being; he was so loving and so caring. His substantial
financial support to her one time ailing business had enabled her
to succeed with peace of mind. Now that it was no longer needed,
Victor still gave Samantha excessive amounts of money. Yes, all of
Samantha's morning thoughts of Victor were all good, which
almost gets us to the point of begging the question: Why in the
hell are they divorcing? Part of that answer obviously lies in the
new ecstatic wetness, Samantha is now experiencing in her hands.
Freer flowing freedom and freedom flowing freer: Sweet-slip-
peryseepagesoiling-satin sheets. When Samantha would tell Victor
of the abundant supply he missed, he merely said, "it was not
there, but let me know the week." Samantha's thoughts continued
on how fortunately she was to have a true friend like Victor, when
the phone rang.

"Why hello Stacy!"

"Hi mother, is father there?"

"No–no, should he be?"

"Well, I tried to call him late last night and early this morning,
without reaching him. He told me to try your place whenever that
happened."

"Oh I see, well you just missed him. Is there something urgent
or something I can help you with Stacy?"

"Well not really–I sort of wanted to talk."

"Oh, I see, well I am listening Stacy."

"He is probably at work now, maybe I can reach him there
Mother."

"Stacy!"

"Okay, Mother, but promise me, you will not get upset."

"Is there anything wrong at school Stacy?"

"No, Mother, there is nothing wrong and I am making good
grades–it's just that–I do not like it here anymore. You would not
understand mother–but it is too country here at Prairie View. Or

maybe, I am just homesick, I don't know."

"Okay, I will tell Victor, we will see you at the end of the semester–in three weeks or so–right?"

"Mother, that is part of why, I am calling, I want to come home now."

"You what! Stacy, you need to get a grip on your life; you are getting entirely too old to continue this foolishness–."

"Mother, you promised not to get upset!"

"Okay, Stacy, I will tell Victor. You will not have to make another long distance phone call; when can we expect you?"

"This weekend mother, probably Sunday."

"Okay, I will tell Victor; say goodbye Stacy!"

Samantha hung up, repeating out loud, "I am not going to let that girl ruin my perfect day–I am not going to let that girl ruin my perfect day!" There was no use in prolonging her agony, she would call Victor immediately. Well, so much for a day of leisure, she thought.

"Hello Victor, could you stop by on your way home this evening?"

"Sure Samantha, what's up?"

"It is your daughter, dear, she wants me to tell you she is coming home this weekend."

"That is great Samantha, I was thinking about Stacy only moments earlier."

"For good Victor, I hope you were thinking about–for good, dear."

"For good! Samantha, you are kidding me!"

"Now–now dear, you promised not to get upset. Yes Victor, you heard me right–for good! Think of all the money you are not throwing away while she is here, dear."

"I hear your sarcasm, Samantha, that is not in the least bit funny!"

"Sorry, Victor but that girl makes me so mad. I was merely trying to find some humor for my satisfaction I suppose. Oh Victor, how is the new secretary working out?"

"Tiffani; not bad, different but not bad, and thanks by the way for sending her. I'll be able to tell you more later on. Are you going to prepare me another one of those delicious meals, Samantha?"

"Two days in a row, you are going to get spoiled again, Victor."

"Think about how I devour your delicious dessert, Samantha."

"You are on Victor, you sure know how to drive a good point home, very–very convincing I–might add."

Yes, it was true, Samantha's dessert, she called it her eboni creme pie, was both of their weaknesses. Victor loved eating it and Samantha's excitement came in watching him do so, much more than an ordinary dish. This is because Victor always held her pie in both hands, pulling it to his mouth, with his tongue hanging out. His technique was as if his lips had to be warned something good was about to enter. Once inside, however, Samantha could actually feel the swishing movement of the disappeared object. Each bite taken made her feel happier and happier that Victor loved eating her sweet stuff. Samantha received her greatest excitement, though, when Victor finished devouring the whole dessert, leaving the container absolutely clean, vowing to her, "I love eating your dessert so much that I could eat it everyday, you put it before me." That, she felt, was a true compliment coming from her true friend. And to think, it was only hours away before Victor would be there and once again gulp down her eboni creme pie or what he sometimes referred to as "his chocolate Samantha's creme delight", but here as of lately, Victor simply referred to such an ambrosial dual sweetness as Samantha's delicious dessert for compelling indulging reasons. The name mattered not to Samantha as long as both of them enjoyed the evening. An assumptive assessment; and be it as she lay, it was Samantha's widespread delicious dessert which now routinely plunged Victor, head on, to the depths of her gorgeous wedge-angled thighs, facing a luscious appetizing delicacy.

Enjoyed the evening they did, especially after Victor convinced Stacy, via telephone to complete the semester before coming home. Samantha told Victor that Stacy was about as conclusive on what she wants to do as those dreams he had been having. Samantha had been inquisitive of Victor's dreams two successive visits without a response, but there was no denying the shattering realization looming before him, one otherwise ordinary Saturday morning, several months later.

CHAPTER TWO

A DREAM COME TRUE

A FAIR MAIDEN

Who had seen
*   A maiden so fair*
She could pass
*   But did not dare*

Some say French
*   Other say White*
The blood 1/8, 1/10
*   She's Black alright*

What a complexion
*   A teasing tan*
This fair maiden
*   Gets any man*

She was not tall, but tall enough; slender but not skinny; but was unmistakably beautiful with a definite aristocratic look. It was the open air or freshness which she displayed. A refreshing lift you might say. Early, this warm autumn morning, there she stood mulling over an array of captivating flowers at the market place. Victor was looking for a potted plant for a friend and co-worker in the hospital, and she apparently was trying to decide what color mums to select. The radiance of her beauty blended with the flowers to form a perfect bouquet. A bouquet which once picked; would give a thousand fragrances and hours of joy to any dull hospital room.

The moment Victor laid eyes on her, he knew she was the one–Victor meant the girl in his dreams. You see–he had been dreaming about this girl; the same one always showed up. No special dream, but always the same girl. Now, here she stood looking at him with those marble black eyes. Eyes which twinkled and sparkled with the brilliance of polish upon her dainty fingers, caressing a promising bud. A set of eyes that smiled, putting Victor in a trance with each blink; and casting a spell upon what, now seemed like a spineless body. What could have happened a fairy or two ago had never before graced his presence.

A woman with the beauty and eloquence of a wind blown silken-scarf. Her brown hair was sheenful–bouncing gingerly upon her naked shoulders. Each strand danced to the tune played by her body's rhythm. Molded into white pants was a shapely figure of delicate proportion–gripping. A slim pointed nose hid between the blushiness cheeks on earth–a rosy red that leaped off the canvas of an artist's masterpiece. A full pair of moist lips surrounded her ivory white teeth. Specks of lipstick adorned the glistening teeth; and seemed to be saying, "I got in, please join me." Her smile, for sure, assisted in the warming of each God given day. "How could any woman be so beautiful, so early in the morning," thought Victor. He was somewhat startled, but felt he already knew her. He gazed imperceptibly at this beauty before allowing himself to utter a sound.

"Good morning, what brings you out so early." Victor spoke cheerfully.

"I am going to see my grandmother in the hospital. What color do you think I should get?"

"Well, what's her favorite color?"

"Green!"

"Both the flowers are green, so you can't go wrong there. So what color do you like?" said Victor.

"I like the purple ones but the yellow ones are gorgeous also."

"Get them both." said Victor wearing a very pleasant smile.

"But I would look funny going into the hospital with two plants."

"Okay, you get one and I'll get the other."

"This is fine, but grandmother does not know you."

"She will when you introduce me—I'm Victor Previtt, what's your name?"

"Angela Lincoln—but that is imposing on you."

"No, I'm going to the hospital anyway to see my friend, Angela."

"But you are a married man, Victor."

"How did you know?"

"I felt it, you are too caring, Victor."

"I don't mean anything Angela; excuse me if I offend you."

"No, it is all right, I just wanted to be sure we both know, Victor. I feel like I know you and I have never seen you before, Victor."

Her face slanted upward as those inquisitive eyes pierced Victor's.

"I'll explain something to you later Angela, shall I follow you in my car."

Victor put the plants in her Mustang convertible. As he followed, her hair sailed through the wind like a sweet melody —so soft, so smooth, and so soothing.

This girl had never appeared in any of Victor's dreams sexually or intimately, so he didn't think of her in that respect. But she was very appealing, saying girl because she looked to be every bit of twenty and Victor was every bit of forty seven. Victor smiled as he thought being labeled a dirty old man; but his dreams had labeled the girl. She was really better looking than the dreams portrayed, and mature indeed. Could luck of some sort be on Victor's side, because in all his years, he had never had a dream come true before. Victor tuned his radio on an easy FM station, and commence to daydream as he followed. Victor's mind spoke silently, "Where did she come from, and why we just happen to meet, and was on our way to the same hospital. A coincidence if ever there was one. I'm not going to get bogged down in all those thoughts and possibly ruin a perfectly good day or worse still, pinch myself and wake up."

Angela half melancholy, half buoyant, grinned warmly as her black eyes stole glances of Victor through the rear view mirror. This hunk of a man was already sending inspirational messages across the inner portion of her upper thighs. These roasty–toasty vibrations had Angela feeling the way she had longed for, in the presence of a man. A stimulative effect. An eagerness and willingness crept over Angela's body, without any hint of mind hindrance or denial. Certain creative urges forced all doubtful hesitation aside, pumping a seemingly new vitality seductively through her. A readiness to respond and succumb to this vibrancy, now consumed Angela's entire brain. Angela's imaginative power felt the morning's breeze caressing her soft lips, cheeks, and naked shoulders in the form of a trailing dark male image. She felt Victor's lips upon her in the most dynamic fashion, as she allowed his strong hands to guide her lubricant human resources to a digestive elevation; delicately holding his lips firmly to that wonderful task with her exciting out stretched fingers. Entertaining stirrings touched Angela immensely; luckily the drive to the hospital was coming to an end.

Victor wanted to run ahead and push the button for the wooden barrier to lift itself for this beautiful lady to enter the covered parking garage. His thought of being a gentleman escalated. Angela circled the garage until finally, there were two spaces together. Such thoughtfulness did not go unappreciative by Victor as he raced to open her door. A flawless – pleasant "thank you" eased out of Angela's mouth. Their corresponding smiles made up for the momentary silence as their eyes met. Victor searched for speech, very much uncharacteristic, but his tongue was still temporarily parked on thoughts–lots of thoughts–until.

"Here, let me get the flowers, you lead the way Angela."

They went to see grandmother first. As they rode the elevator to the sixth floor, Angela appeared subdued.

"What's wrong Angela?"

"Nothing, Victor, it's just that I am very uncomfortable in hospitals."

"I know what you mean, but pretend you're somewhere else, Angela."

"Does that work, Victor?"

"It doesn't for me," and smiled.

Angela smiled and said, "I am glad you are here. My parents are deceased and my grandmother reared me, she is all I have."

"Oh, I see, you will be all right, Angela, don't worry."

Angela caught Victor's arm as the door opened, "Her room is this way." She continued to smile as they walked through the hallway.

Victor thought, "she's glad I came, but Angela is terrific company, a dream girl you might say."

"Hi grandmother", as they entered the room, "this is Victor."

Angela kissed her and Victor shook her hand and exchanged the customary pleasantries. Grandma appeared to be about sixty five, and was overjoyed to see Angela. She thanked Victor for coming by and bringing the flowers. She also wanted to know more about him. Angela interrupted saying, "he is just a stranger I met at the market who assisted me in selecting flowers." They both laughed and continued to chatter for the next hour. Grandma; however, had immediately noticed the wedding ring on Victor's finger, but because of her background, refused to acknowledge anything of the sort to Angela. She had experienced–TIME–as a healer and solver of situations and did not want to prematurely deny Angela any of her natural instinctive female rights. After all, grandma thought, "Angela was of the age now where learning would have to come in the new form of a testing the waters." Grandma promised herself, from this moment on, she would carefully watch Angela wade in. Monitor Angela's safety from a distance. "At least Angela is not hiding anything of this magnitude from me," was grandma's last thought on Victor, before getting consumed in Angela's pleasant visit. Grandma forgot Victor was even in the room, which was all right with him. He did not know or care what to expect in coming, but was not exactly ready for a bunch of loaded questions. Not only was it too early in the morning for such, but it was no time for a mood swing. The day was lovely; thus far, and you might say, the flowers were just settling down to bloom.

They later visited Victor's friend and co-worker, Ralph

Krendec, who was highly sedated and fast asleep after a delicate male operation. Afterward, Victor invited Angela to have lunch.

"I am not very hungry, Victor, but what do you suggest?"

"There's this small French restaurant nearby which has pretty good food. We can get a light lunch and…"

"And what Victor?"

"Well, talk – talk to that stranger."

"It was true, Victor."

"I know Angela, but do you think grandma believed you?"

"No, she is pretty sharp, but she did take it as my not wanting her to bother with my affairs."

"Shall we take my car Angela." Victor opened the door and Angela suavely got in.

"I love your taste in music Victor. It is perfect for the perfect day."

"Thank you Angela, are you always this cool and easy going?"

"No, quite the contrary, Victor, but you relax me, and grandmother always said, never act up on someone else's turf."

"Grandma is probably right Angela, but feel free to change to whatever station that suits you."

"No, really this is fine, Victor, I am going to also let you select my lunch for me."

Angela had a hearty smile, one that said you're driving, but I am in control. As it turned out, Angela was twenty two, and had just graduated from college with a degree in Marketing.

"So, what are you going to do now, Angela?"

"Well, I have two offers, so it is decision making time all over again, Victor."

"What do you mean again?"

"Nothing, except I had a tough time deciding which university to attend. Maybe you can help me decide which job offer to accept, Victor."

"Maybe, Angela, are you leaning any particular way?"

"Sure, the one that is out of town, Victor, but with grandmother not being in good health, I fear leaving home at the moment. I love San Antonio, but I would love to travel to another place."

"It appears to me, Angela, you want to travel, I thought you were talking about work."

"I am, Victor, but, if you can go somewhere else, wouldn't that solve it all. I would be in another town, with an opportunity to see different sites."

"Not really, because you wouldn't be traveling after you got there, Angela."

"True Victor, well, that is settled, I will stay here and take a real vacation later."

"Wait a minute, Angela, I didn't say to stay in town and take this job."

"Yes, I know, Victor, but you helped me decide what I think is the best thing to do."

"It was certainly fast enough, Angela. Do you always make decisions that fast?"

"Yes and no. Yes, if my helper gives me a good analysis, and no if he says the shallow thing."

Victor was more and more enthralled by Angela with each passing moment. Once at the restaurant, Angela waits patiently for Victor to open the door, both on the car and the restaurant. Displaying such mannerisms of a lady; it did not take Victor long to relate Angela to the old bourgeois families back home in Atlanta. His wife, Samantha, being one of them, with an automatic air about certain gentlemen duties. It's bred in them, a way of life; so there's never any ill will intended. "Maybe Angela," thought Victor, "is really a Georgian by birth; nonetheless, she has the style, class, and grace of one." Such refined qualities in form and movement assured her of lineage to an excellent bloodline.

"What was this that you were going to explain later Victor?"

"Huh!"

"Remember, Victor, when we were leaving the market?"

"Oh, it's only about a dream Angela."

"What!"

"I'm sort of embarrassed to mention it; but, you probably felt you knew me because you're the girl, that's been in all my dreams, Angela."

"I do not understand, Victor, what that has to do with my knowing you, maybe the reverse would be accurate."

"That's what I surmised at first, Angela; but somehow, it must have mirrored into you."

"And how do you figure that Victor?"

"I don't know, but it must have been instantaneous, probably upon your first glance of me or my good morning to you. If you can recall Angela, not one time did you ever appear frighten or consider me a stranger–well not until you were riled by grandma."

"Oh Victor, I did not mean that then, but do tell me more about these dreams."

"It's really nothing to tell, Angela. The dreams were all vague, but you were always clear–your face that is. You never said anything, but you were always there."

"Are you sure that you are okay, Victor, that is a little spooky to me–not the dreams–but me not saying anything."

"Maybe it's better that you didn't talk, Angela because I recognized you upon first glance–those black eyes and that stern look."

"Is that good or bad, Victor?"

"It has been good so far, I've really enjoyed your company, Angela."

Angela smiled and said, "Victor, you could be one of those smooth operators with a secret scheme trying to prey on a poor helpless creature."

"Now you consider yourself poor and helpless."

"No, just joking Victor, you have not been overbearing, but just really nice. Maybe after graduation and grandmother's illness, I was looking for something or someone nice."

And with elbow on the table, Angela stopped talking, placing her chin in her left hand, her eyes fell upon Victor in an amorous and passionate fashion; nothing moved except an occasional flicker, and it too was suggestive. Victor turned and looked across the room, what magnetism those eyes generated within him.

"Well Victor, for sure, you know how to select restaurants and order, the food here is superb, certainly better than that cafeteria food, I have been eating for the past four years. Maybe this is my initiation to the real-real world."

Victor turned back, and the stare was gone, but he could still feel the intensity.

"It's a beginning, but the real test will come after you start working Angela."

"What do you mean Victor?"

"I'll let you tell me later, Angela."

"That sounds like an invitation to me Victor."

"It's not, but I would like to see you again, Angela. Do I make an appointment now?"

"Can if you want to Victor, but it is not necessary, I live with grandmother. I will give you my address and phone number, better still, you can take me home later."

"What about–"

"About someone coming by, I have friends but I am not dating anyone at this point Victor."

"No, I meant what about your car at the hospital, Angela?"

"Oh my, I had completely forgotten about my car. Forgive me for jumping the gun Victor."

"That's okay, Angela, I'm anxious to see where you live, we can pick your car up later."

The house was on the other side of town, about twenty miles from where Victor resided. Located in that wealthy neighborhood with the large lawns and old stately homes or mansions, more appropriately put. The lawn consisted of at least five acres with a long winding driveway galloping toward the four huge white columns glorifying the red-bricked luxurious estate. Angela pressed her monitor unlocking the decorative wrought iron gate. Victor drove slowly toward the massive structure, quickly noticing the well maintained area. Except for the darting about of a few birds, there was no brisk activity, it was a peaceful setting. Flowers, what looked to be thousands of them in bloom, added to the peacefulness. Tall pines and oaks appearing to be hundreds of years old bowed a welcome sway as Victor proceeded; the trees foregrounded and backgrounded the mansion which stood proudly displaying its ancient age. Victor couldn't help but think of the old colonial styled mansions, his grandpa told of working in, during his lifetime. The difference being, the Big House, he so often related to was part of a plantation. A slave plantation where peace and tranquillity never equaled that of today.

"You didn't tell me you were a little rich girl."

Angela frowned and said, "you did not ask me. After all you were the one doing the dreaming. Maybe you should be careful who you dream about. I guess now you want to take your flowers and lunch back."

"Oh, Angela I didn't mean nothing by it."

Victor tried to calm her down saying, "I must be careful, now that you're getting close to your own turf."

Angela starting laughing, placing her hand on his thigh. "Grandmother said that Victor and she is not at home."

Victor was beginning to wonder now about Angela and how she was interpreting his dream. It was not intimate and he had not thought of her as a sex goddess. Maybe, Victor thought, "his being nice was too overwhelming for the young mature lady."

"There must be thirty rooms in this house, Angela."

"Close–there are twenty two and the servants quarters out back."

"Where are they?"

"They are probably out back, but could be anywhere; Saturday is their off day. Come on in Victor."

"I've always wanted to see inside one of these homes. It's even finer than I thought it would be, Angela."

"Thank you, but it is not mine, it is grandmother's, and to answer your earlier insinuation, I am not rich, at least not yet. There is a trust fund set up for me, but I cannot get anything from it until I am twenty five. There is a clause, even then that I must be employed and fully responsible, whatever that means. How about a tour, Victor?"

"I would like that, Angela, but how about a raincheck; you are going back to the hospital, and I should be going."

"Okay, if you promise, maybe the next time, Victor."

As Victor drove back to the hospital, they did not do very much talking. Matter of fact, they did not say anything to each other, just sort of drowned themselves in an old tape Angela found and inserted. Roberta Flack's "The First Time Ever I Saw Your Face" sort of set a sensual mood. Victor is thinking that he knows what she's thinking and want that intimate dialogue to dissipate. They came to a stop at the hospital's entrance.

"A penny for your thoughts, Angela."

"Can I meet your wife, Victor?"

Victor was stunned because his thoughts of her thinking was way off base.

"You see Victor, I feel you are attached to me, but you look at me as a daughter. If that is so, I want to meet your wife; if not I am further confused because my real world on men has not come together. I have never kissed one or had sex or nothing. I feel very comfortable with you and I admit my mind wandered a bit, starting in the restaurant."

"I appreciate your honesty Angela, but to be honest with you, I'm a bit confused myself. My dreams didn't spell all this out or you might say they were shallow dreams."

Angela smiled, and said, "you have my number, keep in touch."

"Thank you Angela, I will."

Angela, with her raincheck, later retired to her new bedroom, located the opposite end of the mansion from her grandma's. Formerly a guest room, Angela, since graduation was stressing more and more of an independence these days. The second floor south-east wing suite overlooked the tulip's breeding beds, as Uncle Lonzo called them. The luxurious newly decorated bedroom also faced Uncle Lonzo's portion of the servant's quarters. Alonzo Simmons, a gentleman, far along in years was the gardener and head groundskeeper of these magnificent surroundings of this powerful architectural wonder. Uncle Lonzo, though not a personal relative, but to Angela, this was all she knew. To her of course, he was more than an uncle or gardener; he was her greatest friend. Ever since, she could remember, Uncle Lonzo provided all the answers of the birds and bees; the ants and the grasshoppers; the flowers and the butterflies. Matter of fact, Angela has confided all of her little mischievous secrets from grandma, in Uncle Lonzo. Of course, he had no doubt forgotten most of them through the passage of time.

Anyway, noticing the light on in Uncle Lonzo's room, Angela slightly wondered what he was doing, as she sat at her jigsaw puzzle table to work on the five thousand piece puzzle of London's Trafalgar Square. This was the latest in many puzzles given to Angela by Uncle Lonzo. He told her puzzles taught patience, his words, "Finding all those itsy-bitsy pieces teaches you patience Angela." Well, tonight, Angela needed patience, lots of it. For today, she thought, "had been really hectic and challenging." Meeting a married man was the sum total of them both. "A man," she thought, "who had almost made her make a fool out of herself instantly." There were no explanations for the swift intimate feelings. Angela knew right from wrong concerning his matrimonial attachments and had mixed emotions, because her body felt soooo-good. If patience could be found in the small pieces of cardboard, Angela had trouble finding it. That is because the more she thought of Victor, the more pieces she found and inserted into the proper open crevice. It was like he had his hand upon hers and she led him to the right spot. Piece, after piece, after piece, fell into place; Uncle Lonzo's light went out, it was twelve mid-night and with each piece, there was enjoyment. Angela smiled as the large puzzle neared completion; it was five in the morning–she wondered if Uncle Lonzo ever had this much enjoyment putting his puzzle together. Being unable to comprehend the old wisdom ways of life, Angela wondered, if Uncle Lonzo meant–learning patience was an enjoyment of life. The activity of the people milling around, the fountains gushing water about, the red double-decked buses cruising through, all displayed signs. Trafalgar Square had now come alive; the puzzle was completed at half past six. Angela, stood gazing at the activity as if it was really moving, when really it was Uncle Lonzo, moving around below, clearing weeds from the tulip's breeding beds; maybe there was some significance between patience and breeding or enjoyment and breeding–Angela laid back onto the neatly blue covered queen size bed–promising to ask Uncle Lonzo later.

Angela tugged at her pants, removing them to get a bit more comfortable in her continued wonderment. She thought of what Victor had told her of his dreaming and wondered if that had anything to do with the way her body was reacting. Angela wanted to touch her beautiful blush-reddened flesh, but was fearful of the outcome. Her girl friends had told her of being alone and wanting a man inside of you–what could and would happen if you touched yourself. A premiere performance, alone, was not her idea of how to start a romance; and the lessons in patience throughout the night began to become effective. Angela told herself, before she soundly fell asleep, "I will have that Victor on his knees, bowed before me, before he knows what struck him."

Without Victor's knowledge, it appears...his dreams...Angela, or both have made him a marked man. His night however, and several days ahead for that matter, had none of the complications being experienced by Angela. He was too busy being consumed with his new position; Samantha's newly discovered dessert filled moments, and Stacy's return from college. One can easily see how Victor, not even, had little thoughts of Angela to surface. There were no signs of weariness or complacency in Victor's daily routine. Normalcy might be the best way to describe him these days; his acceptance of the three challenges above relieved his brain much more than they burdened it. Samantha was happy – her needs were being met; Stacy was happy–mother had not started talking about her going back to college, and finally, Victor was happy that everyone else in his family was happy. This left him with plenty of quality mental time to develop plans and procedures in his new position.

Being busy has its advantages or disadvantages in this case, because poor Angela was left completely out of the immediate scenario. It is fortunate though, for people like her, that other's brains, have an excellent subconscious state. Sooner or later as one would have a good story to go, one's joyful memories are bound to surface as in Victor's eventual recall of finally meeting his dream girl. Angela. Extraordinary circumstances could not possibly stay suppressed forever or for that matter–very long. Of course, none of that ultimate recall power helped Angela for the period in which she heard absolutely nothing from Victor. Her thoughts of him went from happiness to anger, and back and forth, one to the other. She even had thoughts of completely scratching men off her list forever. Uncle Lonzo was the one person who saved her poor mind from insanity, "Child, you got to have patience–you cannot live happily without patience." So Angela waited, waited patiently on Victor to call.

Victor intended to call Angela the next day; now a week had gone by and he still had not attempted a call. Victor thought, "for all I know I could have been hallucinating the whole thing. But I do know, he continued, I have been doing a lot of thinking about what she said, being a virgin and all." Now it's into the third week and he has been shipped out of town on company business. Victor called the number, but got no answer. It was early evening, he would place it again after dinner.

During dinner, all kinds of things filtered Victor's brain. "Nightmares of what if there is no Angela, and it was all a bad dream." All of a sudden he was not very hungry and would have to talk to her tonight or he was going to be a nervous wreck. He went back to his room about 9:30 p.m. and tried again–still no answer. Victor thought, "after three weeks of not doing anything, why would I get bent out of shape." Just the thought of Angela not being real, was more than he could bear. Victor must have dozed, but awoke at 2:00 a.m. to find the TV on with the programs asleep for the night. He placed the call.

"Hello Angela, where have you been?"

"I beg your pardon," the other end said; "who is this?"

"It's me–Victor!"

"Oh, I have been in the bed for a while, after going to the hospital earlier; grandmother is not doing too good. But the question is, where have you been and where are you now? It has been almost a month since you promised to keep in touch. Then you call at three in the morning, like it is some big time emergency. Victor, I have thought about you daily, but you did not give me a number where you could be reached. Maybe you should do that now. Because I am sure you are not calling me about fatherly concerns. Victor, are you still there?"

"Yes, here's my office number–I was just listening and glad to hear that you're okay. I'll be home tomorrow, I'll see you then, Angela."

Not to Victor's amazement, but a pleasant surprise, none other than Angela was waiting as he departed the plane.

"What are you doing here Angela? How did you know how to find me?"

Angela smiling said, "In which order do you want those answered, sir? Aren't you pleased to have your niece picking you up, Victor. I told your secretary, Tiffani, I was your niece and was suppose to pick you up, but had misplaced your flight schedule."

"I must admit you're the prettiest niece I've ever seen. But I don't have a niece, Angela."

"You do now"–and they both laughed. "After your morning wake-up call, I did not want to be late Victor."

"Oh, I'm sorry about that, Angela but you were heavily on my mind."

"That goes doubly for me, how about lunch, I am buying Victor."

"At the airport! Okay, I guess anything will beat those roasted peanuts."

"There is a hotel on the premise, how about that Victor."

"A hotel!"

"Yes Victor–a hotel that serves food–they do have restaurants, you know. You are safe Victor, I promise not to seduce you before lunch."

As they ate, Angela was all chatter. "Your call surprised me Victor."

"Why–I told you I would call, Angela. You said keep in touch, and its only been three weeks."

"I had written you out of my dreams Victor." Angela said with that fun look–those beautiful black eyes of hers were gleaming with joy.

"I've been thinking about you Angela, it's just that I've been busy lately."

"Victor, if you care, you do not get busy."

"Well, to be honest I was debating at one time whether I should talk with you again, Angela."

"You mean, pursue your dreams, don't you."

"Well, I did call, Angela, please don't let me regret it over lunch." Victor suddenly, slightly irritated. "What's been going on in town?"

"I am sorry Victor, but I do have feelings too. It might not seem like it, but I am so glad you called. And it seems like you take it a matter of, oh so what."

Victor thought, "Angela might be a virgin but she's certainly not unspoiled to the other female characteristics. I'm sure none of her rudeness is rehearsed, it's just that lady inside of her. She's such a charming person, even when she's upset with you. Of course I wouldn't want to take too many chances on that side of her charm."

"Why are you gazing at me Victor?"

"Just admiring the other side of you Angela."

"There is still another side Victor; why don't we spend the rest of the day here," as she rubs his hand.

"Here!"

"Yes, here–I mean at the hotel, preferably upstairs in one of those luxurious suites; lunch is over–you know. I could express how I really feel, in a more relaxing state of mind. After all Victor, you have been gone all week, and should want someone to exhibit their feeling of compassion. What a perfect time for you to rise to the occasion. I want to demonstrate my feelings and stop my imagination from going crazy."

Without a doubt Angela is breathing fire and is ready to explode. "Maybe a little extramarital loving would be nice," thought Victor, "but I'm still not sure this is the answer. After all I'm not looking for that at this point in my life."

"I know how you feel Angela, but I have an appointment at the office at 3 p.m., that I must keep. I parked in the long term lot; take me by there, it's 2:15 now."

"Okay, but consider yourself unlucky for today Victor."

Victor thought to himself–"sometimes it's lucky to be unlucky."

"I'll talk to you later, Angela; thanks for the lunch," as he closed her door.

"Hello Angela, how about some tennis this morning?"

"I did not expect to hear from you so soon Victor; I guessed another three weeks, but I am probably heavily on your mind, huh! It is a little brisk for tennis, isn't it?"

"If you're outside, but it's at the country club Angela, my partner can't make it."

"Sure, I will be nice Victor–see you there."

"That was quick, Angela."

"Well, I was already up Victor to run a few errands prior to going shopping."

"Anything particular?"

"No, just browsing mostly, but you never know. I am not good at tennis Victor, but I am sure you invited me for my company, at least let us hope so."

"No, I hadn't thought about it Angela," as she throws a ball at him.

"Is this how you keep your body in shape Victor?"

"This, bowling, and cycling is about as strenuous as it gets for me Angela."

"That is what I figured, but before it is over I am going to have you doing some more exercises Victor."

"Is that right Angela, sounds like you're pretty sure. What kind did you have in mind?"

"Let us just call it push-ups for now; you will be fitter afterwards, I am sure of that Victor."

"They have an exercise room here with all kinds of equipment Angela, but I've never used it. I usually use the whirlpool or steam room when I finish."

"Yeah, Victor, but that is not exercise."

"I know, Angela but it helps to make the ole body feel good."

"What about massages Victor?"

"The club does not provide those, Angela."

"I do Victor, maybe you should join my club."

All of a sudden Angela's mind had become one track and Victor was cornered on ever turn.

"What do you say Angela, I tag along on your shopping spree."

"Fine, Victor, I was going to ask you anyway. I am going to the new mall on the river. Have you been there?"

"I went the first week it opened but haven't been back. It's a little bit chic for me Angela."

"Mr. Country Club man, I can hardly believe that."

"Well, Angela, maybe it was all those first time gawkers for the opening."

"How much longer are we going to knock this ball around Victor?"

"Are you ready to go Angela?"

"Do not let me rush your weekly exercise Victor."

"No, I've had enough, Angela. I'll show you the showers and meet you in the lobby later."

"Angela has made a perfect partner for tennis," thought Victor, "much prettier too than the guys I normally play with. And also a lot healthier. It didn't matter what time my male partner and I stopped playing; we always capped it off with a few beers. My stomach is beginning to show it; I suppose, as long as I can see toes, with little difficulty, it's not too bad. It's a wonder anyone would find me attractive in this condition; certainly gluttonous, even by a hog's standard. I'll think seriously about not indulging on all the luxuries of consumption after the first of the year. I'm only fooling myself, on these exercise excuses."

"This is a beautiful mall, Angela, I'm surprised I don't come here more often. It appears that the gawkers are gone."

"That is generally how it is with new things Victor, hot and heavy, then nothing."

"That remark does not include me, does it Angela?"

"Means by no means, Victor. You certainly did not start out hot and heavy, just lukewarm to warm. I am going to be patient and just keep on pushing. Sooner or later Victor, you will give in and succumb to my heat waves. You are short on the subject, but something tells me you are long on the experience side."

"No comment, Angela, I'm going to buy you a present. What would you like?"

"You do not have to make-up for not touching me Victor. I am sure your reasons are valid."

"No, Angela, I want to give you a gift. There's a jewelry store, let's go in there. Since you don't want anything, what do you need? Where's your watch?"

"I have one Victor, the band is broken."

"Sure, let's just look at some anyway Angela."

"If you insist, Victor, but my watch works perfectly fine."

"Sir, could I see that watch—no—the other one. Here Angela, try this one."

"See, it will not fit."

"Oh, I'm sure the jeweler can make it fit Angela."

"I will not take it Victor, it is far too expensive; that watch is over three thousand dollars."

"Yes Angela, but it also has your birthstone on the dial."

"Rubies and diamonds are my favorite stones Victor, but it is not me."

"I do believe you'll grow into it Angela."

"Oh, I know I will Victor–you are so wonderful–I could love you to death."

"If you don't stop squeezing me I'm going to keel over right now. That's a good way to go Angela, but please, not in the mall."

Across the hall peering anguishly through the jeweler's window was a feminine observer unbeknownst to the happily embracing twosome.

"Victor, you are not slyly telling me to watch the clock or something, are you?"

"No, no devious hints are intended Angela. I am just being nice because you're nice and extra special to me. In other words, you're priceless and timeless to me."

"That is strong language from someone who has been restrainfully evasive on the affectionate side Victor."

"Sorry about that Angela, but sometimes haste makes waste, you know."

"Oh, I see, you are trying to make sure I do not have AID's or something, huh Victor?"

"You never know!"

"No, I am just joking, Victor."

"Seriously, everything will be all right; I'm slightly turtlish and snailish, but I'll get there, Angela. That's something I wanted to do, now what do you want while we're here?"

"Nothing Victor, I am satisfied. I do not even want to browse any more."

"Okay Angela, then how about some cookies from that concessionaire; my sweet tooth is acting up."

"I would say, your sweet everything is acting up today Victor; you can be considerate, if you want to, I see!"

As they sat down near the ice skating rink, "Victor, have you tried staking before?"

"No, it looks like fun though."

"I understand there are classes here for adults; how about us taking a lesson or two, Victor?"

"I don't know Angela, that's not stable like a tennis court."

"Yeah, but look at the fun those people are having Victor."

"Okay, Angela, why don't you check it out and I'll see."

"Do not worry Victor, I will be responsible for your ineptness."

"I wonder if you can use pillows for padding Angela?"

"Victor it is not a Santa Claus rehearsal–you will be fine–it will help that athletic body you possess."

"Come to think of it, I believe you're absolutely right Angela. You're really good for my ego."

Victor thought, "why do I have this feeling, Angela is trying to mold me into a slenderrella, all of a sudden. Of course it wouldn't hurt. Over the years, I have just let myself go; I'm probably pushing around two hundred fifty pounds. At six feet, that's not real bad, but it has moved the old waistline by a considerable margin. Angela has smoothly made me aware of my unhealthy look by not calling me a pig. Angela's maturity is definitely above her years."

"Victor, you are aware that I am secretly trying to seduce you, but I do not want to be considered as your little whore or first class prostitute. Of course the thought of being a dedicated mistress would solve my problem."

"Well, I've never thought of you Angela as any of the three. You mean more than that to me."

"Victor, I guess what I am saying is, I want to experience what my girl friends are telling me. Is there anything so complicated about wanting to be held, caressed, and have soft words of assurance spoken to you. I am okay, when I do not think about it; however, when I get around you Victor, my body seems to be moving in so many directions. I am sure you can calm me down and give me that satisfaction I am growing to expect. You can have me anytime you get ready Victor; so what are you waiting on! Is it my virginity?"

"No Angela, to the contrary. I have often wondered what it would be like to make love to one for the very first time. I understand I would have to be gentle, but that does not propose any problem. You're so special to me, that I would take extra care and patience."

"That sounds like a proposal Victor, if so, let us go to my place, I am ready."

"Angela, you're just horny."

"Well Victor–is there anything wrong with that?"

"No, not really, but we'll–or–I'll get there. Why don't you think of something else, Angela?"

"Oh, sure Victor, but it is not that simple; why don't you stop eating! Anyway, thanks for the watch, I am going home, I will talk to you later!"

On that last note, Angela bolts from the table. Victor told her she was special to him, but he did not mean sexual special; although her firm pointed breast were tempting at times. Victor thought, "my lips twitch and my salvia glands act up, just looking at what must be the most delightful set of tits in the world. Although, it would be for a short time, I'm not sure I'm ready to lead a dual life. Having a mistress is not a dream to me; that's pure fantasy. Some guys would jump at the opportunity. I was somewhat surprised to hear Angela bring that up."

Victor continued thinking, "she's young, but is she ever advanced. And to be honest, I'm not adept at handling a young hot mama. I have two–well–three options. Go on and love her; tell her to forget it–or keep on stalling. Telling her to forget it, is out, because Angela is the girl of my dreams. Either, we're going to be friends or we're going to be lovers. Of course, her actions today indicated we're going to be lovers. Angela is pretty adamant about that. She'll be okay, once she simmers down. I'll call her later."

DREAMS ARE REAL

That's something, I never knew
Pleasant dreams, will come true
Again and again, mine did appear
Never dreamed, she was so near

Over and over, dream was back
Pretty thing, gorgeous in fact
A touch, and one could feel
Dream was true, dream was real

Saw the face, and nothing more
A lovely creature, one could adore
No words, did we exchange
Not even stares, isn't that strange

And until, that Saturday morn'
I never knew, dreams were born
Standing there, so much alive
A dream girl, before my eyes

The flowers blossomed, so did she
An unbelievable, sight to see
A pinch to test, my awaken
Temptress beauty, can't be mistaken

Such colorful bouquet, in my view
Proves dreams, can come true
Talks, walks, moves at will
Dreams come true, dreams are real

It was my dream, but her advance
Which opened the eyes, into a trance
A kiss, a caress, to this point nil
Why couldn't the dreamer, be for real

Reality sets in; we run and hide
Doubting our dreams, pushing them aside
She wasn't bashful, she wasn't naive
Dream girl meant business, I do believe

Like a falling star, she truly fell
Into my life; never hesitant to dwell
Words were clear, more than a jest
Settling for nothing, short of mistress

Dare to believe, when the dream comes
Exciting, intriguing, pleasant ones
Next move; what would I do
Now that my dream, had come true

CHAPTER THREE

STACY'S STATIC

What Angela did not know and Victor neglected to tell her; his wife–Samantha, and himself had already decided on a divorce, which would be final in six to eight weeks. They had been trying to wait until their daughter–Stacy got her act together. Stacy had gone to Howard University, out of high school; transferred to Prairie View A&M, the second year. The third year she was back home working as a cashier in a supermarket. Then she takes a computer course and lands a mediocre job. Later Stacy marries a young man, she had only known four months. Stacy told Victor after her annulment, that it was for spite. "Mama, just put so much pressure on me, I had to get out of that house."

Getting out of the house was what Stacy had in mind, when she got married; but marriage was not the solution. Immaturity has its drawbacks in matrimony; especially if you are as headstrong as sweet little Stacy, never wanting to give an inch. Plus, its been proven many times before, doing something to be spiteful, merely hurts yourself. Although one must admit, there is a lesson to be learned. The lesson for Stacy was, her own apartment, by herself. This too, had its shortcomings, because Stacy knew categorically nothing about cooking, not to mention grocery shopping. Stacy's idea of having fine meals, waiting on the table as she ran in and sat down, soon dangled no more in that cranium of hers. And it was not long before she was always stopping by her parents house to say hello, and to eat, of course.

They could not understand who that child took her habits from. Stacy defied everything they were for or tried to tell her. A good example of getting too much love and not enough discipline. Of course when Samantha and Victor realized that much, it was too late, even at the tender age of eight. The child was spoiled by two sets of grandparents, and even more by a loving set of parents. Everyone laughed at the little nasty cute behavior too long. For the grandparents, that works wonders, because they can always send the child home.

And that's exactly what they did; after weekend visits of trips to the ice cream parlor, hot dog, cookie, and other junk food stands; trips to the zoo, aquarium, and of just riding around town, not to mention Stacy's excessive toys; of which there were tons of play things at each grandparent's house. Stacy, generally had her way on these miniature excursions; and why not, because the point of it all, is to be happy. Grand mom and dad had enough friction rais-ing their own kids, and they were not about to start over again with this darling, cute little kid. The word was, enjoy her; the unspoken word–spoil her and send her home.

So the years sailed by, and the cute little kid became a monster, like overnight. At least it seems like it; but a gradual process of a few months, then a few years skyrocketed into high school gradu-ation. Those years went by so fast. What seems like today was yesteryear. Those beautiful years of mainstream America; living, taking vacations and having fun. Victor and Samantha even believed they were the ideal family with this intolerable brat. The grandparents gave, the godparents gave, and the child received an abundance of love.

Love flowed to Stacy like rain from a lovely spring cloud–show-ers and showers of it. And, as with the weeds, Stacy was growing each day, uncontrollably. Oh, the parents saw to it that Stacy got her homework. They were educationally conscious, because their parents had bred that into them. Matter of fact, they might have been too focused on education or more precise, grades. Victor can remember as Stacy got older, she got away with murder, simply because she made excellent grades. And to be honest, again Victor said, "we didn't realize what had happened until it was too late." Too late for discipline is what he is saying. Samantha and Victor knew it would take something else to rein this headstrong filly in.

Samantha had the idea that her Ph.D. in Psychology would come into play. She tried it time after time but it did not work. Now don't get it wrong, Samantha was as sharp as they come, but you have to understand, Stacy was not seeking help or counseling; she was simply rebelling. Oh, before you get any ideas; this uncontrollable brat had nothing to do with their divorce. At least not in their conscious state of mind.

Samantha said, "they were not a failure as parents." Her theory was that Stacy had received a good dose of rebellious genes from their forefathers some generations back, and it was probably on Victor's side of the family.

"Well," Victor stated, "I don't dispute that theory; never have, and never will, because I'm no expert on genes. I'm just glad Samantha didn't do a psychological analysis. Of course I have a theory; being of unquestionably sound mind and character."

His theory was rather simple, "Stacy got away with too many ass whippings." Just pure and simple–no discipline–no total respect from the child. What Victor is talking about is the first time they throw a tantrum, you get them; when they snatch the hand back to hit you at twelve months, you got to get them; when they use that sassy "ain't" in those early words; you got to get them. You have got to get them early on by spanking that little hand to correct those mischievous cuties. And early on, you got to spank that butt instead of smiling. As Stacy got older, she had the Ph.D. in Psychology and was using it on them. The ole pupil outfox the teacher theory.

The sad part is, Stacy did not realize what hit her when she went to college, because she was use to manipulating people and having her way. If Stacy had gone on through college, Victor and Samantha would not have experienced a double dose of this mild misery. They as other parents, always hope for the best when kids leave for college–like please do not return until you graduate, and have several job offers–of which you are going to take the one in another city; and what a relief–we can walk around the house nude again.

Stacy went to Howard University, not because she wanted to,

but because Samantha wanted her to go to her alma mater in Atlanta, Georgia. Most parents want their children to follow in their footsteps or be what they want them to be. Stacy was content on doing the opposite. During Samantha's and Victor's parents time, it was sort of understood that a certain tradition must continue. What they told you to do or go was the last word. One might have sulked; but it was always with your back turned, or when you went to your room. Never in their sight or child, did you ever have a good whipping coming. Can you believe Samantha and Victor actually got whippings for looking ugly or puffing up the ole jaw. They worked though, because they did not grow up with no serious attitudinal problems.

Well, Samantha was no different on the college tradition, and of course that is were the tradition ended. Anyway, Stacy, just to be spiteful, was not going to no Atlanta. Her reason for leaving Howard was really twofold. She did not like the city and she did not like the setting of the school. None of this was upsetting to Samantha because she knew her alma mater was back in the running. But Stacy disappointed her again by choosing Prairie View. Samantha, determined not to be outdone, tried a little reverse psychology; telling Stacy that she loved her choice, but if it did not work out, to come on back home. Stacy, true to form was back home as we now see after one semester, with the excuse that she did not like the country. That was okay with Samantha, until she found out Stacy was not going back to college. Now they were back at each others throats after only a brief honeymoon. Two grown opinionated women cannot live under the same roof in peace. It's easy to figure the next move, Stacy decides to get married. Samantha wanted to provide a lavish ceremony. Stacy, of course, would have no part of that and got married at the court house. All of this happened within six months of Stacy being home. Details would have been provided except for the boredom which often exists in weddings of that sort. Non-church ceremonies where mother and daddy cannot strut their stuff in front of close snooty moral dignitaries (we all have them in our midst–you know) actually merit the lack of highlights and dullness that it really is.

Samantha and Victor have taken a new approach, that if nothing more is again different, they treat Stacy as an adult, even in her childish fronts.

Stacy deserved a background check to interpret any future erratic behavior. Specifically, her actions below:

"Hello, Angela, I want you to leave my father alone."

"Who is this?"

"My name is Stacy Previtt, and I'm demanding that you leave my father alone. I know you and your kind. You were a cheap little skunk in high school and you're even worse now."

"I do not believe I know you—are you sure you are calling the right person?"

"Look, bitch, don't try to play dumb on me. You're seeing my father, Victor Previtt. He is a happily married man and I don't want no trash like you interfering with that. He is a perfect father and husband. That shouldn't be so hard for your dumb ass to understand, but then again, you never did care anything about other people's feelings. I saw you at the mall, hanging all over my father. What were you trying to buy him? You have bought everything else in your life."

What Stacy had reference to was her feelings on not being selected as a majorette. This was way back in high school. There was one remaining spot to fill the squad. Of course the candidates involved were Stacy, a freshman and Angela, a senior transfer student from a private academy. Stacy as you have already guessed, became angry when she lost out to Angela for the final selection, Stacy contended then as she is still contending, the spot was bought off by Angela's grandma's dollars.

Grandma was influential in the community and certainly wield considerable financial clout. A phone call or two on her behalf could have induced those in charge to give the spot to Angela. It was highly likely, because grandma knew the right people. It also was no rumor that Angela was grandma's life, and would do anything to make her happy. Not that Angela needed any help, but to be in a judging contest against her, with grandma's knowledge was a sure defeat. It had been the same way in private school where grandma had been matched against the wealthier class, and fine tuned her skills.

In most of those cases, they proved no contest to grandma's power. She always managed to know the right button to push or string to pull. No one knows for sure if any funds exchanged hands illegally; but grandma's name always surfaced for supporting the school's programs. We are of course talking about substantial financial support. Others did the same thing, so it's not like grandma was an isolated case. She merely looked after her own, like everyone else, who could afford to play or pay big league ball. Grandma's description was not one of ruthlessness–just protective. But rightly or unrightly so, such actions spells out correctly the aspersions alluded to by Stacy, though probably only in her flouting brain matter.

And whether grandma did anything or not, Stacy believes she was deliberately passed over in favor of a little rich girl. The facts do not wholly substantiate Stacy's point. The girls as it turned out, were equally talented. And as the story goes, Angela got the nod because she was a senior. Stacy, of course made the team the next year, and went on to become a celebrated majorette. However, deep in her mind she never forgot about Angela stealing her position with the almighty dollar.

"My father is not for sale, so why don't you take your money and your tired ass ways where it's appreciated."

"What are you talking about, Stacy?"

"Look heifer, don't try and play dumb again. It's time you wake up and accomplish something on your own merit. You can't buy your way through life and money sure can't buy you love."

"Stacy, I do not have the slightest idea of your fabrications, nor do you believe such lowdown insinuations."

"Don't try and get cute with me honey, I'm going to expose you for what you really are."

"For your information, Stacy, it is called sophistication and minding one's own business."

"Why–why you little bastard, I've got a mind to come over there and kick your ass right now."

"Stacy, I do not believe you are capable of elevating your mind that high."

"Don't push your luck honey, neither grandma nor daddy will be able to save your ass when I get on you."

"Well now Stacy, if I…" Click!

Angela's face redden as the hum of the disconnection penetrates her ears. Lack of an opportunity to deliver some more parting words were even more irritating.

"Wow, I can not believe this. That girl is mad at me after all those years. And of all the men in the world. I am in love with her father. How do you like that for rekindling an old wound. This is incredible. The point is, what am I going to do about it. Oh, well, I will just call Victor and he will talk to her."

Certainly, Victor did not know of the above startling developments at the time; but future developments should make it all the more interesting. It is amazing how coincidence's seem to happen in one's life.

Whether one is stumbling through life or is on a wayward binge, like Stacy currently seems to be, it helps to have supporting parents. But it also hurts, especially the child, because the maturation process appears to slow down while the dependancy level seemingly speeds up. One would think that is the case here, but there is a bit of a different twist. Stacy's current problem actually stems from not living up to expectations—not great expectations—just a simple expectation of going to college and remaining there. The situation, however, complicates itself when we start talking about the expectation of really–what college. Stacy, down deep, has no problem of going to a family member's alma mater; and the preference is that of her loving father; which is impossible–a male college. Now the choice is limited, she thinks, and she actually feels–unrightly so–pressure coming from mother to attend her alma mater.

The above trail leads us to where Stacy is today–rebelling, rebelling against what she feels is the great expectation and pressure of attending mother's school. The solutions are, of course fairly simple to an outsider; go to the college of your choice or go to your mother's alma mater. Until Stacy realizes, her life is virtually on hold due to her own stubbornness and self inflicted rebellion; will a solution wander into her path. Otherwise, insignificant particles of nature's matter will forever toss her the way of their own floating, winding, uncharted course; and incidences such as dropping out of college, defunct marriages, and grudge holding, to name a few will become common place.

Stacy wanted to tell her father that Angela was no good, but she knew the truth; concluding that a furtherance of her own cause might be better served, if nothing was mentioned to him at this time. Ironically, Stacy never considered the resisting of her mother's urges and getting back at Angela, as a hindrance to life's successful moving parts.

"I'm going to get even with that heifer, if it is the last thing I do"; were the lasts words off Stacy's tongue when she hung up on Angela. Strong words–strong sentence–especially from the off-spring of the "ideal couple". It is difficult to visualize, but most of those who know Stacy, view her as "a nice girl". Surely, finer char-acterizations have been bestowed upon finer people, and all ended well, after a flare up or two; let us hope history repeats such wonders with Stacy.

CUTE MONSTER

Spare the rod, spoil the child
A saying, all too familiar
Accurately measured; the term defile
Never sounding, any more peculiar

Punishment–what might that be
Discipline, the child knows not
Cute monster, for all to see
Too much love, is what she got

"Ain'ts, pleasingly smiled away
No spanking, did we administer
It wouldn't haunt, until this day
Too late, much like the spinster

All isn't lost, psychology abound
Let's use it, to perfection
Ah! Cute monster has us down
Waited too long, for correction

Coping today, the best we can
Hoping for, a change somehow
Cutie, eventually will understand
One day! Doesn't help us now

CHAPTER FOUR

ANGELA'S VICTORY

Angela had decided against calling Victor about Stacy; but had promised herself on their next meeting, the topic would surely surface. There was no way this concerned daughter was going to interfere with Angela's very first encounter with the opposite sex; though stubborn as he was. Angela had become impressed by Victor's caring and sweet ways and wanted more of the same. She knew it was only a matter of time before he would be conquered with her persistent persuasiveness. A man it seems can only evade beautiful charm for so long; at least that was Angela's thinking.

Now, Angela sits in her office reviewing next quarter's travel itinerary. The more she looked at it, the more upset she became; it was pretty much identical to the dissatisfied one she received last quarter. Out of the six trips, all were local, with the exception of one in Dallas and one in Houston. Last month, every trip had been local of the seven, except one in Austin. The problem. A new co-worker as she again observed had the better or more glam-ourous travel schedule. Last quarter, Angela complained to her boss, Larry Trebor, of the co-worker's trips to St. Louis, Kansas City, Topeka, Nashville, Memphis, Oklahoma City, and Tulsa. And this quarter, to her surprise, the co-worker's trips, in her opinion were even better; Baton Rouge, New Orleans, Denver, Colorado

Springs, Albuquerque, and Louisville. Angela, irritably thought, "either Trebor did not fully understand where she was coming from or he totally ignored her complaint of not getting some out of town trips in another state." Water appeared in her eyes, dropping on the light blue itinerary. Each fallen drop turned its stained spot to a much darker blue, which incidentally was Angela's true feeling–light blue and bluer. Retrieving a handful of Kleenex from its crystal covered container on her dark walnut desk, Angela gingerly dried her eyes and nostrils, which seemed to be flooding water also.

With the flood gates closed, Angela turned her complete intellectual comprehension to what possibly could have happened. Because it was clear and clear without a doubt, Larry Trebor understood her comments concerning last quarter's itinerary. She recalled and carried her statement to him, through her brain over and over again. Each tine it came out clearer and clearer; "Trebor, for the next quarter, I would like to get some out of state trips on my itinerary." Angela thought, "it cannot get much clearer than that." Then she thought, remembering Trebor's actions, he made no comment after her remark and had only grinned. Was it a sarcastic grin–Angela could not remember. No matter how hard Angela tried, details of the grin would not come forth. She really wanted to believe Trebor had forgotten, but her brain refuse to give him benefit of the doubt, telling her; "it seems highly unlikely, an intelligent being could prepare three whole months worth of trips and forget to schedule, even one out of state trip. Even an accident would land you at least one." Angela's brain further told her; "do not cry about this any more; do not shed another tear."

Angela remembered something Victor had told her when she mentioned how fortunate it was to have a job with a window overlooking the Riverwalk. "I will let you tell me later", was his reply. That remark, she thought now calls for an explanation from him. Then Angela began to smile as she thought of how nonchalant Victor was when it came to even talking love making. "How could any man be so stubborn to inactions when he virtually has been given the green light;" she whispered to herself and continued, "he is not the only one who can be stubborn; I will show him who is stubborn–he wants to wait–I will make him wait", and her smile grew wider. Angela reiterated her threat of having Victor down on his knees, bowed before her, before he knew what struck him. She tightened her legs together and squirmed her bottom tightly against the soft cushion seat. Angela now felt extremely warm, saying, "whenever we make love, I will be stubborn and make Victor follow the direction of my hands. He will obey me; that will teach him to be stubborn." Before Angela could devise any more schemes on Victor, the phone rang.

"Hello Angela."

"Hi Victor, I have been thinking about you a lot. I had you on my mind this very moment."

"I never would have known; why didn't you call me Angela."

"I just did not want to bother you; plus the way I left you at the shopping mall last month, I was too embarrassed. I promise, I am not going to pressure you again. I will just let nature take its course, if that is possible."

"Thanks Angela, you're wonderful. Did you check on the skating classes?"

"Sure, either two hours on Saturday for two months, or one hour each week day for two weeks."

"The hour per day sounds good. What do you think, Angela?"

"That is fine, I will set it up. How about lunch, Victor, I need to talk to you."

"I can't today, Angela, but, what if I stop by this evening.

"Sure, that is even better."

"You sounded rather solemn on the phone Angela. Is there a problem?"

"No, not now, but there could be later. It is on my job. There is this guy who came two months after I did, and the boss is giving him the best assignments."

"What do you mean, the best assignments Angela?"

"It is this Victor, I get ninety percent of the in-house assignments, while he gets most of the outside assignments. Some of his outside jobs are out of the state, while the few I get are never out of the city."

"Angela, have you discussed the situation with your boss?"

"I mentioned it last week Victor, and he smiled without making a comment."

"Do you think he was being evasive Angela?"

"I can not really say Victor, but the more I think about it, the more upset I become."

Angela was just beginning to feel the ways of the real world. No more false pretensions of a classroom or campus life. No more casual relations of make believe in a fictitious social atmosphere. The college scene was–no more. Angela would find these same people to be different when you are competing for a buck rather than a grade. Larry Trebor, a young decolorize-complexioned fellow, about five years her senior, reminding her of something yet to put her finger on, had welcomed Angela into his department. There had been no problems until now. Angela did not quite know what to think; and because of all her sheltering; certainly did not know how to handle a first offensive.

"I would hate to think he is using this to leapfrog his gender for a promotion ahead of me Victor."

"That could be the case Angela, but if it's bothering you real bad, tell him tomorrow, you would like to see him in his office for a new minutes. Sometimes, that male chauvinism takes over and women are taken for granted. Subconsciously, he might feel like he's doing you a favor, keeping you off the road. But, the only way you'll know is to approach him directly. Tell him your aspirations Angela, and impress upon him your capabilities. Talk to him like you're talking to me–like a real diplomat."

"Yeah, but you are so understanding and easier to talk to Victor. I would love it if you were my boss, plus I probably would not care as long as I was near you."

"I'll keep that in mind Angela, and I want you to know I appreciate that. But I know you'll handle tomorrow well."

From Victor's experience, Angela's appearance alone could never cause an eruption between two people, especially if the other was a male specimen. If so, her reason for existing might offer insight and bridge any assumptions or cultural diversity among us. Angela is young and naive; void of a self-identity;

unaware of barriers and limitations; therefore a new found knowledge of the majority people, darts any direction on healing a rupture.

"Are you ready to skate Victor, the classes start Monday."

"Sure Angela, and only because of you am I looking forward to it. Not that I don't like a challenge, but ice is slippery. We had enough of that on the streets last winter."

"That was nothing, Victor, but if you promise to be more passionate in the future, I will let you off the hook."

"That's okay Angela, but that's the challenge I needed. I'm going to skate rings around you Miss Smart Lady."

Angela, smiling, says, "is that standing up or lying down."

"Laugh if you want to Angela, but I once did some skiing in my dreams."

'We will see if that is enough to keep your feet out of your mouth next week, Victor."

"How is your grandmother?"

"She is better Victor, and would probably be much better if she followed the doctor's orders."

"I think most people have trouble following orders Angela, even if it's for their own benefit. Maybe it's just the idea of changing your life style after so many years. Sometimes, what once worked for you still does."

"And sometimes, Victor, it does not. Aryway, I get her to do most of the things she is suppose to do."

"That's probably because she respects you Angela."

"Oh, Victor, is that how you get people to obey you?" Angela, kisses Victor on the cheek, saying, "I will keep that in mind. I hope you are talking about a hundred percent obedient ratio, Victor. Because this fifty percent stuff is keeping the body out of kilter."

Angela's now holding Victor's hand and has directed her kisses to his mouth. That was kind of sudden, and Victor admitted, kind of nice. Angela is one satiny operator, as she pushes Victor back on the sofa, with that sultry body pressed to his. Victor wants to resist, but cannot. Angela is so soft and undoubtedly in heat, and Victor is not exactly passionless. Victor unbuttoned her blouse and commenced to caress her pointed breast as Angela hasten his lips upon them.

This was the opportunity Angela had longed for, and she was seizing it to prevent Victor from suddenly coming to his senses. Anything to keep him moving in the right direction. Angela was a virgin, but know enough to encourage Victor. If it felt good, she promised herself not to let him stop, no matter what. That is why she only allowed him to move his lips from one breast to the other. Victor was smothered somewhat, but obeyed her command.

Angela is having a feminine tantrum as she claws Victor with her sharp fingernails. He continues to undress her, pulling her skirt off. Angela is breathing hard. That body of hers is simply beautiful. Angela is not only hot, but is also extremely moist; the sweet odor of womankind had now aromatized the air. Victor, originally had no intentions of accommodating Angela; but the sweetest of aroma's emanating near her virgin pubic hairs, captivated his taste buds; simultaneously activating his right hand which found its way, rolling Angela's panties beneath interference. Victor gently placed his hand upon the soft curliness, calming the rage in Angela with his tongue gliding over the nipple of her firm tender breast. Suddenly, Angela's self-promise of having Victor down on his knees, bowed before her, before he knew what struck him, had quickly come true. Victor was perplexed at Angela's maturity; there had been no intentions of gliding his tongue any further than her gorgeous breast. He was now bowing bewilderingly before Angela, awe stricken, mouth opened; his tongue hung freely like a panting German Shepard's. Angela clutched and held Victors head upon her curly cavern until she felt voluntary movements. A stimulating relaxation occurred as Victor held her behind tightly in his hands with a firm gentle grip. Angela gasped silently with each touching, guiding the smooth swirling object each place a tingling arose. Knowing little of what to expect, Angela enjoyed several minutes of warm gentle swishes all through her curly cavern before crying out softly. Angela is beginning to overheat as grandma calls her. Victor snatched his head away as Angela yelled to grandma, "I will be there in a minute"; putting Victor's head back saying, "please obey". Victor's warm gentle swishing continues a few more minutes as she's saying again "please obey" before letting out this deep sigh. Momentarily dazed, Angela is overcome by a new and ecstatic sensation as her body sinks unenergetically into the sofa. Then she quickly grabs her skirt and heads upstairs to see what grandma wants. She motions for Victor to stay right there.

When Angela came back, she was all smiles.

"Well, Angela, did I obey enough?"

"Yes, Victor but grandma sort of foiled things on the end. I am not sure if I got the full effect of this ecstasy."

"Don't look at me Angela, I was just following your command."

"Thanks for being gentle with me. I will sleep good tonight. You are good for me Victor. Look how quickly you solved two problems."

"Those were not my intentions when I came by Angela."

"Neither were they mine, but who is complaining Victor."

Angela had no discomforts for complaints. Victor was now in the palm of her grasp and she felt at ease. She knew his body still had a lump in it from today; and would throb with pain until he eventually completed the task she started. Angela knew enough about nature to know hungry animals had to have food. She smiled as she thought; "Victor was now in that category."

"I'm really fascinated with this mansion, Angela. My first impression was that its size made it impersonal. But with its twenty five feet or so vaulted ceilings and huge crystal chandeliers falling downward; this room closes in romantically around you. Those chairs near the fireplace and the lamps and small tables must be hundreds of years old."

"Grandmother said practically all of the furniture in this house was imported from France and England. She knows the history on most of it. Of course I have never been off into furniture Victor, other than that huge sofa just now."

"Come Angela, don't you ever think about anything else?"

"Is that before or after you, my dear?"

"Look Angela, at the workmanship on all these pieces of furniture. Without a doubt, it was distinctly hand carved by the best craftsmen of the period."

"I remember grandmother saying something earlier, Victor; I merely use what is available. If you would like, I can have grandmother to come down. By the way, she told me to tell you hello, and to make yourself at home."

"Little did she know that you had already made me feel at home Angela."

"Now Victor, look whose mind has strayed."

"Angela, I must say, you're rubbing off on me."

"And as far as I can tell Victor, it is all good. At least you rubbed it good today;" virtually giggling.

"One can swim against the tide for only so long Angela."

"True, Victor, and I love you when you go with the flow. I just hope this is an indication of what is to come."

"I can't comment on that Angela. I'm just glad you're happy."

"Well, do not look so sad Victor when you say it. Would you care to see the distinctly superior and more useful furniture in my bedroom, now? I am happy, but you appear to be a little bit on the grumpy side or should I say unfinished business side."

"Oh, I'm okay Angela, there's plenty of time for that later."

"Let us hope you are right, Victor."

"After all, Angela, maybe it's best that you lose your virginity in stages."

"Is that what you call it; I think the first stage was highly successful. I have never felt that good before. I know you did not do anything, but is that the way your body should feel, Victor?"

"What do you mean Angela?"

"Well Victor, it was sort of like a shock wave bolting through my body and mind simultaneously. That is when I sounded rather loudly. Prior to that it seemed if though my body was heating up or swelling up like a thermometer or balloon, and then I exploded."

"Well, I think that's pretty much how it is Angela, especially if you let yourself relax and concentrate on what you're doing."

"Well, I could see and feel nothing but you Victor, so I guess that is pretty good concentration. But, as a warning Victor, I am going to concentrate on more activity from now on."

Angela thought: "I want to mention his daughter, calling me, but after such a wonderful night, I do not dare. That Stacy is not going to ruin my relationship with her father."

Angela's tolerance of Stacy was about normal. Most of that was due to the safety valve of turning the brat over to Victor. Otherwise, there might have been an immediate explosion with

Victor caught in the middle. Angela's intimacy for Victor was growing. She felt she was close to getting all her desires fulfilled, and no one was going to threaten this erotic link. Stacy's static would have to wait.

"Victor, let me apologize for any inconvenience, I might have caused you tonight. I promise you, the next time, grandmother will not interfere."

"What do you mean Angela?"

"It was all my fault; grandmother had asked me to get her prescription filled, and someway, I forgot. The next time, I will make sure there are no outstanding prescriptions; and also the next time, since you have broken the ice, I am going to lead you straight into my bedroom. We will just call it an extended furniture tour. And Victor, thanks again for the job counseling session."

As victorious as Angela was this evening, she was humble enough to know Victor had much much more to offer. She looked forward to many future hours of laying all her problems before him for a solution. As stubbornness goes, Angela thought, "today's performance by Victor was miraculous." She further noted that his mouth or vocal skills were truly an asset any woman would want around her. Victor had wasted no time in solving two of Angela's problems with his skills; immediately upon discovering the urgency to do so. Angela both enjoyed and loved his quick and timely response. Victor graciously assented. after a bewildered moment, to the task before him, under soft feminine hands crying out for obedience. He met the challenge admirably, closing gaps of potential explosiveness by meeting them head on. Angela appreciated Victor's no struggles approach to mending her unique gaps; even praising him for being so gentle. She was young, but old enough to know one did not get that type of positive pleasant action from someone who did not have your feelings at heart. Impressed with Victor's smooth medium of delivery, Angela vowed to seek his valuable experience during any comparable inequities. She even felt an urge at this moment to find something for him to sink his head into. Good problem solvers, she thought, "are so difficult to come by; so their talents should never go underutilized."

Angela had found the evening's exchange with Victor quite

wholesome and exceedingly rewarding. And though he never said or commented one way or the other about pleasantries; if Angela had to guess, she would say he received a handful of treasuries coupled with a sweet taste of success. The exchange reminded Angela of a toast of love; she filled her cup and offered it to Victor to drink–he accepted. The puzzled look on his face afterward, Angela assessed, as his being somewhat disenchanted with a continuous refilling of the toasting cup. She agreed; however, to remedy that deficiency if he would consent to involving her, actively in his love for the mansion's antique furniture. Of course, he declined; and any gentleman would have done the same. But Angela, being the warm blooded lady that she was, simply told him of her courtesy to lure him into her bedroom, onto furniture, distinctly superior and more useful than any he had viewed so far. Victor had bowed before Angela, like a servant before a queen, and for that, she would always be gracious; and for that he deserved the queen in her queen-size bed.

And at this very moment, Angela's visage was indeed that of smiles and pleasantry; thoughts of having Victor's smooth tongue slushing through her curly cavern and receiving other caressing from him on a permanent basis was now more than a Saturday morning's memory ride in an open convertible. Angela realized immediately that Victor's tender kisses and gentle touches, upon and inside of her, was also more than an experiment; and plans for a repeat performance was quickly being planted in his mind.

CHAPTER FIVE

INTERVENTION

Spare time was never at a premium; however, Angela was trying to get all of the extra minutes. Angela, without realizing it, was demanding more and Victor without thinking was giving more. After the divorce, he needed time to himself and he also needed someone. Angela would have been glad to console him had she known. But, Victor did not need more cobwebs cluttering his brain. Nor did he need sympathy, because of Samantha, and their amicable breakup. They were constantly talking on the phone to assure each other that they were doing fine. Obviously the best solution was to leave well enough along and he would not have to explain his comings and goings.

Angela was nonetheless, happy about the amount of attention she had been receiving lately. Victor had devoted enough time for a complete tour of that large mansion; of course, he had not used it for nothing more than further explorations of her bedroom. And might add, found the furniture there was in good taste, and again represented another century in time; a much earlier period than any of his grandparents could probably recall. Victor also had not gotten around to discussing these antiques with grandma; and Angela's views on such, still had not changed—a bed was a bed and a sofa was a sofa—as long as the fine furniture accomplished its mission. The only period important to Angela, was that they could make love on it–period.

Angela's virginity had long ceased to be that, so most of her questions on marvelous body discoveries had also dissipated. Complete happiness and satisfaction obviously had a lot to do with that. What few questions remained, they too slowly disappeared, because on numerous occasions, for one reason or the other, Victor spent the night with her. Of course, he will admit, the stays were generally at her request. Angela would always turn her head to one side and look at Victor from the corner of her eye, upon such a request; but she would never utter a word. She never orally encouraged him to stay. Sort of a mutual eyeing of things. The first time Victor stayed, it caused a few minor inconveniences. It was a week day and he had to leave early for a fresh set of clothes. This problem was solved by Angela who delighted herself in filling, his portion of the closet as she calls it, with an entirely new wardrobe. Victor complained only from the cost point of view; because Angela's taste in men fineries was first-class. Angela's remark was; "top executives like you are suppose to dress nice." Angela had not been working that long, but was observant enough to know a key feature.

Angela was indeed happy over the turn of events happening in her life; notably, there was now a man around to accommodate a dire necessity. She smiled when she thought of the smooth and gentle manner her body was handled by Victor. Angela could feel his tender touches as she lay sprawled upon her bed each night. The bright ceiling lights no longer affected her disposition to that of moodiness; when the colorlessness of her body was exposed. Victor's caressing had given flesh tone to every inch touched by his lavish kisses; they were warm, moist-butter like, extremely mild; pushing a redness to the skin's surface; exciting all of the body's sensual working parts. Tonight was no different, Angela thought of Victor and watched her nude body blush. Her nakedness became excitable as she watched her breast rise like the blossoming beautiful red tulips outside her window. Angela slowly thrust her legs apart, only to discover a love mark vividly displayed upon her inner thigh. It had been left by Victor earlier that evening as he made his way home–home to their private castle with the moat around it. Angela smiled more, as she remembered this stop; the closeness to her vibrant area had made her ecstatic. She could still feel Victor's soft lips as he made the love mark and traveled on to their nearby final destination.

Yes, Angela was happy, but she was also skittish; much like a young deer drinking at a pond, constantly raising her head, listening, sensing, wary of approaching dangers. Victor made her feel good–real good, but the thought of dating a married man had its uncomfortable moments upon her. It was her idea she thought, to be Victor's mistress, but living with that kind of happiness was doing nothing for her real world confidence; and more puzzling was Victor plunging his love deep inside of her as if there was not a guilty bone in his body. Victor obviously had his reasons for not divulging his new single status to Angela. Don't we all keep little secrets from those whom we care for? Angela thought of her boss at work and then thought of Victor again, saying "man can be so cruel in the real world". Before drowsiness and sleep overtook her for the night, Angela felt Victor busily within their final destination, and she softly uttered, "man can even be real good".

True, it seems a bit unfair, especially to Angela, not divulging his new found freedom. However, Victor's life was in transition and really deserved latent hours for retreat. He was able to catch up on his leisure reading and enjoy it more. Also, more details and imaginative ideas were going into his managerial skills.

Samantha and Victor talked about not letting their job performance suffer. They agreed not to call each other during this time at work unless it was an emergency.

And there were occasional emergencies; each pertaining to Samantha's desire for Victor to get his fill of her delicious dessert. After all, what are true friends, if one cannot share a sizable piece of her delicacy with he who was more than willing to taste the enjoyment of it. Samantha loved this part of their marriage contract dissolution agreement, which had substantial climatic rewards. Samantha's delicious dessert in comparison to Angela had the same sugary flavored sweetness, but Samantha's serving was much larger. Victor; however, enjoyed the contrast because it gave him an opportunity for the first time in his life, to be adventurous. Coincidently, he held both to his mouth the same, but

dined on them quite differently; Angela's dessert was more delicate and compact; therefore, taking Victor less time to consume.
A bite or two and a slight tongue manipulation of the seized obstacle was generally all it took, before Angela's dessert was all done.
Whereas, Samantha made sure Victor was more deliberate, ensuring that he savored her delicious dessert from the time the
sweet-scented aroma filtered through his nostrils, (holding it
before his nose like a connoisseur of fine wine) to the time his
tongue slowly tasted the expected goodness, to the time the nourishment flowed noisily down his throat. In reality, Victor did enjoy
Samantha's delicious dessert more, because in his honest opinion,
more was just better with his huge appetite. When Victor left
Samantha's place, he always left with a full stomach; Samantha
made sure of it, and Victor you might say was enjoying the short
and long of it these days. Needless to say, he was as satisfied as
one man could be with true inner peace or more definitively
put–two inner pieces.

Anyway, job performances on both their parts, were found to
be at a much higher level. It had more to do with being focused
than with more time spent on the job. Because in actuality, they
were spending less time at work than ever before. Harmony was
working for them, and normal casual routines were becoming a
standard.

Well, that is, until Carolyn and Helen popped into Victor's life.
One thing he learned very quickly was that married friends do not
want you to be single very long. And single aggressive females will
not let you forget they are available. Now this sounds like there
would be complaining–and if it was–what beautiful complaints.
These were two of the most beautiful women in the world, along
with Angela and Samantha, that is. And if the truth be told and
lets tell it, Victor indiscriminately love those beautiful Black
women. His opinion, "God just made them finer and gave us any
size, shape, and color we wanted. Now, if those are not heavenly
blessings, there just aren't any." But unlike Angela and Samantha,
Carolyn and Helen were suffering from, in their words "the right
attention", or better worded, attention from the right person.
Now, that the big picture has been narrowly focused; this is where
Victor comes in.

Each felt they had a hold on Victor from the very beginning; though, it might be added, they expressed it both verbally and physically different. Both had an uncanny way of driving their point home. Of course, having the body tools to work with generally added a bit more credence and confidence to one's techniques. They were not facing unsurmountable odds, but we must remember, Victor was not looking for anyone either; and too, was very satisfied with dream girl Angela.

Oh, supposedly the subconscious reason for not telling Angela about his divorce, could have been because of these two women trying to nudge and force their way into his life. Carolyn, at work was doing the nudging, and Helen at church was doing the forcing. Carolyn did have a little help from their mutual married friend and co-worker, Ralph Krendec, who insisted Victor date her. Carolyn Gulbsy, was a divorcee like himself and was apparently looking for someone, but it was never obvious to Victor.

That was until that certain day she stopped the elevator between floors and pressed those luscious lips and curvaceous body next to him. Carolyn was at least six feet in height and had the grip of a hungry tiger or should one say tigress. Her body was exceptionally warm as she firmly embraced Victor, murmuring something about, "wanting to do this for a long time." Victor thought, "why hadn't she mentioned something to that effect at lunch earlier. She had been so calm, discussing nothing but work and her two children."

Carolyn had two girls; Sharonda and Tasha which consumed all her time. This had been one of several lunch dates between them; and as usual there were nonchalant feelingout remarks between them. No off the cuff or aggressive words were thrown at the other. Carolyn generally talked about the activities involving her two daughters; and when Victor got a word in, it was usually concerning some company activity. These were wholesome conversations which gravitated them safely through a lunch hour. This was fine in victor's opinion; her love life appeared rather private, and he was content on not exchanging a page for page of his prolific affairs. And now, all of a sudden, Carolyn's spontaneous notion to grab him broke the safety barrier wide open.

It is difficult to imagine anyone in their right mind, leaving

Carolyn. She was not only tall and pretty, but had one hell of a shapely body. One that if you were not careful, always caused an additional crease in your pants. Carolyn Gulbsy was a corporate attorney and also had a lot going for her financially, owning a large three bedroom condominium, two blocks of the downtown office, moving there, "upon starting over", she always said.

Startled as Victor was in the elevator, he couldn't help but respond; grabbing Carolyn's well-rounded buttocks, as she unleashed her tongue in his cheek. Her behind was now moving in his hands, as she twirled and pressed it to his mid-section; and Victor responded graciously. It's not like he had a choice, you know.

Victor thought, if not for the legitimate nature of passion, Carolyn's powerful grip would have been considered a lethal weapon. Such forceful contact was made, that Victor could feel the softness of Carolyn's body through their business suits. He also felt the atmosphere in the elevator's small space turning humid as Carolyn began to breathe hard, sending hot sweltering steam into the air. There were even timely whisperings of words spoken: "Hold me tight Victor, I need you…if you only knew how much…I have wanted to do this for a long time…" Victor made no remarks in return; how could Carolyn expect him to give coherent replies in his condition. The hundreds of tiny bulbs providing light atop the elevator really seemed like heavenly stars to Victor as his oxygen supply diminished. Carolyn's long impenetrable arms had corresponding long vigorous fingers which punctured Victor's back in ten–clenched separate locations. Each spot sensationalized vibrations, shooting energized spurts sharply through his body like Victor had never experienced. Talking about making an immediate impact. Carolyn had done just that. On the elevator's mirrored wall, Victor could see Carolyn gyrating, twirling derriere underneath his hands. He mentally undressed her and hung on for dear life. Then suddenly, Carolyn sensing what could have happened, abruptly turned Victor loose, pushing him away with the same initial powerful force. That was a good move too, because he was hot enough to screw her on the elevator. Victor thought, "Carolyn's not only tall, but extraordinarily strong." If a beautiful, strong, and exhilarating woman does not start a man's blood to boil; life has already ceased.

"I am so sorry Victor, I can explain!"

It seemed like an eternity; the door to their floor was opening; Victor had quickly turned the elevator back on, and outside stood a crowd of people. Some who knew them smiled widely. Rumors of office togetherness gets around pretty quickly, you know.

Carolyn and Victor split to go in opposite directions, but not before Carolyn winked her eye saying:

"I will see you later, Big Boy!"

"Thank you Carolyn!"

Those remarks bothered Victor when he returned to his office. He could not figure out why he had thanked Carolyn; that almost signified an invitation from her again. He did not want to give Carolyn the impression he was hard up for any of her advances. Prior to sitting down, he smiled and said; "that is a dynamic woman; what strong powerful grips; I wonder...", then he shook his head and flopped down in his executive chair.

Carolyn strolled into her office, smiling more openly than when she left Victor in the hallway; and more so at the expression on his face when she gave him, in her opinion, his most worthy title, and compliment. Before sitting, she looked at the old faded sofa across from her desk, talking lowly and pleasantly, "ump, ump, ump–it is wonderful to be working with a man sporting a large tool like that. Girl, is he ever, well endowed. Just think, if I had not been feeling on him I never would have known; that rascal must wear jockey shorts. That Victor is the best kept secret at this company with equipment like that. And to think I had only been looking real hard at those smooth broad lips of his: this guy has unmistakably the ultimate complete package. All this time Ralph and I had only been casually talking about our mutual co-worker. Little did I know, my days for suffering are over; Victor is mine. You are mine Victor, baby, you are mine!"

It appears Carolyn's remarks to herself had a convincing effect upon her. Luckily for the sofa, Carolyn's eyes were not a beam of fire or it would have been torched by now. She had her thoughts and she had her wonderings, as to Victor accompanying her on those old worn out cushions. Loose papers and several pens were lying upon her desk as Carolyn finally sits down. From her desk drawer, she removes some legal documents, holding them in front of her face; and she knows she should have been working, but the way Carolyn was smiling and moving the hair around on the right side of her head; reminds an observer of someone planning something.

Carolyn's white-walled plain office had no windows, but the fluorescent lamps overhead gave off plenty light. However, within minutes of sitting, Carolyn arose and raced to the table lamp by the sofa and turned it on. Then she stepped briskly toward the door flipping off the light switch which controlled the overhead brightness. Carolyn looked pleased, shaking her head in agreement saying; "there–there, now this dump does not look like an office. As a matter of fact, it is down right cozy." Carolyn's last reply as she returned everything to normal was: "I do not want to miss seeing that man!" Then she pulled off her jacket to the navy blue suit, picked some lint from her knee length skirt and grabbed a paper or two upon her desk; which apparently, too flimsy to fan with, discarded it for the sturdier document. Seemingly, unimpressed with work, she sat on the edge of her desk and stared some more, at the sofa, still fanning.

Carolyn was in her mid-thirties, but passes for twenty-five any day of the week. Her complexion matched the color of her blouse, a beautiful autumn leaf-golden brown, which also seemed to change daily, as different shades of blush high-lighted her high round cheeks. Undeniably, an impressive lady who spoke with clarity; not authoritatively as one's first glance would characterize. A serious undertone; however, would sometimes give one, the Carolyn they first perceived. In other words, she could be awfully mean and demanding when she wanted to. Of course, at her height and size, clarity usually worked. For some reason, Carolyn wore those large gypsy–looking earrings everyday. Regardless of hair style, dress, or makeup, those large circled gold rings dangled from her long peanut shaped pierced earlobes. That is peanuts as while still in the hull–reader. A curiosity, mind you, but they did look very good on this tall-shapely woman.

Victor thought of Carolyn as being experienced and did not want her to shatter his dream with Angela. For a moment; however, that appeared in jeopardy, exiled in that elevator with a beautiful woman in transformation. Carolyn had smiled and offered an explanation; and of course Victor had smiled and not asked for one. Victor thought, "some behavior at its worst, I have found to be satisfactory." Carolyn's adorable actions at this time was pure justification of that theory. Her actions were too quick and too sweet to be objectionable.

Victor, also having problems getting work going for the afternoon, said out loud, "this is one exciting Tuesday", not knowing at the time, he was in for one exciting week because the next evening, Wednesday, he received a phone call at home from another interesting guest.

"Hello Victor, this is Helen Tafeel, sorry to hear about your divorce, but it could not have happened to a better guy. Do not worry though, I am going to be another one of your friends, but nicer."

"I don't understand Helen, what are you talking about?"

"I know about Angela and Carolyn and you might say I want a piece of the action."

"If you know that much Helen, wouldn't you agree my hands are already full."

"Not yet Victor, I will talk to you later."

Helen was very attractive, about thirty short curly black hair and complexion; a body on a 5'6" frame that matched or exceeded Angela and Carolyn in the vital hip and breast area. Helen's greatest attraction other than her beauty was her derriere which was like a basketball. It was that small waist that did the trick.

Helen, the nurse, both professionally and personally, as it pertained to Victor, could really call some shots. She was one of the more domineering women he would ever meet. She was also very nosey–especially about his affairs.

What, talking to Victor later would solve was beyond him. You would have to be blind, not to have noticed Helen. She was by far, the blackest lady in the congregation and true, probably the finest; but Victor certainly had not placed her on any agenda of his. From her initial remarks, it sounded like trouble. He had known Helen for about a year; but the only exchanges taking place were of the "hello, how are you doing" category. She always seemed very cordial; but had never said anything of a submissive nature.

A few days had gone by and Carolyn only smiled and spoke as they passed. Her professional image was at its best. Today, though, Friday, she asked Victor about attending a sorority banquet on Saturday. He envisioned what was on Carolyn's mind and told her he was busy this weekend. Too bad Victor did not attend the party, for there was an interesting guest who did attend. His imagination, now, always went crazy around Carolyn; and the thought of having sex with her had entered his mind. He always got horny upon seeing Carolyn, but refused to let her know. Thoughts of her, lubricated parts of his body. Victor was so close to an orgasm on the elevator that, he will probably never be the same. And one thing had definitely not happened; Victor had never put Carolyn's clothes back on. His mind still saw his hand holding her nude gyrating behind. Every time he saw or even thought of Carolyn, he wondered what her twirling movements would be like from the inside.

Victor had an idea that staying out of close confines with Carolyn was his safest maneuver. Action speaks louder than words, we are reminded; and Carolyn's action had spoken very loud. Carolyn was smart enough to put something heavy on Victor's mind and body; and now, she was really just waiting in her lair. Working in the same company did not allow Victor daily excuses for not seeing her. All and all though, Victor was flaring pretty good.

It looked as if things were going to work out without an elaborate plan. Being elusive to Carolyn and silent to Angela had his life in order, until pesky Helen stormed in. Storming, in this case becomes very appropriate. Just as Victor was getting out of his car, the following Monday evening, Helen drives up.

"Hi Victor, how was work today?"

"Not bad–what brings you over this way Helen?"

"You will be glad to hear Victor, that I have moved about six blocks over. May I come in?"

"I don't see why not Helen, as long as you're here. What's on your mind?"

"You seemed puzzled the other day Victor, so I will get straight to the point. You are now an eligible bachelor, but not an available bachelor, if I follow your hesitancy. I have heard about and watched you for sometimes Victor, but I do not date married men."

"You're correct on my not being available, Helen."

"Except for me Victor. You have one opening, now that you are divorced and I am going to fill it."

"You seem pretty sure of yourself Helen. What makes you think I'm in the market for someone else?"

"You are probably not, but I feel we can be helpful to each other, Victor."

"How's that—more companionship, more sex—I have enough of that already Helen. As a matter of fact two friends are quite enough. Your problem Helen, is that you need someone."

"You are right and I have chosen you Victor."

"Why me Helen, you're attractive enough to have any man you want."

"That is just my point Victor, I am tired of having these unfaithful relationships. With AIDS spreading at an epidemic proportion, it is not worth it. Being a nurse, I an aware of the number of heterosexual blacks coming down with AIDS. The percentages far exceed our population rate. This is something that needs to be talked about in the black community. The increasing number of cases are due to a lack of education and also to bad or misinformed education among us. For some reason, we think we are immune to it. It is not just a gay honky disease. I have been giving seminars to this effect, but it is going to take more. As a matter of fact Victor, you will be helping me do that, your voice is very convincing."

"Yeah, later for that; what you're saying Helen, seems sort of contradictory with me already having two women and all."

"Yes, but you are faithful to them Victor and they are faithful to you."

"But Helen, how do you know that, and if it will remain that way."

"Believe me Victor, I know about your women, and you have a pretty good record yourself. Or at least you are more stable than those dogs who have been flooding my doorstep."

"Are you the FBI or something Helen?"

"No, you appealed to me and I checked you out. Think about it

Victor, I am attractive; I am intelligent; have excellent communication skills; and I know anatomy. All those are assets that will benefit you. Plus, I am going to be all yours."

"The "yours" part is what has me worried. Helen, I'm really not interested. Is that so hard for you to understand?"

"Yes, Victor, it sure is. You are not being very neighborly. Besides, Victor, I do not think you understand; I am not asking you, I am telling you. You are going to oblige my desires and I am going to be whatever you desire to call me–a third woman, a nuisance, or a bitch; I am not going away. Later on you will appreciate me, as I am going to quickly dilute all your fears of me. It is obvious to me you have never had any real loving anyway, Victor."

Victor had never met anyone so insistent as Helen, to give him a piece of her body–or should say–more vocal about it.

"Generally Helen, there's nothing to people that pop off or run off at the mouth about their sexual prowess."

"Look at it this way Victor, I am here to help you, so do not fight it. If I find that you are absolutely miserable after my amorous actions, I will leave you alone. Is that acceptable to you?"

"I'm not sure, Helen; all the presentations being made are yours. My point, is not to try anything with you."

"I do not remember giving you that option Victor. I am not going to leave you alone unless you agree to my terms."

"When is this compatibility study suppose to take place Helen?"

"Do not sound so disappointed Victor; I can assure you, I am not always as harsh as I sound today. Call me an experiment Victor", as she crosses her legs, showing the bottom of her large black thighs. "I am in no hurry to make love to you, Victor, I merely want to know you are here when I need you."

The more Victor looked at Helen's thigh, the more he was wanting her to need him now. His attitude was calming and a warming and comfortable feeling was telling him this dark beauty had selfishly–sexually spirited herself into his life. However, he was not about to let on at this point, she had conquered the mighty Victor.

"Okay, Helen, I'll be mulling your proposition over."

"Think positive Victor, think positive."

Helen was so asserting–always getting the last word in, as coercive an individual as Victor had ever encountered. She had undoubtedly, mistakenly entered the field of nursing. Victor's idea of a profession for Helen would propel her into a sales career. "Maybe, she could not sell anything but sex", he thought, "but I would hate to face her peddling anything." Helen would look you straight in the eye all the while, letting you know she meant business. The most fascinating part about her sales pitch, was she never smiled. Those eyes put you in a preoccupied position and demanded your attention on her soft mesmerizing voice. It was like Helen, waving a magic wane and that old black magic putting you under a spell of the sensuous black beauty.

There was nothing flirtatious about Helen, and of course, Victor would tell you he was in control all the while, but would readily admit, partial control was lost when his eyes would only move in an upward and downward cylinder. Could Helen have known his thoughts were slowly plunging to the depth of her intriguing performance. He could see that Helen possessed a look of confidence as she got up to leave. She flashed the most gratifying smile upon his body. A smile which had been disguised during her serious impromptu speech. A smile hidden upon a lovely face, that earlier showed no signs of divulging any noticeable delightful expression. A smile so warm, so delicate, so caring; a bubbly smile with a dimple to match. Helen squeezed Victor's hand as she left. He somehow sensed it was her way of casually saying, "Victor, you are mine."

Possible interventions or distractions to Victor should present no problems; being the strong-willed man, he had always prided himself. In his businesslife, standing his ground and making the best decisions came as natural as combing the soft wiry-textured hair upon his head. Every short-gray-black strand did exactly as commanded during each morning's one time pampering for each day. In fact, so definite was Victor's hair hygiene techniques, that rarely if ever did the weather's daily changing elements affect his neat groomed appearance. Of course, his extremely short sides which required only a swift brushing, did help somewhat. A man obviously in control, and why wouldn't he be; he was a vice president at the corporation in which he worked. Peopled looked up to him and valued his opinion; normally listening or pretending to do so, when he spoke. Victor was his own man all right; he even thought little of what the corporation's bigger wigs would say when he hired his secretary–a frisky youthful looking dark-skinned beauty. Tiffani Dotson, however, was not just a pretty face and fine body, she had excellent credentials. She had come to Victor, highly recommended from his wife, Samantha. Samantha called it a trust and loyalty thing, whatever that meant; Victor never asked for an explanation. Plus, Samantha added "you will never be stressed out with Tiffani around." And she was correct, Tiffani had a sense of humor like none other.

On some of Victor's toughest days, Tiffani always came through. For instance, when she noticed his lips, parched dry, hanging below his belt, and his eyes the color of his burgundy desk top; she simply smiled and said, "Fred would run away." Tiffani was well read in her heritage, with her favorite name from the past being, Frederick Douglass. She had his autobiography and at least five volumes of his speeches and lectures. The reference to running away had to do with young Frederick being whipped by his slave master; turned on the master, whipped him, and ran away. This always brought a spark to Victor's eyes and a big silly cackling sound to his mouth. Part of the laughing was due to the way Tiffani had made the statement; always in a low–highly distinguishable susurrus voice, with her eyes widened, looking either toward the door or out through the large window. The other funny part was due to Victor knowing, he did not have to run away.

Tiffani's historical awareness had made Victor conscious of one fact; he did not ever have to run, because Frederick Douglass had done it for him. Victor promised himself with his new education, no one would ever make him run away; and if he decided to leave, it would definitely be for something, much bigger and much better. He often thought how fortunate he was to have Tiffani around (she was only twenty six) and how blessed he was, not to have to run away. "Yes sir", Victor told himself, "Tiffani is certainly worth the huge increases she gets each year." At times, when Victor was truly aware of the mean–ugly look on his face; before entering the office, a huge smile automatically came, just thinking about

Tiffani's anticipated remark. During certain stretches, it seemed to Victor, like he was getting whipped everyday. The medicine Tiffani provided though, made him a pillar of strength. An iron man.

Well, so much for the on-the-job-business-stress anecdote; a new challenge had now suddenly arrived. The iron man promised himself, he would not directly involve Tiffani with non-business or his personal affairs. In all fairness to Victor, he never expected to get deeply involved with anyone else, other than Angela. And at his age, you would think, he had a greater awareness of the opposite sex's—well—power if you will. Victor did not realize, NO to them really meant ON–RIGHT ON. He would have to learn; anything a woman, young or old, really wanted from a man, she normally got. To Victor, and rightly so, an unattached woman has little power; after all neither of them was Samantha or Angela. But from all indicators, the new distractors, Carolyn Gulbsy and Helen Tafeel had devised some feminine refreshments or pleasant abstractions to become attached.

CHAPTER SIX

A REQUEST AND A VISION

Victor was doing a masterful job of not succumbing to the advances of Carolyn and Helen. He was also doing a masterful job of suppressing his subconscious sensational wonderings of Carolyn and Helen into two women with whom he had daily casual contact, Samantha and Angela. Never before had Victor met two women who were so powerful in getting their message across to the male of their choice. Each was very persistent in not letting Victor forget their initial advancement. They could tell by his attempted avoidance, he was weak, and was easily their next prey. Victor's body had been bitten by their powerful sting, but he found a way to outsmart them; he suppressed Carolyn and her long legs into the almost as tall Samantha, and suppressed the shorter Helen into Angela. Victor was nobody's fool and he was not about to let two sexually starved females take advantage of him. Everyday he now came into the office, there was a reminder of their presence; Carolyn made special trips into his office, some days as many as ten times, to impress her beautiful tall statute upon him. Helen was equally persuasive, calling Victor, now in the office as well as at home, continuously telling him what her anatomy could do for him.

Samantha and Angela were getting their wishes met with

practically daily visits from Victor. Samantha's urges the day after was being solved; and Angela who wanted to see him everyday, anyway, was happy. Victor made love to Samantha as if he was making love to Carolyn. It was so good in fact, Samantha had her comments:

"Victor, we should have divorced years ago!"

"Why is that Samantha?"

"Because you are more active in making love; I use to have urges the day after, but now I am completely drained. It is now almost impossible to love you two days in a row. I am not complaining Victor; I love it and I love the way you do it; making me stretch my long legs through the air and gyrate and twirl in your hands. You also seem to be enjoying my delicious dessert more; at least you are getting more of it."

"You are worthy of everything Samantha; and I am enjoying it more; appetite seems to be better."

"You also get more of me the other way Victor, touching a few unknown spots; have you been taking exercise or something?"

"No, Samantha, definitely not; well, I have been working out in the weight room once or twice a week." (Thanks to Angela)

"I knew it was something, because you are not only bigger, but longer."

"Oh, Samantha, you are probably imagining that; grown men like me do not do any growing in their middle years. The working out has made my arms stronger; therefore, I can hold you much closer, getting more of your delicious dessert without interruptions. Remember, when I use to do half as much and you were still horny?"

"Oh yeah, I do remember, it happened a few days ago; when did you start this weight training?"

"At least a week now, Samantha."

"Isn't it funny Victor, you have strength and you are taking my strength; the other day I was so drained. I did not get to the office until eleven in the morning. Even then, it was a real struggle Victor, I felt like you had loved me the equivalent of two people; you are really getting twice as much as normally."

"Whatever happened to you needing it for a week Samantha?"

"Maybe, my old age is telling off on me Victor, but it seems like you are getting greedy. Are you extra horny, because Angela is not giving you any?"

"Not really, accept the fact Samantha, your stuff is just getting better. It is your fault if you give me a double dose at a time."

"While I am thinking about Angela, when will I get a chance to meet her?"

"Soon Samantha, do you want to compare notes?" Victor laughs.

"Laugh if you want to Victor, I just might do that. I am curious anyway, as to how she is able to take that large tool of yours. Remember, it was several years after the birth of Stacy before I could even take half of it. Maybe that is why I am so drained now."

"Why is that Samantha?"

"Well, maybe I am giving you more, because for the first time ever, I am able to take all of you. And it feels so good. Victor, you are touching more spots with your tool and tongue than ever before. As a result, you will attest to the fact that I am flooding."

"There is no doubt about the floods Samantha; enjoying it more, huh, giving double!"

"Double if you say so Victor, but that truly is because you have been something else lately; getting older and getting better, I suppose."

"I suppose, Samantha!"

"You are coming by quite regularly; is there any other reasoning behind it?"

"Sure Samantha, to see Stacy and help her make the transition since our divorce."

"For my sake Victor, give me a week or two interval, from now on, And Victor, please make Angela take some of that large tool, if she is woman enough to." Laughing. "Under the circumstances, I do not mind sharing."

Victor was digging and manipulating his tongue into Samantha's delicious dessert like never before, but he could not tell her, he was trying to outsmart a lady at the office. A lady that makes him want to lay between her long outstretched legs and help himself, every time she comes into his office. A lady that made him hold her twirling, gyrating derriere in a locked elevator; and which he still feel vibrating all through his body. A lady named Carolyn who he loves, every time they made love. Victor was not about to tell Samantha, he had met a woman that powerful. (Samantha vaguely knew Carolyn, from a few corporate outings). Victor also could not tell Samantha, Angela was getting a double dose because of Helen. He actually felt Helen was going to be a thing of the past with all that cheap chatter of what she could do. And seeing the bottom part of her black beautiful thigh was slowly wearing off or losing its grip.

As a mater of fact, Victor thought he would be able to blow Helen away, like dust on a pair of his shoes. "Women such as this," thought Victor, "was a dime a dozen; no special ingredients of any lasting effect." He promised himself, he would be nice to Helen a few more days; if she persisted, then he would tell Tiffani to reject all of her calls. And when she called him at home, he would politely, then rudely, tell her where to go, if she persisted. There was absolutely no room in his life for Helen. Victor's prior thoughts concerning Helen, he told himself, of possibly loving her, was as dumb as the thoughts in her head. Why would anybody want a woman, so demanding anyway.

And there was no need to tell Samantha, she need not laugh at Angela taking some of his large tool; she was taking all of it. Victor had prided himself in gently breaking Angela in. Plus as Angela put it, "I want every bit you have to offer, Victor." Well, now she was getting it and loving every moment. A double dose; what is that? Angela has as many doses available to Victor as he could stand. She had plans for Victor; plans on putting some of that good sperm to other uses. Reproductive uses; he found out the very next evening.

This attention worked quite well with Angela, making her feel closer and closer to Victor.

"Victor, we have been seeing each other steadily several months, and there is something I need to discuss with you."

"What's that Angela?"

"Well, Victor, you are not around all the time, and I do not need a lot of sex and all, but I do get lonely. What I need is someone to love when you are not here."

Rather rude like; Victor said, "just what do you suggest Angela?"

"Do not look so perplexed Victor; I am not saying I need another man–not a grown one anyway. I want to have a child by you."

"Oh, I see, you had me worried for a moment. That's different, but tell me Angela, how much thought have you put into it."

"For a while Victor, off and on. I tried to say it was stupid and a bad idea, but I have come to the conclusion that it is the only solution for my loneliness. I tried reading a good book, but you were always on each page; and I keep going over the same sentence, without understanding a thing I had read. Television works for a while or until one of those love scenes appear. Victor, you are continuously on my mind; so I figured if you could not be here, I would at least have a piece of you nearby. I am sure, it is not the most original idea Victor, or for that matter the simplest solution; but it lit a bulb in my head."

"It's not exactly a fusty idea either Angela; I'd say your mind is working pretty good despite its bemused state."

"If you knew what I go through when you are not here Victor, you would understand."

"Oh, Angela, I'm not dissenting; I merely wanted to peer into your mind."

"So, what do you think Victor?"

"I suppose it has been done before–I just hadn't thought of me being in on the act Angela. Could you give me some time to digest this brainstorm?"

"Sure Victor, you can tell me tomorrow."

"Oh, thanks Angela, but I was sort of thinking about a longer period–maybe a year or so–after all you've been thrashing it about for several months."

"Not a year Victor; okay, there is no time limit as long as you are reasonable."

"And what might that incredible time constraint be Angela?"

"Do not make matters difficult, Victor; use your own judgment. I do not want you to embrace the idea until it is the same as one of your own. We could be talking about considerable time or considerable thought; that is your decision Victor. Your sensitivity will go undisturbed by me, until I feel robins singing in your heart."

That's one of the things Victor enjoyed about Angela was her patience. She always put pressure on you by not putting it on you. You know, like hitting you with a sledgehammer and then soothing your wound until you relaxed and completely forgot about the grimacing pain. Somehow, Victor knew what the answer would be. He really did love Angela and would do anything for her, and of course, she knew that. But this was something new to Victor; but when you think about it, the entire relationship with Angela was new. Certainly, as each day passes, we continuously break new ground. It's just that some ground appears to have a harder crust. Victor wondered if this was her sole idea or if Angela had some help. "This," he thought, "sounds like some of her grandma's old wisdom."

Angela felt grandma's wisdom was invaluable and sought advice earlier; what she should do about the enormousness of Victor:

"Grandmother, what would you do if a man appeared to be unusually larger or oversized?"

"The fit is not comfortable yet, huh. Sometimes it takes time Angela; you must remember, he was your first; your body will adjust."

"How long is it going to be before that adjustment occurs grandmother? Are there some kind of stretching methods I can do?"

Grandma laughs, saying, "sounds like you are in a hurry child!"

"Not really grandmother, but I do not like being so sore afterward. Victor is extremely gentle with me, but that man is enormous."

"I understand Angela; the solution is simple, practice makes perfect, but you must be practicing the right thing. Do you remember, when you and Victor first started making love; how excited you were when you told me how you had made him bow down to you, and how good you felt until the end?"

"Sure grandmother, I remember all of that, and it still feels good; my whole body gets so excited, I feel like bursting loose, but that is something different, his tongue is fine."

"Angela, you have to realize when you are that excited, you

have expanded for an entry. So the thing for you to do is to practice until you find the proper expansion that adjust to Victor."

"By that time it might be too late." Laughing. "Seriously grandmother, you mean it is that simple; just keep Victor on his knees, holding his head to the task until it expands. So, what you are saying grandmother, is that I am in control of my body, merely having Victor bow as I please."

"That is correct Angela, also control of his body and all of his future actions. You will be able to make him do anything you want, but you must practice what you preach."

"Oh, I get it, "turn about is fair play and what is good for the goose is good for the gander".

"There you go Angela; please your man in bed and you will never lose his head, neither one of them I must add. In your case that is extremely important, because Victor has broken you in with his enormous size and his outstanding manipulative tongue movement. I can tell you now, that man will be very difficult to replace. But on the other hand and in your favor, it will be very difficult for Victor to replace you, if you do what is right. One thing you have to remember Angela, all women's pots, recipes and ovens are different. The secret is putting the right ingredients in your pot at the right temperature. Your man might stray, but you can bet your last money; he will be back. There are times honey, when the competition looks tough; and there is really nothing to it, if you take care of your business. The simplest thing Angela for pretty women to remember is that old saying: It ain't the beauty, its the booty."

Grandma had given Angela some of her good wisdom and Angela had listened and applied some of it. The initial results were gratifying; Angela for months now, had been taking all of Victor's enormous tool and was truly pleased. She had measurable success. So you see, that old saying had some pretty satisfying features already.

That old wisdom which was always resourceful, benefits one at the appropriate time—usually Angela. Wisdom which steered in the right direction, helping to overcome short-spoken people like Victor. Any cynical remark by Victor is softened with Angela's masterful usage of grandma's ways, Angela was as quick-witted as grandma was wise. The impression coming from Angela suggested using all the time you want–today and tomorrow. Be reasonable–make your mind up tonight and give me the answer I want, the first thing in the morning.

Angela thought the world of grandma, though. What she said was law. However, grandma gave Angela no trouble. She also gave Angela all the liberty she wanted. And anytime Victor was over, she never came into the room un-announced. But one had the feeling of her dominance. It was like a mother cat with kittens. The kittens can do anything they want to do, but as soon as one strays away too far; mother cat either looks it back in place or grabs it in her mouth and brings it back. But either way, the power is exhibited, and there is no question as to who is boss. Do not get it wrong; Angela was treated like an adult, and her privacy was not tampered with. So what we are talking about here is the greatest respect among two people.

Respect mutually shared. Neither camouflaged this respect or infringed upon the other. No harsh words were exchanged between grandma and Angela. Their conversations were of the type where one would refuse a comment if a sharp reply became necessary. Boundaries had obviously been established years ago and neither grandma nor Angela seem likely to go beyond the imaginary limit. But they enjoyed the other and got along extremely well; and that is all one could ask of two women in the same household.

Grandma was extremely nice but she did not smile and carry on a lot, at least not in Victor's presence. She was just a no-nonsense firm woman. You listened as she spoke, and when you spoke, she gave you her undivided attention, It was as if what you said was the most important thing on earth. Of course, somehow, you got the feeling of being studied. In other words, you would feel guilty if you did not know what you were talking about. Grandma would never dispute you though. She'd just say uh huh–uh huh–uh huh. Victor was quite leery of her until he figured out those uh huh's.

With one uh huh, she either did not believe you or felt you did not know what you were talking about. Those are the one's you did not want to get. Ultimately, Victor learned to ask questions at this time or explain his position. With two uh huh's, you were doing okay, but nothing to brag about. And with three uh huh's, you were cooking; and she was in total agreement and very much pleased. At this point, grandma's wrinkles smoothed on her forehead as her jaws opened into a loud chorus of uh huh, uh huh, uh huh. After one conversation with grandma, you forever chose your words carefully. Or did what Victor did; know your subject thorough or ask questions and keep her talking.

Because if grandma had one weakness, it was talking. She love to talk. The first thing one would think about in a woman gabbing all the time was gossip; but grandma was different. Grandma, a woman of seemingly highbrowed wisdom, though she talked mostly, only when the subject was immediate at hand. It was almost at times, like she had nothing to say, but when her small perch mouth got going, there was plenty of chatter to fill the air waves. Listening to Grandma was like prying an old stone monument to speak; you expected something historical to surface and guide you through the current moment; be it ever wholesome or troublesome. Grandma had an easiness about herself which transformed best things better and bad things, best things. This all seems especially difficult, since her demeanor is all the more serious, than one normally associated with such a casual nature. If your subject matter appealed to her, and it usually always did; voluminous words flowed across the top of her squirrel like teeth, occupying your attention until silence once again strayed into the area. Generally, the duller the category, the more interesting grandma's dialogue became. She was extremely versed in business—subscribing to the Wall Street Journal and other business magazines. She also took the New York Times, which sharpened her knowledge about the world. So Victor got into some high level discussions with her. Her other favorite topic was politics. And Victor hasten to admit, when grandma wanted a lively discussion, she always invited him over. She called them her summit conferences. "Believe me," Victor said at times, "when I say the lady is sharp."

But grandma oftened talked of her handicap; not being formally educated. She had not finished high school and always reminded herself of that fact. But Victor noticed high-spiritedness in most of her functioning. In other words, if one did not know grandma was not college trained, they would think the opposite. She was well read and probably through the years, had exceeded the requirements or at least the knowledge of a basic college liberal arts and business degree. Grandma matched smarts with the best of them.

Grandma was a stout built woman at 5'4", a few inches shorter than Angela. Her voice though feminine, had a slight bass tone in it. This sound coming from a buxom frame sort of demanded your attention. Time after time Victor seriously mentioned to her about running for public office. And she always said; oh, I am not educationally prepared, but if you ever run, I will back you.

There was this one day, Victor decided he had had enough of this educationally prepared stuff.

"Ms. Lincoln, I believe I have a solution for your deficient educational qualifications."

"Do not tell me Victor that I should start to school at my old age."

Oh, age is just a mind thing, I hear of cases where people do it all the time; some of them much older than you. Plus, my solution calls for you to forget about school as such and start college by taking the GED.

"Uh huh, uh huh; that sounds good in theory Victor, but I am not sure if I am ready for college, even if I pass this GED."

"In my opinion Ms. Lincoln, I feel that you are more than ready; why, you know more now than most college graduates."

"Uh huh uh huh; that may be true Victor, but you have to pass all those exams in order to graduate. I am not confident enough yet for a go of it."

"Oh, passing those exams with your knowledge will be the easy part Ms. Lincoln. Promise me you will look into it when I get you pass the GED."

Victor had heard plenty of "uh huh, uh huh;" those two variety kinds all the while he was talking, but suddenly she ceased using them all together; that generally meant she was thinking hard on what you were saying.

"Victor, I do not know if I should go around making promises, not likely to be kept."

"Look at it this way Ms. Lincoln, what do you have to lose?"

"There is some merit in what you are saying Victor, but I would need lots of help; I am sure of that."

"Consider it done; help is on the way; I will help you, plus Angela will help too. You'll see Ms. Lincoln, it will be as easy as they say; "falling off a log.""

"You make it sound so easy Victor; do not say anymore; let me think on it, this education thing for awhile."

Victor had been around Ms. Lincoln long enough to know, she was seriously considering something when the words; "think on it," came from her mouth. He also knew enough to drop the subject until she brought it up again.

Grandma could have been successful at anything she wanted to do; but she was content in living her life in. and for Angela. She wanted nothing but the best for Angela. By the way, grandma's name is Hattie Lincoln. Victor always addressed her as Ms. Lincoln. But for convenience sake of identification, we'll continue to refer to her as grandma.

Victor thought, "I could give Angela an answer now, but I'll wait a day or so."

"A penny for your thoughts Victor, you have been staring at the ceiling for five minutes. I hope I did not upset you."

"Oh, no–I was just daydreaming about my night dream girl, Angela."

"Victor I wanted to mention it sooner, but I did not want to burden you with more of my problems."

"It's all right Angela, we share everything else, why shouldn't we share each others difficulties."

"The time is really flying by fast Angela, you've grown to be a gorgeous woman."

"And you have grown to understand everything about me Victor. I love you so much."

"So you think you're ready for parenthood, huh?"

"Not just parenthood Victor, but your child. I want a specimen of you near me every moment of each day."

"Sounds like a pretty strong conviction to me, but I'm sure after careful consideration you're up to the test Angela."

"I know it is not going to always be easy, but I am ready to meet the challenge Victor. After all I do have you to help smooth the rough edges. And life is not worth living if you cannot get some of the things you want or need."

"Now that you put it like that Angela, it sounds like a can't miss proposition."

"There's pros and cons as in everything else Victor; but your blessing is the clincher. Although I thought about it, I would never ease a child upon you. That is heartless, selfish, and would not be satisfying for our relationship. Though, precious, an unwanted newborn would threaten the bond between us. Victor, I would rather live my life alone, than destroy your trust in me. I discussed this with grandmother and she opposed the idea. However, she consented to do everything possible to make me happy, if that is really what I wanted."

"What else did grandma say Angela?"

"Well Victor, she thought there were more important things in the world than a bunch of brats running around the house. She basically wanted to let me know that she did not approve of all my decisions. Grandmother stated that some decisions, though bad at the time, turn out to be pretty good later on. She further stated that decisions are all learning experiences for future corrections or adjustments. In other words, grandmother says you make a decision today based upon the known or unknown, sound as it may be, and hope that it turns out the way you wanted it to. Grandmother says, if it works, you are a genius, and if it does not, you must be smart enough to learn something, and make that correction or adjustment."

"Okay, Angela, what did all that mean to you?"

"It meant, number one, that I can cope and two, she believes in me, Victor."

"Angela, that's a rather brief, but accurate summation."

Victor in principle; however, agreed with grandma about "a bunch of brats running around the house," thinking very little of Angela's puerile persuasion, but in a different light was trying to remain positive toward her.

"Well Victor, I have two good teachers in you and grandmother.

I do not always appear to be listening at grandmother, but I hear everything she says. It might not make sense at the time, but I have always been able to recall and apply it later. And you Victor, you are always so complimentary; but you make me think through a project, just to make sure it is workable. I want you to know Victor, I appreciate your guidance. And speaking of guidance, I need your help."

"What's that Angela?"

"I want to give grandmother a surprise birthday party Victor."

"So what's the plan?"

"I told her, we were taking her out to dinner Victor."

"A surprise, did you say, and you told her Angela."

"Yes, that is just the plan to get her dressed and out of the house. We will actually have dinner, so pick the restaurant of your choice Victor. By the way, she normally eats early; no later than 6 p.m. While we are gone, her card playing friends and all will decorate the house and prepare for our return. I understand they are going all out Victor. With hors d'oeuvres and several dishes for a full course meal. Champagne and all. Grandmother should be full; so we will try and skip dessert. That way she will have room for some of their hard work. But it is really the surprise that is the key."

"That's true Angela, so, when is the party?"

"It is next Wednesday night Victor."

"You mean in the middle of the week?"

"Sure Victor, that is the 16th of May, her 70th birthday. It will be over by twelve Victor. Hardly, any of them work anyway. You do not have to stay Victor. As a matter of fact you can leave as soon as we return. The way they will be carrying on, no one will notice you, I am sure. They will have the party professionally video taped; so you might want to miss the grand entrance. I will go in with her and you just walk in following all the hoopla."

"Sounds like you have everything figured out Angela."

"Well Victor, I sort of thought you would not want to be a permanent fixture on a video, in which everyone at the party received a copy."

"Thanks Angela, I never did want to be a movie star. Tell grandma to be ready at 4:30 in the evening. Is that okay?"

"Sure, have you thought of a place Victor?"

"Not really Angela, but I'm leaning toward the Oyster Bar–the seafood restaurant. The food is exceptionally good and they give you very small portions. That way, within a short period of time, she'll be hungry again."

"Victor, you are wonderful."

Angela called Victor the next day saying: "Victor, I wish you could have stayed at the party last night. Grandmother and the old guys and gals had a hellacious time. I mean that was a real party. They were dancing and telling stories like you would not believe. As a matter of fact, grandmother did not miss you until she told the story about how her future son-in-law tricked her into going to that fancy restaurant. She said, "it was the finest place in town, but they were going to go out of business, if they did not stop serving food on those saucers."

"She went on to say, "that she was as hungry when she left as when she arrived; and was going to fix her a tuna sandwich before going to bed." Grandmother said, "she should have known something was wrong when everybody looked starved and nobody ordered dessert." But she decided to be nice because it was her birthday; "after all, it was the thought that counted." Of course she said, "she was going to tell us about it later." That is when she looked around for you Victor. I never laughed so hard in all my life. I mean they really had a good time. Several of then planned a trip to Las Vegas next month."

"What did you say about the son-in-law bit, Angela?"

"Not one thing Victor, because wisdom had the floor. There is a time to listen, you know. Anyway, that was grandmother's vision and she seemed pretty certain of it. I sort of hoped that her crystal ball was clearer than mine. Oh, I suppose I could complain Victor, but I am basically happy. You have really been more than a husband to me. You have been my friend–someone to lean on–someone I could talk to and discuss things with. I have married girl friends and they seem to be bitching about something all the time. Maybe you can say I have accepted my role graciously."

"And what's that Angela?"

"I realize I am the other woman; your mistress in real terms, but I feel fortunate to have met someone like you. There might be someone out there single, just like you, but I have never looked. It does not matter because I am basically happy like I said earlier. You give me everything I want."

"Angela, you never really ask for anything."

"Oh, I do not mean materialistically–it is the satisfaction I am talking about. Plus, you are a good love maker. Maybe I am happy because you got my cherry, so to speak." And smiles sensually.

"Probably so Angela, but do I detect you getting a little horny at this point."

"Just a little, my dear."

Victor spent the next several days with Angela and it dawned on him along about Saturday night, Helen would become a thing of the past. Victor's decision on Helen seemed pretty definite. After all, he was not seeing her everyday as Carolyn and the appearance of one black juicy looking thigh had all but lost its appeal. Even the sweet sensuous phone calls had become a bore. And as far as promises go, in his opinion, he had no agreement with Helen to become her fantasy beau or sexual whipping boy. "Those notions of grandeur concocted by Helen," thought Victor, "were only pro-posals of a horny lady's standby operation." Being on standby meant taking a number and waiting; Victor wanted no part of such wishy–washiness. "Helen could and would," thought Victor, "find another male to help her out, as he remembered suggesting." Somehow though, on Sunday, one lady would have thought, upon seeing her; an immediate positive response would come forth.

"Good morning, Victor, how are you today? Please follow me."

"Oh, Hi Helen."

Helen was all cheers with that bubbly smile and dimple show-ing as she ushered Victor down the church aisle to a choice seat. Helen was beautiful today, but Victor paid no attention. And if her legs were gorgeous, he never noticed as she walked dutifully within his sight. In fact, there was no reaction from Victor; agree-able to his decisions to be null and void of Helen. Unless, as Helen thought, "Victor really has on his religious church–face this morning." Just to be on the safe side, Helen touched Victor's arm upon his entering the pew; and sent up a little pray. She actually asked God for help in accomplishing her goal. Never mind, what she said, it was sincere; sincere as that genuine bubbly smile upon her face. Okay, if you insist; Helen eloquently said: "Lord, please send me a caring man like Victor." This morning had suddenly become special to Helen; people in the pews became a blur on her return to the rear of the sanctuary; a joyful wetness welled in her eyes. One would have thought there would have been stumbles on this short wayfarer's journey, but there was no weakness in Helen's legs; she felt extraordinarily strong. That bubbly smile never left her face as one of her fellow ushers furnished her with a tissue. And Helen never lost a beat from her earthly–heavenly chores; merrily ushering others along their way.

Helen had been in town a long while, long enough to be considered a native. During this time her acquaintance list had grown, mostly from her occupation as a nurse at one of the local hospitals and through her health lectures, traveling throughout the community. She had also met her share of men on this same route; none of which she was looking for or really interested in, but there had been a date here and there. And as odd as it may sound, as bubbly as Helen was, she had few friends in town to date; to be specific, she had one good girl friend. Of course her lack of friends had more to do with the constant moving about of the people she met at the hospital and her continuous movement within the city, than with her beautiful personality. Her personality did sometimes scar a bit in her lectures due to the sensitive material and the serious approach she usually took. Victor had seen this side of her during their mini chat.

And speaking of Victor, his decision on Helen had not changed during today's religious ceremony. To be truthful though, the latest comment to himself was sort of mixed, it seems; "Helen is one more, beautiful black lady, but I am really not available." Helen made a point to acknowledge her presence to Victor when the service had terminated. She stepped into his path as he entered the foyer, headed for the exit doors.

"Victor, it is so good to see you again."

That charming bubbly warm smile and dimple of hers was at its best. It was not only warm enough to knock a little chill off Victor; it was warm enough to knock thirty degrees off an iceberg.

"It is good to see you too–err–Helen!"

"You look real nice today Victor; that tie goes well with that suit; it is really gorgeous!"

"Thank you Helen, I picked it myself, but speaking of gorgeous, you are more than that today; even in–."

"Excuse me Victor, I have an immediate errand to run! I will see you later."

"NAW SHE DIDN'T." You mean Helen left the man she is seeking in the middle of a sentence. Those are precisely a viewers comments. Indeed she did, but with a simple message; I will see you later. Now to most people those are just words used in departing or leaving someone, but to Helen they meant much more. And to Victor, well, they meant more, but he was puzzled as to what. The first time she used those words to Victor was over the phone, and she showed up later, only to make an impression upon him, with the underside nakedness of her digestible looking black thigh. This had not only left Victor horny, but had caused him to wonder about being inside of her; and later made him love Angela, double because of it; only later to change his mind about Helen's dessert as Samantha loved to call it.

Victor's eyes followed Helen to her car and continued following her bending over, as she accidentally dropped her car keys, while trying to open her door. His sensual imagination suddenly loomed as big as the bulge in his pants. Victor looked in Helen's direction until her car was out of sight; then he completed his sentence: "Even in your black and white usher uniform, you look gorgeous today." Helen would have loved to hear what seems to have been a positive mulling over of her proposal. Victor now wondered about Helen again. He wondered about her on his way to his car, and all the way home; he wondered about Helen as he tried to sleep that night, and wondered more so when she no longer called him at home or the office. Victor, even told himself; "She probably saw the writing on the wall and decided to give up." He even tried desperately to forget about her, but it would not work. Helen was on his mind again, equally as much as the powerfully gripping Carolyn. Along about Tuesday into the next month, the feeling was with him so bad, he inquired of Tiffani:

"Tiffani, did Ms. Tafeel call today?"

"No Victor; Helen–I mean Ms. Tafeel did not call today; as a matter of fact, she has not called in over two weeks. Is she still in town?"

"Oh, I suppose!"

Victor really did not want to involve Tiffani in his personal affairs, but she knew more than she let on or more than he thought she knew. Private secretaries always do–you know; don't they? When Helen use to call and Victor was not in, she chatted with Tiffani a minute or two each time. She could let on more when he knew that she knew that he knew that she knew that he knew. I hope you understand that without me having to write a paragraph explaining it.

"If you like, I will try and call her Victor."

"No, Tiffani, it is not important, another day perhaps."

Victor was not about to open up to Tiffani just yet; if that happened, he could hear her saying: "Fred ran away; Victor must run away; run away quickly and leave all of those beautiful black women alone." Admittedly, sound advice, which at this moment Victor would not heave or for that matter wanted to hear. Because deep, deep, down, Victor was loving the challenge and enjoying the heck out of being chased by a bevy of beauties. One get's the idea though that anxiety was building up faster than pressure these days.

CHAPTER SEVEN

DIET FIT FOR A QUEEN

Victor's rare evening of idleness began when Carolyn stopped by his office on her way home. And speaking of rarity, this was Carolyn's first time today to bug or stop by his office; a change certainly from her numerous passes. Saint Patrick would have easily welcomed her entrance upon seeing the bright green suit upon this tall shapely corporate attorney. The short jacket allowed a spectacular view of what was in the shorter than usual skirt; at least a full ten inches above her knees, exposing those long hairy legs. Victor often complimented her on the woolliness as he often surveyed the pair of them.

"Hi Tiff, is Victor still here?"

"Oh, hello Carolyn; sure go right in, I am on my way outta here, love that suit girl." Each smiling and winking an eye at the other.

"Hello Carolyn, come on in; whoa, I love that suit; man you look wonderful!"

"Thank you Victor, that is by far the best compliment given me all day; that made my day. It is too bad I waited so long to come by; it would have been nice if you could have made my day earlier."

"Have a seat Carolyn, is there anything wrong?"

They seated themselves across from each other in Victor's large office's lounging area. Only a glass circular table and three feet of distance separated the two in the low luxury cushioned chairs. Carolyn crossed her beautiful woolly legs at the ankle, placing both arms on the chair's arms, immediately raising the left one to the left side of her head; and commence to play with her large loop earring and hair surrounding it. The earrings were completely hidden prior to this time; also completely hidden prior to Carolyn sitting was her upper thigh which now lay exposed to a viewer's delight. She drew more of Victor's attention to them as she slowly moved her right thigh inward and outward.

"Until now Victor, I have felt sort of out of it all day; I suppose it started early this morning, when I could not find anything to wear."

"Well, you certainly found something nice, I see Carolyn."

"Oh Victor, this was just something I threw on at the last minute; after giving up on everything else. Now, I dread going home, my bedroom is a mess."

"I see what you mean!"

"The bed is full of clothes Victor."

"I can understand!"

"Shoes are all over the place Victor."

"That is awful!"

This was beginning to sound like a session in the psychiatrist's office. A bit difficult at this point though to tell who exactly the patient was; as Victor was mesmerized by Carolyn's constant thigh movement, which seemed to be going faster and faster.

"How about a soft drink Carolyn?"

"I would love it Victor."

Victor had began to heat up, mostly around the eyes, as he was not certain if they were telling him the truth. It was obvious to him, Carolyn had on no pantyhose, but his eyes due to the reflections from the glass table was probably deceiving him on the extended view. Victor returned with two glasses and two napkins setting them on the table, leaving, returning later with a bowl of ice and a large Pepsi container.

"Here Carolyn, let me pull this table over so you can have more leg room."

"Thank you Victor," as she moved to the front edge of her chair.

Victor seated himself and began to pour until he looked again in Carolyn's direction, obviously at her stockingless and uncovered legs. To his amazement Carolyn's bottom was uncovered; she had on no panties whatsoever. She was aware of Victor's awareness of her because his hands trembled while staring underneath the short skirt, which got shorter each time she scooted forward in the chair. When Carolyn reached for the soft drink, there was little to hide; the skirt had rolled far enough to expose what Victor's burning eyes thought they had seen earlier. Carolyn coolly placed both feet wider apart which gave him a clearer and more unobstructive view. Victor attempted to drink from the glass, but it kept bouncing against the front of his upper teeth. He finally gave up setting the glass down; figuring conversation to be steadier. Victor's stares to Carolyn's woolly center had not ceased, but intensified, dropping his quivering lips wide open.

"I really love your green skirt Carolyn; green means go—you know."

"Except for you Victor; you seem to have a problem with going or for that matter, coming to."

Carolyn rose an inch or so, adjusting the well discussed skirt upward. Now, there is nothing covering her curvaceous hips or anything else. The chair is now holding a nude derriere; no green skirt or reflections from the glass table can even block Victor's view any more. He is stunned; Carolyn notices a tremendous bulge in his pants.

"I believe I can see the green go signal a bit clearer now Carolyn."

"I certainly hope so. I misjudged you Victor; any other man would have been using my bedroom on a daily basis by now. You are one tough nut to crack. And just for the extra suffering I have endured, you are going to suffer a bit also."

"What do you mean Carolyn?"

"Well, they say a man has to crawl before he walks, and for the pressure and stress you have put me through, I think you should crawl a little bit Victor. Do you know how to crawl Victor? Do you know how to get down on your knees? And you do not have to answer that today, because I am not asking you to do it today, but I want you to think about it. I have a lot to offer as you can see;

and having generous portions available makes me a very generous person; that is if you let me. Grabbing you in the elevator was no play matter Victor. I need that bigness you are showing off over there, inside of me, and you are going to give it to me; the decision is really not yours to make; it has been made already. So you might as well quit being so stubborn. Mr. hard to get; men quit acting that way when high top shoes went out Victor."

Carolyn did not wait on Victor to give an explanation, because she was not looking for one. She had accomplished another phase of her mission; "maybe this one," she thought, "would work on this dumb fine man." Before standing, Carolyn quickly looked into her woolly center and then straight into Victor's face, his mouth was still hanging open, and remained open as she left his office. A few minutes later, Carolyn stood in her neat and order (not messy) bedroom. She smiled, removing some black panties and pantyhose from her purse.

Victor's rare evening of idleness continued; he was drinking Pepsi as he arrived home. To be honest, Victor had not gotten over Carolyn's initial gripping claws, and had loved her each time he loved Samantha; but apparently that was not good enough for Carolyn. Victor thought, "he had never seen Carolyn that salty before; she was really irritated, but extremely cool about it. She raised her voice a time or two, but she threw no tantrum, and she definitely got her point across this time." Victor's first move was to take a shower, a rather cool one, which helped a little temporarily, but probably spoiling his appetite for the evening more than anything else. Victor was not hungry at all, at least for that steak and baked potato, he had craved all day, and planned on preparing. There was a craving for what he had seen earlier, inside of Carolyn's sensuous appetizing thighs. Victor talked aloud to himself; "Do I know how to crawl; do I know how to get down on my knees. Man, that fine sister is something, talking about bold; little did she know, in a few more seconds, I was going to have my long-roving double-edged tongue gliding over everything in sight, caressingly devouring her alluring sweet-scented flavorful-tasteful looking woolly center; talking about making me suffer, this sister knows how to deliver a message for sure."

The most suffering Victor was doing was right now; he could

not get Carolyn out of his mind. He wondered what she was doing as he tossed and turned all night. Thinking instead of sleeping. Talking to himself instead of snoring. Constantly going to the bathroom to urinate, letting go of that Pepsi, just when it seemed like his eyelids were getting heavy. Then it was morning, and guess what; Carolyn was still on Victor's mind. Talking about long suffering; what a miserable night.

Victor had his morning's coffee black; his appetite still had not returned; four cups of coffee, before leaving home, had to suffice though. Tiffani arrived to the office shortly after he did. There was a large grin on her face, larger than usual, Victor thought.

"Good morning Victor!"

"How do you do, Tiffani?"

"Wonderful, would you like a cup of coffee? Oh, Carolyn told me to tell you "hello and Thanks;" we came in the building together. She is so nice, don't you think?"

"I guess; what did she mean, Thanks?"

"I have no idea Victor." Grinning even more.

"Did she say anything else Tiffani?"

"No, not that I remember Victor; she seemed awfully happy though; what about the coffee?"

"Yes Tiffani, I'll take a cup, black, no sugar, no cream!"

"Here you go Victor," and heads for the table where the ice bowl and two glasses remain.

"Oh Tiffani," waving his hand toward the door, "I will get that later."

"Okay." Tiffani pulls the table back into place, grinning again as she strolls from Victor's office into her place of domain.

Victor was heavily off into his work and seemingly had forgotten all about Carolyn; but ever so often, the "Thanks", ran across his mind. He thought, each time, "what did I do to deserve a Thanks." Otherwise the morning went smooth; Victor accomplished the share of work he had earmarked and more; quite a productive morning. Then suddenly the coffee appeared to be getting to him; he could feel himself vibrating, but his hands were not shaking as he held them before his eyes. His stomach growled reminding him that he had not eaten breakfast, nor dinner the evening before; and it was near lunch time, his watch said eleven o'clock. Victor wondered what Carolyn was doing for lunch, punched in her extension.

"Hello Carolyn, how's lunch shaping up today?"

"Hi, whose turn is it Victor?"

"Oh, I don't know but I've got it Carolyn."

"Okay, meet you downstairs at 12:30, how about the Snacke Shoppe Victor, they have a good salad bar."

"That's not what I had in mind Carolyn, but all right."

"By the way Victor, what are you doing in this heap–where is your company car?"

"It's at home Carolyn, I drive my car at least twice a week to keep it from getting lonely. It's like any woman you know, need a little attention every now and then."

"Now, I can relate to that brother."

"And what do you mean, heap! Heap! Is that how you refer to a classic automobile, Carolyn? Remember it's not called a Champion for nothing. And 1954 was a very significant year in terms of our history."

"Victor, driving a 1954 Studebaker Champion is no more significant than a girdle on an elephant."

"That's not what my father thought; anyway, I only have 201,000 miles. From what I understand Carolyn, some of these early American Classics get as much as 700,000 miles or more."

"Surely, you aren't thinking about–"

"Why not Carolyn, with tune-ups and oil changes, it's virtually maintenance free."

"Victor, you are a strange person. If I read you correctly, you care more about this heap than you do your own body."

"Please, Carolyn, I don't want to discuss your–no more beef fitness program again today."

"Okay, the auto show is in town next week. Mr. Selfish, how about going?"

"Carolyn, you're not going to make me feel bad, I'll go. Maybe I'll find one that will do a million miles. Seriously Carolyn, I think we as black people, should keep our cars longer. Think of the economic impact we could make on our community. More money for things of real importance, like better housing, education, not to mention further developing our own businesses."

"That sounds good to me Victor, but start telling that to the average Black on the street, or for that matter, the highly-educated Black, like you and me, and see how far you get. We have been deprived so long, that when we get a chance, we are going to buy that Cadillac or BMW."

"I don't see anything wrong with that Carolyn."

"Then what are you talking about Victor?"

"I'm saying, buy what you can afford, but think about what you buy. We cannot continue buying items that depreciate. You don't have to be a financial genius to know it's better to invest in a house than a Mercedes. However, if you can afford both, buy both. In our company Carolyn, I'm looked upon as a fiscal conservative, and it has helped me move up. It goes further than driving a relic like this, but let's face it, that's part of it."

"Before lunch is over Carolyn, I must say you look terrific today and you smell so good. That red suit is saying as much as the green one yesterday. Red means stop, you know."

"Yeah, I know, but for you Victor this signal means go; and while I am thinking about it, stop by a little after the hour, I have something to give you."

"Is it a surprise; can I use it daily; will I enjoy it; and will I like it?"

"Let me think for a second Victor–no, yes, yes, no–you will love it."

"It sounds like I will really be missing something significant if I fail to show up Carolyn."

"Believe me Victor, you will."

"Anyway, I must compliment you Carolyn. You're a woman in every sense of the word."

"Well Victor, I am glad you finally realized that."

"No, I'm serious Carolyn. You're head and shoulders above most women."

"Victor, what have you been drinking or are you buttering me up for something yourself later on?"

"Hmmm, I'll take whatever you give me honey. No–I've watched you–your hair, your makeup, your fingernails, your clothes–your everything is in place. And speaking of clothes Carolyn, are you still buying them from your no beef Boutique friend?"

"Victor, you wouldn't be getting jealous, would you?"

"Well, not too jealous Carolyn considering I don't know quite what I'm missing."

"Believe me Victor, a lot. Yes, I contribute a great portion of my success to Gerald's Boutique. He actually dresses me. All of my clothes for work are his choosing. I have some leeway in my church clothes, but not much. He does not sell casuals, so I have him there. But, then I do not have a need for a lot of casuals either. It is just mostly old jeans and shorts in that department."

"Shorts—please don't tease me Carolyn."

"I do not see where it would do much good Victor. I keep inviting you out and each time I am turned down. For some reason until just today, you avoided accepting an invitation to anything, but lunch."

"That's true Carolyn; let's just say I'm still adjusting from my divorce."

"I understand Victor, but being wifeless is not the end, you know. I welcome being accompanied by a handsome fellow like you anywhere. With a little cooperation Victor, your days of hesitant female relations could be short-lived."

"Oh, it's not that Carolyn, but your openness is appreciated."

"Anyway, Gerald has been dressing me since graduation from law school. It has been a few years and it has paid off. The clothes are not cheap; but all my promotions and employment moves have been rewarding. He knows my size, my body, and exactly what I need. That is why he is so concerned with my weight and eating habits. Gerald use to get upset, when I gained several pounds."

"And now?"

"Now Victor, I do not have that problem since I became a discipline eater. Since we are on the subject, let me show you my dietary plan, Gerald wrote for me."

NO MORE BEEF

My breakfast was really fine
I did not get out of line
Lunch was tough, but it was fair
"Should have a burger; who will care"
Fish at dinner, gonna give myself an A
Made it honey; ate no beef today

Staying off beef is quite a feat
...must realize, there's other meat
Giving up steak is the ultimate test
Me...I'd rather have chicken breast
At first, its very difficult to do
But remember, Gerald is watching you

"Liver, meatloaf; maybe a little bit"
Oh no; DON'T even think about it
There's one thing, you must realize
Don't know weight, but I know your size
You can not cheat and get away
Gerald is watching each and every day

Few years ago, was a size ten
"Huh, I'll never see that again"
Hold it, one step at a time
Have Faith; keep the goal in mind
Losing pounds is like brushing teeth
Daily honey–just stay off the beef

"Spend money on diets, doing all I can"
Problem honey; giving to the grocery man
Buying ground chuck, then and now
Tell me, why eat an old dead cow
Sure envy; most popular of the day
Watch out OPRAH, move outta my way

I'll succeed without a doubt
Just keeping roast, out of my mouth
Still eat dessert, bread, carrots and peas
GERALD's watching: He is really pleased
Discipline's the key, in helping one's self
Really doing this for me, and no one else

Eat more tuna, salmon, spinach and bean
Don't fool 'self saying sirloin is lean
Forget beefburger, throw away rib bone
Not fat; but its injected with hormone
Used, to rush a poor cow to the market
Be sensible, don't be the next target

A ten, twelve, fourteen, sixteen and all
You'll reach the size, lay off beef meat ball
your number will come, you're eating less
Pounds off; way they went on; that's best
Take your time and patiently do it right
Remember–NO BEEF PERIOD–today or tonight

You're not on a diet; just changed eating habit
Don't eat like the cow; eat like the rabbit
Chorus: "She sure is pretty, nice personality"
Heck with that, how about my body
Doing this for me and not old Joe
Remember–a day at a time is the way to go

Months later: Feeling healthier and looking good
Leaving cows along; letting them chew their cud
I did it all for me; but others sympathized
Even my mate helped and compromised
Poundless life, is as beautiful as can be
GERALD–you can now, stop watching me

"I keep a copy of this in my purse and on my refrigerator door to serve as a reminder. When I look good Victor, I feel good. What do you think?"

"I'm sorry I teased you about the No Beef Diet Carolyn. There may be something to it. Gerald might have a valid point. It definitely hasn't hurt you."

"Gerald is like my beautician. She does her thing with my hair; and he does his thing with my clothes. It really works Victor. I have been trying to educate other sisters to dressing–expertly–is what I call it. It's expensive, but it is cheaper in the long run. Take the suit I have on, it is five years old. He knows what he is doing with clothes and I truly admire him. And most of all he's a brother, which is an added plus. And it gets down to what you were talking about earlier–putting those dollars back into the community. I know personally that Gerald puts money into scholarships and employs two full-time and one part-time worker, whose a student. When I first started patronizing his Boutique, it was only him. Of course I still only allow him near me. So I understand what can be done if we as blacks support ourselves, as Oriental people do. It is really like blacks aren't aware of what is going on about them."

"Oh, I'm not so sure, Carolyn."

"Victor, I believe a lot of our non-community support stems from a lack of education."

"Don't lay that on education Carolyn, we've been educated for centuries.

"Not scholarly, Victor, I am talking about parental education. We as mothers and fathers must start schooling our children on buying habits. We must endow them with these, support your community values. I have a duty, I believe as a parent to instill such values in my girls. Then when they are educated and on their own, they will help move the twenty- first century where it should be. Thanks for the compliments Victor, but I did not hear you say anything about my physique."

"That was by design Carolyn–the least I think about your body, the better my body will be–if you know what I mean."

"Thanks also for lunch Victor, I will respond in kind the next time. And please do not forget about this evening."

Carolyn was looking exceptionally good during lunch, and that evening, Victor's mind kept wandering away from the work on his desk, trying to figure out what she was going to give him. Her perfume had captivated him. The sweet aroma was still with Victor, except now it appeared to be even stronger. It was like he could taste the fragrance. His clothes were scented from being in her presence. His hands were scented from having touched Carolyn. As Victor's mind wandered wildly and his body heated, the scent became stronger and stronger. He felt like a bloodhound hot on a trail. Victor thought; "I love Angela, but Carolyn really turns me on; the goddess of love has made me lose control." Victor said to himself; "Well, it's almost closing time, I'll pick up my gift and say goodbye to Carolyn on my way out."

"From the looks of your desk Carolyn, I'd say you are working late. Man, it looks cozy in here, that lamp really changes things." Carolyn had already cut the bright overhead light off. The old sofa looked even better, now that Victor had arrived.

"Hi Victor, come on in," as she closed and locked her office door behind him. "I had a few things to wrap up;" and in the same breath was unwrapping her jacket. Parts of her breast showed as she pulled Victor in closer. "I promised my girls a movie tonight," as they kissed.

Carolyn's upper garments were quickly dispatched by her as she led Victor to that old faded sofa begging for more wear. He commenced to squeeze those lovely breasts. Her nipples staggered between waiting lips, pressing against Victor's nostrils, smothering out the sweet fragrance which filled the room, and moments earlier had made a furnace of Victor's body's pressure.

Victor did not plan on anything like this, but this was working out fine. The ever present aroma was causing his nose to breathe fire. Carolyn's bottoms were off and she was pulling at Victor's shirt. What he is seeing now is about as picturesque as it gets. Carolyn is as pleasantly woolly below, today as she was yesterday, looking everything like a bronze sculptured statue. Victor thought of how Carolyn was suppose to make him suffer. "It is just a matter of time," he thought, "before he conquers this fine stallion; his way." Victor was trying to take his time for the moment. Wanting to make sure Carolyn enjoys this as much as he was, Victor slows down, and continue to admire and caress this soft, beautiful copper body. Victor can feel Carolyn getting ready, summa libido, as she laid back upon the sofa pulling his head downward into her woolly center, to let him sample what she knew he would certainly love. After all, love to Carolyn was making a man of Victor's caliber sank his tongue or tastetester whichever you prefer, to stimulating depths; moving it about only as directed. Victor was trying to savor Carolyn's sweetness, following her hands and slowly allowing his tastetester to swish about and into those stimulating depths. All the time Victor was hoping Carolyn had forgotten about making him suffer. She appeared in no hurry, letting Victor do his enjoyable thing, luring him deeper and deeper into his false security, until her sensitive areas reacted throughout her body. Then excitement began building, Carolyn's, twirling and gyrating had started; her powerful claws pulled Victor's head in closer. Victor knew now, Carolyn had not forgotten and he must prepare himself to suffer; (Carolyn's interpretation) to crawl before walking; to get down on his knees. Both their reactions; however, were overwhelming as Victor generated a powerful thrust; and Carolyn held on; not letting go of this sumptuous sat-isfying union until the phone rang; right in the middle of, and cutting short, Carolyn's sweet liquid adventure.

"Oh my, that must be the girls....yes, I forgot, I will be right on."

Carolyn throws on her skirt and jacket; throws her panties and bra in her purse as she leaves the room, saying;

"I'm running late for the girls movie. Sorry, I will talk to you later."

Victor was left stranded in mid-air; kneeling on his knees, horny, shocked, and puzzled as to what happened. Carolyn had given him just enough to whet his appetite. Suddenly, she reap-pears in the doorway and says,"THANKS", then she's gone. Hunger pangs set in as Victor watched her scurry on her way. Carolyn's sophisticated look toward Victor told the story; "A taste of honey, darling; savor the sweetness upon your tongue until I need you again." Victor smiled to himself as he swallowed a sug-ary flavored substance saying; "so that is what the "Thanks" was all about."

Victor felt this brief contact with Carolyn was a sweet relief say-ing: "Carolyn really put some pressure on me the past few weeks; next time there will be no phone interruptions giving me only half of what I expected. Half of Carolyn though is worth more than a hundred percent of the average woman; and she was correct in answering all my questions, because her gift was not a surprise; it can be used daily and if available, I will; and I did enjoy and love her sweetness, even for that short duration." He loved the excite-ment generated by Carolyn, without any of that outrageous noise; she did it all with her lubricious body twirling and gyrating and with vigorous sharp clawing which directed him between her large thighs and within the confines of her luscious woolliness, where he truly enjoyed himself. "There is no denying it," thought Victor, "and I would never tell her, but Carolyn could make me do anything she wanted me to do."

Victor smiled, thinking of the bigness, Carolyn said she wanted from him. He could hardly wait until the next time as he continued enjoying the small bits of sweetness trickling down his throat. Victor was more than pleased with what little he obtained from Carolyn, because in his opinion, "she was excitement, excitement, excitement;" and to this day, he had never met anyone who put such fire in his veins.

CHAPTER EIGHT

FED UP

Victor arrived at the mansion about eight in the evening; grandma was in the downstairs library. She had been spending days at a time here since Victor's lecture on her eventually going to college. The twenty or so books read during this time, in her opinion, was leisure reading; however, grandma felt a dual purpose could be served; she also wanted to test her retention ability. She knew it would do no good attempting college if she could no longer remember what she had read; saying, "I would never pass an exam." Laying upon the reading table when the door bell rang was a book entitled DARKWATER by W.E.B. DU BOIS. This book had been given to grandma years ago, by a friend back in Ohio, who had made the greatest impact upon her life and changed it forever. And to be honest she was half reading and half reminiscing; thinking and smiling about those strange eating habits of her belated friend.

Grandma was still smiling, holding the book to her side, when she opened the door for Victor.

"Good evening Victor, come on in."

"Hello Ms. Lincoln; anybody I know?"

"I beg your pardon!"

"The book; do I know the author?"

"Oh, excuse me Victor, I am sort of spaced out right now; here, take a look for yourself."

Victor took one glance, saying, "extremely good author; I recently finished, "The Suppression of the African Slave Trade", by him."

Victor opened the cover where his eyes fell upon an inscription reading; "To my Greatest Friend and The One I Truly and Will Forever Love. SIGNED, J.B. TANKERSTROKE."

He smiled, handing the book politely back to grandma, hoping not to interfere too much with her daydreaming, as he saw it.

"He was a dear friend Victor; we will talk about him sometimes." With a solemn expression.

"Sure Ms. Lincoln....Angela is expecting me."

"Go right on up; and Victor, confide in me if there is a problem. I saw her talking with Alonzo Simmons the gardener, earlier. Sometimes they maintain little secrets among themselves for too long."

"I understand; your interest will be protected, Ms. Lincoln."

Grandma managed a grin, the best available, considering the mixture of her feeling; a solemnness from the later thought of her friend and a happy response of Victor's remark. She trusted and respected Victor and could be assured of his word. If there was anything of great concern with Angela, he would let her know. Grandma, without thinking, and an unusual display for her, stood and watched Victor as he climbed the curving flight of stairs toward Angela's bedroom. Victor sensing something upon his back, turned to see grandma staring at him. Giving her the thumbs up sign, she laughed heartily re-entering the library.

"Victor, I talked to my boss several weeks ago. Nothing has changed. As a matter of fact it has gotten worse. I have not even had an assignment out of the city. Now, I am getting nothing but in-house duties. It is like I am being punished for questioning his decisions. I graduated from Yale, and I have to put up with this bullshit. Do you think it has anything to do with my race or is it another one of those old sex games, I have heard about? Either way, I am not going to stand for it. I have worked and studied too hard getting my degree, and I am not letting these ass-holes take advantage of me; I an fed up to here." Throwing her hands over the top of her head.

Victor had never seen Angela this angry before. Whatever the reason, her boss, Trebor, had really riled Angela. Talking to him had caused more ripples than Angela cared to swallow. He had not abused Angela verbally, but handed her the silent treatment, and lambasted her with deceitful actions. It appeared as though a serious problem was developing; however, only time would tell if it was of a racist nature. Angela's instincts has already raced in that direction. Little did she know that black males have had to deal with that racism on every turn.

"Of course in most of our cases," Victor thought, "we didn't even get hired. Now it's beginning to get bad for our sisters. With the Republican President's allowing affirmative action programs to become weaken and non-existence in most cases; we are now beginning to feel the pinch across the board. Where and when will all this discrimination end. All we want to do is have good jobs, get equal treatment, and live our lives like any other American or should I say white American."

Angela had not had to deal with adversity of the color kind before; and was not quite sure which way to explode–outward or onward. The only sure thing–a blow up–was within that gorgeous body. It was enough to cause those black eyes to beam into a distant–seemingly a place of intolerable treachery. It was a mind-blowing experience; a stunning perception.

"I went skiing with these people on weekends, Victor, visited their home, went to beaches every spring break, attended parties and games together; and never had any problems. I have never experienced anything like this. It is as if whites are a Dr. Jekyll and Mr. Hyde all rolled into one. Was my college days a make believe situation and just a dream, or am I dreaming now and having a nightmare."

"Angela was right in one respect;" thought Victor: "It was a nightmare, but a real one, that had been with us for over three hundred years. Now, it was catching up with the entire African-American race including our lovely black women. It didn't make any difference whether they were black, chocolate, coconut, coffee, honeycomb, or what; they were all African-American beauties experiencing hell on their jobs. The exclusive club of white men/black women was finally breaking down. What was causing this phenomenon after so many decades of advancement for these lovely sisters is not only amazing, but down right scary. Our women have been thoroughbreds, carrying black men on their backs; carrying little black children on their backs; and just bearing whatever the load. Their load and burden has been unusually heavy. They did what they had to do, supporting their man and their family; often when there was no man even around."

Victor's thoughts warmed up: "It has been hard and it will continue to be hard. What did happen? What caused this abrupt cruelty to these beautiful black creatures? There is one theory that the white man found out that instead of being the user, he was now being used. Of course that's his terminology–we call it getting what is rightfully ours. Regardless of the semantics, we were forging ahead. When he got a Cadillac–we got a Cadillac–and he smiled; when he moved to the suburbs–we moved to the suburbs–and he grinned; when he joined the country club–we were teeing off or already on the tennis court–and he became pretty damn angry."

Victor continues: "Another theory was that the white woman was tired of sitting at home and attending frivolous meetings. So she came out of her cocoon to see what was going on. She found these beautiful black women getting royal treatment from her man and she did not like it. Not having to work or really wanting to work; felt she had lost control. So she pushed for women's rights to reclaim the hierarchy. That meant one thing, the sister's job was in jeopardy. So you see it's really the white women who have all the power. It's a proven fact that they control the wealth in our country. Its been rumored that they have threatened the white man with putting the black man in power. Now if you want to really dream, think about that day. Anyway, whatever she wants, she gets, and it's not working too good for Angela."

Victor's thoughts conclude: "The realization, is that the black woman was providing that old one-two punch of income to go with the black male's. This gave them more money for educating their children, taking vacations, and obtaining other niceties, that before was only a dream. Now this was beginning to really threaten the white male dominated society and the rebellion is on. Why can't we just have equal rights and justice for all. Is that really asking too much?"

Angela knew her grandma had sent her to the finest schools money could buy. From the charm schools in the south to the boarding schools in the east. And she also knew she was not going to start being no second class citizen at this point. Angela, like grandma, was very sharp, with an even higher degree of common sense. She realized now that she had been sheltered. School was the real world, but not the Real-Real World. She had been sheltered and it was all make believe.

"Victor, I am sure grandmother knew of the problems I would face upon entering the real word; why did she not say something or warn me?"

"She did, Angela."

"What do you mean Victor?"

"Grandma sent you to the best schools in the country; she gave you the best education that one could have; and in the process, you had the opportunity to mingle with races of people from around the world Angela."

"So!"

"So Angela, you successfully completed that phase of your development; you learned how to get along with people–period–and you learned that people are people regardless of their color. You were in an arena were academics and intellect was the judge; and in my opinion and grandma's opinion, no doubt, that is the way it should be. Grandma saw that you had the best tool to go to work; and the best weapon to go to war. She saw that your brain was equipped with the right knowledge. She prepared you for the struggle, Angela. You see, no one can take your brain from you."

"Prepared! If I am so prepared, then why am I having these problems? I hear what you are telling me Victor, but there is something missing. It is difficult for me to cope with what is going on in this job arena. In college Victor, we had many projects where we worked as teams. We had a project to complete and everyone worked together to get the job done. Our concentration was on the task before us, and we were always successful. In my opinion, there should be no difference in the real world–you have projects to complete–and you work as a team to accomplish them. Now tell me, what am I missing?"

"Everything you just said Angela was true, and that is the way a color blind society would work. But you will find out that there are those who cannot tolerate a black person being their equal. And that is where we get the tragic–race discrimination–it has nothing to do with your education and ability–it's a race thing. Grandma steered you in another direction, probably, hoping that being academically qualified and white in color, you would escape all the evils of racism. Yet, there were those other ancestors who taught their children about racial hatred, thereby creating ances-tral racism."

"What do you suggest I do Victor–fight, or leave it alone?" The last remark startled Victor and his look must have shown it.

"Okay Victor, I will do something, but what? This is really con-fusing."

"In answer to your earlier questions about what is missing Angela, I want you to have this."

"What is it?"

"It's an autobiography of Frederick Douglass, Angela. It is important for us as blacks in this society that in order to know where we're going, it's imperative to know where we came from."

"What do you mean, Victor, I believe I know where I came from."

"That's what I thought Angela, you're overdue for some good education. Please read the book. You are really naive as to what's going on in this country."

Angela was going through the worse time of her life; never before facing an obstacle so great or complex. She felt when you do what you are suppose to do, accomplishing your job task and more, that was the necessary road for advancement and moving on. Now with her first job and her first boss Larry Trebor, it was nothing like that. She had approached him diplomatically, follow-ing Victor's instructions, and instead of improvement in the volatile situation, it appeared to have antagonized Trebor, making her travel schedule worst. It was obvious now, Trebor did not like being told how to do his job, and it was now obvious, even to

Angela, Trebor had a problem seeing another race making any type of financial strives. Angela avoided jumping to conclusions on Trebor after her diplomatic contact; preferring to watch scheduling for two more quarters. Her co-worker, the white male and Trebor had lunch together, and he continued to receive the best of the trips and finally all the trips. The age old questions Angela asked herself; "why in the hell would they hire me in the first place." She was too young, but more so, too sheltered to know the answers: "We tried one Black, she did not work out." What happened after that meant no other African-American getting an opportunity in that department. Multiply those incidences across the country and you have qualified black men and women never getting the same opportunity as their white college classmates.

Angela was not savvy enough to know Larry Trebor was trying to force her out; get her to get fed up as she stated and quit. Because he neither had the grounds or balls to legally dismiss her. She was no madder than anyone would be, black or white, who knew an evil was deliberately being cast in their direction. Victor had weathered and was still weathering these racism storms everyday; but he never told Angela, "they keep coming at you honey; you have to either defend or prove yourself every second of the day, in most cases, both." He thought of the devastating effect those words would have on a young sheltered naive, first time employee of America's labor force. So Victor elected to let her prepare herself, the way he had been helped; knowing where you came from, knowing your black history; reading Tiffani's favorite, first. That is when he laid Frederick Douglass' autobiography at her feet. After all, it was helping him daily, keeping him from running away.

Victor felt bad seeing Angela go through these changes. Until now, he knew she was surviving only through the consolation of receiving the double dosages of loving from his renewed Helen's wonderings. He also knew, more than his loving would be necessary to sustain Angela and prevent a total resentment toward the white race. She would have to learn to weather Larry Trebor and racism storms wherever she found them. Knowing about her heritage was the first step in that direction. Victor thought to himself and became as perplexed as Angela, saying: "Why in the hell do these racism storms continue." And being the seasoned person that he is, all types of answers, good answers came into his mind; but for the sake of getting fed up like Angela, Victor merely shook his head and smiled. "If he could help Angela get to his status," Victor thought, "the world would be a better place in spite of Larry Trebor." The point being, you cannot let one such racist idiot get you down.

Angela, now, had her new ammunition and Victor knew she was smart enough to digest and use it wisely. He also had a gut feeling, Angela would triumph over Trebor; good always triumphs over evil. If there had been some way Victor could have smoothed Angela's work life out in one blow, he would gladly have done so. Victor realized that he was the man in her life and with that, came a great deal of dependancy. Living up to that dependancy for one as sweet as Angela was by far the easy part; trying to explain America's continued racism storms was a bit more difficult.

Grandma had done what she was instructed to do; "send Angela to the finest schools in order for her to get the best education possible." Education was looked upon as a cure for the inequities of this country for African-Americans. It was looked upon as a way for the talented tenth to help their own race of people. That is why grandma had been the recipient of such instruction, more than twenty years ago. She neither questioned or second quessed the instructions or the instructor at the time, because, she too, knew they were sincere, well-meaning words of wisdom for the Black race of people. The caretaker from that bygone era had looked into the future, into Angela's future, forecasting the best for her. He knew, with an education, Angela would have the road paved, never having to travel the ruts they did. He knew, an education, was the one thing worth fighting for.

Now that Angela had received the necessary education, she was expected to gain experience in a corporate setting and move on. And like Victor mentioned, because of her bright, light, and damn near white complexion, she was not expected to have any problems. Of course the problem of all problems was the fact that nobody told Angela to expect the unexpected. Nobody told her to expect evil people like Larry Trebor to be standing in her pathway. And nobody ever told her, one's race could hold them back regardless of the color of their skin. It appears that Angela is going to have to be re-educated; educated as to the ways of the "Real–Real World," as she puts it. To date, there had only been hints and wishful thinking of those around her. It was now evident, Angela was due some super training from somewhere.

The most interesting thing about Angela is that prior to her joining the labor force, she was totally unaware that prejudices could exist so strong. You heard her: she went to college with these people; she went skiing with these people; she visited the homes of these people; all without incidents. It was obvious that her color helped her then; so much for color huh; so much for college days. Let's face it, until this point, Angela was really "the little rich girl," as Victor once referred. It can be taken even a step further, the little rich white girl. Now that we have everything in its proper perspective, we can sympathize as we wish for her rude awakening. Forgive me, if I mislead you; Angela never tried to pass, she merely went through living and enjoying a carefree, normal, non-race discriminating life, like all human beings would love to do. There are very few of us who would trade places with Angela for those twenty something years, especially if we knew we would wake up to a hysterical nightmare. That is really Angela's status today.

Speaking of today and feeling blue; Angela at this moment stood before Victor in a sheer pale blue, mid-thigh length gown. This was her normal attire when he visited with her in the bedroom. Getting and keeping Victor's attention when he came around was Angela's strong suit. She was young, but because of grandma's wisdom, she had no problems in this arena, and was far ahead of most women, twice her age. Angela had learned how to make Victor do the things she wanted; that is why she constantly told him, when he helped her with this employment problem:

"Victor, I wish you were my boss!"

"Yeah, I know Angela, so you would not have to come to work."

"Well, what is wrong with that Victor?"

Victor could only laugh, saying, "nothing Angela, nothing."

And like always, Victor prepared himself to solve two problems for Angela in cases like this; not that he would mind. He had sensed it for a while and had finally come to the conclusion; Angela's bedroom was her calming domain.

CHAPTER NINE

ANATOMY LESSON

Helen had been extremely busy since her last contact with Victor at the church. She had thought of him a time or two, but deliberately refused to call him, because in her words: "Victor really needs to believe in my honesty; that I too am busy and have no time for foolishness; that he is the one chosen to share my sexual desires, fulfilling all those needs in that regard. He needs to understand, my work needs my concentration, but my body needs the appropriate attention to keep me fully concentrated and focused." So, going about her work as if Victor did not exist was fairly easy. Helen had promised herself, "after a few weeks of disappearance, Victor should be ready," because something had told her: "Victor was her man; he was the guy to take charge in her life; he was the someone, whose arms she would lie in and find comfort after a tiring day."

Helen was being truthful with Victor; she only wanted him to be with her, when she really needed him. Well, I suppose, every woman will say, that is all they want; big deal. But, are they serious. Helen had no problems with satisfaction, she could and did take care of that herself, if need be, but psychologically she felt the presence of a man eliminated the constant desire for sex or lust, which sometimes consumed an entire day, night, or whenever her mind thought crazy things about what her body could do with someone else's body. And like all of us, at least those of us who think positive, Helen too felt and knew, "she was the only woman capable of completely satisfying Victor."

Helen knew there was not a man that walked on earth with her which she could not get; simply due to man's nature: They crave black things, either conscious or subconsciously. Blackness reminds them of personal possessions around them, such as their black shoes, black belt, and black wallet. Black reminds them of falling into a black pit or black cavern and whether they are man enough to get out. Black even boosts man's vulnerability when he thinks he can get one piece and not want another. And lastly, for purposes here, the curiosity of that powerful black vaginal elasticity which can drain juice out of a toothpick or the last bit of juice from a cucumber, and everything else in between; plus a grip and suction with strength to lead a man involuntarily around the room by his tongue. You jet black women out there, of course have many more and are not afraid to use them on whomever you want. Helen knew all the truths, myths, and mystics, be they craven, personals, manhoods, vulnerabilities, or curiosities; they worked. She knew, her black smooth shiny skin demanded attention by its mere presence. In other words, it was real easy to get hooked on that sweet black magic.

There was no doubt, Victor was hooked the last time he saw Helen, and it was all by design. Helen interrupted Victor in the middle of a sentence, which ensured an eagerness to follow her to her vehicle with his eyes widely focused. She knew he was still looking when she purposely dropped her keys before entering the car. As the long black skirt tightened around Helen's curvedness, Victor imagined himself standing closely to her bending round derriere; he had those lustful cravens which captured his imagination. Helen originally had a one step plan for Victor; be honest, tell him he can have your body; and it did not work. So she developed her three step plan: Show the front, the rear, and then combine the two if necessary. Victor had taken a nibble when Helen exposed her sensuous black thigh; he took another nibble, off of her bending rear, when his imagination was totally blown. Helen had really expected Victor to call her immediately. He did not. No problem, Helen had another step to go; the deadly combination. She was positive, Victor would be inside of her bedroom and inside of her bald volcano by the weekend; today is Wednesday. Victor, at the moment, is busy solving Angela's problems, giving her a double dosage–one called Helen. NO problem for Helen; she had promised Victor, "he could have his cake and eat it too."

Thursday morning, Victor had a message awaiting his arrival into his office.

"Good morning Victor, Helen wants you to call her."

"Hello Tiffani; did she say what she wanted by any chance?"

"Well, yes but...we never discussed Helen or Carolyn, and I would rather not say, Victor."

"Those are personal items Tiffani, which you probably already know." And laughs.

"Well, yeah...women do talk from time to time." Smiling also.

"Okay, what did she say or want rather, Tiffani?"

"Helen wants you to come by her place after work today; are you going Victor?"

"Why? And why are you so excited, Tiffani?"

"Well, I have talked to her on the phone and she seems like a very nice lady Victor."

"Yeah Tiffani, you said the same thing about Carolyn."

"Yes I did and she is, but Helen seems nicer than Carolyn; and I really like Carolyn, but she is a little bossy. I actually believe she could make you do anything she wanted you to Victor. That is not all bad, because she does look nice all over."

"Just between you and me Tiffani, that Carolyn is nice everywhere."

"Yeah, she said you were no slouch.....oh, Victor, I did not mean to say..."

"Yes, go on Tiffani!"

"Victor, you should not pressure me about a private conversation."

"Oh, I'm just kidding with you Tiffani."

"Well, Carolyn is really funny; she refers to you as big boy; where did she get that from?"

"Oh Tiffani, you mean she did not tell you; it is only a private joke."

This morning was funnier than any lately; even when talking about running away. Now that they both knew, the other knew; maybe Carolyn and Helen could be discussed and Tiffani could help Victor with his problems…well, whenever he gets any from them.

"Victor, are you going to see Helen this evening; you never did answer me–you know."

"You would find out anyway, I am leaning hard in that direction." Tiffani laughs.

"What's so funny, Tiffani?"

"The way you said that leaning–"

"Oh, don't say it Tiffani; get your mind out of the gutter. Helen, like you said is a very nice person."

"Okay!" Tiffani still laughing. "Well, do you want to go Victor?"

"What troubles me is why I should go; which has little to do with me wanting to go, Tiffani."

"The two might be closer related than you think Victor; what does Helen look like?"

"She is a beautiful black woman….."

"Well, knowing you Victor, I assumed as much myself."

"No, Tiffani, I mean in complexion; she is beautiful and has the smoothest black skin I have ever seen; she reminds me of a doll."

"That is probably it Victor, you find her appealing because she is gorgeous."

"I already considered that Tiffani, and I do not believe so."

"Have you touched her or been touched by her Victor?"

"No– not that I can recall. What would that have to do with my going by there Tiffani?"

"To possibly finish what you started; like sometimes people kiss or hold each other in a manner, which they know a follow-up will produce more of the same enjoyment and much better results, Victor."

"You mean sexually, Tiffani!"

"Victor, you are sharp today–now what else would a follow-up entail! How about lustfully touching her?"

"Well, I did look underneath her black thigh once Tiffani, and sort of let my mind wander; but I have since discarded that."

"Sounds like you thought you discarded it Victor, but in reality it is still with you."

"How is that Tiffani?"

"Listen at what you said; not thigh, but looked underneath her black thigh. You buried that intriguing black thigh in your subconscious; and now you want to go further, go beyond that black thigh to a black something else. You would even settle for the black thigh again, because you have become fascinated and completely overwhelmed by Helen's blackness. Even in your description of her Victor, you started out by saying; she is a beautiful black woman."

"You might be right Tiffani, what do you suggest?"

"Stay away if you can; you are asking for double trouble Victor; Carolyn will be leading you around by the balls, while Helen will be leading you around by the tongue; either yours–hers, or both."

"Now that might not be so bad Tiffani." Smiling.

"As long as you know what you are in for Victor; after all, it is your body. The choice is probably no longer yours; sounds like you are already hooked. Answer me quickly, yes or no."

"Okay, Tiffani."

"Do you want to go by Helen's?"

"No!"

"Are you going by Helen's?"

"Yes!–I mean I don't know yet; you tricked me Tiffani."

Tiffani laughing. "Let me know about your visit tomorrow Victor."

"You really think I'm hooked, don't you? No woman can hook me that quickly Tiffani."

"Carolyn did!"

"Well, that was different Tiffani; Carolyn had those strong grips and forced me into it." Laughing.

"Yeah Victor, you men are all alike; one whiff and you will sniff at anything. I will be waiting for your report tomorrow, Mr. Tough Guy."

Helen asked Victor to stop by her place. "Maybe she has come to her senses," he thought. As soon as he entered the door, Helen proceeded to undress. As she removed each garment, his mind wondered. He wondered if he would see the same lovely kinky nest as Carolyn's or the large black curly locks that adorned

Helen's head. Helen had the thickest, curliest hair, he had ever seen. Victor's imagination was enraptured as he watched her slowly remove each piece and lay it aside; each being neatly folded.

Victor sensed Helen was deliberately doing this to prove his other women were commoners. So far she was right. Helen had the grace of a queen. Now down to her panties and bra; that eye-filling black body was glowing like fiery coal on a grill. Victor's body was as hot as a straightening-comb, but he did not dare touch her. Never before had a lady caused his hands to water. Helen knew what she was doing as she unsnapped her bra, only to have it hang on one shoulder. Her pointed breast darted free as she caressed each nipple with her thumb and the tips of her fingers. Now Victor's mouth was beginning to water.

Helen paid little attention to Victor as she continued to cuddle and squeeze her breast. Suddenly she gasped as secretion gently flows from the erected nipples. She fondled and massaged her breast like he had never seen before—so meticulous, so indulgent, so caring. Now Helen glances at Victor as she slides her palms down her stomach inside her panties and gradually glide them over her smooth round buttocks. As the panties and bra fall to the floor, Helen bends over as if to pick them up. Helen's now frantic, with eyes closed and mouth open, as her delicate fingers tenderly rub her vital organs. She screams and quivers with intensity as an orgasm occurs.

While Victor did not know what to expect, not a pubic strand resided there. There it was, a perfect rosy and black bald volcano staring him in the face. It was extremely wet and gapped wide open; then it was shut; now it was open again. What body control as splashing sounds drowned Victor's ears with each opening and closing. He had risen for the occasion and his tongue was also swollen. He did not quite know what to do. The glistening moisture on her labia majora beckoned a kiss, but Victor did not move. Helen was in no hurry to raise up as she peered at him through her magnificent black thighs. Several more openings and closings as she slithered her tongue across her lips, was all Victor could stand as he ejaculates in his pants—ejaculatio ante portem.

Helen had loved herself and raped Victor with unyielding

sensuous erogenous movements. Now he was wet all over. She knew he was done for today. Helen smiled and said "the lesson on copulation, fellation, and cunnilingus were to come later." Whatever she meant it was all right with Victor.

Helen had proven she knew anatomy; at the same time making herself irresistible. As bad as Victor wanted to originally tell Helen to bug off; he now knew it was impossible to say no. The lady had a seductive body. In Victor's wildest dreams, this would have been farfetched. Without touching a hair on his head, Helen had become overwhelmingly convincing. "Helen might not be so bad after all," he thought saying, "Whoa, is she ever overpowering."

Curiosity had gotten the best of Victor–he wonders what else she knows. Now he wants to love every inch of Helen's body. "Maybe she is not from this planet," he thought. And today she dared Victor to spend the weekend with her.

"Victor, you will be hooked forever, when I get through with you."

Victor, was still trying to be cool and little did she know, he was already hooked.

"Victor, I want to share you. Please promise me that you will not leave Angela and Carolyn. I will show you how to satisfy all three of us."

"I'm pleased to know you have so much confidence in me Helen. Are you sure a weekend is enough schooling for me?"

"I hope it takes a lifetime Victor; but you will know enough to give lessons when the weekend is up."

That kind of talk coming from a woman could piss a man off; but from Helen, Victor truly wanted to listen and learn. At his age, he already thought he knew everything. However, Helen had proven, that you never get too old to learn.

Victor, talking lowly to himself said, "one thing I do know Helen, whenever we do get together, I'm not having another orgasm in my pants. No more of that psycholagny. I had something to do this weekend, but I suppose it can wait. Helen has me on fire."

EXHIBITIONIST

On display, a body, so revealing
So beautiful, so black, so real
In me, arose, a sensational chilling
I dare, not touch, nor feel

Movements-meticulous, tender-caring
Assets cuddled, and fondled-so fine
My presence, no notice, of such staring
Motionless, gazing she didn't mind

A body, so dark, yet glowing hot
Smooth lines, and curves-so round
Appearance, a statue, reality-its not
Suffering, but ecstatic, me-she found

Passion, anxiety, the room did fill
Quite, an anatomy lesson; and next?
Much to learn, each day, you live
Doubly indeed, from opposite sex

Determined, showing, others a commoner
Dazzling, pleasant, voluptuous outburst
Heart-pounding, eyes-glued on her
Much watering; her body-I now thirst

Yelling, screaming, heard only inside
A weakling, I could not let on
Conquered; to myself, I did confide
Somehow, black beauty, must have known

Moving, grooving, giving me an eye
Much teasing, and pleasing, I get
On and on, she performs, my oh my
Not stopping, until, we're both wet

Victor had now taken a good look at Helen and her blackness; man, he said to himself, this child is really black. He remembered what his grandmother used to say about that black berry and its sweet, sweet juices. His mind went rampart. Helen he thought seductively, as he had stared at the glistening moisture, had to be really–really sweet. If Victor had any myth concerning Helen being anything but sweet, it was quickly dispelled with her mouth-watering strip tease. With his saliva glands secreting heavier than ever, he could taste the sweetness as streams and streams of sugary juices flooded his mouth. Now, obviously was not the time, because he was trying to be–well, cool, but Victor knew, down deep, all the way to the wetness in his underwear, Helen was truly appetizing and worthy of his dining pleasure.

Helen knew what she wanted, and now Victor's little Pekingese curious nature had rapidly squirted forward. He needed Helen, like he needed another hole in his head; however, as we see, the decision made was not done entirely on his own. Coercion. It is amazing how outside forces can affect one's life…body…feeling…thinking…; the message is so clear. Victor's illusion of Helen being good and tasty is one presumption; but before the readers get another presumptive idea…Helen is really good…at heart.

It was seven o'clock in the morning and Tiffani was already in the office and going about her day as usual. Getting to work an hour or so earlier in her opinion always seemed to make things run smoother, if nothing more she always avoided the busy rush hour. Somehow, it all balanced out, because on Friday's as today was, Tiffani left the office at noon. Victor, even told her she could leave at three o'clock in the evening all the other days, but Tiffani rarely if ever took him up on it; she loved working for Victor, stating on numerous occasions, "I could not have a better person as my boss"

Besides the workload going on, Tiffani also had the two coffee pots going on, and today as most of the last days for the week, she had picked up a dozen old fashioned donuts. Victor was spoiled to sweets, plus it was Tiffani's way of telling him weekly how much she appreciated his kindness. She generally ate one, while Victor and people going and coming consumed the rest. And speaking of coming; drawing nearer, in the outside hall was a harmonious whistling approaching. Tiffani heard it and did not hear it, continuing her work, until the office door opened. It was Victor, whistling up a tuneful song; much unlike his normal self.

"Good morning Tiffani!" Continuing his song of, Old Man River, into a croon as he went into his office.

"Good morning, my, aren't we happy today; Mr. Tough Guy must have things going his way."

"Tiffani, you are so nosey; okay, bring one of those pots and we'll talk now; otherwise, we both know, we'll never get any work done…don't forget those donuts."

Victor definitely knew Tiffani; she would have bugged him until noon. Walking faster than she had earlier, Tiffani hurried into Victor's office with the tray full of goodies, smiling as she entered, wasting no time, saying:

"Okay Mr. Tough Guy, what happened?"

"Tiffani I am only sharing this information because you do not know Helen from Jack-in-the-Box and to satisfy your snoopiness."

"Victor, you are sharing this information because I am your private secretary, who will be better able to advise you further during current and future affairs."

"Well…yes, that too! Anyway, I do not know how much you know about my visit from Carolyn, and what she did and all, Tiffani."

"You mean, having no panties on; she told me those were her intentions to get your undivided attention and hold it. Did Helen do the same Victor?"

"Uh huh, sure did, if I did not know any better, I would say they knew each other or do all you women treat prospective male friends the same Tiffani?"

If Victor had been listening, he would have known Helen and Carolyn knew each other. Honest Helen told him a while back, she knew of Carolyn and Angela; who knows what his mind was on at the time. And if he had gone to Carolyn's sorority party, he would have known the two were sorority sisters. Helen and Carolyn were not only sisters, they coincidentally found out both were pursuing the same fellow. Neither wanted to give up, because both felt they had discovered the right fellow to take care of their sexual needs; after all, in their opinion, "girl I just need somebody to knock this dust off, every now and then." So they agreed to share him, if they were both successful, henceforth the similarities. Tiffani was not aware to date Helen and Carolyn were friends.

"Not really Victor, I would never do anything like that, unless I felt I had to. Knowing you and your stubbornness, that may be the only way your attention span could be expanded. Well, did you put up strong objections or what?"

"Tiffani, I wanted to, I really wanted to, but that Helen put on an exhibition which would have made a blind man take notice."

"Well, what did she do Victor?"

"Helen not only pulled off her panties, but every stitch, and paraded around in front of me with sexy antics with her fine black body, and let me tell you Tiffani, that area was like a bald volcano, but I was the one spitting and breathing fire. At no time during this exhibition did I touch her; however, I wanted to so bad until–"

"Until what Victor?"

"Promise me Tiffani that you won't laugh or tell anyone else; the girl had me so hot, I did it in my pants."

Tiffani was laughing so hard, her side begin to hurt. "Oh, do not worry," still laughing, "I would not tell anybody that, Mr. Tough Guy. So if I follow you correctly Victor, you are now hooked on Helen like you are on Carolyn; unless you refuse to see her again. When are you going to see her again?"

"Well...I promised her...this weekend Tiffani."

"Tomorrow! What are you to going to do Victor?"

"Well, tomorrow, today, and Sunday; at her place Tiffani."

"Victor, you mean the entire weekend; have you lost your ever loving mind; nobody's stuff is that good."

"I tried to tell myself the same thing, but Helen is still parading around in front of me with that beautiful black clean- shaven body. It feels like I am craving this woman Tiffani."

"Victor, that is nothing but lust; I am sure you were the same way after Carolyn showed you her naked body."

"That is true Tiffani, but this is worse."

"Mr. Tough Guy, huh; Victor you cannot go around catering to every woman who bares her bottom to you; women will use and take advantage of you, if you let them. Pretty soon, this Helen will be making you do anything she wants, like I feel Carolyn is already doing."

"Maybe so Tiffani, maybe so."

So much for the coffee and donuts; the coffee was gone and only three donuts remained. Victor's appetite increased somewhat, just thinking about the two most powerful women he had ever met in Helen and Carolyn.

The weekend spent with Helen was one of the most exciting and exhilarating weekends ever. Helen took one look at Victor and said.

"Victor, you have one gigantic molly-whooper on you. I tell you now, there is no way I will ever try to take all of that, but I love it; it will be so easy to get a grip on. Do not worry Victor, you will always be satisfied each night with me; leaving the next day completely drained. That molly-whopper of yours will look like a used dish rag, when I am done with you."

And was Helen ever right, Victor was truly happy the entire weekend, but was happier when he limped out of there.

CHAPTER TEN

GETTING ACQUAINTED

"Victor, I am picking you up for the auto show; what is the best night?"

"I'm available all week Carolyn, so make it convenient for yourself."

"Okay Victor, see you about seven Friday evening; we will grab something to eat on the way."

Victor hoped Carolyn was not too preoccupied with that dumb auto show, because he was going to surprise her with a seafood candlelight dinner. He thought, "I deserve it–she deserves it–why not."

"Hi Victor, are you ready?"

"Well Carolyn, yes and no, come in."

"Why is it so dark in here Victor, did you pay your bills this month?"

"Just hold my hand and follow me Carolyn. I have a surprise for you."

"I'd say you do Victor, who prepared all this food?"

"Never ask a lady her age and never ask a man his secrets on fine cuisine Carolyn."

"Okay, then, what's the occasion Victor?"

"Honey chile" don't spoil the evening. You said we were going to grab something on the way, so prepare to dine."

Ever since the unfinished evening in Carolyn's office, Victor had jitters when she was nearby. Tonight was that special time to get his body back on the normal side. Easing into dinner and following it up with something naughty seemed like the correct protocol. Victor was guessing that she's no more interested in that old auto show, as he was. Victor's mind went crazy just looking at Carolyn: "Lets hope our bodies are the right model and year; a bit vintage perhaps, but workable. Carolyn certainly has a lot more mileage in that motor of hers. Tonight's a night for park anyway. The only cruising, will be down the hall into my bedroom." His thoughts clearly saw him continuing the enjoyment of Carolyn's digestible juices.

And, about the dinner. It's amazing what guys go through to impress their female companionship. One thing Victor can do is cook. Preparing the finest of cuisines is a trait he was blessed with. When it comes to taking vegetables from the garden, and making their true form disappear onto the table, that's Victor. Carrots become radiant jewels; potatoes are like pearls, onions twinkle more so than diamonds; beets will have an appraisal to match the most luxurious ruby; and his greens and beans, set sparkling to that of an emerald.

What are vegetables without a main course——meat! Beef was out——at least with Carolyn——and what a shame. But with poultry——just mention quail, pheasant, Cornish hens and the like, and ducks; these feathered friends are all dying to get on Victor's table. Fish and all sea foods——a specialty of all specialties. French chef's have been known to ask for his secrets. Fish and fowl alike volunteer for his oven, begging for more seasoning.

And tonight——their meal——well it came from the Oyster Bar, the finest seafood restaurant in the city of San Antonio, Texas. Well——what did you expect him to do——lie about a substitute. Let us hope Carolyn is as pleased eating it as he was in ordering it.

"Victor, before you get too romantic, I am on my cycle."

"WHAT——I mean——you are?"

"See, I knew you were up to something. And it is not a bad idea, but you cannot fool with mother nature. Relax Victor, we will get around to that again; I want it to really happen more than you do."

"Sure Carolyn."

"That is right, "honey chile", don't pout and spoil the evening."

"I've been acquainted with you about a year Carolyn, but it seems to be so much longer."

"Is that good or bad Victor?"

"Good I suppose, depending on how you look at it."

"Is that a singular or plural you, Victor?"

"Carolyn, don't be so technical."

"Oh, I am just having fun. Now that I know you can't seduce me, I feel safe. Again I am just kidding Victor; this food is magnificent. Other than what Ralph told me about you Victor, I do not know a lot; but so far, you are the nicest man I have ever met."

"Do you want to learn about me in bunches or little by little, Carolyn?"

"If it is all like tonight and in my office the other day; I will continue to take it step by step. You know, slow and easy is always much better, Victor."

Victor thought to himself: "That's sort of what was in my mind——slow and easy. But tonight we are pretty much stuck on slow. There ought to be someway a guy can tell when mother nature is calling——I mean before time——like before the dinner is all prepared. Maybe one day, some smart scientist will develop something to warn us poor fellows when the old period is near. We'll simply point it at the woman and it'll beep twice——maybe three times. Just a thought——we must think of the safety of the fish and fowl——you know. Well, learning about Carolyn this way might not be all bad."

"Why are you so quiet Victor?"

"Oh, just thinking Carolyn. What about your girls, I've never met them; where do you hide them out?"

"They spend almost every weekend with their father Victor. They are nine and eighteen, so it gives me much needed relief."

"Why is it that you've never married again Carolyn?"

"I have only been divorced three years. And really Victor, I have not been looking. The girls and work take up most of my time. My spare time is generally spent reading and exercising this tired body of mine."

"I can see the results on the latter Carolyn."

"Oh, yeah, what about the reading Victor?"

"Oh, just kidding, but your body has a way of blocking the other views Carolyn."

"I have met men, but I have not been interested. I have not had sex or any intimate relations until I met you. That is why I asked Ralph to introduce us. You appealed to me, and afterwards I found you interesting. My body starts vibrating, even at the thought of you. I just hope I have not made a fool out of myself. You got short changed in my office Victor, but that was a welcomed relief for me. I promise, I will make it up to you."

"I did not want to, but I had to divorce my husband. He was extremely jealous, Victor. He threatened Gerald and any other man that even looked at me. Any woman that takes pride in keeping herself fit is going to look good. My mom raised me that way. So I have always received considerable attention from the opposite sex. And I will be the first to admit, the stares and goo-goo eyes are pleasing to me. I just do not know any other way. He married me like that and then wanted me to dress and look like a plain Jane. I suppose if I had not been so independent, wearing those long cotton dresses would have worked."

"Men are naturally going to notice a woman that is dressed well and maintain her body in a streamline position, Victor. My husband knew that and became angry when I received compliments. I laughed about his moodiness until it started happening often. Then I saw he was serious and did not want another man smiling at me, let alone talking. I felt sort of special about my husband thinking his love was just that strong for me. He had always been extremely possessive, even prior to getting married. It never dawned on me, the strong love would change into jealousy."

"I can't say I've ever been around anyone Carolyn, who is extremely jealous; but I suppose a few problems could develop."

"You bet they can Victor. You are watched all the time; and what few social events you attend, you are never out of their sight. My husband constantly made excuses about attending affairs; even parties given by our best friends. To attend anything, I was having to put my foot down and say; I'll go alone.... That was out of the question, so he would agree to go."

"His traits were somewhat peculiar Victor, because he never said a word if I did not dress up. For instance, when I went shopping in a sweat suit or baggy pants, sneakers, and a scarf on my head; not a word was said."

"Maybe it was the high heels that made him act up Carolyn, I've noticed you, walking around the office; high heels causes your body to move a little different than most women I've seen. Sometimes I wonder if you aren't putting an extra swirl into that motion."

"Victor, you are kidding me."

"No Carolyn, but I figured it out; it's your height. No one notices hedges blown by the wind, but a pine tree swaying, generates much attention. And let's face it girl, you be wearing the hell outta those clothes."

"Jealousy Victor, of course was only one of his problems; the other one was a bit male chauvinistic. It had to do with me making more money than him. At first it did not bother him or at least, it did not show. Maybe it was eating at him from the inside. It became real apparent though, when he got a second job. He made a few excuses why we needed the extra money. Then my salary began to take off, after the first job change. It got to the point where I could not share the joy of my promotions with him. It became worse when I shared them with the girls, by going to dinner and shopping. As a result, my girls and I are extremely close. I don't see how I could live without them. Most of the time, he was at work, so I did not think it mattered. He then accused me of turning the girls against him. I told him that he did not have to work so much, that we did not need the money from his damn extra job."

"I found myself getting off the floor Victor. That was the first time he hit me. I forgave him that time because I was sorry for saying what I did. The second time he hit me was after a banquet. The couple on my left, somehow reversed seats during the night and the husband ended next to me. He was a big talker, a very jovial character, and I was laughing the rest of the night."

"We argued all the way home Victor, and he decked me in the driveway. I forgave him this time because he convinced me he was protecting me. That was how many women got raped, he said. After that I lost count, and the reason, and why I forgave him. It seems like he was beating me everyday for something I did or did not do. The girls were becoming terrified and I was fearing for my life. This seems to have all happened so quickly that I did not know what to do."

"Some people told me to get him to seek help Victor, but I got a beating for that suggestion. Then something just clicked; I have lost all my independence with this man. The only way out is to take my girls and leave. Waking up is what probably saved my life. He begged me to come back; that he would change. I attended a battered wives seminar, and the conclusion was; "don't go back". "Once a wife beater, always a wife beater". "Someone will get hurt". "Either, you'll kill him or he'll kill you". There was not one positive quote for going back. So I forgave him one last time via telephone, and divorced him shortly thereafter. It is funny, but since that time, we get along so much better, but I am never going to get cocky and spend a night with him."

"Speaking of spending the night Victor, it looks like I have spent the most of it talking about me."

"That's fine Carolyn and if you like, you can spend the rest of it here."

"I would not want to impose on you Victor, the dinner was more than enough."

"Remember, you said you had mother nature protecting you, Carolyn."

"Now-now Victor, I am not afraid of you."

"Well, why not, you can sleep in a pair of my pajamas Carolyn."

"Oh, I don't know Victor, I don't like bottoms; I cannot breathe that way."

"Okay, leave it off Carolyn and I'll suffer."

"You do not have to suffer Victor, just pretend I an not here; I can use your guest bedroom; that way, you will never see me. It is only ten o'clock Victor, but for some reason I am bushed. If you do not mind, could we get a fresh start in the morning."

"Sure, why not Carolyn, let me show you where the towels are; I will lay those pajamas on the bed, while you're in the bathroom."

"Thank you Victor, and please leave the bedroom door open."

"Excuse my French; damn," said Victor to himself, "this is not exactly how I drew up the plans."

Victor was far from sleepy, so he sat in the family room and scanned through the news on TV until the Tonight Show and Jay

Leno came on. He heard Carolyn splashing in the tub and humming some tune as she washed that fine body of hers. Victor thought about yelling to her to see if she wanted a back rub; but decided against it just as quickly; since she had made it pretty clear, a fresh start in the morning.

"Victor, what are you watching?"

Victor looked up to see the tall beautiful Carolyn, with his long pajama top hanging over her gorgeous body, showing only a portion of her large thighs and all of those long hairy legs. Victor had simmered all the way down, but Carolyn's appearance caused an immediate swollen bigness inside his pants

"Hi Carolyn, I thought you had turned in; would you like to join me?"

"No, I do not wish to disturb you Victor, but I want something to drink, like milk or juice."

"You're in luck Carolyn, there is some milk and orange juice inside the refrigerator, help yourself."

Carolyn was smart, knowing her presence in the same room with Victor was enough to disturb him; and here she was, in the same room, half dressed, returning with a large glass of milk, sitting opposite him.

"Mind if I finish my milk in here Victor?" Crossing her legs and looking Victor directly in the face.

"This is your palace for tonight Carolyn, make yourself at home." Looking hard at her legs, trying hard to see further, but his pajama top hung entirely too long in his opinion.

"Knowing she was safe," thought Victor, "he expected some antics from Carolyn any moment." She did gap her long legs apart, placing both feet on the carpet, as wide as she was comfortably capable of spreading them, but she pushed the loose pajama material upon the sofa, hiding that woolly center, which she stunningly displayed to Victor in his office. And oddly enough, Victor could not help but think of that very moment. Looking at this sensuous woman made him feel silly at his current thought: "She is the only woman I would gladly love on the rag."

"You have a nice place Victor; it could stand a little of the woman's touch though."

"Maybe I can borrow a suggestion or two from you Carolyn."

"Sure Victor, if you promise to invite me back."

"How about, when you are available Carolyn!"

"I understand Victor, the bulge in your pants makes it obvious; there is more to life than that you know, I lasted three years, surely you can last a few more days."

"Carolyn, I cannot help it if my feelings are showing, but you are one sexy woman, and I wish we could make love tonight."

"Thank you Victor and I wish I could help you, but my husband forced me into doing that once and I have hated it ever since; there is still a bad taste in my mouth. Please do not ever ask me to do you Victor. Having a cruel man in my life has spoiled me to a number of good love making features. It has even made me somewhat selfish; sometimes wanting to tease and not give up anything. Fortunately, that does not apply totally to you."

"What do you mean totally Carolyn; seems like I will get the partial selfish person, huh?"

"That is true; however, I will change in time, you will be a big part of it too, with that load you are carrying. Being out of commission tonight is as hard for me Victor as it is for you; I can hardly wait to have your bigness inside of me. And on that note I am going to bed. Goodnight Victor."

"Goodnight Carolyn, see you in the morning."

Carolyn strolled into the bedroom with Victor watching her every step of the way. He still was not sleepy, so he decided to cut the TV off, remain on the sofa and meditate. And it seems now, like there was more than ever to meditate about. Carolyn, in his opinion, had had a rough go of it, with that husband of hers. "Thanks to him," Victor thought, "I am not getting some of Carolyn's loving right now; men like that should be hung or shot before a firing squad." He wondered if this crazy fool had done something else to Carolyn which she had not mentioned. "It would have never dawned on me" thought Victor, "a woman could become skittish on making love because of a bad husband experience."

More thoughts went through Victor's mind, thinking of a beautiful Carolyn in his bed by herself. There would be no sleep or rest for him tonight; he had already come to that conclusion, as the hour eased onward toward two in the morning. Carolyn was snoring loud as a wild boar and seemingly on her way to a restful night, until words began to come forth with jerking movements. At first Victor heard only a murmuring of sounds which turned to intelligible words of "NO,....I wont go....NO....NO." Concerned and wide awake, Victor rushed to his opened bedroom door to find Carolyn screaming, jerking, still saying "NO....NO....NO." The covering had all slid onto the floor and Victor's long pajama top was completely unbuttoned and too, had slid off her gorgeous body, to each side. Carolyn woke up when Victor yelled, "Carolyn," simultaneously cutting the light on; jumping on the bed, grabbing her into his arms, to comfort her. It was minutes later that Victor discovered the nakedness within his arms; however, he immediately felt the warmness of Carolyn's large rapidly breathing breast pouncing into his chest. Carolyn was shaking as she embraced Victor, holding him even tighter than when the elevator stopped. This however was no love hold, but one of fear. There was no crying. Victor gently patted and rubbed her back as he would have, during her bath. He held her affectionately, the same, if she had been lying there within his grasp all night. Victor also spoke soft, kind, comforting words, just as he would have done, if they had been making love to each other. When the shaking ceased and Carolyn's breathing was closer to normal, Victor pulled back to look at her face and inquire.

"Are you okay Carolyn?"

"I think so....I will be all right."

"You were apparently having a nightmare; do you know what it was about Carolyn?"

"Maybe some little old green man was chasing me Victor; oh my, I do not have anything around me. Excuse me Victor, let me button up my top and get some cover on me. I will be okay, seriously, don't worry," leaning and kissing Victor lightly on his lips.

"It does not seem like something to be taking lightly Carolyn."

"Okay Victor, if you are worried, why don't you stay here with me the rest of the night; and protect me from the little old green man."

"Those were exactly my thoughts Carolyn; I'll have a quick shower and be right back."

Victor quickly removed his clothes, going through the shower even faster, returning at once to further hold and comfort Carolyn. Victor's body was moving quite rapid, and his mind was going just as fast; thinking about his house guest. It seemed to him, Carolyn was concealing something from him; and his mind flew to that no good abusive husband of hers. Now he knew, there was more to Carolyn's story on him than she had told him only hours earlier. "Well", Victor thought, "it is none of my business, and since they are divorced, she will undoubtedly be okay, just as she said." No sooner than Victor crawled in beside Carolyn, did she wrap those long arms and legs about him. The warmth and softness of her body made him forget the earlier incident. Carolyn could feel Victor's bigness pressing against her woolly center. She let him know of her willingness to be more than a partial lover, pulling him even tighter and holding and rubbing his behind with those delicate hot hands of hers. Before going to sleep, she whispered to Victor, telling him, "she would be ready, and back in his bed in three days." It appeared, both of them had comforted each other.

Morning's light came and the two were still bound together with their embracing arms and legs. There was no mentioning of last night or hours earlier by either of them; for they were too busy concentrating on three days away, which calculated, according to their estimates, to be Tuesday. Carolyn's awakening felt Victor's bigness more than ever, still resting firmly against her woolly door.

"It is too bad we have to wait until Tuesday Victor, I can hardly wait."

"Good morning Carolyn; I was thinking Wednesday," and laughs.

"Oh no you don't Big Boy, you are not putting me off another day for this." Caressing Victor's bigness with her soft warm hands, making sure he remained focused. "I am looking forward to coming here."

Well, nothing of any consequence happened between today and Tuesday. Tiffani did tease the both of them Monday for not knowing anything about the auto show. Neither, mentioned their park-in or automobile show the following evening.

Tuesday, true to form, Carolyn made her way to Victor's place; following him all the way from work, no sooner than the closing minute approached. Both were eager to get even further acquainted, and this they did; going through the shower faster than Victor had, early that memorable Saturday morning. Missing their evening's meal to be devoured by each other had many more nutrients; each would have quickly conceded. Their nude bodies clasped as soon as they fell upon the bed; each holding the other tightly as if this was the first time ever, being with one of the opposite sex. Carolyn wanted to relish this moment, asking Victor:

"How long can you hold on inside of me Victor; I want you parked there all night long. I want to feel and enjoy what I have been missing the past three years."

"That is a hard one Carolyn; probably a long time, if you do not move."

"You are so right Victor, it is really hard." Laughing.

Carolyn had no problem taking all of Victor's bigness; and as much as she wanted to she did not move. She was calm, never thinking of making Victor suffer, but praising him for ending her suffering of three long years. Their unique togetherness lasted until five in the morning, when the alarm sounded for another work day or day at the office. Both Carolyn and Victor; however were completely satisfied, and neither had moved. They teased each other as they showered and dressed for the office saying; "somebody moved." All during the week as they met each other; their private joke had become; "somebody moved".

CHAPTER ELEVEN

ADVICE

"That is a great book Victor. My question is, where has it been. Do you realize that it was originally published in the nineteenth century, It should be on public schools required reading list instead of Mark Twain's Huckleberry Finn."

"Now, Angela, you're beginning to understand. Twain's book continues to perpetuate the system of degradation, while Frederick Douglass's book is geared toward upward mobility."

"That is true Victor; here is a man born a slave and went on to become a free man, and a real somebody. He taught himself to read and write. That book stirred my curiosity, so I am reading other books about our black heritage. One thing I have learned already: With my fair complexion, I am a direct descendant of that cruelty upon our black women. They were raped and molested against their will. We were really treated bad. My mind has been enlightened Victor, I want you to read my poem."

AM I BITTER

You brought me here
  Against my will
My sister died
  My brother was killed

You destroyed family unity
  As we cried
We couldn't escape
  Lord knows we tried

Mama to New Orleans
  Papa to Charleston, S.C.
Highest bidder
  Got the body

Property indeed
  Is what we were
We begged to stay together
  But you didn't care

We worked with mules
  Like mules before day
We were your slave
  So forget the pay

You breeded us to
  Get a stronger stock
You raped our women
  Every chance you got

Who in the hell
  Do you think you are
Loose ass morals
  And all thus far

You were superior
  Had lots of fun
You still have the whip
  But I've got the gun

Am I Bitter!

"Whoa, your mind is more than enlightened Angela, I'd say it's boiling."

"That is just the way I felt at the time, Victor. You would have to agree it is better than screwing someone around on their job everyday. Maybe from now on, I will take my frustrations out with the pen."

"Do you think that will work Angela?"

"I do not know; but I do know Frederick Douglass was a fighter, and he has become my hero. We as a people must believe in total freedom as he believed; and have the determination to achieve as he achieved. Because of you Victor, I will never be the same. All blacks must realize that until equal opportunities are attainable without double standards, caused by our skin color; we will never be free. We must fight daily to eliminate those barriers. I have come to the conclusion Victor, that it is not going to be an easy task, because we are up against the ancestral racism, you spoke of."

Angela had come to the right conclusion, it would not be easy. But with young people like her trying to make a difference; it was a gigantic step forward. The old adage of "not knowing where you are going until you find out where you come from," had come alive. Angela had got a taste of where she came from with her brief study of black history. The knowledge attained had made her "Bitter" as she puts it; but it had really done more, because Angela was now forcing herself to read and learn more. She now knew where her people came from, she now knew where she came from; and evidently, did not like the beginning; and was now on her own mission to change the present and future.

"Victor, what did you guys do in the olden days about frustration?"

"I wasn't living then Angela." Laughing.

"I do not mean it like it sounds Victor, but you know, during your younger days."

"Oh, let me see Angela if I can remember way back then."

"I am serious Victor, there is so much racism—causing so much inequality in this country."

"The first thing we did Angela was vote. Are you registered to vote?"

"No, I do not see where that will do much good—a few people

getting elected to office. I am not talking about political gains, Victor, but economic gains."

"Angela, the two can't be separated, they go hand in hand."

"What do you mean Victor? I do not quite understand."

"Well, for example Angela, take the Mayor's Office and City Council person and Alderman in most cities; they see that certain appointments are made to fill high level administrative positions. Other positions are filled on important boards and commissions. This translates into us getting better jobs and in many cases, a first time job. It also helps the black business man or woman; because we could be talking about sharing in the millions of dollars being spent on city contracts."

"In any case Angela, we are talking about obtaining positions and money, in which we were formerly completely shut off on. As a matter of fact, we didn't even know about most of this money. All the years we paid taxes and were denied any equitable sharing, simply because we didn't vote. So Angela, before you do anything else; register to vote and vote. Voting is probably the single most important thing a black man can do as an individual. Taking voting for granted is like granting yourself and future black generations to a life of poverty and disparity. You're really telling yourself and others, by not voting; you're not worthy of a chance to improve your small dwindling share."

"I mentioned some elected offices; but County Commissioners and other local elections are very important. Take school boards; look at the educational system and curricula that our community can be stuck with. Angela, you mentioned earlier the famous classic of Mark Twain. To make a black child read that in class filled with white children is embarrassing. Because after class, you have opened the door for so called intelligent whites to feel, they can use these racial slurs and get away with them."

"Now Angela, we are talking about education and developing the minds of little children today and forever. You are what you read. So with inferior textbooks, inadequate programs, and lackadaisical teachers; we can breed a generation of stupid, ignorant, or unprepared children-both black and white. The future and hope for tomorrow lies not only with our children Angela, but also with us. We must do our part."

"I understand a little bit more Victor, but how about the private sector?"

"The private sector is a bit tougher to crack. Because we're leaning more so, for the corporate or company officials to voluntarily implement programs to hire and promote black employees Angela. And to award franchises on an equitable basis. In the olden days as you say, we pushed the Federal Government for affirmative action programs. This worked to a certain extent; mostly for lower paying clerical type jobs. Also, some professional jobs such as what you have now, opened up, but not many. And if one of us were fortunate enough to get hired in a department; they would deliberately not hire another black in that area. Every now and then, one of us like myself, managed to hang around long enough, to get a management position. Until recently most of those positions dealt with minority affairs."

"Well Victor, there is no one at our corporation in a management or executive position but white males. And we are talking about a retail corporation, located in most of these United States."

"That's about par for the course Angela. So you see, your road ahead is going to be even rougher. Now that affirmative action programs are drying up, it's really going to be tough."

"We also tried such tactics as boycotts Angela, which seen to be pretty effective. Boycotts would work today if administered properly. White people are like mules; stubborn as hell. So in order to get his attention and gain your respect, you have to jolt him into it. Get him to the bargaining table, explain your position and see that changes have taken place before you relinquish your position."

"Boycotting Victor seems like it would be too long and cumbersome; and look at the number of people one would have to get together."

"That's partially true Angela, but with mass communication and a little organization, it can be quite effective. But the whole problem in all of our struggles has been getting black people together."

"Why is that Victor?"

"Oh, for a number of reasons; but I'll let you tell me about that later on. But believe me Angela, boycotts work, especially if you're talking about not buying a particular product or using a particular service."

"Picketing is another method of getting your point across Angela. Especially if you can draw good national media coverage. A combination of boycotts with pickets is also highly effective."

"Why is it Victor, that we do not have black organizations addressing these problems today?"

"Complacency, for one Angela. We think we have arrived when we can afford a pair of reebok's, a designer suit, or an European luxury automobile. We'll work two jobs to obtain and maintain this false sense of arrivalty. So advancement or real upward mobility is no longer important or for that matter essential."

"Secondly, the old I got mine, you get yours theory comes into play Angela?"

"What do you mean Victor?"

"Angela, life is about sharing and helping people, especially those less fortunate than yourself. For example, if you can afford to help a kid through college, who otherwise would not go; do it. And it might just mean helping your neighbor in times of trouble. But you have those of us who really struggled, and against all odds and adversity; made it. A selfish individual in this category takes the attitude that, if I can struggle and get mine, you can struggle and get yours."

"Thirdly, Angela, there's a theory that we have been bought off, killed off, or put in jail. Good people, speaking out, cause problems attacking the ills of the world. There have been many of us hushed by a lucrative paying job. If that does not work, we're either disposed of, or jailed on some jumped-up or fabricated charge."

"Lastly, but not all Angela, because I'm sure there's myriads of others. People your age, not taking part in our society, thereby creating a permanent void. Most of you are still riding the horse your parents struggled to get. You don't know how they got the horse; you don't care how they got the horse; and, you don't really give a damn about nothing but yourself. In other words, you're laying back, waiting to reap a harvest and you haven't planted one damn seed. Angela, I can really appreciate your concern."

"Thanks Victor, but I would be like all the others if I had not become so frustrated on my job."

"Angela, you would be surprised the number of blacks

frustrated on these jobs. It applies to most, but they have learned to cope. Of course, anytime you can't get a job or you can't get a promotion, when whites all around you are moving up; you should be frustrated."

"I want to do something on my job Victor. Because I am in a better financial position than most of my cc-workers; I thought of a better plan that might be workable."

"What's that Angela?"

"Like I said, there are no blacks in management or executive positions. They have a management training program, but no blacks have been accepted. Several have applied, including myself, but no success yet. We see whites in this program moving on to higher levels in the corporation, and we cannot even get in. We are tired of it and are thinking about forming an African-American corporate organization to address this issue. What are your thoughts on that Victor?"

"You have to start somewhere Angela. I think that's an excellent idea. The old, two heads are better than one, theory works. You'll have an opportunity to toss ideas around and formulate your next move. Trying to correct a wrong is always a good idea Angela, but you'll meet with resistance."

"We met that Victor when they would not acknowledge an applicant for the management training program. It is not like, we are not qualified. Some of those white guys accepted do not even have college degrees."

"As you go through life Angela, you'll find this old double standard being used. The white man has been using it successfully for centuries. It has worked for him. And let's face it Angela; unless he's forced to share the pie, he's not going to."

"But Victor, we are talking about right and wrong."

"You're right Angela, we are talking about right and wrong; but the white man is talking about giving up power. And, believe me when I tell you, the two are not synonymous in the white man's mind."

"Victor, couldn't the white man see that he is improperly or under-utilizing valuable human resources."

"Nope, I don't think so. You'll have to remember this thing is new to him. New in the sense Angela, that he's been doing okay without our brain input. Our muscle power of old was the great benefit. Plus, the ole slave mentality of "whites are suppose to rule and blacks are supposed to be ruled by whites" is still with us."

"Angela, I had problems when I became a manager. But to be honest they were minor—nothing that I can relate to racism. And a lot of that had to do with my being around for so long—like you know—ole Victor ain't bad after all. But when I became a Regional Vice President, I had a white manager tell me point blank, that he was not going to work for no G.D. nigger."

"What did you do Victor?"

"I told him I understood Angela, but to think about it before you tender your resignation—the company value your input and I value your input."

"You were too damn cool, Victor; I would have told that honky where to get off."

"Don't think I didn't think about it, but there's a thing of over-reacting. I was in the driver's seat Angela. The company was behind me and they wouldn't have selected me if they thought I couldn't handle the position. Some companies recognize talent and utilize all their resources—black or white. My company does that and we are blowing the competition apart. Blacks are not only hired, but promoted as well. We have a mentoring program that is unreal. I'm talking about whites being mentors to blacks and vice-versa. But in order to have this type of thing, it must start at the top. We have one of the best CEO's in the world. His motto is "Human resource is a terrible thing to waste." You and I under-stand the take off."

"Who knows Angela, I might replace him someday, and that's not a dream."

"That is terrific, but what happened to the white manager Victor?"

"You're not going to believe this Angela. He apologized later and is still with us. As a matter of fact, I'm his mentor and con-sider him a real friend. Just two months ago, I recommended him for a new District Manager's opening, and he got it. He's also a mentor to, get this, two black supervisors. The bottom line is prof-its but you must give people a chance regardless of race; and in our case, because of race; otherwise we'll never get in the door.

That's why affirmative action programs are so important—they will get you in the door. Because let's face it, some companies are not going to voluntarily hire blacks. Others will hire, but only for menial and clerical jobs."

"But Victor, don't they know they are losing a valuable resource."

"I know Angela, but they're too racist to give a damn. So when is the first meeting Angela?"

"I do not know Victor, because we are talking about a national meeting; so it is pretty involving. We just completed a list of all the African-American employees. We told personnel what we were doing, and they have been very cooperative. As a matter of fact, they have obtained the corporate cafeteria for our usage. We are talking about 850 people, but out of 48,000. That is some percentage, huh."

"It's about par for the course Angela, but whether you know it or not, there's strength in those numbers."

"We have been trying to decide the date; whether we want it on a holiday weekend or another weekend Victor."

ADVICE

Given gladly only upon request
Ingenious for a mind to seek
Solace in the heart that confess
Painful landing upon your feet

ADVICE upon your toes——ouch
Scold conscience until its clear
Hand from face, undo that crouch
Sound advice is nothing to fear

Impolite to touch cold feelings
Were they not in the way!
Listeners often times go ailing
Snooping distastefully so astray

Advice——half-heartily meant for you
No reason for lips a pout
Much mettlesome work to do
Unprejudiced——help us carry it out

Advice kind and ungrudgingly used
Can change one's woeful heart
Honest-decent-just, not to refuse
Thank yourself for being so smart

During Angela's short time in the work place, she was learning fast, especially to the adverse ways her people were being treated. First, she could not believe the small numbers of blacks hired and the lower positions they were hired for. Then she was surprised, there were no upward mobility in the corporation's plans for them; and worse the plans in place were for white workers only, even inferior educated ones. And all of these new developments in her life had made her frustrated and, well....bitter. There is really nothing revealing about her attitude; she is reacting like the typical African-American who finds themselves denied advancement, immediately after they are employed; which really begs the question asked by all of us; "why in the hell did you hire me in the first place." With the help of Victor, Angela was determined to channel her bitterness into a positive; to make things better, not only for herself but the masses of blacks working at the same company. Angela's greatest asset for this endeavor was her ability to listen, and later try and sort things out. She sought special advice from Victor, inquiring about "olden days", and listening to his reasoning as to why the work place for blacks was the way it was.

Angela was unique; she asked for Victor's advice and also asked his opinion on ideas of her own. Yes, young Angela was in the process of devising plans for strategy to combat problems for blacks at the corporation where she was employed. She was aware of Victor, frowning on her, for not doing something, taking a stand, being a fighter; she will never forget the look he gave her; it was like...are you crazy lady. Angela loved Victor for his brain and to be honest, she really did look up to him. But she had some ideas cooking in her head, and wanted to run them pass Victor. She knew he would go along if the ideas were basically sound, because Angela had found Victor to really respect her brain and ability to think. That is another reason she wanted him for her boss. She obviously would be able to do her thing without fear of reprisal. Oh, she knew, she would always hear his favorite words: "I will let you tell me about that later." Angela had figured out this line to mean: "Go for what you know, see the results, and get back with me." She had not known him to be negative about anything; objective yes. Angela was not just forming ideas and plans in her head, she was putting them down on paper; and we shall surely hear of them in the weeks and months to come. Stay tuned is probably the best summation.

Another interesting point about Angela was her ability to follow through on suggestions made to her by others. She recognized early in life, that nobody knew everything and she could learn from others. So Angela would take the time, follow a suggestion to see if it had any merit. In practically every case, she either found the suggestion worked or led her to something else even more dynamic or both. For example, Victor's suggestions to read the book about Frederick Douglass had led her to start reading all the books she could find about her African-American heritage. Angela read fiction as well as non-fiction. She found herself learning the ways of her people and why they did certain things, but also learning the ways of the slave master and why the white race of people in power today, as a whole, still want to hold African-Americans in an inferior role. Angela found there was a wealth of knowledge to be learned. Useful knowledge for blacks and whites too, who were concerned about respecting all races of people as equal human beings. Never reading anything before on the black experience; Angela now had allocated an adequate portion of her free and leisure time to doing just that. And oddly enough the readings became invaluable in assisting Angela develop her upward mobility project for blacks at their corporation.

Talking about upward mobility for masses of her people was a favorite topic with Angela, but the big score for the evening was a little upward mobility for herself; Victor consented to them having a child; yes, a real live baby. And believe it or not, they would start work on this project immediately. Angela had been patient in waiting for Victor's answer, in which she knew would be, yes, all the time; her response indeed, still was a happy one.

"Victor, I love you so much; now we have a reason to make love."

"Excuse me——a reason?" Victor laughing.

"Victor, you know what I am talking about; you know I am not saying we made love for the fun of it–I mean–we did but we did-n't–Victor–you know what I mean–quit trying to confuse me."

Victor laughing real hard and loud said, "Angela, I did not say a word!"

"Yeah, but that look inferred—"

"Inferred what; so you haven't been having fun huh; I must do better Angela."

"Victor——Victor, I am not talking on this subject anymore; your kidding is bothering me." Angela even looked irritated.

Victor's attempt to have some real fun with Angela was short lived. Angela was sensitive about some things and this just happened to be one of them. Her number one priority in life, it seems was having a baby by Victor. Angela walked over to the window and looked out upon Uncle Lonzo's tulip bed; she had wonderful thoughts of having a beautiful reproduction, the same as he did with his lovely colorful blossoms each year. She could only think of how invigorating the flowers always made her feel and how a little one, peering through her life center, crying and cooing, would make her feel the livelier. Angela's head was filled with thoughts of a tiny girl on her lap, wearing dainty pink, yellow, and blue dresses. She wanted a child and she wanted a girl mostly, because it reminded her of the pretty dolls she played with when she was so much younger, but right now seems like yesterday.

For two minutes now, Victor had joined Angela at the window, looking over her shoulders, with his arms folded tightly around her waist. She could feel his warmness and bigness penetrating through her usual sheer gown. As Victor kissed her gently on the neck and raised his hands to lightly touch her breast, toying with her ever hardening nipples; Angela felt this was a good moment to make that baby girl. She felt the inside of her, throbbing, getting wet, and anxiously awaiting the sweet arrival of all of Victor's big-ness. Angela was   proud   now   that   she   had   listened   to grandmother's suggestions on the full consumption of Victor, because it was about to reward her with huge dividends. From now until she gets pregnant, Angela envisioned having all of him for every love making session. Her sensuous body was currently overheating as she whispered to Victor:

"Victor, let's get in the bed."

And Victor, quickly lifted Angela onto the spring like flowered comforter. There was no time to pull anything out of the way, but the sheer gown, covering Angela's naked body. Only moments went by before Angela, feel all of Victor inside of her and what seemed like, lots of little girls running through her body. Angela was more than a hundred percent sure, her tiny wish was on the way. Never before had a quickie given so much pleasure and over-whelming satisfaction. Victor had not planned on spending the night; and after a throughly fulfilling successful act, there was no need to anyway. Even Victor was happy; this session for some reason had more than surpassed any of their double doses.

"How do you feel Angela?"

"Extremely good Victor, I feel like you have made my wish come true."

"In order to be sure, maybe we should fiddle around all this week Angela."

"That is absolutely not necessary Victor, it would be a complete waste."

"Excuse me——waste!"

"Oh Victor, I am so sorry, you must forgive me; in my bedroom with you, I think less before I speak. You will forgive me for let-ting my guard down around you, wont you!"

"You are lucky Angela, I am drained and not horny anymore." Laughing. "Or else we would now be in the process of making another one of your wishes."

"Victor, you are so nice and understanding."

"So are you Angela, plus I like the way you sugar coat and clean up your act; love or instinctive!"

Both Victor, instinctive love!"

Angela and Victor are both smiling, which is the way friends, lovers, sexual partners, should be after a delightful evening. Angela loved Victor's departing ritual anyway, and looked forward to it when he did not stay. They always showered and then Victor tucked Angela into bed and showered her with luscious kisses upon her lips and curly cavern. He told her this was to ensure her not forgetting him until he returned. Angela, naturally believed Victor, because she thought of him constantly. Tonight's kisses; however, did much more to Angela; they rejuvenated her.

"Victor, you will come tomorrow evening won't you?"

"Sure Angela."

"Thanks for coming by Victor; you are so considerate, I will see you tomorrow, right,"

"Sure——where's grandma, I haven't seen or heard her all night."

"She ate and went to bed early Victor. I told her you were coming by. She said to give you her regards."

"Thanks for dinner Angela, and please keep me informed."

CHAPTER TWELVE

STILL ON TRACK

Victor returned from an early morning meeting and was given a handful of call messages by Tiffani. He stood there, going through them one by one; Samantha called, please call; Helen called, please call; Carolyn called, please call; Angela called, please stop by immediately after work. Taking in a deep breath, puffing up his jaw, letting the air out again, all before saying, whrrr; sounding like a tired north pole breeze. Victor suddenly felt more than important, more than challenged; more like no rest for the weary. He looked at Tiffani, who smiled saying.

"Problems Victor?"

"I hope not; ironic huh!"

"Angela called for you to come by yesterday, didn't you go?"

"Yep, I guess something came up Tiffani."

"It looks like your agenda is becoming crowded Victor."

"Yeah, fortunate for me it is Tuesday, which should eliminate any scheduling conflicts; three can certainly be a crowd Tiffani."

"Have some of your fingers been cut off lately Victor?"

"Huh!"

"My count comes to four; has someone been eliminated since yesterday Victor?"

"Oh no, you see Tiffani, I don't count Samantha, she is my one and only true friend."

"Oh——I see; well tell me something Victor, you still service her don't you?"

"Sure Tiffani, whenever she needs it; she is my best friend, you know. And friends must take care of friends. Our relationship is sort of different from the others. Samantha, you see, would never let me down and I feel the same toward her. I probably will regret telling you this but Samantha comes first behind Angela, and maybe first in some instances. The point is, I will never have a problem with Samantha because she is very understanding."

"The point is Victor, you missed the point! "How long do you expect to continue servicing all four of these women?"

"Well, until now Tiffani, to be honest, I never thought about it. I suppose it could become hectic; which reminds me, from now on, I will be spending more early mornings or lunch hours in our fitness room."

"Why is that, if I am not getting too personal Victor."

"No problem Tiffani, it appears there are no more personal secrets between you and me. To answer your question, my body seems to respond better and--"

"You need not elaborate Victor; I believe I can figure out the details myself." Laughing.

"I appreciate that Tiffani, but in short, the bottom line is favorable and the compliments I'm receiving are fantastic."

"Well, speaking of favors, do me one, do not bite off more than you can chew Victor."

Victor starts laughing, holding his side, and seemingly uncontrollable, but finally regaining his composure. "That is the funniest thing you have said lately." Laughing hard all over again.

"I do not see the humor Victor." Somewhat perturbed.

"Oh, its nothing Tiffani, please excuse me, maybe I do have a personal secret; boy, that was funny."

"My point Victor, in case you missed it while clowning around, was to promise me, you would not add another toy to your playhouse."

"I understand Tiffani, and thanks for the concern. I promise, there will never be anymore women in my life, maybe less but never more. You can be assured of that."

Victor turned and headed to his office, smiling real hard now, and talking out loud to himself: "That was funny, man that was funny, I could never make it without Tiffani, she is hilarious at times, without even trying, boy oh boy oh boy;" shaking his head and looking at his other messages, all business–business, of course. Victor returned the seven or so business calls, before turning his attention to deciding which toy, according to Tiffani, would get the first call. He tried to tell himself, it really did not matter, but Samantha won out; after all, it had been at least two weeks since they were together. Normally, or at least here lately, Samantha had used the pretense of wanting to talk about Stacy, and getting her back in school; but when Victor called today, she simply said; "I need you one day this week, and before Saturday." Victor knew her urgency agreed to see her early Thursday evening.

Helen got the next call; she mentioned nothing about making love, but pressured Victor vehemently on giving her a yes answer to work with her volunteer AIDS awareness seminar and fund raising group. She told him, "people were dying while he was saying "maybe". "Victor became somewhat peeved, telling Helen, "Maybe", was the best answer he had for right now." With a slightly louder voice. Helen; however, was not threatened by his tone, saying calmly, "Victor, I will be on your doormat tomorrow evening at six, expecting a much better answer; I will see you then, okay;" as mild as Victor had heard any female sound lately. Well, what was Victor to say, but okay. He was fuming though, when he hung up that phone; saying, "that Helen; that damn Helen; who does she think she is; bossing me around." His voice must have been louder than he realized, because Tiffani, now stood in his doorway.

"Victor, are you alright: Is there something wrong with Helen?"

"Oh, I'm sorry Tiffani, that woman makes me so mad! I mean, Helen is a very beautiful person in every respect, but she has one problem, she does not know how to take, NO, for an answer."

"Pretty persistent, huh; it looks like you are the one with the problem Victor."

"Okay Tiffani, what would you do if somebody insisted you volunteer some of your leisure time, for their pet projects?"

"Depends on the person, depends on the project, what is the project Victor?"

"It has something to do with giving AIDS lectures and fund raising speeches for the same cause."

"That is definitely a worthy cause Victor, do you realize how many African-Americans are dying from AIDS today?"

"I hear the rate is growing higher daily Tiffani, but I'm not off into that; I do not know any of those people; and I don't want anything to do with that crap. Helen has been trying to get me to volunteer my spare time ever since we started talking."

"Well, that is a pretty sensitive area; pray about it Victor, you will reach the right answers." She then turned and slowly walked to her desk.

Victor, even found Tiffani's voice mournful at this moment, but as sermonizing as Helen. He thought to himself, "these women are all alike, they stick together, no matter what." Victor had detected what he assumed was a sympathy vote toward Helen's position. He shrugged it off, picking up the phone and calling Carolyn, who had not wanted anything other than to say; "good morning; how good and relaxed she had been since the other day, and how she was looking forward to his continued support." Carolyn's cheerful voice was a welcome relief after the preachy mannered Helen and Tiffani.

Hanging up, Victor noted it was time for lunch, thinking how Carolyn's sweet disposition could not have happened at a better time. Ironically the same could not be said of Tiffani, who had strained to hold her composure; only to break down and cry, as soon as Victor left the office. Skipping lunch, Tiffani laid her tearful face into her folded arms upon the desk.

Victor returned from lunch in the same festive mood as before; never knowing of Tiffani's sorrow, or ever noticing the tear stained blotter upon her desk. After about two hours of pretending to be her old self, she told Victor, "she was not feeling very well and was going home."

The rest of the evening passed quickly for Victor and before long, he was on his way to Angela's; he could not help but think how unique Angela was.

One unique characteristic of Angela was her ability to become focused on more than one thing. She would become obsessed with whatever it was. She had the trait of her grandma about listening. But her strongest feature was planning. Angela could plan all these projects in her head, and know exactly what the next phase should be on each one. She kept the projects separate, working on them individually, but steady pressing forward on all of them. And of course, Victor thought she wanted to talk more about them.

Grandma had a good description for Angela, "The girl has a one track mind". Grandma was partially correct; the girl has a multi-track mind. Her mind was constantly working on each project, be it business or personal. And her personal goal for the moment was making sure there were extra little Angelas and Victors around the house. In the midst of all those problems, you would think child rearing would be on her back burner. Victor did not mind it so much because it would have its good features.

Angela had called and asked Victor to stop by, as if he had forgotten. It's funny, he used to be inquisitive and ask why; and she used to ask him nicely to come over. Now Angela politely demand Victor stop by. That's what happens when two people get used to each or develop a good understanding of the other. Of course, now it seems like Victor was always anxious for Angela to call. And with her alluring tone, it always has the sound of ravishing urgency. As compelling as she is at times; Victor was probably more eager to abide. Angela is such a sweet insistent person, he does not feel annoyed by it.

"Well, it's no need of me speeding," Victor talked aloud: "she'll certainly be there. Sometimes, or should I say, here lately, I've been going at a full gallop whenever she called. What use to be once a month or so has now turned into three or four times a month. The door is opening; Angela must have been waiting on me——this could be serious."

"Hi, Victor you are here quick."

"I did say I was coming right over Angela; where are you going?"

"Nowhere, I promised grandmother I would water all her potted plants Victor."

That was one of grandma's personal chores. She cared more for her plants than anything. And she had a way with them. The plant

Victor gave her in the hospital had died out and come back a hundred times from her seed cultivation. The lady had a green thumb for plants. She often brought her friends sickly looking flowers home to nurse them. Of course, grandma had lots of time for talking to and pampering her many potted plants. That is because the flower beds on the immaculate grounds were expertly maintained by Uncle Lonzo. Grandma's wanderings in this area was impeded somewhat by his preoccupation.

Alonzo Simmons, the gardener was every bit as caring about the flowers and plants as grandma; but was more picky. He had a ritual of supplying the house with freshly cut flowers and did not want nobody, including grandma, cutting on his flowers. Grandma respected his wishes; well most of the time. Anytime you saw him fuming, it generally had something to do with someone interfering with his beautiful flowers. Alonzo, an elderly gentleman, about grandma's age had been with her ever since she owned this mansion. His silver hair only added more distinguishing character to the age-old setting. Handling plants was all he did, day in and day out and he did it well. That is why, all year round, the magnificent grounds had blossoms everywhere.

"They left for their trip this morning Victor."

"I completely forgot about it, Oh, the Las Vegas trip—that time sure did come quick."

"Yes, it did Victor, but they changed and went to Monte Carlo instead."

"They what!"

"That is the fickle mind of a lady at work, grandmother says. Some of them had been there twenty years earlier and suggested it. So they changed horses in the middle of the stream and away they went Victor."

"Angela, do I see a mischievous look in your eye?"

"Victor, either you know me, or you are the best mind reader in town. I figured we could be playful today and run around the house in the nude. I am feeling that urging you left me with last night."

"Sounds like you have seduction on your mind instead of plant manipulation Angela."

"Maybe I should have warned you Victor, but grandmother will be gone a month, if you prefer another time."

"When you finish your watering Angela, I'll be inside taking a bath. I'll prepare the cold shower for you." Victor thought, "he should be horny too, but last night still had him a bit drained."

"Move over Victor, so I can scrub behind your dirty ears."

"That sure was some fast plant watering Angela."

"I will finish tomorrow Victor; first things first, you know."

"Okay, I'll settle for a back scrub Angela, and while you're at it, massage my shoulders."

"Will I get my favorite massage later Victor?"

"That depends on whether the kinks have been removed from the ole body Angela."

"Don't you worry Victor, I will also do your favorite head massage."

"Okay Angela, let me dry you off. Lie on the bed, face down—where is the massaging oil?"

"There is a new bottle in that paper bag, near the bottom shelf Victor."

"Let me straddle this hot body Angela and rub it down until it cools off."

"That feels good Victor; can I turn over now?"

"Sure, you know when you've had enough. Your front is always harder to massage Angela."

"It would not be if you kept your mind on what you are supposed to be doing Victor."

"I try, but you're no help Angela; your nipples always get hard."

"Well now Victor, if you were not so good at your trade, that would not happen."

"Angela, you're suppose to relax."

"People relax in different ways Victor. Anyway, you spend too much tine around my breast—you will never finish the massage. But somehow Victor, I do not think you intend to finish."

"Oh, I don't know about that Angela, my mind is clear today."

"It is always clear Victor, but is it clean."

"So far, so good my dear, you're perfectly safe. My lips are sealed against any thought you have on further caressing. What's all this about parading around in the nude? You're not getting sadistic on me, are you Angela?"

"No Victor, I happen to think that is absolutely normal for a woman. We like to show off our bodies. Also, I feel carefree in the nude. With grandmother gone I felt this was the perfect opportunity to really relax for a change. We can skip all over this house."

"You are safe today Victor, because I started on my menstrual cycle."

"You what!"

Victor thought; "I appear to be running into a lot of these cycles lately."

"That is right, so you can put those sexy penetrable emotions aside for now. But I still like my body caressed when I am on my period. What is wrong with that Victor?"

"Nothing Angela, its just that I didn't know. I'm learning more about you each day. Grandma should leave more often."

"Leave grandmother alone, you know she never interferes with us in my quarters."

"Oh, I was just kidding Angela."

"Anyway, grandmother is counting on you to look after me while she is gone Victor. I told her you would be with me everyday."

"Did she believe you Angela?"

"I am not sure Victor, but I convinced myself of it–you are going to spend most nights, aren't you?"

"Well–er–why not–I was just telling myself the other day, I wish grandma would leave town so I could walk around the house with Angela–in the nude. It's baffling to know my responsibility increased when grandma left."

"Isn't that interesting Victor, but so did mine. I am going to spend all my free time making you feel ever more special. Thanks for finding my love parade amusing."

"Angela, why is it that I'm getting a feeling you're up to something."

"Nothing other than my normal sweet self, dear, except I am in good spirits, thanks to your kind deed last night Victor."

"Angela, I was thinking today about something, concerning the child."

"What is that Victor?"

"I thought about you having a natural child birth and me helping with the entire procedure Angela."

"Oh Victor, I think that is wonderful; I love you so much. I am enjoying being off those contraceptives. They work, but I have felt nauseated ever since. I wish there was something you men could take to give women relief every now and then."

"I hear they're pretty close to getting something for men Angela. But I think it will be too late for us."

"Why do you think that Victor?"

"Well Angela, you said you wanted children."

"Wait a minute Victor, I said a child; there is a difference between the two you know. I only want one. After that it is back to the pill again."

"We can solve that Angela."

"How?"

"By not doing anything Angela."

"Not on your life Victor."

"Oh, I was just kidding my dear."

"It was me at first Victor, but lately you stay horny."

"That's because you entice me to be naughty Angela."

"I do not necessarily want sex Victor; I just want you to be around me, hold me, and be affectionate."

"I haven't seen you fighting to turn me down Angela."

"That is because I do not want to hurt your feelings Victor."

"Oh sure, is that like hurt my feeling on your warm breast or your soft body Angela."

"Victor, you know you want sex twice as much as I do."

"Oh, I don't deny that Angela. I'm just saying you love it as much as I do. Anyway, who is keeping score as long as we're both satisfied. That should be all that matters Angela."

"True Victor, so very true. I am going to be more considerate Victor, now that you consented to the baby. That is the only way to be successful in that category. Of course, there is a certain time when I can actually get pregnant."

"You told me you felt it last night Angela."

"Women say things like that in the heat of battle Victor; you have so much to learn."

"I have an idea Angela. Let's just do it everyday, then we can't miss."

"Thanks, but I know when. Just promise me Victor that you will love me during that time."

"Angela, that's the least of our worries."

"It will be several months anyway Victor, before my body is receptive to the pregnant mode."

"Say what! Does that mean we're back to our once every now and then loving Angela?"

"I am afraid so Victor, once a month is all I really need. There is more to life than screwing you know."

"True Angela, but there's also more to life than waiting."

"This is a new day Victor; I did not think the time would ever come when I had to actually run from you. What has gotten into you——are you taking pep pills or something?"

"I'll tell you later Angela."

"Hand me my robe, Victor, I will be ready again in several days. You can come back then, with your horny self."

"Angela, now you're talking my language–good ole fashion body english."

"Victor, have you thought about your responsibility?"

"Much more than you'll ever know Angela. That's part of the reason I needed some time before saying yes. Of course, my responsibilities were easily defined, once the decision was made. It is that of any other father–child rearing, love and devotion, and in these days, lots of financial obligations for daily needs and future education."

Overall, this had been a pretty good day for Angela. From the beginning, the thought of having Victor spend the entire night with her was enough within itself. Then with the thought of having the house all to themselves, brought smiles upon her face, making Angela happy, even at work. Of course, her mind was certainly not at work, it was solely on Victor. She had even called Victor when she realized, she had forgotten to tell of grandmother being gone. Angela could not remember, the last time she had been so excited. It had nothing to do with sex, because she knew mother nature was prevailing, but more to do with how Angela imagined life being in the future. The thought of pursuing Victor and having him all to herself one day did enter her mind every now and then. But the musing was generally short lived, because of the guilt attached already to her pursuit of a married man, and her convincing Victor to give her a child.

Having the house to themselves was a rare luxury and a relaxation easy to define; carefree and joyous togetherness. Victor was even enjoying himself; Carolyn and Helen no longer presented a fiery challenge as they once did, especially when an initial sex arousal caused havoc with the old imagination. Notions crossed Victor's mind several times during the evening, to confessing his one secret to Angela. The thought of coming home to her every night and living happily ever after, seemed to have an appeal greater than his current hap-hazardous lifestyle. "Let's face it," Victor said to himself; "Angela was getting to the point where she almost made love as good as Carolyn and Helen." He did concede; however, "Angela could not match Helen's sex appeal nor Carolyn's fine body; but then again," Victor reminded himself, "he had not met anyone else who even came close to those two ingredients." Doing without two such pleasers would present a great challenge and challengers, for that matter; for neither Helen or Carolyn has been informed of even a remote possibility of Victor relinquishing their rights and his duties. Terminating their hard fought gains would not be easy; Victor obviously had a plan. The only problem, plans do not always work as conceived; Victor's hope was, when in Helen or Carolyn's presence again, he would not be overwhelmed by these unyielding bronze idealized credentials.

Spending the evening and night with Angela was pretty much like spending it with Samantha and almost as settled. These two were so similar: pleased to have your company; a flair up or two; and then an easy time of it for the rest of the night. It mattered not how heavy the love session was, they generally wanted to sleep in peace; and this is where Angela is for the moment, lying on her side of the queen sized bed, fast asleep, enjoying the comfort of having Victor nearby.

CHAPTER THIRTEEN

LOSS OF A FRIEND

Victor was as jovial entering the office this morning as he was leaving it yesterday. And why not, there had not been anything between then and now to make him any other way. Even Tiffani appeared to be in a better mood; at least she was smiling when she spoke to Victor.

"Good morning Tiffani; feeling better today?"

"Hi Victor, sure, I feel fine."

"I thought about you a time or two last night Tiffani, and come to the conclusion it was something I said that upset you. Do you have any skeletons in your closet that I should know about?

"Not in the manner in which you might be thinking Victor, but yesterday was stressful for—" phone rings. "Sure, hold on for a second; it is for you Victor."

"I will take it in my office Tiffani."

Tiffani went about her work, but she could hear Victor's voice rising and falling, getting silent and going through exclamation points; rising and falling again. One time, she did hear him say; "Man, that can't be true!" Several minutes later Victor stood in his doorway.

"Tiffani, I can't believe it, one of my real close friends has died of AIDS."

"It is happening to everyone these days Victor; everyone is being affected by a friend, relative, or love one dying with this dreadful disease."

"That may be true Tiffani, but I never figured it to happen to me."

"Yeah, I know, you made that pretty clear yesterday Victor. None of us will be able to escape this epidemic entirely because it is all around us."

"It hasn't affected you, has it Tiffani?"

"Sure Victor, that is why I became so upset yesterday; my first cousin, Kasandra Dotson died with it three years ago. We were like sisters; I miss her so much. I cannot help but shed a tear when I think of how young Kasandra was; only twenty three and just beginning to live her life; and boom, like that, life was snubbed out."

"Please forgive me Tiffani for being so rude; I didn't know."

"I wanted to tell you yesterday Victor, but I was overcome with sadness before I had a chance."

"This is too much Tiffani, please hold my calls for the rest of the day." Victor turns, closes his door, and heads to his desk.

Tiffani made sure there was plenty coffee, but Victor never came out to get a cup or asked her to bring a cup in. She could see his phone light on, looking at her extension; never no more than a minute or two at a time though. When the phone light was not lit, it was quiet in Victor's office—real quiet. Tiffani, worried at this extraordinary silence peeped in several times to see if he was alright. Each time, she noticed Victor writing something, and each time, Tiffani noticed that far-away thought look on his face, when he looked up to see who was there. Victor made several calls; one of which went to Helen who was going to storm his doorway at home after work. He wanted to let her know he would not be there and why, but would be over to Samantha's. Helen was so understanding, telling Victor, "she would be there for him if he needed her." Victor also called Angela, telling her practically the same thing. Oddly enough, these calls were made before he contacted Samantha; that is how much confidence Victor had in Samantha.

Samantha and Victor had agreed not to call each other on the job unless it was an emergency. Little did he know it would be him calling her for none other than a consolation. She agreed to him stopping by her place after work. We all have sorrowful times in our lives and need comforting from someone, just to make it through. Victor was fortunate to have that someone in his ex-wife, but friend forever. In the worst of times they promised to be there for each other. Pacification from an understanding source was heart-warming. Samantha knew Victor best and also had met Joseph.

Joseph Adams, a friend of theirs in Dallas, Texas had died with AIDS. Joseph and Victor had become instant friends upon entering college and had remained so throughout the years.

"Are you going to the funeral Victor?"

"No Samantha, it's the first time I've lost a friend. It's hard enough as it is. I just talked to him last week and he was doing okay. I would prefer to remember him alive and well. So I'm not going."

Two old buddies, Ringo and Chuck called and wanted Victor to go with them. Each one of them had the same impression of Joseph. It seemed like only a few days past since the four of them roamed the campus. Throwing those funky fraternity parties and getting invited to those raunchy sorority parties. Those celebrations went on every weekend; starting on Friday evening and not winding down until late Sunday with a jazz session. When there was a football or basketball game; the partying was delayed, but nevertheless, went on. Those were really the best kind because they lasted all night long. We're talking about organized parties and not just something thrown together. To describe what went on at these parties would tarnish their reputations today as outstanding citizens.

Atlanta, Georgia was probably the party capital, when they were in college. Joseph and Ringo were from Texas–Dallas and Houston respectively; and they said these parties were small time compared to those in their home towns. Victor could not have expected anything different from them, because he knew Texans were known for having everything bigger. Joseph and Ringo swore they had parties like these in high school. Victor and Chuck teased them about Texas, and they gave them more and more layers of bull manure. They were the greatest of friends, which is partially the reason Victor eventually moved to the Lone Star State. Twenty five! Those few days past had turned into years.

"I have written a letter to include a poem to his parents, Samantha, and I want you to go over it before its mailed."

Dear Mr. & Mrs Adams

I met you many years ago when a group of us from college came home with Joseph. Joseph will be missed by all of us. It was a loss to you; to me; to the city of Dallas and the community at large; and to all who had ever met him. But everyone's loss is someone's gain. This gain belongs to God and the Kingdom of Heaven, where Joseph is certainly smiling upon us today.

I met Joseph at college thirty years ago and we along with countless other freshmen became instant friends. His philosophy to us was that we could make it with a little, but consistent effort on our part. That we were there at college to graduate, and if it took us ten years, we could do it. "Don't give up, and let those who sent you here down". Those words stuck with me and I passed them on to those behind me. Joseph had an immediate positive impact upon me and all whom he came in contact with. He got the point across without seeming boisterous or like a braggart.

Joseph also had a special gift of reading people's needs, without them directly quoting their problem. I remember needing a hundred dollars for tuition, to get in school one semester. Walking down the hall, not knowing where it was to come from, when along came Joseph. I never mentioned my problem, but Joseph sensed something was wrong. He let me have the money. That was important, but the most important thing was what he said, "Don't pay it back until you can afford it." I enrolled in school and was able to pay him back that semester.

That was the type of person Joseph was. That was only one of many such stories. I'm sure he helped many people through turbulent times——not by always doing something, but by his advice or that rare philosophy. Joseph had traits we see in an individual, once in a lifetime, if ever. He had the uncanny ability of making one feel important from just talking. He could converse on anyone's level, about anything, or he listened patiently for your view point.

We became friends and remained friends over the years. My wife Samantha, and I stayed with Joseph when we visited Dallas. She liked him the instant he opened his mouth. It's rare for someone to have an immediate positive impact upon strangers; but that was Joseph's gift from God. He succeeded in touching many lives while he was here, and I'm sure his mission was accomplished. He helped so many as he passed along. The world will truly be a better place, having had Joseph walk among us. His philosophy is everlasting in our presence and he lives forever in our hearts.

Sincerely yours,

Victor Previtt

P.S. The poem enclosed, entitled My Friend, could have been written by any of the many people that met Joseph on his journey home.

MY FRIEND

I lost a real good friend this week
Maybe he's not dead, but fast asleep
I'll just call him on the phone
He's surely there, in that heavenly home

We'll chatter and laugh about things past
Nothing heavy, just pleasant thrash
A solemn note about next years election
Who'll run, and the party's selection

Twenty five years and he never changed
Always treating everyone the same
Trying to be fair, and giving of himself
Doing right, being honest, if nothing else

Joseph would say "move on, keep going"
There's lots of work you could be doing
I'm safe now, God has my hand
Keep pulling weeds and plowing the land

Lift up that heavy heart and mend others
Along the way; your sisters and brothers
Remember, just treat everybody right
I'm resting now...so you can rest tonight

"Victor, there is not anything I would or could change in either the letter or poem. Those words come from the depths of your heart and should not be tampered with. This is a sad day for me and you; but especially for you, because you two were so much closer. You are taking this pretty hard Victor; are you sure you shouldn't go to the funeral?"

"I'm sure Samantha."

Joseph's death had really dampened Victor's spirits. To lose a friend to a disease with no cure in this day and time just did not seem right. Victor thought: "I can see what Helen goes through everyday in her nursing of AIDS patients. She has talked of her frustrations, I have heard her, but until now, I don't think I really understood. That's why she's always so emotionally drained. Helen is doing what she can for her patients, but it's not good enough—they're still dying. I now see why she feels so helpless."

Samantha consoled Victor as much as she knew how. It affected her greatly too, because she knew Joseph also. But her heart felt sorrowful for Victor and the loss of his real good friend. "It makes a difference," she thought, "when its more of an acquaintance than a friend." Samantha made Victor spend the night; after all, she had put in a request for his services. Now, however, neither she nor Victor was in any lovemaking mood. "It would have to be put off for another time," thought Samantha; "probably sometimes next month." Samantha was reminded how they discussed helping each other in times of need and this was one of those times; Victor had come to her for comfort.

Samantha handled her role with ease, fixing and making Victor eat a ham and cheese sandwich, when she found out he had not eaten anything since breakfast. She impressed upon him, not to punish his body or allow it to suffer because of one misfortune; "do not compound a bad situation," she said. Samantha let Victor talk as long as he wanted to, which ended up being until about twelve midnight, then his voice and body petered out, and loud snoring replaced the repetitive sentences about Joseph. Samantha pulled off Victor's shoes and clothes and covered him for the night, slipping into the guest bedroom herself. She knew with the snoring he had going on, there would be no sleep by his side tonight.

Samantha would set the clock early for the next day and repay Victor for some of those breakfasts he had left behind, while she laid in the comforts of a bedroom. She had no idea whether he was going to work, but would try and get him ready for a normal day, if that was possible. Samantha would be encouraging Victor as much as she knew how, for him to remain on schedule and let the past be past. "Moving on with one's fruitful life with those loved ones around you," thought Samantha, "is more important than dwelling on one's past, who more than likely has eternal rest."

CHAPTER FOURTEEN

ANOTHER FIGHTER EMERGES

Samantha did manage to get Victor going for the day, but there were so many things playing on his mind by the time he reached the office. Tiffani was on his mind and how her cousin Kasandra's death was still affecting her three years later. He wondered if Joseph would be affecting him, years and years down the road. Victor knew what was best, and that was to follow Samantha's suggestion, at breakfast: "Victor, you must be strong and move on, life is for the living, you know." To Victor that made sense, life is for the living, and the question jumped into his mind; "Victor, what are you going to do about it?" That question weighed heavily upon him, helping him make the decision to help Helen with her seminars and whatever else she wanted.

"Good morning Victor, you look much better; will you be okay?"

"Hello Tiffani, I feel much better, but again let me apologize to you for my actions a few days ago. I now understand the impact of your loss; it all seems so senseless during this day and time for an epidemic to be raging. You would think doctors, scientists, or somebody could come up with a cure."

"Maybe God is trying to tell us something Victor!"

"Maybe! Yeah, maybe, like telling each one of us to do our little part Tiffani."

"What do you mean Victor?"

"Well, now I realize why Helen has been bugging me about volunteering some of my leisure time to this cause Tiffani."

"Of course, that is not what I meant Victor but I suppose it will work also. You should do something worthy with your spare time Victor; what did Helen think about it?"

"Well, I haven't told her yet; I only reached the decision on my way to work this morning. Could you please get her on the phone for me Tiffani?"

Victor poured himself a cup of coffee, adding both sugar and cream, and stirring lightly as he waited.

"Sorry Victor, there is no answer!"

"Thanks Tiffani, I will try again myself later."

Victor walked sluggardly into his office, this time leaving the door open, sitting down at his desk, looking intently into the large coffee cup as he slowly took sip after sip. There was nothing in the coffee cup, other than what he had poured into it, only moments earlier, but his eyes still focused on its sweet creamy mixture, sometimes holding it with both hands. Victor's countenance only meant one thing; he was thinking, yes doing some serious thinking.

Joseph had come and gone like the flicker of a light. Victor talked about serving a purpose and truly believed those graceful words; but there was nothing graceful about AIDS. No matter how you addressed it; there was no glamour. It could not be dressed up and made to look like a king or queen. It could not be played as a harmonious melody, becoming pleasurable with each note. It could not come in and out of our lives like a common cold. When AIDS hit, it hit like a thunderous blow from John Henry's hammer. DEATH! The spike pierced your body to the stake, and you were doomed.

Helen's lectures and seminars on AIDS now took on a greater meaning. Victor now also understood her position on not having time for those, do nothing sexual friends chasing her. Her dedication to this cause was genuine. No personal friend had to die for Helen to become a fighter against this Deathly disease. All whom had it, was her friend and her fight to do something. Victor understood now the helplessness she felt as the number of cases soared in the hospital. Helen took them all personal. Before, he could not understand why she was so perplexed and mentally exhausted after the loss of a patient that she did not even know.

In her mind Helen knew them. She knew of their personal ordeal. She knew of their will to live against all odds. She knew of their desire to fight when they had no punch left. Helen was trying to fight each one's lonesome battle; and she along with them was losing each round. It did not matter whether they went one round or fifteen rounds, the results were always the same——a knockout.

Each knockout was also taking its toll on Helen. But she kept coming back for more. In the back of her mind there was hope. Hope for a split-decision that she would win. Hope for even a draw for the patient. Hope that was always fading in the end for each one. But somehow Helen was not going to give up. Each day she was eager to start anew, because the glimmer of hope could mean victory.

A victory so overpowering, it would sweep the country like a mighty drought. Our throats would be parched from our displays of exuberance. Our eyes will be strained as if a dust storm had oozed out every tear. We will be speechless and sightless as we lift our hands in a heavenly direction. No words could express the joy and happiness of the world. The Helen's of the world could lay down their battle armor, and rest from so weary a journey.

Someday, somebody, some country, would find a cure, and Helen could rest. The mere thought of a breakthrough in modern medicine was enough to be optimistic. It was enough for Helen to wake up with a smile on her face. Helen was far ahead of anyone Victor had ever known, because she knew the meaning of life. Nothing was taken for granted. It was really the little things that kept the big smile coming back. Helen knew the meaning of each day and took advantage of it.

A MEANINGFUL DAY

None lives on earth forever
With some it only seems that way
Long lifers bucking the weather
Others with meaning in each day

Its not such a rugged chore
To put a sunrise in each day
Its been done many times before
...might not live to be old and gray

Would you rather have them say
You thought of no one else
He just passed his time away
Helping no one but himself

Or do you want your light to shine
From just a mere simple endeavor
And whether you're nine or ninety-nine
You'll live in their hearts forever

It matters not how long you live
But what happens during your stay
Not what's received, but what you give
Just putting meaning in each day

Victor had managed to get Helen on the phone, and she agreed to have him over to her place later on that evening. Seems that he just needed to talk to Helen as he had with Samantha. The necessity; however, had expanded from being comforted to that of providing assistance. Victor had thought of a number of things and he wanted to discuss an item with Helen.

Somehow, Victor felt Helen needed more. She definitely deserved more. And with his new understanding, he was going to do something about it.

"Helen, I don't know what your schedule looks like, but plan on taking the next two weeks off, after this one. I am going to arrange a trip for the both of us."

"That is a nice thought Victor, but I have an important luncheon near the end of the month. As a matter of fact, my main speaker cannot make it. Will you help me out Victor?"

"Sure Helen, if you agree to the vacation."

"It's a deal, Victor."

It is so funny how things turn out. One event can alter the course of one's life. One event can alter the course of history. Just six months ago, Victor would have said no. Sixty hours ago, Victor would have said no. Six months ago Helen had asked. Six months ago, Victor's fondness for a stranger's life had no meaning. But in the last sixty hours, unlike the prior six months, Victor's awareness for human suffering awakened. His answer had been a resounding yes. He did not know what he was going to say. But whatever it was, a new meaning had been spirited in him.

Victor prepared an eloquent speech, loaded with statistics of the AIDS sufferers and survivors. It gave the epidemic rate and quoted percentages and numbers after percentages. He let Helen review the speech and she said; "you have the facts down," and handed it back to him. Victor felt pretty good about being prepared. On the morning of the luncheon and right before he was to speak, something came over him. Victor was introduced, but as he arose to go to the lectern, there was a numbness in his entire body. It was not a numbness of stage fright. It was not a numbness of fear of any kind. It was not a numbness of a physical defect. It was the stunning numbness of impersonal factual statistics he was about to exclaim.

Victor stood there a few moments to gain his composure. People in the audience had began to look at each other. He heard Helen in the background saying; "take your time, take your time." Helen, a woman of compassion must have known what he was going through. Then Victor cleared his throat, and looked up saying:

"Good Morning, I hold before you today, a speech filled with the cold hard facts of AIDS. It quotes every conceivable statistic on HIV (the human immunodeficiency virus) and AIDS (acquired immune deficiency syndrome) as we commonly call it." He balled the speech up and tossed it to the floor. "What that speech did not cover is my personal frustrations of losing a friend to this DEATHLY disease. That speech does not cover frustrations shared by Helen and other nurses, as they watch thousands die across the country each year. That speech didn't cover the frustrations of the many doctors and scientists that are tearing their hair out, because no cure can be found. The speech failed to mention the hopes and dreams of someone who could be standing before you today. The speech forgot the plans that had been made by so many and will never materialize. That speech didn't tell of the talents we'll never benefit from. And no where in that speech did it explore the achievements by anyone; of which a cure could have been found by one of the many."

"And what about the many loved ones that will prematurely lose a young lady in her teens or a young man in his twenties. And what about the mother that will never see her child. Think of the child that will never bring joy to the home of a grandparent; a child that was introduced to the horrors of the world through no fault of its own; a child that never had a chance to smile. That speech lying there did not address that. That speech failed to mention the personal stories of those affected with this Deathly disease."

"The seriousness of this epidemic cannot be taken lightly. Today we need your help. I'm not going to stand here and tell you to wear or buy a condom, although you should. I'm not going to stand here and tell you to stay away from the high risk groups, although you probably should. I'm not going to stand here and tell you not be promiscuous, although you probably shouldn't. I'm not going to stand here and tell you, an ounce of prevention is worth more than a pound of cure, because you know that already."

"We need your help. We need your help in terms of dollars. Dollars for research to fight a disease that is claiming so many lives. You can help, you can make a difference. This weekend there is a concert in town supporting this cause. Go out, enjoy yourself. Your dollars can and will make a difference. Next month there is a national telethon addressing this Deathly disease. Please call in and make a generous pledge. You can make a difference. Let's change the course of history today. And remember, this is not a white disease or a black disease, this is a DEATHLY disease."

"Thank you for your time. Thank you ever so much for your patience."

As Victor sat down, he received a thunderous roar of applause. Then people began to stand all over the place. They clapped until he stood up for that second time. A glance at Helen showed a smile and watery eyes.

On their way home, Helen said; "I knew you could do it Victor."

"Yes Helen, but I sort of sensed you weren't satisfied with my handwritten speech when I showed it to you."

"No, it was a good speech Victor. I never question anyone when they are doing a favor for me. But the speech you made today was a great speech Victor, because you made it for you. I have never been so proud of anyone as I am of you today. You not only reached the audience; you touched the audience."

"The speech touched me also Helen It was the therapy I needed. The vacation will solve the rest. And speaking of rest Helen, you're overdue for a much needed rest. You have been going twenty four hours non-stop. You must remind yourself that you cannot save the world all by yourself."

"I am not trying to Victor, but I must do my share and a little bit more for the weaklings of the world. It is work, but it is the satisfaction that outlast any tired body and depleted mind that really counts. The sacrifice of one's self to benefit an unfortunate person is not only a gift—but a God given gift—to the recipient, and a blessing to the giver. Victor, my rewards are many, compared to a few sleepless nights. I am blessed to have had someone like you to have helped me out of my precarious predicament. I thought at one time about canceling the luncheon. I am so pleased you helped me out Victor, thank you."

"I hadn't planned on getting all worked up Helen, but I couldn't help myself."

"You were great Victor. Sometimes God takes over in our stead. God was in control, when you might have thought you were out of control. But you see, you had help today Victor. You graciously accepted the challenge and you were also rewarded. God soothed your pain and lifted your burdens. Your heavy load is lighter."

"Helen, I believe you're right, I feel so much better. It's like a ton has been removed from my shoulders."

"Victor, you must remember, God always works things out. Even when you pray for the wrong things. He just knows what is best. You do not have to give me an answer now Victor, but I would like for you to help with future lectures and seminars."

"I'll be more than glad to help Helen. I want to help you in other ways also."

"What is that Victor?"

"Well, I've heard you mention several times about going to Med. school. Are you still interested in pursuing that goal?"

"Yes Victor, but that is out of the question, the cost is prohibitive."

"I know Helen, but I lost a friend to AIDS; and now I understand your frustrations. If you really want to go, I'm prepared to send you."

"But Victor, I could not do that; that is not your responsibility."

"If it's not my responsibility Helen, then whose responsibility is it to try and save lives. That is a small price to pay for what has already been given."

"Victor, I cannot believe what I am hearing. The Lord works in mysterious ways. You will be blessed Victor—you will be blessed. OH——THANK YOU——THANK YOU."

CHAPTER FIFTEEN

CRUISING AROUND

"Victor, I am so glad you planned this cruise."

They took the Cunard Liner that took them to eleven different ports. These islands consisted of San Juan, St. Maarten, Antigua, Martinique, Barbados, Grenada, St Lucia, Guadeloupe, St. Kitts, Tortola, and St. Thomas, which they visited within fourteen days.

"You deserve it Helen. We have not been together lately, thanks to your dedication. I was getting a little edgy about it. Not to mention seeing you drag your body around. Even your face Helen, was beginning to show the stress. But that's not going to happen again. From now on you're taking at least two weeks off every year."

"I do not know about that Victor."

"Helen, I feel you're killing yourself. I'm going to look after you from now on."

"Thanks Victor, you don't know the satisfaction that gives me."

All of a sudden, looking after Helen had become a priority. After Joseph, they appeared to have so much in common. Victor had not realized the importance of her work before and how stressful, ordinary life could be. Now he found himself wanting to make up for the neglect, and times he unsuccessfully tried to avoid Helen. Helen did not want or better still, have to make love often; but when she needed it, was she ever persistent. It's not that he did not want to make love to her, because she was the most fulfilling. But it was nearly always at an inopportune time–like twelve, one, two, three–in the morning. Helen explained before; "that is when her body settled down and begged for affection." There was never a time that Victor regretted doing so, other than a major physical workout from exertion. Only now after peering into Helen's devastating days does he understand. The girl just did not have the strength nor energy.

Victor wondered; why had he waited so long between vacations. His recollection says it has been at least three years. And to think if it was not for Helen, he would not have taken this one. That is much too long to rejuvenate the body or mind. Carolyn was right, "Victor has been caring more for his old car than himself." You would have to think, his body needed a tune up or oil change before now. The rigors of daily work, as taxing as it is sometimes, did not appear to be affecting Victor that much. Maybe he would have passed out on his feet if he had not observed Helen or Joseph had not left us.

Victor wondered if Joseph had taken a vacation lately. "Probably not," he said, "if like himself and his ever hard working Helen." What is the reason for us continuously abusing our bodies? Victor did not consider himself a workaholic. And it's not like he is a pauper, so he can afford one. Victor's only excuse is, "I was busy." But the truth of the matter is, you should not get too busy to take care of your body. There is more to life than being busy and hard work. It does us no good to move mountains, if later on, they push us down. So, Victor made a promise to himself that every year from now on, he is going somewhere on a vacation. And he did not mean that weekend and long weekend stuff with the Fridays and Mondays. We must learn to take notice of a body pounding to minimize latent fatigue, be it work or love.

The cruise was going pretty good. Helen's body was so run down, she slept through the first port–St. Maarten. Victor tried to wake her up, but she said, "I'll catch you later–my body is so tired." So Victor's initial assessment of Helen was correct. She was beat.

"Victor, you are going to be sorry, because I am eating and

sleeping like a pig. And please forgive me for sleeping through today."

"That's okay Helen, you didn't miss very much. Of course, it was difficult carrying on without you."

"Sure Victor—I will make it up tonight. I have not been this horny since I forced my way into your life."

And boy was she ever correct. If it had never been done before, they did it-they rocked the boat—that night. Turbulent waters and blistering waves would seem calm amidst their storm of love. Singing endless loving, would be the song. With no competition, Helen lost all her sophistication and became a barbarian each night and some days.

It must have been the ocean breeze. A far away freedom wind that enslaved the nostrils. A breeze with an aroma that floated upon your taste buds and made them howl a whispering note into your lovers ear. If you were not in love, you would fall in love, or in the ocean, after getting carried away. Intoxication at its best.

It was definitely something in the air, because each day Victor's body tingled with more ripples than the Liner made as it split the jubilant waters. He wanted to make love every day as bad or worse than Helen. You might say, they were a wild pair. Swooning over each other like the seagulls overhead. Victor had never exchanged that many kisses before in public. They were acting like newly-weds on a honeymoon; like love birds on a spring day. Their savagery instincts forced them to let themselves go. There were to be no thoughts of tomorrow. Only this moment counted. If they had to love once, they were doing it now; they were also storing up a treasure of sweet memories.

Victor and Helen made some acquaintances. One in particular that stood out—Mr. & Mrs. Knusant; a retired couple in their late seventies, it appeared. The Knusants said they reminded them of a young black couple they knew back home in Chicago. For some reason they liked Victor and Helen and attached themselves to them the entire cruise. They were very nice people. Helen jok-ingly (I think so) referred to them as Mr. & Mrs. Nuisance. Helen wanted Victor to herself, and was always in an avoidance mode, where company was concerned. But it was no use, the Knusants always found them after a while. Victor told Helen it was all her fault. With that big bubbly smile, she attracted people toward her and made them feel at home. However they respected their privacy and never bothered Helen and Victor in their room. In there, they both were the Captain; and Victor can recall only two nights, that they did not help the other captain, rock them to the next port.

"The Islands are all nice Victor, but so far, Barbados is my favorite."

"I was thinking the same thing. You're rubbing off on me Helen."

"Good Victor, maybe you will let me rest, part of tonight."

"Nope Helen, you can have all night when we return home."

"Victor, what has gotten into you?"

"It must be the ocean breeze; I wish I could bottle some and take it back Helen."

"Not on your life Victor; I could never defend myself from your amatorious vicious sexual attacks. Let us hope that your stream of air has subsided by then. If not, you are going to blow me away. Don't pay me any attention Victor; those were only wisecracks; you are wonderful——simply wonderful."

"Helen, the thing I like most about this vacation is not having to worry about changing hotels."

"It would not have made any difference Victor, with all the energy you have. What I like most besides being with you Victor, is the food. Does it look like I have gained weight?"

"If so it must be in the right places Helen. Did you notice the goo-goo eyes on you at pool side?"

"I bought those bikini's especially for this trip Victor."

"There was one guy that turned his drink over at least three times Helen."

"Victor, why didn't you tell me all this several days ago?"

"Well, because, I was getting a big thrill out of it. You have the sexiest walk in a bikini. I even lost my drink once Helen. Are you sure you weren't putting a little more into that back motion. That black body of yours was the most beautiful figure at pool side. Do you remember when I put the suntan oil on you?"

"Yes Victor, you said it was to protect me from the sun rays."

"That's partially true Helen; it made you glisten and sparkle like the ocean when the sun danced around it. All eyes were on you. I was patting myself on the back that you belong to me. Girl, you are so fine, it's pitiful. I can imagine what those women were saying as their men focused on you. You didn't make it any better Helen, because you love to walk around. And those shorts you were playing tennis and volleyball in–they looked as though you were melted and poured into them. Did you notice that you never had a woman partner playing doubles?"

"Yes Victor, I did notice that, they were all gathered around you."

"Well, so much for the observations Helen."

"Not yet Victor, how about the dance floor, those women kept you dancing all night."

"Okay Helen, but we're still not even."

"What about that day in the casino, when that guy let you roll his dice as he watched you–from behind. You rolled them dice for at least thirty minutes Helen and never won nothing. Each time you bent over to throw, I bet his shorts got wetter and wetter."

"Okay, that is enough Victor; I was here to be with you and have fun, and I did that. I am yours and yours alone and there is no guy in the world that will ever change that."

Helen, on these cruise days was sailing about as high as one could, without actually flying. She realized how special this event was in her life and also realized how special Victor had become. Somehow, she knew there would never be another moment like today, and if so, because of her busy schedule, there would be precious few. Knowing what more she wanted from Victor; today's nature timing was right, and she must take advantage of it. She must not waste the perfect opportunity. Her plans were to slip away from the Knusant's and everyone today, with Victor of course. So after breakfast, she simply said to Victor:

"Victor, my body feel strong today, can we retire to our cabin for awhile?"

There was nothing Victor could do, for he felt Helen's body heat and smelled her special alluring body fragrance.

"Why not Helen, you deserve it." Not fully aware of what was at stake.

Helen, not only wanted today to be one for conceiving, but wanted to show Victor, how appreciative she really was. No sooner than they entered the room and stripped, Helen was upon Victor; holding him within her palms, admiring his most animated position. Victor lying sprawled upon the bed was at Helen's complete mercy. He relished the idea of her boldness, bracing himself for her eloquent touch. Helen knew Victor would be inside of her twice today, and this moment could be the most important. She also knew, they had made love a lot lately; so it was essential for this occasion for Victor's supply of wetness to be strong and plentiful. Helen purposely teased Victor for an hour, concentrating on an inch only, but repetitively, until he was seemingly wild and crazy. She had never made love to Victor in this manner before and it showed upon his face. His eyes were shut so tight, it looked as if his eyelids would push his eyeballs into his skull, and Victor's mouth was wide open, with him appearing to need the extra wide passageway, to get a decent breath. Helen's lips, filled with more than a broad smile enhanced Victor's enjoyment and encroaching weakness, as he started begging her to end her head-throbbing ecstasy. Helen could feel his bigness was ready for her other inside, and she smoothly made the transition, politely going against her wishes for the first time, taking all of him. Victor was overwhelmed by Helen's tremendous body heat, which ended his begging. Helen felt good also, because she knew, she had thanked Victor properly; and she also knew, more life, or for clarity, more little Victor's were truly on the way.

Turn of events the past several weeks had thrown Victor deeply into Helen. Helen thought, "this is truly a miracle, and I am merely a vessel to be used." I mean, it is not like she had not tried, but there was no way she thought, she could have worked a plan this elaborate. Helen again, sent up a prayer; but this time, she thanked God for sending Victor to her.

CHAPTER SIXTEEN

THE ACCIDENT

"Hello Victor, this is Ralph, I have been trying to reach you since yesterday. I know you have been on vacation, but Tiffani said you were due back on Friday."

"That's true, but I was delayed somewhat. What's up?"

"It is about our friend Carolyn..."

"Hurry man, has anything happened to her?"

"No, not Carolyn, but her oldest daughter, Sharonda, was killed late Thursday night in an auto collision. It is the headline story in the Friday morning's newspaper."

"Ralph, I saw that, but had no idea Carolyn's daughter was involved."

"Yes, Victor, she was just a passenger and was the only one injured. She was killed instantly. The driver of the car failed to realize a car on the freeway had stopped. No passengers were in the stalled car. The driver and owner of the car in which Sharonda was riding, Victor, did not get a scratch on her."

"Those things happen Ralph; I guess it was just not her time to go. Have you talked to Carolyn, Ralph?"

"No, I talked to her ex, who said she is taking it pretty hard. As a matter of fact, they had to take her to the hospital, shortly thereafter. And she is still in there, so Victor, you might want to try and see her."

"Thanks Ralph, I'll see you Monday."

Victor said to himself: "This is a hell of a way to come off a vacation. I know Carolyn is devastated, because that's mostly all she ever talked about. Her life was wrapped up in her daughters. And while I didn't know her daughter, I can't help but feel saddened by this unfortunate occurrence. The loss of a friend, and now the loss of a friend's daughter. Tragedy strikes us all. No one is immune to it. I would rather do anything than make this trip. What will I say? She was only a teenager; she had so much living to do, but apparently destiny wanted her to live forever."

As Victor is stumbling around, trying to get ready to go to the hospital–the phone rings again.

"Oh, Hi Helen. Yes I heard. I'm going to the hospital to see Carolyn as soon as I get dressed. You're not serious, Helen. You are! Okay, I'll pick you up."

Victor thought: "Now isn't that something, Helen insists on going to the hospital with me. I feel better already. Helen is so caring. The caring mold was thrown away after she was made. An asset to have in anyone's corner. I suppose I'm a very fortunate fellow after all, to have her as my friend. Helen's weakness and strength is the same–she is just so forceful. If I had told her no, I'm going alone; we would have still been on the phone."

Victor had been too busy thinking about Carolyn's terrible disposition to wonder what type of reaction their appearance would make. Well, it was too late now, because Helen and Victor were about to make their debut. Carolyn was asleep as they entered the room. As they talked lowly, with Helen holding Victor's hand; Carolyn awakened. He introduced Helen. Carolyn did not seem startled or anything, but the effect of whatever she was under had her a bit drowsy. Victor was sure there was as blank a stare on his face as was the hollowness of his insides. You do what you have to do—but Victor had no experience at being a comforter. Talk: He wanted to say something, but there were no words. His mouth received no command from the brain to speak. His communication system had broken down. Surely, silence had its rewarding moment and domicile; the time and place on this fateful day seemed appropriate. A gaping look was all that could be mustered. Appearance: Sure, that counts for something. Just being present was all that was necessary—his mind kept reverberating. Was it enough; could silence be enough.

Victor could not help, but to think of Stacy and her childhood. All the sweet moments of growing up. The good times they shared with each other; without an interruption of unhappiness. None of his dreams had been shattered with the loss of a daughter. Stacy was still able to walk in and say hello–daddy. Stacy could still smile and be with him, to either, her or his choosing. He had managed to escape the sorrowful pains of a departing youth. He had managed to elude this disheartening ache. No woefulness crept into his body, from earth's removal of a young and innocent love one.

What could be going through Carolyn's mind but sweet-sweet memories. Joyful days of nursing her first womb's blessing. Happy days of kindergarten and elementary school; pretending to love those weird drawings, she brought home. Placing each on your bedroom wall until the room's decor was modified; no longer was there a lone picture of grandma and grandpa. Now, peeping at you each morning and night, in your most private gathering area; were those big sunshine faces with even warmer sunshine smiles. They were all a different color, expressing Mr. Rainbow's greatest wish. There was no room in this room for nothing but cheerfulness; but the faces ended and the cows, horses (more like donkeys), elephants, and myriads of other animals started coming in. Still, buoyancy overflowed within the setting, as the child development ran its course. Lasting and pleasant thoughts of Sharonda would now live with Carolyn forever.

Carolyn and Helen with her huge bubbly smile hit it off immediately. Victor thought: "I tell you that girl is like magic the way people take to her. And I was worried about what to say and all." The nurse came in and Victor stepped out of the room until she left. When he came back, Carolyn and Helen were laughing and talking. He looked somewhat puzzled and they burst out laughing again.

Carolyn said, "I see why you like Helen, Victor, she is so lively and cheerful."

"Oh, I'm glad you approve; those would be my choice of words Carolyn."

Victor's mind was thinking; "there was something going on here that he didn't know about."

"They are going to release me Sunday morning Victor. Could you pick me up?"

"Sure Carolyn, I'll be glad to."

As they left the hospital, Victor asked Helen what the chatter was all about.

"Oh, nothing Victor, I will let Carolyn tell you tomorrow."

Victor was still a little bit somber in his thoughts of Carolyn's daughter. "And tomorrow, when Helen is not there, what will he say; those thoughts kept coming back to him over and over again. Every time he and Carolyn had lunch, Carolyn always talked about her daughters. He could not sleep at all. Finally, he got up and wrote this poem for Carolyn.

OUR CHILD

Dear God, you'll love my ebony child
I know...she was here for a while
She is lovely, sweet and kind
And you got her, while in her prime

She's safe with you as I write this letter
Sobering thought but, it makes me feel better
I know...I've shed plenty of tears
But what joyful times in nineteen years

Forever in my heart; Forever in your care
...beautiful qualities, that often seemed rare
I can never repay the blessings you gave
But I thank you, for the life you save

Life will go on——someway——somehow
Our child is happy...see her smiling now

On their way home from the hospital, Victor presented it to Carolyn. She started crying before she finished it. She told Victor everything was going to be all right and thanked him. He did not know quite what to say, so he just held her in his arm. After they got home, she thanked him again, and said "the poem had made her cry." It was the first time Carolyn had cried since the tragic ordeal.

"Victor, I tried to cry before, but it would not come out. When I was first told, I must have passed out; because when I came to I was in the hospital. I understand I passed out several times. I will always cherish this Victor. As a matter of fact I am going to get it framed, so I can hang it on my wall."

"If there's anything I can do Carolyn——"

"Oh, you know I will call you. Just hold me Victor."

Holding Carolyn between the long periods of silence became Victor's easiest chore. If only they made sentences this easy during spells of bereavement.

Victor stayed with Carolyn the rest of the day or until Helen came over. Some of Carolyn's others friends also came by to pay their respects and bring food. Carolyn, seemed to be taking the loss of Sharonda pretty good at this point. Victor thought: "Much better than I if it had been Stacy. The crying was probably what she needed, although crying cannot replace nineteen years of happiness. Crying relieves the pressure momentarily but memories last forever. Let's hope Carolyn's memories are full of priceless treasures. Treasures which send thoughts of Sharonda smiling across her face. Treasures, though locked in the heart explodes through her bosom for enlightening and gladsome meditations."

Besides the guest coming by, there were phone calls, numerous calls; Carolyn was on and off the phone like a switch board operator. Some lasted much longer than others, and most appeared to put Carolyn in a happy mood; but there was this one, that seems to antagonize her. Matter of fact, even when the call was over, she was down right incensed. That is when Victor inquired if she wanted someone to screen her calls and volunteered to do so. Carolyn gave him a somber smile, held his hand for further assurance, telling him; "just one of those things; I will be alright." Victor fixed his mouth to inquire further, but just as Helen showed up. The conversation was dropped in the shuffle, and Victor's anticipated question of, "who the hell was that," never left his lips; but it also never left his mind. The call appeared to have set Carolyn back some ninety digits on the one hundred digit mood meter. Yes, she was darn near batting zero.

The arrival of Helen was perfect; that bubbly dimpled smile of hers was usually enough to charm a vicious rattler out of his venom. As Helen lit up the room, so did the glow appear upon Carolyn's face. They greeted each other warmly and sisterly, as genuine friends normally do; embracing and kissing each other affectionately. Victor knew he was no longer needed and bowed out gracefully. He thought to himself as he left; "there is just no substitute for a real friend; realizing even more so, Helen was definitely a special person." Helen's entrance brought the type of warmth and happiness in the room and around her which penetrated through one's heart and to one's soul. You did not have to touch her to feel it, but if you were fortunate enough to do so, as Victor; it left you with a happy numbness; you were happy and you did not know why. Victor walked out of the house on a high; looking staringly like, as if he was in search of something.

Victor spend the rest of the evening wandering slowly through Brackenridge Park. He was looking for anything peaceful to address his mood. Birds: They are always happy and busy; singing and hopping about; scratching and eating; or just flying around with a twig in their beak. Always watch the birds; they are the source to a new beginning. You will escape with one as he soars through the sky. Your mind becomes wings and moves with the wind as you glide into an unconquerable arena where only you will triumph.

The funeral was on Tuesday and we shall not get into that. Other than to say, Helen and Victor attended it together; and that Victor and all attending was truly saddened by such youth. Helen remained with Carolyn for the rest of the week.

The following week, Carolyn asked Victor to spend a night or two with her; but he moved in for the week, and became her chauffeur and guardian angel. It was her first week back to work and Victor got a thrill out of driving Carolyn around. He felt sort of important. To be honest with you, it was sort of like being married. She cried a bit more in his arms at night. She talked a lot and he listened. Victor had become the benevolent comforter. And finally Carolyn was smiling more and more. She even broke into a laughter when he asked her about Helen.

"I wish you could have seen your face Victor when you tried to introduce Helen at the hospital. You were so scary looking."

"Well, what was so funny, Carolyn?"

"Helen and I are Sorors and friends, Victor. We had already met at a sorority meeting. Somehow we got to talking and found out we were after the same fellow. Since neither one of us had time or a big need for sex or companionship, we agreed to leave it like it was, even after winning you over. However, if you start dating someone else other than Angela; we have already decided this town is not going to be large enough for all of us, especially you."

"Did I miss something, somewhere, Carolyn? You mean——you two actually knew each other——and me!"

"That is right, but like I say, Victor, you are available not only when we want you, but when we need you."

"So the jokes on me——right!"

"No, it is not a joke Victor. And if you think that, you have another thought coming. Believe me Victor, it is no joke when I am making love to you. Nor is it a joke when we are involved in an intellectual discussion. We are very serious. It is a neat arrangement and it is convenient. I am sure we both love you, if you are worried about your ego. Helen and I admit that you are the best thing that ever happened to us, as far as a male is concerned. Both our situations are unique and you fill the bill. A word to the wise; you just continue doing what you are doing and everything will be all right. In other words Victor, relax and enjoy yourself."

"YES MA'AM—I caught your directive and it don't feel any less funnier."

"Why Victor, because we know."

"No——I guess——because, I know you know Carolyn."

"Now Victor, that is funny. So, I suppose what you are going to say now is that women are treacherous."

"I wouldn't label it that harsh, Carolyn, but I'll accept your terminology."

"Victor, we are no more entitled to bad labels as "men are dogs.""

"Let's just say you're consumer interested, Carolyn."

"That might be a good choice of words Victor, depending on

how you mean them. If it is from the point of the consumer as a worthwhile selected buyer, that is good. However, if you are talking about the consumer as a user through begging, borrowing, scheming and conniving, you are off your rocker."

"You don't have to get upset about the issue Carolyn."

"Victor, life is a give and take situation. And I would like to think that we are taking no more from you than you are taking from us. And the same holds true in giving. I just want to clarify the issue, so there are no problems in the future, Victor."

"Your choice of, or succumbing to the chivalry of three well-endowed chicks should not ruin your reputation, even if disclosed. You could not be dangled by a more caring trio. So you are in a controlled environment Victor, so what. You are allowed to roam around at will within our perimeter. You are respected for the latitude given you, so it should not matter to you what minor constraints there are. Your mind, Victor, will stay focused on the complete satisfaction of a trio——Helen, Angela, and myself, as long as we deem it necessary."

"There will be no wavering of your responsibility to the three of us. Victor, you will love each equally and respond as we command your body to ravish us with delight. No other woman will be able to manipulate the entanglements of your mind. You will be free to love–love–love, the desirous three now in your possession. We are yours; we belong to you; you cannot deny us. Your honor is to Helen, Angela, and myself Carolyn. Victor, you will be faithful and we will protect you from other beautiful women who are there to harm you. Their bodies and beauty will only remind you of us as your eyes roll upon them in a rapturous state. The three of us can do no wrong, as you will cater to our every whim."

"Don't worry Victor, we don't go around comparing notes on you. Your bedroom business is safe. But to explain what I am talking about Victor; you can probably count the times you have had sex with us anyway. You provide that need, but we don't need that need, that much. Oh, sometimes I will get horny and think I need it the whole week, but you are so good, it's short lived."

"I love you Victor for more than your body. You are everything a friend should be. Do not destroy that. Keep on being there when you are needed. This week was one of those times and I am so thankful to the kindness and thoughtfulness you tendered to me. The affection you have shown is spoiling me, but I should not allow myself to become too fond of you."

"And why is that Carolyn?"

"I thought we covered that a moment ago, Victor——anyway——you are being shared by a trio of intimacy; and I would fight to maintain my one third slice. So neither one of us should become too selfish."

Victor thought: "Empty. That's the feeling inside of me. A space crowded with emptiness. I felt used, then dejected, then empty. Carolyn and Helen in some ways had slid the carpet from under me; they had let me down——hard; they had pulled a fast one; they had stolen my thunder. Ego. That's it——my inflated ego had just come crashing down upon me. These two beauties punctured my bubble. And neither acts if though they've done anything blameworthy. Which means, there will be no apology; no words of regret; no expressions of being sorry from either of them."

Victor continued thinking: "Sure, Carolyn expressed her dictatorial gratitude——keep on doing what you're doing brother. Yes, don't change a thing——keep on being a sucker for our benefit. We love the arrangement just the way it is, and you'll have to learn to deal with it. Didn't I hear little voices inside of me telling me those things. Mine. It's difficult to determine whose funeral I just attended. I'm grieving for myself; and there's no one to comfort me. There's no one to console and lift me through my suffering of self-pity."

And through all of the emptiness and self-pity, Victor could not help but feel obligated to these women. He hears other little voices telling him to love–love–love. They are telling him to cast his personal agenda in the direction of those now soliciting his attention. Those little voices are telling Victor he was needed by them and any desertion would destroy a bond of happiness. It seems as if, he had been asleep in a garden of paradise; and no one was there but Helen, Angela, and Carolyn.

Victor was now trying to figure out which word described this situation the best——disappointed or betrayal. Of course, the disappointment pertained to himself. Helen and Carolyn had exposed (to say the least) him to undue naked physical pressure and he had succumbed; not without a small fight, mind you, yet he ultimately did give in. There really was no point in looking back at events which were surely to happen only once or twice in a man's lifetime; so Victor was fortunate to get his two at the same time; why be disappointed in that. And there is the part about being challenged; what real he-man would pass up such a rewarding task? Even a narrow-minded man would find justification for mingling with exclusive feminine hierarchy, who would belittle him? Opinions of other women, also should not carry any weight; Tiffani's warning to Victor, that Carolyn would have him doing anything she wanted, was merely an envious woman's viewpoint. Afterall, what do women know about other women. Victor searched and searched and could find no reason whatsoever, why an intelligent man of his caliber should be disappointed in himself, for probably one of his finer decisions.

So obviously, that left betrayal as the likely reason for this debacle. Betrayal from Carolyn and Helen, of course. Well, after Victor's very careful consideration, his thoughts were in agreement, with all other men; of which neither of them could fault these lovely ladies for fending for themselves. So what, if their tactics were brutally savage with abusive sensuous attacks; they were sensibly trying to level the playing field, because of this stigma as being the weaker sex. And whoever said that women were smarter and could outwit men, knew absolutely nothing of what they were talking about. There is no denying, prettier brains, sometimes do have the edge, but every man knows that already. There is also this story going around about women having more convincing sexier voices, which leads men behind them like little puppy dogs; a fallacy for sure; that story was started by those jealous of men, being better listeners. This leads us to another story about women coaxing men to trust them, deliberately setting a trap to eventually betray him; which is absolutely absurd; no man in his right mind is going to blame a beautiful woman for trapping——petting, caring, and providing necessary body nourishment. Yes, Victor looked high and low, and he could not find any reason to blame Carolyn and Helen for any problems, past or current, directly attributed to them. Certainly, he thought, their lovely attributes did spur him on, to do constructive things, which just happened to be helpful to their self interest. Victor insist, all his endeavors, involving these gorgeous women was done of his own accord and further insist, he was always in control.

Victor, again, after a careful thought process, "feels Carolyn was correct in reading him his rights; he had no reason in the world to think of them using him; if anything, the reverse was true. Carolyn and Helen had a right to sic their womanhood upon him, and make that powerful gentleness, prevail over his sensitive receptive manhood.Afterall, they were only doing what he allowed them to do." Victor, now recalls, "getting more and better good-goodies, than he had in his life. And not only that, was still receiving all these delightful treats." "If anybody should be complaining, on second thought," Victor knew "it should be one of these women. It was he who should feel guilty for using them to his advantage." Victor's head is a bit clearer, now that Carolyn talked to him man to man, well——woman to man. And to think all the time, he is really the fortunate one. "Sometimes," Victor thought, "we men, all need a little talking to——one on one, of course; for you see, men are much better listeners."

After spending the week with Carolyn, Victor realized how important he was in her life. So what, if Carolyn and Helen had pulled a fast one on him; he now felt strongly, that he had a place somewhere in their lives; and he would prove it to them. Somehow, he now felt extremely relevant in the lives of the trio (as Carolyn had put it). Yes, this new trio of women were impacting his life like he could not believe. Carolyn's words thundered through his brain; "he needed them like they needed him." His thinking was getting firmly entrenched in that direction. "Who would help them if he didn't;" was his persuading remarks to himself. "From now on," Victor told himself; "I will be there for them when they need me; I will do what ever is necessary to make them happy."

Victor suddenly sounded like a sentimental vowing machine. Those could become mighty big orders, he was getting himself into. But, men understand, there are times when men must make sacrifices, and bear the brunt of the burden. And this is what

Victor was doing, through no additional pressure from anyone; it was Carolyn though, who got him going. Once he put two and two together, he saw the trio in the pot; then he threw himself into the mix as they all held their extended pleading arms and hands out to him. Under those circumstances who would do the opposite and better still, who would blame Victor for his new approach to existing on earth's planet.

Well, Tiffani for one, objected. She constantly told Victor: "Victor those women are just using you; Helen, Angela, Carolyn; even Samantha, they are all using you to their satisfaction?"

"Is that right Tiffani?"

"Ask yourself Victor, what benefit are you receiving?"

Victor smiled.

"Well Victor, I mean other than all that sex; look at Carolyn, she is using you in sympathy from her daughter's loss."

"I understand what you're saying Tiffani, but everyone needs help in their hour of bereavement."

"Yeah, Victor, hour of bereavement, not days and days of bereavement!"

"Well, Tiffani, it does take longer for some; I am just glad to make myself available."

"Think about it Victor, I have noticed you going into her office after work, almost every day since she has been back; how many times have you been on that old sofa of hers?"

"Tiffani, I am doing no more than what you would do; helping out where I am needed; but if it will make you any happier, I will quit the office routine."

"Please do Victor, because I do not want my boss to have the worst image among top executives."

"And that Helen, she seems real nice and all on the phone Victor, but she is using you too, in the name of sympathy for Joseph's death. I can tell just as good when you have been by her place; you have those large bags under your eyes; pretty soon, they will turn into big black rings. Don't kill yourself, excuse my french, over a piece of ass Victor; it is just not worth it."

Victor started to laugh, but when he looked into Tiffani's eyes and the seriousness they displayed, he cut it off immediately. This was the first, she had expressed down right anger with Victor.

"It seems to me Victor, you learned nothing in Joseph's dying."

"I will try and do better Tiffani, but Helen gets home late. Anyway, it was you who said, I should volunteer some of my leisure time to a worthy cause."

"Victor, you know damn well, what I meant? It is just not worth it man; think of your own life. You will be looking seventy five by the end of the year." Tiffani starts crying and Victor holds her in his arms.

"Now, now Tiffani, it is not that bad; I promise, I'll do better."

"Victor, you are making fun of me, and this is a serious matter, you are a good man——a good boss, and I do not want to lose you." Tiffani quickly regains her composure.

"Don't worry Tiffani, I am not going anywhere, but Helen is sort of special to me."

"It looks to me, like they are all special to you Victor; look at that Angela, you spend a considerable amount of time going by there in the evening. She calls, asking me to tell you to stop by almost everyday. What did you do to that young girl and what are you doing to her now; or better still Victor, what is it she is doing that makes you jump every time she calls."

"Well, Angela has a problem or two which I have been personally helping her with Tiffani."

"Victor, you do not know it, but you are the one with the problem; what are you going to do when you collapse?"

"Don't worry Tiffani, I will slow down eventually."

"Eventually, might be too late, Victor; you are not a machine, you know. Tell me, what does one woman have, that the others do not have?"

"I never thought about it Tiffani."

"That is part of your problem Victor, you are not thinking; and the answer to the question is——NOTHING. Neither has nothing that the other one does not have. Believe me Victor, if you closed your eyes during the process, not knowing, who was who, you would not note a dime worth of difference; and the result is always going to be the same."

"Maybe so Tiffani, I never thought about it like that."

"That is because you are letting those women do all your thinking for you Victor. What are you going to do when they use you up?"

"I don't know, I never thought about it Tiffani."

"Man, you better get a grip, and I do not mean on one of those chick's behind. And Samantha, I love her like a mother, but now, she is using you. She did not want you and now she is making more demands on you than a married woman. Tell me Victor, what it is about a damn near fifty year old outcast pussy that turns you on? You need to get your act together and move on; stop all this shucking and jiving and bullshitting around. And pardon me if I sound harsh, but I mean every word I'm saying."

As to Samantha, Victor really wanted to tell Tiffani; Samantha's stuff is by far sweeter than any of the other three combined, but saw no point in rubbing salt in a wound; so he just left that alone.

"Tiffani, Samantha is the mother of my child."

"Fine and dandy Victor, I am the daughter of my divorced father, and he is settled again with one woman. So don't cop out on me; that is no excuse; probably the one Samantha is giving you, but definitely, no excuse."

"In time Tiffani, maybe things will change."

"I certainly hope so Victor, I certainly hope so! I love you Victor, but you must take care of yourself and not let everyone else take advantage of you. At your age, you need to be settling down, not gallivanting from watering hole to watering hole."

"I really appreciate what you are telling me Tiffani, and I know you would not tell me these things, if you did not love me. Please bear with me, maybe it'll work itself out. I do not know all the answers, I wish I did."

Victor should have been despondent, having his rights read to him again, in such a short period of time. But, he was not, because like he told Tiffani; "he did not know all the answers." And he was not going to complicate life by looking for any answers. One thing for sure, he knew what he knew; his current status was what it was because of circumstances beyond his control, and he was going to deal with it to the best of his ability or to his dying breath. Because unlike Tiffani, Victor knew it was not all about watering hole to watering hole; and maybe, he was being used; he did not have the answers. From now on though, Victor promised himself, he would try and understand things as he went along and explain them to Tiffani, to the best of his ability. He felt good, to have another woman in his corner, looking at things from the outside. If Tiffani has done little else, her fiery talk will definitely cause Victor to think more. The phone rings.

"Victor, it was Angela, she told me to tell you to stop by this evening."

Victor could not do anything but smile and shake his head as he waltz to his desk. Even Tiffani smiled and shook her head. He wanted to tell Tiffani this moment, the problems he was helping Angela with, but somehow it did not seem like the appropriate time. Seeing Angela this evening; however, was appropriate.

CHAPTER SEVENTEEN

JUST PISSED OFF

There was little wonder what Angela wanted; discussion of frustration in the workplace; but she always made the evening interesting and exciting; thanks to grandmother's wise counsel. A sumptuous meal was usually waiting, followed by generous love making. Angela had learned the give and take aspect of making love as schooled by grandma's wisdom; and Victor was more than eager to come running when she called. In other words, Helen was not the only one popping his eye socket and making his brain feel silly; and Samantha was not the only one with a sweet dessert; and Carolyn no longer had a patent on taking his bigness all the time. Yes, Angela was the new kid on the block and was making great steps forward, but her expertise level was not that of a Helen, Samantha, or Carolyn. Keeping everything in its proper perspective; Angela was a highly prized rookie in a big league arena, competing and doing everything well; developing the complete package; and in time, if successful, would probably put the others out to pasture. Victor, however, thought nothing of the sort; for he was much too busy, hopping to all of their demands. Tiffani had been right in her assessment of the four women; they were all special to Victor. Victor himself had put them in special categories, without realizing the significance of what he had done.

Today, as the revolving, special treatment goes; happens to be Angela's turn.Victor gave no further thought of Tiffani's remarks pertaining to his reaction, to the ladies whims and fancies. Their concerns were his concerns; meaning Angela's cry for help today, entitled her to be rescued by Victor. To Victor, no trip to this mansion is ever considered anything other than a routine visit. He loved listening to Angela and helping to solve her every problem. His arrival this evening found her in a jovial mood; greeting Victor downstairs, and sitting on the same sofa where they first made love.

"Why are you so happy Angela; no problems today?"

"No more than the usual Victor, but I am learning to cope more, thanks to you. That translates into happiness; life would be so difficult without you Victor."

"Don't keep me in suspense Angela, what did I do that was so spectacular.?"

"Well, you got me reading and I cannot seem to stop. It has helped me somewhat, but I am still steaming. For this evening, though, I thought I would at least appear to be happy when you arrived, because I know you get tired of me greeting you with a tired ugly face."

Victor kisses Angela's lips, saying; "You have the most beautiful "tired ugly face", I have ever seen."

"Keep that up Victor and I will forget why I asked you over."

Victor kissed her lips again, smiling, saying; "this is my lucky sofa, you know."

"Yes, how well do I remember that night, Victor; and if I recall correctly I was truly happy. You really taught me something on this old sofa and I have been loving your techniques ever since; matter of fact, how about a refresher course right now."

And how could Victor forget that night; he remembered how annoyed he was when he was unable to get all of Angela sweet liquidity. And since that day Victor has never been able to get enough of Angela; no matter how much she gives, her liquid production comes up short. On each successive effort, Victor has been unable to get that extra little bit which he feels still remains. Even when the double dosage was coming his way, the supply was inadequate, because his mind kept telling him; there is a sweeter bit of her wetness remaining. Maybe this was what Tiffani hinted at, when she wondered what Angela did, which made Victor jump whenever she called. Deep down, Victor was chasing something, which he knew was there, but could never get. Maybe, it was this extra bit that remained behind which kept Victor jumping when Angela snapped. Angela knew what she was doing then, because that old wisdom of grandmother's was in effect. Angela had made Victor bow down before her, because she was the queen in charge. She knew to give him just enough to have him craving her forever, and bowing forever when she called. Coupled with her give and take stranglehold, Angela knew to give just enough; Victor was truly hooked. Victor was fortunate, Angela did not abuse her wisdom power; he was fortunate, she did not want him twenty four hours a day. Victor was unaware why he jumped when Angela called; he only knew, he did, and he loved it.

Victor sat on the sofa today like an humble servant; fuzziness surrounded him; this was one of their few times here, since their initial sexual orientation. A feeling was coming over him which he could not interpret. He kept wanting to bow down upon his knees at Angela's feet, even seeing himself doing so. "Your majesty," formed in his mouth and he heard himself constantly saying these words over and over again. Commands were being given to him, but he could not hear them, yet he kept saying, "yes——your majesty." Victor did not know what to do; if only he could hear the commands. "How am I going to please my mistress," he thought, "if I can't hear the command." Victor could see her dainty alluring feet move and he wanted to kiss it, but heard no command. Suddenly the pretty petite toes beckoned for him to come forward and touch them; this he did, kissing them all over, placing each delicate object within his mouth, hoping to satisfy his majesty. Victor looked up, hoping to hear a command; hearing nothing, but seeing two smooth shapely legs, moving firmly against his jaws. No command came, so he kept kissing, going upward until he reached the queen's knees. Looking forward along the lovely thighs pathway, Victor listened faithfully for a command, hoping it would not stop him from, continuing to kiss. He paused, slowly moving forward along the tender pathway, inching ever so close to what appeared to be the end. A beautiful unique aroma was telling him to continue kissing, keep coming forward, keep kissing; and suddenly he was commanded to "stop." Victor was close enough that he could feel the beautiful aromatic flavor upon his tongue, but he had to stop; the command to "stop," by his majesty had to be obeyed. He was close enough that he could even taste the sweet wetness looming digestibly within his eye sight, but his majesty's command was to "stop." Cravings began to set up; cravings to continue kissing, cravings to move a little bit further, cravings to settle where the beautiful fragrance scent emanated from, cravings to kiss the sweet wetness before his eyes. Little did Victor know, these cravings would always be with him, because his majesty had stopped him at the height of a most enjoyable moment. Curtailment of satisfaction leaves one in a desirous state. That is where the queen——Queen Angela has Victor; and that is precisely the reason, Victor jumps when Angela calls.

Victor can remember the queen being happy, he can vaguely remember his irritability. Victor can remember Angela placing her hand on his head, telling him to please obey, but scarcely remember if he did. Slowly, his fuzziness began to fade, and the real live beautiful Angela appeared in his view. Victor noticed he was not bowed down before Angela, upon his knees, but he wanted to do so, as a craving crept into him. He noticed he was not kissing Angela's lovely thigh pathway, but he wanted to do so, as saliva flowed heavily into his mouth. Victor also noticed, his head was not inches away from Angela's curly cavern, but he wanted it to be there, trying to get that little bit extra and more. Victor noticed Angela was fully clothed and he commenced to unbutton the row of round objects that held her skirt together; until it was a mere piece of cloth lying loosely upon the sofa, and her sensuous thighs opened as wide. Only a pair of black panties separated Victor from satisfying his cravings. And like before, he found himself bowed down before Angela, upon his knees. Angela had already laid back upon the sofa and placed her hands upon Victor's head. He could hear her telling him to quickly remove her panties, and get started; he could hear Angela telling him to please obey; and he could feel the cravings deep down inside his throat. Victor felt a readiness in Angela that was sure to leave them both happy. However, this time he thought to say:

"Where is Grandma Angela?" This broke both of their concentration.

"Grandmother is upstairs Victor; the same place she was that night, remember?" Sounding half disappointed.

"Yeah, now I remember Angela; that is the night I got short changed. And for your information, I am still running in the arrears, so you better be real careful."

"In that case Victor, we will wait until we retire for the night; you did say you were spending the night, didn't you?" Reluctantly releasing Victor's head.

"Sure Angela, those were the first words out of my mouth, when I came in the door; remember?" Both Angela and Victor are laughing as they hug and squeeze on each other.

"Maybe, we should make love now Victor, because when I finish with what's on my mind, I might not be in the mood."

"It has never stopped you before Angela; if anything, you are generally more lubricative and succulent. But don't you worry about the love making, I have enough mood for both of us tonight."

"Victor, that is why, I love you so much; you make up for all my deficiencies. Anyway, like I said earlier, the reading has really done something for me——and to me, I might add."

Angela had been reading very heavily about her black heritage, and she was a little upset. Angela's frustrated mind vented the following long slow thought out monologue:

"Slavery was the cruelest form of conditions to ever stranglehold the Black race of people. We pray that those who killed themselves, rather than die a slow merciless death at the hands of a slave master or overseer; somehow will be shown God's mercy and entered into his kingdom, on the highest throne. They truly deserve the highest honor shown to mankind. They were the strong——they were the weak. They knew about freedom and made death the ultimate sacrifice. They set the tone for others to endure the duration of struggles and sufferings which is lasting for centuries. Yes, they set the precedent for freedom and others got the message."

"Somehow, hope burned in the others hearts, and survival became the ultimate sacrifice. They prepared their minds and backs for the suffering. They sang when they were happy and they sang when they were sad. And right now, there is a song in my heart for each and every one of them. They were now the strong——they were now the weak. Grandmother said in all of her wisdom, "the Black race of people are God's chosen people". I cannot dispute that. The slaves never knew they would endure so much and survive——they only knew they would survive. But not only did the Blacks survive, we thrived and multiplied. My ancestors survived because they heard there was freedom on the other side. They could smell that freedom; they could taste that freedom; they could feel that freedom; and oh yes, they could see that freedom. That's why we kept on singing; that's why they kept on going; that's why we keep on going.

"Some say, why rehash the past and bring up slavery. I am not a slave, they say, in abrasive language. My parents were not slaves, they say; spoken in a highly intelligent voice. These eloquent sure fired up present day twentieth century blacks, all have one thing in common——they are still slaves. We are——all inclusive——still slaves. Abolition of slavery declared in the great Emancipation Proclamation on January 1, 1863, did not do away with slavery. Not to mention in Texas where we did not even hear of the signing of the document until better than two years later, on June 19, 1965. Heretofore, the origination of the popular holiday "Juneteenth", still celebrated all over Texas by African-Americans. It is so ironic that President Abraham Lincoln, the issuer and signer, of the Emancipation Proclamation, had himself been assassinated by April 1965; still, before we in Texas received news of our so called freedom."

"The so called freedom that was suppose to make us respectful citizens of the great land we had cultivated with our laborious sweat. The so called freedom that was to give us equal rights in all arenas of America. The so called freedom that was suppose to protect us against inhumane injustices. The so called freedom that was suppose to end all singing. What happened to that freedom that we SUPPOSE to have gotten. Free? Black men and women——where are you? Freedom! What damn freedom."

"You see, we did not really get freed; slavery merely changed forms. We now have two forms of slavery. No longer are blacks bounded and chained; sold as property against our will; tortured physically with beatings, brandings, and rapings; and abused mentally because of the loss of a wife/husband/child in a slave sale. But if the truth be told, we are all still slaves. Not one of us in our right mind can stand before the masses and honestly say——I am free. You can't say it because I still hear the singing."

"Slavery in its old form was a denial of our birth rights—freedom and its inherent liberties of humanity. We are still denied those inherent liberties. We are still being denied those equal employment opportunities of hirings and promotions. We are, you see, still slaves to the lowest paying jobs. And on a so called equal job, we still get a lower, yes, a different rate of pay. We are you see, still inferior in the same discriminatory system."

"The system continues as we speak, because of the black color of our skin or in my case, because I am of the Black race. The big questions before America today are: Can a racist heart change? Can the ones who are trying to perpetuate this racist system change? Will they stop teaching their offspring a different set of rules to apply to the Black race? Will the twenty-first century survive without another civil war? History recorded the first one pretty good and showed that many thousands of people lost their lives."

"Questions——questions that can be answered and solved with the usage of equal human rights. It will be difficult for the African-American people to overcome this form of slavery without the oppressors attitudinal adjustment. Because of the same old tactics being used by the oppressors, of making and changing laws to their advantage; it will be extremely difficult to eradicate a racist society by or any time during the twenty-first century."

"But our struggles will continue and we shall overcome. As oppressed laborers, champions of minimum wages, if you will, we are gaining strength daily to fight on. And for all those that say——have patience, you're moving too fast; I say——over five centuries of patience is quite enough. I calculate my patience from the fifteenth century. You have to be awfully naive to believe if Columbus, supposedly, discovered the New World in 1492, slaves were not brought over until the year 1619. Patience should be banned from our limited vocabulary. Take patience and stick it where it can't breathe."

"When things got too tough for the slaves on the plantation, they ran away. They ran away, following that north star to freedom. Some made it while others were caught and brought back. Thanks to the Fugitive Slave Law——yes a law to the oppressors advantage. The first Fugitive Slave Law was passed in 1793. And if that wasn't enough, a new Fugitive Slave Law went into effect on September 18, 1850. For those of you who are not familiar with the Fugitive Slave Law; in short, it meant any runaway slave, anywhere in the United States could be returned to the slave master. My studies show that often, free blacks were caught and sold back into slavery. There is a lesson here. Because they ran, we don't have to run."

"I am tired of these bullshit games anyway. No more running; no more inferior ass wages for me. Being a nice patient guy has proven one thing. It does not get the job done in your lifetime. This is a new day and must be treated as such. We as a people have economic power and must use it as a negotiating tool."

"A tool which says we stand on equal footing and bargain from strength. A tool which says we have clout. A tool which attack racism wherever it is found in our society. A tool which says I am not and will no longer be treated like a second class and no class citizen. A tool which says no more abuse from you or your offspring. A tool etched deeply, inscribed with immovable words——ENOUGH IS ENOUGH. A tool which stamps out all the new Fugitive Slave Laws. Oh, I know, some of the laws were already on the books. That is true, but they were not enforced before and against the oppressor; why should they be enforced against us. All recently enforced as well as new Fugitive Slave Laws must be banished."

"This form of slavery is alive and well. These new Fugitive Slave Laws are not always on the national level. Some of the most damaging ones appear on the local level, in our back yards, so to speak. And as usual they are very well camouflaged. As blacks move up the economic ladder and become more middle class, we naturally want to move from the urban area to the suburbs. The inner city has become crowded and congested and the surrounding suburbs look attractive and ideal for raising these beautiful Black children. But when that child walks in and greets the instructor "Yo, what it is teach", or "Kin I set inter dis here chair", or "Whut is de signment fuh themorrow"; they just got put in a Special Education class."

"Your child has been erroneously and deliberately assigned to a slow learners group where they get farther and farther behind. After a couple or three years, you have a lost generation. The assignment occurred, all because of ethnic and cultural diversity, and that ever present racist slave mentality. You must understand; that mentality was for Blacks to never learn to read or write; must less get an equal quality education. We become too much of a threat with an education."

"And then there is the teacher's verbal abuse which is often perpetuated upon the outstanding Black student. Reported incidents of what should I call you——colored, negro, black, african, or what; punishing a Black child by making them write an essay on how they are not going to be anything in life; and later canceling a spelling, math, or science contest, after it was won by a Black child. We are sorely mistreated in the suburbs, because we are simply not welcomed. We have penetrated the oppressors pure haven and they just don't like it. Such insensitive verbal abuse and actions, whether intentional or the refusal of an attitudinal adjustment, must cease. We must learn to live together in peace."

"The new Fugitive Slave Laws accomplish the same devastation as the Fugitive Slave Laws of 1793 and 1850. It brings the runaway Black back into his so called "place", and again under the dominance of the oppressor. Our freedom and independence is again stifled. So be wary and attack the new Fugitive Slave Law wherever you find it."

"Look about you——oppressor——and you will see. You don't! Oh, I see——then maybe you should open your eyes before looking around. Still, others must open their minds. And all must open their hearts. We the oppressed will continue to help you see the light."

"The other form of slavery deals with us as a Black people. The kind we are perpetuating upon ourselves. The most common of them all, is voting or in this case, not voting. All, we are out of here, is a little time to visit a nearby precinct, usually less than four blocks away. Now you talk about being lazy and shiftless. It's

quite simple, you high five slapping brother——lower your hand—
–pick up a pen and register. Then at the appropriate time——get
your tired ass up and go vote."

"Our forefathers died for that right. So before you do anything
else today, register; register your sister, register your brother, register your neighbor and your neighbor's-neighbor, register your
friend and so called friends. Then get yourself and all other slaves
together on election day and go vote. On that day and at that
moment you become a free person. This without a doubt is the
easiest form of freedom."

"The other slaves are those of us carrying those credit cards.
Each card is maxed out. Almost an entire check is used to make
monthly payments. In some cases we even use one card to pay the
other card. We have no discipline, and those cards, like the
bondage chains are dragging us around. So put down the credit
card and pick up the voter registration card. Become debt free
and become free."

"Debt makes us slaves. The luxury automobile owner knows it
best. Before I step on too many toes, let's talk about the ones who
cannot afford it. Affording it means, first, that you are buying
your own home instead of renting. Next, it means that your life
style should not be altered deleteriously after purchase. In other
words, if you have trouble buying the basic necessities——food,
toothpaste, soap, and gasoline to fuel that sucker; then you can't
afford it. And last, your children's college should already be provided for. You can add to this list, I'm sure."

"We are also keeping ourselves slaves because of the jealousy,
envy, selfishness, and hatred, we hold for one another. For some
strange reason we are crabby by nature. If we see our brother and
sister doing something to succeed, we do everything we can to
pull them back. From putting the bad mouth on them and telling
lies, to actual destruction of their property. We must learn that as
one of us succeed, we all succeed. We must learn to support one
another; whether it be social, education, or business. Look at it
like this——if we do not support us, who will support us. Most of
us however, think of support as a one way street. You give it to me
and I never give it to you."

"Taking advantage of what is available to us is also of immense importance. The most critical in this arena is education. We are becoming more and more each day, slaves of ignorance, because we are not taking advantage of educational institutions. How in the hell do you expect to learn to read and write if you keep dropping out. Our forefathers taught themselves to read and write, because that was the only way. Remember——they did it for us. And we at times will not even stay in high school or go to college, when our parents have already paid for it. You are helping to create a permanent underclass. What you are doing is throwing yourself and your offspring right back into slavery. So get that education at all cost——stay in school."

"While we are attacking us; now is the time to address the latest entry which gives us no respect. We are making ourselves slaves to the Oriental, Korean, and other foreign stores relocating in our community. They take our dollars, but refuse to hire blacks or make even minimal donations to charitable benefits. When asked for such, they often laugh in our face and tell us to move on. We don't tolerate this kind of treatment from our brother; so why would we let, Johnny-come-lately, make a fool out of us."

"And finally, our Black organizations have institutionalized slavery all over again. We spend so much time either partying or fighting among ourselves that we do not have time to properly address the above slave issues. Some of this has to do with a constant power struggle over leadership, while the other have to do with our leaders being bought for. We must remember that in order to gain our freedom, we must gain our independence. As long as we are the puppets, we will dance only when the other guy pulls the string."

"In concluding my monologue, it appears that retrogression sets in every day; politically, economically, educationally. If I was a fool, I would say socially; but everyone knows partying for us will never be jeopardized. Oh, the day of reverting back to barbarity slavery and slave trade, is not a threat, nor or we close to it. What is at stake though, is the deprivations of privileges gained through years of suffering of our forefathers. Are we to make them turn over in their graves from our complacency and do-nothing attitude? Should we just apologize and ask their forgiveness for our status quo? Do we accept the color blind society, some oppressors would have us believe is in our best interest? We must keep our forefathers happy by choosing alternatives which keep us moving forward."

"It has always been my belief that pleasant dreams should not be allowed to turn into nightmares. If you do not care about your forefathers because they did not leave you as a millionaire or a wealthy snobbish bourgeoisie fool; think of your siblings, and what more, think of your damn self. Open your eyes quick and see the real pot of gold left by grandma, grandpa, and the like. Come out of that shell you're in; and heaven's sake, come down off that high horse. Or your dreams will turn to nightmares. Our children might never dream unless we give them a glimmer of hope. Don't let it be said that we are our own worse enemy; and please don't let it be true."

CHAPTER EIGHTEEN

PASSING THE TEST

Tiffani had been feeling real bad since talking to Victor the way she had; accusing him of letting himself be used by all of those women; those three plus his ex-wife Samantha. Tiffani was especially downhearted for talking against Samantha, because she was the one who got her this excellent job, working for Victor. Each day afterwards, she came into the office, she felt worse and worse; and each day's end, leaving for home, Tiffani felt even worse and worse. Three work days had passed and she wanted to apologize to Victor, but did not want him to think she was giving in to his way of life or approving of his daily frivolous actions by any means. Working in this office had become a chore; the work was so much more difficult; it now seemed like she really worked for her money. Her job was even becoming tiring and boring and what more, she hated to come to work. Part of that——or let's face it— –all of that was due to what seemed like strained relations between she and Victor. And it was probably, all just her guilt complex, because Victor still acted the same as usual. Tiffani had thought of taking a few days to a week off, or until she felt better, or at least half of her normal self. "That's it," she said out loud, "I will take a week off; Victor will not have to know why I am doing it." Tiffani now felt better; she even sang as she made the morning's coffee; her melody flowing with such vigor, she virtually danced to the phone when it rang.

"Oh, hello Victor——is there anything I can do?"

Victor had called to inform Tiffani, he was taking the day off. There was no point in him talking about her staying busy, she had a whole slew of work to do, with that special project he gave her the day before. Working for Victor, Tiffani always had work to do, but it was still a relaxing office, for the most part. "Maybe, Victor is feeling guilty too," thought Tiffani; "he sounded so tired." Tiffani looked at the two pots of coffee, saying; "maybe I will have company today; that is entirely too much coffee for me to drink." So, for the first time in three days, Tiffani could freely happily smile; she had been faking that happy face around Victor during that time; "that was the least she could do," she thought; "after all, the misery upon her, was of her own doing." Nobody had told her to open her big mouth and stick her nose far into Victor's business. Tiffani talked lowly to herself saying; "if I had it to do again, I would——"

"Good morning, Mr. Previtt's office! Hello Helen, Victor called earlier, he is taking today off."

Helen could only laugh, telling Tiffani, it was all her fault; her day had been so exciting, yesterday, she wanted to share it with somebody, so she asked Victor to come by, sort of late last night. Then she proceeded to tell Tiffani, apparently the same thing; sounds if though Helen was still excited. Tiffani did not have to say anything; Helen went on and on about some, Mrs. Garley, that had recently inspired her. You would have thought this Mrs. Garley had given Helen a million dollars, she was so excited. Tiffani listened attentively; there was little else to do, with Helen's mouth going a mile a minute. Tiffani's ears perked up though when Helen told how happy she was, that Victor was sending her to Medical school. Tiffani thought, "now Helen, you are talking the kind of stuff I want to hear;" afterall, Tiffani had already guessed Victor was tired from staying at some woman's house; and further guessed it to be Helen. Tiffani inquired, "how long had the medical school deal been in the works, and whose idea was it, and what type of strings were attached for such an outlay of funds." By the time Helen and Tiffani got off the phone, the morning was shot. "One day," Tiffani thought, "I would like to meet Helen; she really does seem like a nice lady." Of course that was besides the point, they had talked on the phone today, as if they had been knowing each other, all of their lives; it really seems now they were good friends already.

Tiffani suddenly felt guilty again, when she thought how nasty she had talked about Helen to Victor. It appeared now, that talk was undeserved and Victor was at least entitled to an apology pertaining to Helen. Tiffani began to sing, as she was feeling good again. She would apologize to Victor, the first thing in the morning; then she would not have to take those days off. Tiffani thought, "Helen is worth apologizing for; she appears to be doing so much good."

On, off days, weekends and just available time, one could find Helen at the Senior Sitizens Senter, or the old folks home to you. Helen referred to them as her golden youth. She often said: "I just love my golden youth, they are so wise. I learn so much from them daily. To me they are crystal balls. They forecast the weather, predict the future and tell you what tomorrow will bring. The satisfaction and enjoyment I receive from the golden youth sustain my usefulness for another day."

Helen usefulness far exceeded the typical getting up in the morning and having a nice day. An itinerary making use of the full twenty four hours was a matter of course. To be habitually busy spelled HAPPINESS for Helen. Because it meant unfolding her gracious arms and heart to embrace another down and out soul. Partaking of others in their need for a helping hand signaled a bilateral geniality. Helen developed lasting friendship among all who had shared in her unconditional outpouring of generous humanitarianism. She never hesitated in extending what had come to mean; doing her part to help the helpless, comfort the sick, provide strength to the weak, and forsake not, none of the aged citizens.

Helen had come to believe these white-headed wonders were simply worn-down, but not worn-out. They were slower perhaps and more deliberate, but there was still a mental sharpness present. Helen spoke wonderful words about the aged: "Just because one walks slow is no reason to not let them finish the race and because they talk slow is no reason to not let them finish the sentence. Speed moves us faster but it does not necessarily, move us farther." Such sentiments were often expressed by Helen in her defense of the golden youth's staying power.

Helen was rejuvenated from her vacation and was hard at work again——volunteering that time. She stepped now with even more enthusiasm because she had been accepted into Med. school. Helen had her cheerful, bubbly smile going again. She just went out of her way to help people period. Poetic justice would read as such:

CAN WE PASS THE TEST

Are we doing our very best today
While sitting pretty in the luxury nest
Did we help——someone, along the way
...other words, can we pass the test

We're tested daily, on every turn
So we must strive, to do our best
...my, we have so much to learn
Think it over——can I pass the test

My neighbor, is down and out
But, I'm better——than the rest
I ignore his signs and his weak shout
Hey, I've made it...did I pass the test

I can lend a helping hand
And share my blessings——more or less
...feels good, to help my fellowman
Maybe...I just passed the test

If you ever——see——that warm smile
Of someone lifted, from their mess
You won't forget it, for awhile
My God!...I passed the test

Helen passed the test all right. She not only spent her time but also spent her money. On almost every visit, she brought flowers. Workers at the Senter called her the flower child. Each worker smiled and spoke when they saw her coming. Helen's appearance put life in the hallway and cheered everyone who was aware of her entry. Everyday was special with Helen, but on the golden youth's birthday, she made it extra special. She always brought that one white candle for them to blow out. The candle always went out; sometimes with a little help, but it always went out.

The light on the candle went out, but the light of Helen and her radiance shined even brighter. Also the light within each person's soul she touched glowed ever so much more. There were no lights going out for the aging women and aged men at the Senter. Helen provoked an enteral flame into their lives.Not all responded right away, but with Helen's persistence; they all eventually responded politely and vibrant. Helen was continuously sharing her God given blessings——the joy of helping people with a smile on her face. A cheerful bubbly smile that made others return the compliment with a hearty smile of their own. Smiles so broad, that they themselves, told the story of Helen's presence.

You could not tell who was the happiest——Helen, the workers, or the golden youth. Helen beamed rays of light that everyone could see. She was a favorite with Mr. Hamilton who was ninety five, and a baseball fan. He talked baseball all the time. Nothing else mattered. He did not care about no flowers. Mr. Hamilton slept for the better part of the time, but was ever mindful of Helen's entry. Helen learned something about the game so she could converse with Mr. Hamilton. He could not see that well, so Helen bought him a radio with a good reception. He was thrilled that he could now pick up the St. Louis Cardinals.His favorite line to Helen was, and, she always repeated it with him at the end of their meeting——no runs, no hits, but no errors. Helen's visit and that line just made his day. That smile pushed her into the next room where an even broader smile was waiting. Another special person, another special story.

Helen would say, "riches like these can not be found in money and wealth. These are the heart warming and everlasting trea- suries. Those divine and glorious riches. The kind no robber can steal from you. The kind of riches which never escape, even if you are lost." Yes, Helen would say, "I'm always prosperous and riding on Easy Street——my riches are unguarded and no one can take them from me." It must be admitted, Helen was not always the easiest person for Victor to understand, with this philosophy of hers; but for sure she was always happier than anyone else, he had ever known.

Helen in making her rounds among the golden youth came across a new resident——a Mrs. Garley. The history on Mrs. Garley was that her husband had passed on several months earlier. Since that time she refused to talk; would hardly eat and refused to get out of bed. She was only seventy nine, with no physical ail- ments. Doctors had checked her over and out, around and through. And they found absolutely nothing medically wrong with her. That led to her daughters putting her in the Senter. Mrs. Garley obviously was depressed and had given up on life. There was just no desire to carry on.

Upon entering Mrs. Garley's room, she just stared at Helen. Helen did not say anything, just smiled, put a red rose in the vase and walked out. The workers told Helen the rose was on the floor that night. The next day Helen did the same, walked into the room, smiled. But this time she put a carnation in the vase, mov- ing it way across the room. The flower again found itself on the floor. Since Mrs. Garley was responding, Helen made it a point to come back every evening with a different flower, smiling and putting it in the vase. All the flowers for two weeks all ended up on the floor; but Mrs. Garley had begun to eat three meals a day. Helen thought, "all that moving around to get at the flower was paying off." She was exerting herself to the point of frustration, because she was not being allowed to continue enjoying her misery.

Then out of the blue, Mrs. Garley stopped Helen as she walked into her room and said;

"Young lady, where are your manners? Can't you speak?"

"Oh, good evening, but they told me you could not hear nor talk. Some said you were deaf and dumb."

"Don't be stupid young lady! Don't ever believe anything you hear. That's what's wrong with the world today. Too many people don't know nothing about nothing. You don't work here; what are you doing here?"

"Please call me Helen, ma'am; I came by to see you."

"Young lady, er-Helen, don't lie to me. Anyway, call me Edna. You mean, you came by just to see me!

"That is correct Edna."

"Helen, please forgive me for throwing your flowers out. I didn't know anybody cared. Why would you come to see someone, you don't even know?"

"It makes me feel good Edna. Look at you. You are now up and about and doing fine."

"Yes, thanks to you, Helen. My husband was my life. I waited on him hand and foot all my life, and all of a sudden, he had a heart attack, and was gone. I just had no usefulness left in me."

Helen was still excited about the progress of Mrs. Garley when she got home; and of course, it is when she called Victor to come over. It was only eleven o'clock in the evening, and he was, still up.

From that point on, Edna and Helen became good friends. She got herself together and got out of the Senter. Mrs. Garley had been forced to take a microscopic look at herself; she had been forced to leap out of her dolefulness. The realization of feeling sorry for one's self, did not aid in one's recovery. Even slyly-begging for sympathy was found to be ineffective against Helen. The spark to move on a life that had been placed on hold, burnt the thickskin of Mrs. Garley. Her stubbornness also was no match for Helen. Mrs. Garley's wisdom told her she was traveling a winding road of someone that truly cared To continue acting in a nonsensical manner served only to bend more, the crooks ahead. Helen had showed her, the toughness she possessed was being withered away between the bedclothes.

Mrs. Garley now lead a productive life doing charitable work herself. Helen's persistence had worked again. No matter. A soft spot, a weak spot——she found an angle to get through. Mrs. Garley, once strengthless is now full of life and useful again. She is no longer an aging woman, wasting vital seconds away. Helen's foresight to restore a seemingly useless person to one of new vigor, not only keeps her going, but it keeps the world going. Call it sanding away layers of stain; grinding into the rust, or oiling a valuable part; it was all the same to Helen——productivity again surged. And all of society was rewarded for her wondrous deed.

Tiffani went to lunch after talking with Helen and quietly returned to her normal cheerfulness. Victor, now would never know she had been under the doldrums. Ralph did come down and spend the greater portion of the evening, as he normally did, especially when Victor was not in. It was as if he had antennae's which signaled him that Victor was out. Ralph was the Corporate Treasurer, so he was always talking about money; Tiffani's money, that is. He invested quite heavily in the stock market and always inquired of Tiffani; what she was doing with her spare money. Tiffani had agreed to look into something like that, but usually forgot about it as soon as Ralph left. Maybe, that is why he kept coming back, because he knew she had not contacted his broker, as she said, she would. Ralph had a genuine interest in Tiffani from that point of view. Oh, he also liked her company and those short skirts she usually wore. Tiffani could tell that in his eyes, which strayed upon her shapely thighs as she sat. She also enjoyed his company, as he never said anything out of the way, and Tiffani loved the way she held his attention; she noticed that his eyes always followed her body when she stood and moved to the file cabinet or some other distant place in the area. She often wondered what would happen if she gave him a clue that she might be interested in talking about something other than the stock market. Of course, Tiffani knew, there was no future in dealing with a married man, as good as he looked, and deliberately shied away from any inclination.

Tiffani was also afraid to tell Ralph, she had no spare money; by the time she got through with the rent, the car note, the food, the shopping; there was not a penny left; and by this time, she was generally off into spending the next pay check's wages. Tiffani did not tell Ralph this; not because she was afraid it might open up a different conversation; as she had heard women talk about, high-salaried men helping them out, but because she was ashamed of not having any money to invest. "Ralph seemed understanding enough," thought Tiffani, "why don't I just open up and trust him. After all, he does seem interested in my financial welfare." Victor had never asked her what she was doing with all that money he kept giving her in those large increases. "Probably figured, it was none of his business" she thought, "plus he was always too busy helping all those other women." Tiffani knew if she asked a question the right way, Ralph would probably come to her mind set.

"Ralph, if I had some extra money to invest what would you suggest? I mean, how would I go about knowing the right amount I needed to invest; how would I get the money in other words?"

"Those are a lot of questions Tiffani, but I follow you; first you must get on a budget. Would you like for me to help you prepare a good budget Tiffani?"

"I would like that very much Ralph."

Ralph's face lit up like the phone lights when it rings. It was probably Tiffani's imagination, but his broad smile with that large mouth of his became sensuous, and his eyes widened, gazing far under her short skirt. Tiffani should have felt uneasy, but his sudden burst of enthusiasm sent an electrifying thrill bolting upon her breast and thighs; she could feel Ralph's hot breath on those areas, and doing quite well. Feeling sort of good, Tiffani raised her legs slowly and crossed them, allowing the skirt to fall away from her behind, showcasing her red bikini panties. Ironically, Tiffani and Ralph occupied Victor's lounging area, where Tiffani's seat was the same as Carolyn's when she displayed her nakedness to Victor. Ralph never pretended to be doing anything other than looking at Tiffani's assets on display. She loved this in Ralph because it showed, he was not sneaky, and would ask for her body if he really wanted it.

"When can we get started Tiffani?"

"Oh, I am ready when you are Ralph; will your wife care if I come by your house, or would you prefer we did it here after work?"

Tiffani thought, "the way she was feeling right now, she had to test Ralph's real interest; stocks, bonds, and mutual funds, or mutually bonding body stocks." Tiffani had wanted to add, her place, to the list, but did not want to seem too eager. "If Victor knew," she thought, "I was sitting here in his office, showing Ralph everything I could without pulling my clothes off; he would kill me."

"We could do it here Tiffani, any day you are available." Never removing his eyes from underneath her skirt.

Tiffani thought; "Ralph had certainly passed her test; giving her the only correct answer. She now knew the answer he would have given if she had included "her place" among the others."

"If it is okay with you Ralph, could we wait until Victor is out of town again?"

"Sure thing Tiffani, if you feel comfortable with that! I will prepare you a list of items I will need."

Tiffani slowly uncrossed her beautiful brown legs, looking directly in Ralph's face. She wanted to catch his expression, to make sure she had gotten his message correctly. Tiffani watched Ralph as his large mouth fell open again and saliva actually rolled onto his bottom lip, and his openness again showed.

"You will have to excuse me Tiffani, it appears as if I am drooling; your legs are so gorgeous." Calmly wiping his lip with one swipe of his tongue, before rubbing both lips together.

"It is amazing," Tiffani thought, "how a woman controls a man, with this thing between their legs; I see now why Victor is so screwed up these days; and Ralph is probably not any different; it is a shame those juicy lips of his have to go to waste this evening."

"Thank you Ralph, I love your sincereness; I hope we will be able to get this done soon, I'm getting anxious myself." Standing up, walking into her office and toward the outside hall door. Ralph followed closely as a faithful dog would to his master. They exchanged handshakes and said; "have a good evening." Tiffani felt a tingling under her skirt as she watched intriguingly, the lean tall sturdy figure walking down the hall. She could not believe how horny she had become in the past few minutes. Neither could she believe how Ralph's tongue had removed the wetness from his lips with one smooth swipe. "He must really be something," she thought. Tiffani felt guilty again, but she closed the door, screaming out loud:

"I love this feeling——I love this feeling!"

There was only about thirty minutes left in the day, but Tiffani decided she needed to work on Victor's special project for awhile. She also decided she would have a few cups of coffee, because it appeared, she was going to be up awhile tonight. At least, this way, she would have an excuse, for lying awake. Tiffani was right, because she did tumble for awhile; she wondered if she would be as sincere as Ralph, and tell him, "it was after three in the morning, before she went to sleep; and he was the primary reason." Tiffani wondered if she could be that sincere and tell Ralph, "she loved the way he made love to her last night;" it was indeed a long pleasurable night.

Tiffani wanted to call and tell Victor, she was tired, and was taking the day off, but the thought of Ralph coming by forced her out of bed; she still was not quite sure, it was really Ralph, who was having such an effect upon her.

Anyway it was bright and early and Victor was energized and raring to go, obviously rejuvenated from a day of rest. However, Tiffani could not seem to get it going; she was already on her fifth cup of coffee, and still sluggish as ever. Victor was busy at work, so he never noticed all her returned trips to the coffee pots. Tiffani knew better than to be downing all this coffee, because she was very much aware of its effect; once she got started going to the restroom, there would be no letting up. She had far exceeded the two cup limit and was still putting it away. "It would not be so bad" Tiffani thought, "if she could just stop yawning."

Lucky for Tiffani, she had finished the bulk of Victor's special project; he did not need it until the next Monday, but she knew he always wanted things as of yesterday. And of course, that is how she got extraordinary pay increases; being much better than efficient; always finishing any project or report as soon as possible, regardless of his stated future date. Yes, she was lucky, because her bladder was now full and the wee-wee trips were starting.

Travel time to the restroom was short, as Tiffani shared Victor's large exclusive bathroom, equipped with separate tub and shower. He had been kind enough to have her own private door cut through from her office. Tiffani had expressed her appreciation to Victor by giving the bathroom a feminine touch, at which he gladly approved. Not many bosses, she told him at the time, would be so generous; and her point was substantiated by this being the only coed bathroom in the building. Tiffani verbally thanked Victor excessively, further telling him; how she hated using the restroom with those other women. After four or five trips to the bathroom, she found Victor standing in her office, waiting patiently, but concerned.

"Tiffani, are you okay? I am sorry, but I heard the flushes."

"Oh, its this coffee Victor; you know I cannot have more than two cups, before my other cup runs overs."

Victor laughed saying; "how many have you had?"

"I do not know, I lost count after four; let's see, one pot is empty; oh, I do not want to think about it Victor; far more than I should have though."

"Why are you drinking so much coffee today Tiffani?"

"Oh, I did not sleep much last night for some reason Victor, and I was hoping an extra cup would keep me awake; looks like I over-did it. Anyway, I am not having a problem staying alert; this moving in and out of there, (pointing to the bathroom,) is keeping me on my toes."

Victor could not help, laughing at Tiffani, the way she rolled her eyes, while looking toward the bathroom. She was not about to tell him of Ralph's investment interest, in her and their budget sessions; not yet anyway.

"The rate you're going Tiffani, you'll have trouble sleeping again tonight, you better lighten up."

"You are right about that; oh, Victor, while you are not busy, let me apologize to you."

"For what Tiffani?"

"For saying the things I said about Helen; I talked with her yes-terday and she was all excited about Mrs. Garley becoming a productive citizen again. Helen is special, like you said, because I would not have had the patience to deal with that old woman and the way she was acting."

"I accept your apology, Ms. Tiffani Dotson! Didn't I tell you?"

"Pull your chest in Mr. Victor Previtt; I am still reserving my remarks on all the others, for now."

"Some people are sore losers!" Victor, looking at Tiffani, laughing and shaking his head as he retreats to his office.

CHAPTER NINETEEN

CHRISTMAS SPIRIT

"Hello Samantha——It is good to hear from you too——yes, Victor is here, but he is in a meeting right now; I am holding his calls——I will tell him as soon as they break up——How is Stacy——Oh, I see; that is not all bad; look at the money you will be saving——I understand Samantha, I will tell Victor——Good talking to you too Samantha——Bye, Bye."

Tiffani hung the phone up, saying quietly: "Samantha needs to grow up and stop using that grown daughter, Stacy, as a means to use Victor; if she had not gotten me this job, I would have told her a thing or two, just now. Who cares if Stacy is going to get married at the courthouse; Samantha should be glad somebody even wants the little spoiled grown-up child."

It is lucky for Tiffani, the meeting turned out when it did, because she was fuming, getting hotter and hotter at Samantha for her abuse of Victor.

"You had only two calls Victor; your ex called; says to come by after work, and be sure to call her, if you cannot make it. It is important, she says, having something to do with Stacy getting married at the courthouse; says she is truly upset——You get the message Victor——please go by or call." Tiffani was getting more upset just being Samantha's courier.

"Simmer down Tiffani, who else called?"

"Oh, I am sorry Victor, but that ex of yours crawls under my skin; I suppose she will want you to service her, while you just happen to be there."

"Tiffani, you are getting upset for nothing; you said I had another call."

"Sorry Victor, yes, Carolyn called; just told me to tell you she would see you at the Christmas party tomorrow."

"I almost forgot about that party, we get off early; are you going Tiffani?"

"You bet I am Victor, it is really the only time, all the executive secretaries get a chance to rub elbows and compare notes——you know. The talk this year, is sure to be about my bathroom."

"I believe the correct wording is——our bathroom Tiffani!"

"Come now Victor, it does not translate that way, when we are talking girl's talk."

"Yeah Tiffani, well, I felt good at the meeting earlier; the guys were raving about it; and it sure did smell good. Matter of fact, they teased about having the next meeting in the bathroom."

"If you think that is something, wait until tomorrow Victor."

"What do you mean Tiffani?"

"Well, there are a few changes, I am going to make; an extra item or two, here and there. The girls will want to see my bathroom——you know."

"Tiffani, are you spending more money out of your pocket on—— – OUR BATHROOM." Victor laughing. "And you are inviting, "the girls", to see it——I see."

"The money will be well spent in my opinion Victor; they will definitely want to see, my bathroom, when I finish telling them about it."

"I see, I'm never going to win this battle with you Tiffani; I give up. Oh, don't bother about cleaning up my office, I will do it after lunch."

Normally, Tiffani might have left Victor's office dirty, but today was out of the question; she had far too much to do for the bathroom-showing tomorrow. She was going to stay late this evening as it was; doing things in Victor's office, her office, and her bathroom. Tiffani was not only proud of their offices, she was extremely proud of Victor; he was in her opinion, the ultimate boss. Needless to say, Victor's office was cleaned during lunch; Tiffani's tuna sandwich in the refrigerator assured her of that. What more, she had in store for this room was definitely beyond Victor's imagination. Victor had come to realize, when it came to feminizing this work area, he was not Tiffani's boss; she was the boss. Firing her would probably not stop her; no doubt, she would do what she wanted to do and then leave. So Victor had learned to give Tiffani a free rein, generally reimbursing her, if she would accept it, which was only one tenth of one percent of the time.

There was no need for Victor to complain, when he returned from lunch; he knew his office would be already cleaned. Tiffani listened for Victor to call Samantha, but it never happened; so she surmised, he would go running over. Every time she thought of Samantha using Victor, she got mad. Tiffani thought, "if she had a magic wand, Samantha would be the first person she would wave it toward for disappearing; Carolyn next, then Angela maybe." Helen was no longer on her bad list for Victor. Angela was getting somewhat of a break these days, after a second thought by Tiffani. The reasoning had to do with Victor deserving everything he got, for messing around with such a young lady; maybe, she could and should teach him a lesson. Plus, Tiffani thought, "Angela was a little (not much) more considerate than the others; she was almost, always, apologetic when she asked for Victor to come by. At least somebody had taught her some manners," thought Tiffani.

Anyway, quitting time came and Tiffani informed Victor she was staying late to help prepare the place for tomorrow. Shortly thereafter, she also informed the florist what kind of plants and flowers she needed delivered early the next day. Then Tiffani started on her cleaning; the dusting and furniture polishing, for she and Victor's office, before moving on to her bathroom. "It is amazing," she said; "how dirty a bathroom can get with just two people." To be honest, it was not really that dirty; Tiffani just wanted everything spotless and perfect, because she knew her nosey co-hearts would be rubbing their fingers and straining their eyes for something negative to talk about later. You would have thought the party was going to be in their office. Tiffani had wrapped a green floral print scarf around her head, to go with white sneakers, a tight T-shirt and jeans; she was definitely prepared for cleaning. What she was not prepared for was what happened next, while she bent over dusting the bottom of the bookcase in Victor's office.

"Excuse me ma'am, I thought the secretary was working late tonight."

Ralph turned to walk away and Tiffani started laughing, saying; "I guess you have never seen, a real clean-up woman, huh?"

"Why Tiffani, it is you; I had just said to myself; that is the finest clean-up woman I have ever seen; and was about to inquire about an opening." Both laughing real hard.

"Have a seat Ralph and watch a real professional work."

"Excuse me for asking Tiffani, but what's the occasion?"

"Oh, I am cleaning up for the Christmas party tomorrow, you know how some of the girls want to nose around."

"Well, it looks pretty good from where I am looking Tiffani. I was unaware you did cleaning."

"You would be surprised; this is how I got my start; cleaning office buildings and working my way through school. And to think, after four years of college, I am right back where I started; of course the pay is a little better." Tiffani laughs, walking near Ralph to windex the glass table.

"Yeah, but do not forget the real difference Tiffani, because I know where you are coming from."

"What is that Ralph?"

"You are a volunteer at this cleaning job; but changing the subject a bit; I have been sitting here Tiffani, trying to figure out, if you are prettier in jeans or a skirt. Maybe, I will have an answer before I leave."

"By the way Ralph, how did you know I was here?"

"It's my spies Tiffani, they are on the lookout for me. I would say their surveillance is pretty good; what do you think?"

"So you are spying on me, huh Ralph; is there anything I should be careful of?"

"Smile when you say that Tiffani, do not take me so serious."

"Nothing personal Ralph; sometimes my humor is dry." Slowly gathering her cleaning material and heading for her bathroom. "You can follow me in here if you like."

"Is there anything I can help you with Tiffani?"

"I never turn down a good offer Ralph; first, the tub and shower, then the commode and wash basin; take your pick, then we will do the floor together."

"Sounds good to me Tiffani, you make your selection and I will take your leftovers."

"Fair enough, I will take the items, I have no problems reaching, like the commode and tub Ralph."

Ralph starts off, cleaning the large mirrored wall over the wash basin; closely watching Tiffani as she bends and swerve inside the tub and over the commode. Several times he turned to look himself, making sure Tiffani's image on the mirror was not distorted. Still, no decision had been made on the jeans over the skirt, but the more Tiffani bent inside that tub with her behind pointing upward and wiggling; the more Ralph's imagination tried to make the decision for him. Ralph was cleaning the mirror over and over, beyond its already clean surface, and having a tough time constraining his thoughts, when he muttered out before he knew it; "damn, Tiffani has a nice ass!"

"Did you call me Ralph?" Hearing her name, but with the water running, not much else; looking in his direction. "Are you still cleaning that mirror?"

"I want to make sure its spotless, Tiffani, you know how the girls like to nose around." Laughing. "I am real professional when it comes to cleaning bright pretty surfaces."

"Yeah, I have noticed, rubbing in one spot; you are going to rub a hole in that mirror. Were you rubbing anything in particular Ralph?"

"What's that?"

"The mirror, you were rubbing it like you had something else in mind Ralph?"

"I did not think you noticed Tiffani, but I was sort of watching you; thinking how good a shape you must be in, as you bent over into that tub. You sure are limber to be able to bend and move like that; fascinating I might also add."

"Fascinating huh! Thank you Ralph, I consider that a compliment."

Again, Tiffani thought, "Ralph's sincereness is beaming

through." Looking at him as she sat on the edge of the tub, she noticed he had beautiful large brown eyes to match his smooth brown complexion. They were glaring (as they were always) upon her from underneath thick black eyelashes. "Ralph is really handsome," Tiffani thought; "too bad he is already taken, though he does appear to be interested in me somewhat. Why doesn't he just come out and ask me for some and quit torturing me, playing on those words of his. It looks like I could easily have another sleepless night, thinking about this man; and I hate to be the one to make the first giant step."

"What will your wife think, with you coming home so late Ralph?"

"It's not late Tiffani, it is only six o'clock, anyway, I worked late."

"What if it took us another two hours, what then Ralph?"

"Well, I worked later; anyway, we should be through in another thirty minutes, Tiffani."

"My-my-my," Tiffani said to herself.

Ralph was almost right, in twenty five minutes, they were headed downstairs into the parking under the building. Tiffani saw for the first time, how Ralph knew when she was in the office alone; his assigned parking space was only two spots over from she and Victor's. So he is the spy, she thought, saying good-bye to him, dryly. Tiffani went to bed angry, saying out loud; "I hope I do not have to pull a Carolyn on Ralph, sitting before him, without a stitch." She even laughed out loud; curled up and fell soundly asleep.

Across town, Samantha was having far more luck. Victor had eaten the sumptuous meal she had prepared and was now lying upon Samantha, enjoying her customary delicious dessert.

Neither Victor nor Tiffani; however, had any problem with loss of sleep when morning came. When Victor got to the office, the plants and flowers had already arrived. In his office was a large diffenbachia, near the window and a vased bouquet of flowers on the glass table; in Tiffani's office was a large schefflera and a vased bouquet atop one of the file cabinets; and in her bathroom was nothing more than a simple green-white leafed ivy sitting on the counter top near the wash basin, with runners which made it appear as if it had been there a very long time. Tiffani had completely changed her original color decor in her bathroom to a bold masculine burgundy and dark green. This included all the neatly strategic placed small rugs, to the monogrammed his and hers towels. Also in her bathroom was a completely new item; a tall dark brown wooden stand, which held two burgundy–green trimmed flannel monogrammed robes. The initial noted on everything, incidently, was that of Victor's and Tiffani's. It certainly looked as if some thought had gone into this preparation.

The first thing Victor saw as he entered the office was an admiring Tiffani, standing in a corner near the door, looking through his office; she had positioned his large plant where it could be seen shortly after coming in.

"Good morning Tiffani—hey, there's flowers in here." Victor called all plants, flowers. "Where did these come from? Man, it smells good in here—Tiffani, what's going on?"

"Remember, I told you I was going to be doing some things for the Christmas party today Victor."

"Yeah, but I thought you were talking about dusting and that sort of thing Tiffani, I want you to give me the tab on these items, I'll take care of them. This place needed a little sprucing up; my body is beginning to feel a little spirited; where's the party?"

"While you are in such a good mood, I had better show you everything; get yourself a cup of coffee and follow me Victor."

"Okay Tiffani; the flowers in my office——looks good——office needed flowers——whoa——look at those colors——love that purple and green."

"The color is burgundy and green Victor!"

"Hmmm—hmmm—a robe huh——initials huh—the towels are the same —TD and VP—hey Tiffani, those are our initials! That's sort of sexy, don't you think?"

"Sure Victor, the robes are just for today; the girls are coming— you know; they will need something to talk about when they leave."

"Oh, I see—I see—we might leave the robes a little while longer; I have another meeting on tap soon; the guys will love it; they'll be jealous, but they'll love it. Don't forget to give me that tab Tiffani. Girl, you're tough." His wide smile turning into an undertone giggle.

Not a lot of work was done in their office, other than more sprucing up. The office closed at three for the traditional Christmas party. Carolyn's car was in the shop, and she volunteered Victor to take her to get it after the party. This party always gave everyone an opportunity to mingle with the upper echelon of the corporation. As a matter of fact, that was how Victor became a Divisional Vice President. Only champagne and cheese was catered, so everyone had a good time, keeping their wits in the process.

Victor still remembered the first one he attended, twenty one years ago. Not a lot has changed in the rapidly fading years; champagne and cheese is still being served. The brands have probably changed and they no longer have to hold their own bottles; as waiters walk among the crowd constantly refilling each glass, nevertheless, the ritual is pretty much as usual. But on one of those yesteryear days, as some of Victor's co-workers and himself stand, huddled and talking; they are interrupted by the President and Chairman of the Board. Once he finished the customary hello's; he says, Mr. Previtt, what do you think of all the hoopla, the papers are making over women's rights these days?

It must have been a satisfactory answer because Victor is still with the company and he has moved up considerably. After that question though, he became somewhat of a celebrity in his department. The other guys all wanted to know how the President knew his name. Victor admits, it dumfounded him at first; because of less than a year on the payroll, and not ever having met the guy. But then it dawned on Victor, he was the first. He was the first Black employee in the corporate office.

Maybe, the reports he had been getting on Victor were pretty good, and he wanted to check him out for himself. And simply put, that is what champagne and cheese and the Christmas party was and still is all about. Victor's answer to his question, by the way was rather brief; "I honestly feel, they're entitled to their rights Sir". Those were Victor's sincere feelings twenty one years ago, and like the champagne and cheese; not a lot has changed, Victor still feels the same.

Women's rights are often taken for granted by men, especially in the work place. Surely, it is due in large part to their gender alone. However, Carolyn had since come on board and had made her presence felt with the best of the men. She was the only woman in her department, but it was known after a few trials and tribulations; there were no feminine chores—only—in the office. Carolyn as you have probably gathered, expressed herself very well and we might add very clearly. Her position was, "that she was hired to do a job—not a female job."

After about two hours Victor asked Carolyn if she was ready to go get her car.

"Oh, I forgot to tell you Victor, they did not get it ready. Could you take me home?"

"Sure, why not Carolyn."

Victor was feeling pretty good, so that was a good move. The champagne had the ole bod going, and he was in the company of a gorgeous creature, who he knew could really make love. Carolyn was rather somber, so the guess is, the reverse was working on her. They arrived home and he invited himself in; Victor was really in a love making mood tonight. They sat at her kitchen table; he drank some freshly made coffee while Carolyn drank scotch and water; well, that is what it was when the few accompanied pieces of ice melted. She was not talking at all, other than to answer Victor's questions. Carolyn's professional image was showing too much, so Victor invited himself to spend the night. Normally, this puts Carolyn in a love making mood.

"That is fine Victor, I am taking a shower and going to bed, I am tired."

"Now, that's more like it," Victor thought; he was aroused and ecstatic as she returned in a sheer gown and says good night. The glimpse of that fine body has Victor throbbing in a conspicuous place. And he can see himself doing something very naughty. Victor thought, "I'll hit the showers now; I've delayed enough already. It's hard to believe I'm acting like a sex maniac. You would think this was some new stuff," but Carolyn's tall body always made Victor horny, just to see it. "Man, she's really snoring," Victor spoke softly, "I'll lay here awhile and wake her up later."

"Is that sunlight," Victor thought, "I must have slept all night. Where's Carolyn?"

"Good morning sleepyhead, it is ten o'clock, how about some breakfast?"

Victor went to bed horny and as soon as Carolyn appeared in that flimsy gown, it was horny time again. "How can one be so sexy, so early," Victor thought, "I'd rather just have her for breakfast."

"Well, what will it be—breakfast or not Victor?"

"Err–sure Carolyn." Victor thought, "she's nice, but romantic she's not, did I do something wrong?"

"Victor, you just stay there, I am serving you in bed."

"Now you're talking Carolyn."

If there is anything worth waking up to—it is a beautiful woman upon first view. Somehow, the focusing of the eyes takes less time—a real eye opener. This precious sense was serving Victor well. With his sights on Carolyn, only her movements were of any real meaning. And movement was showing through the gown as she heads for the kitchen. The red transparent garment clearly made Victor as wide awake as she was visible. Carolyn's tall frame was circumgyrating with each step. Such motion was building Victor's appetite—his recommended breakfast would be scrambling in bed with meat only.

As Victor eats, Carolyn is sitting on the bed; her gown opens, and those firm pointed breast illuminate the room. They stood out just like Angela's. Victor thought; "I'd love to nibble on those right now instead of this bacon."

"Here, let me get you some more juice, Victor."

When she returns, the gown is completely open. Carolyn thinks nothing about what she is doing because they have been around each other so much. She is teasing Victor without vulgarity and acting if though they have been married for years.

"I see the exercise program is paying off at work Carolyn."

"Yes it is Victor, but I also use my exercise equipment more; and most of all, I watch what I eat. No beef or pork, remember, and lots of rice and poultry."

"What about this bacon Carolyn?"

"Oh, that is turkey Victor. It took me a while to get use to not having red meat and pork, but now after seeing the results, I love it."

"I love the results I see too Carolyn?"

"Thanks Victor."

"Carolyn, I don't know if I can do without those juicy steaks and chitterlings. And what about hamhocks and pigfeet—you have got to be kidding."

"I can tell you indulge pretty heavy. Look at your stomach Victor, plus you are overweight."

"Oh, that's a few beers Carolyn."

"That is another thing Victor, you should not be doing all that drinking."

"Carolyn, you're the health nut—not me. And look who's talking about drinking; what's that you're fixing?"

"It is a Bloody Mary—I understand they are good for hangovers."

"Oh, I see."

"Do you want one Victor?"

"No Carolyn, it's a little too early for me. Aren't you going to eat?"

"No Victor, I am not hungry."

Carolyn did not have to eat; Victor's appetite was big enough for the both of them. Breakfast was one of Victor's favorite meals; lunch and dinner were the other two. He would not characterize himself as a big eater; he like to use the terms–consistent or regular. Between Victor's observations of Carolyn's appetizing body, he consumed his share of the kitchen. But in all fairness, Victor eats more when he is horny. Besides, Carolyn forced him into it with her nourishing-alluring service. Anytime you're served on a silver platter, you have a tendency to lose track of your helpings.

"I am curious Victor, why are you in the exercise program at work, if you are not going to at least try and watch what you eat."

"There's an unwritten rule Carolyn, that the CEO frowns on any management person not involved. You might say I'm doing what I have to do."

"That is nonsense Victor, it is your health and your life."

"I'm enjoying myself Carolyn, believe me."

"You are slowly killing yourself, you mean. Take pride in yourself Victor; no one wants to be under the shade of a blimp all day. You look like a stuffed animal."

Samantha and Angela had told Victor when he was getting too heavy, but not this rude. And there he was in Carolyn's bedroom, nude; being virtually handfed and talked to like a complete idiot. This health nut was making Victor damn mad. He was now doing everything he could to hold his composure. What was her motive for coming down on him like that. Victor thought, "Was she sincere or was it her way of getting out of making love." In that case, it was working because a dish rag had nothing on him now. To be embarrassed is one thing, but to be ridiculed was not Victor's idea of life's simple pleasures.

"Carolyn, what works for you does not work for everyone else."

"I am not saying it does Victor, but it might work for you. Why don't you give yourself a chance."

"If I agree Carolyn, can we drop this subject before you piss me off."

"Sure Victor, but it sounds as if you are already upset."

"I'm sorry Carolyn, the breakfast was real good."

Carolyn in her directness could inflict pain upon your feelings. And that is what Victor had just undergone. He wanted to tell her, she scratched his feelings, but his pride would not allow him to confirm what he felt she was aware of. It's possible she did not deliberately try to hurt Victor, but to let him know as a female, she controlled herself and was in charge. Carolyn is a competitor in her professional arena and that is good; however, sometimes there is a spillover of the rivalry into their merry-making sessions. Victor's mind tells him all is well if he appears well on the surface during her aggressive moments. The adjustment to Carolyn was one of toleration and pretense. Accepting the bitter with the sweet is a more delightful way of stating it.

"Don't you think you're drinking too much of that stuff Carolyn, that's your fourth or fifth glass."

"Victor, I can take care of myself. Hurry and get ready; I have to pick my car up before one o'clock."

Victor thought, "now how in the hell was I to know her car was ready; it's just as well because I've long since ceased to be in a love making mood."

"Sure Carolyn, I'll be ready in a minute."

Victor thought, "Carolyn doesn't seem like herself today. She has always been straight forward, but today, there is an overwhelming abuse in the air. And all those Christmas spirits could dampen those Christmas cheers. I can understand why she didn't say a word about her daughter; however, Christmas spirits will not drown her sorrows away. This will be her first Christmas without Sharonda and it has to be hurting."

The effects of the hurt was apparently surfacing in that whisky bottle.Carolyn it appears was beginning to torment herself. Because that is the only thing which can be found within those ounces. Not to mention the destruction and disaster it can do to one's own body. Tragedies such as Carolyn's could pain for awhile; but alcohol as a remedy is not the road to travel. In time her depths of despair will no longer be raging. The doom and gloom will no longer be as acute. And dreariness and booze will no longer be her main diet. Alcohol will slowly end one's problems forever. One must give oneself a chance without such toxin.

CHAPTER TWENTY

TWO ON THEIR WAY

Free for the weekend with Angela in charge.

"I will tell you later Victor. Meet me at 74 Joplin Place after work."

"What do you think Victor?"

"It's nice Angela, are you buying this hotel?"

"No, just a suite for the weekend. Wait until you see inside. There are only fifty suites, but it is like a grand palace; complete with a restaurant and real French chef. I understand the food is magnificent. We are in Suite Elizabeth–7."

"Sounds lucky enough Angela."

"Here we are. Well, what do you think, Victor?"

"It's fantastic, but I'm still puzzled as to what you're doing."

The small hotel must have been built before the turn of the century--that's the nineteenth—you know. It had the type of architecture found only in European cities. There were curves and designs, which could have only taken place from a person with immeasurable pride. Pride of artistic lines. Starting with climbing the front ten steps into the archaic structure. Each step was shaped like a lucky horseshoe with the smallest one being on the top. A pyramidal escalation from the cobblestone walkway. Each step formed its own character as the reddish colored rocks accented one's ascent to the arched doorway.

"Victor, this is a special day for me, and I wanted a perfect setting for the occasion."

"I assume you're going to tell me in due time, right. But let me guess Angela, you got that promotion."

"Warm Victor, but not quite. You will know in due time; I can assure."

"Due time. Is that like during this lifetime Angela or what?"

"Oh, don't be funny Victor; you will know before the night is over."

"Okay Angela, I'll stop my relentless pursuit of guessing."

"Now—you're being a good boy. Think of yourself as being in captivity for a weekend Victor."

"Is this going to be a sadistic adventure? Am I going to be tied to the bed and all Angela?"

"No, nothing like that Victor; just going to captivate you with my love. A weekend of reassurance of my total appreciation for you. I thought of a thousand oddities and flattering things to do, but the hotel won out. It is all on me, so relax and have fun. After all, Victor, you work hard and you are exceptionally nice to me. My version of "Gather ye rose buds, while ye may", Victor."

"Angela, I don't know what to say. If the food is even close to this room, you have a winner."

"I hear it is superb Victor, which was the key to selecting this small quaint hotel."

"So if I'm disappointed in this retreat, it's whose fault Angela?"

"Mine of course; the room is fine, the food is fine, everything is fine Victor."

"You can say that again. That sexy body of yours is unrivaled for fine lines. From your fine pointed breast to your curvaceous rounded hips. Down to those shapely thighs and legs. Finery revealed at its best Angela."

"Victor, that is not exactly what I meant."

"Yeah, I know, but man cannot survive on food alone. I'm going to love you roughly every night Angela, starting right now."

"Rough, did you say Victor?"

"Well, endlessly is what I had in mind, you know. Like several times during the night Angela, from different perspectives. You'll be tired, but will want more. You'll beg me to caress you, again and again. Your body will be limp, but, continue to explode with short bursts of energy. You'll be sore, but, still have the fire power to give me five full courses of sheer delight. With every course, Angela, you'll go from a pet pussy cat to a tenacious, ferocious tigress. You'll scratch and claw and we'll both be screaming with ecstatic fits. Temperatures will rise and perspiration will flow so; we'll need linen service time and time again."

"That is why I asked for two queen size beds Victor, but I guess I should have ordered adjoining suites on each side of us. Those love making feats you propose sounds good, but I think those are classic examples of delusions of grandeur. I am not sure you could withstand the excitement anyway Victor. Besides, we did not just come here to screw. I want us to be fulfilled, but also learn more about each other; not merely to explore our bodies and have a sexual revolution until the end of time. Let me show you the rest of the hotel Victor, before you capture me. Come on tiger, let's go. And remember, you are the one in captivity."

It appears that Angela had put considerable thought into her special rendezvous. And Victor was the captive to be preyed upon. From the exquisite surroundings he had already become winded. Relaxation was settling upon Victor as they moved about the grandiosity of the antiquated hotel. From the tall Black doorkeeper in his gold-trimmed red suit to the brass doorknobs; everything was standing tall and immaculate. Angela was smiling assuredly because she knew this highfalutin place had met with Victor's approval.

"Besides the restaurant Victor, there is only one other spacious area, and it is out here."

"Whoa, an enclosed flower garden with palm trees. This is breathtaking Angela."

"There is suppose to be over one thousand plant varieties from all around the world. The magnificent thing is the different colors in bloom. I understand it is like this year round Victor."

"This is one huge bouquet; and look, there's some butterflies Angela."

"There is suppose to be about fifty different species of butterflies, but come over here Victor."

"An aquarium! Now that's relaxing——this whole garden is

tranquil——let's sit here Angela. This is a small eighth wonder of the world."

"And it was an accident Victor; this area started out as an indoor swimming pool. I understand the original owners ran out of money and over the decades, the garden slowly evolved. The aquarium was added last year at no cost, by the local University's science department. Now the entire garden is maintained and funded by the University."

"I could sit here for hours; look at those fish Angela."

"We can always come back Victor; the restaurant stop taking orders at nine o'clock."

"You have filled my life with excitement this day Angela. Since you've pleased me, I'll let you order for me."

"I like duck, so I am ordering the roasted duck. I understand everything is good and prepared as ordered; I am ordering the rabbit for you Victor."

"Oh, I don't know about that Angela. I've never tried that before."

"Yes, but you have never been here before either. And anyway Victor, you promised to let me order. If you do not like it, you can have some of my duck. I am sort of curious about that rabbit myself."

"Then why don't you order the rabbit Angela, and I'll give you part of what I order."

"Victor, we did not come here to argue."

"I know Angela; you said it was to learn about each other, and you have just learned one of my non-eating habits."

"You are my prisoner Victor."

"Okay, Angela."

Angela was not about to let Victor forget her charming persuasive powers. And being cooperative for the most part around Angela is never all that difficult. She leaves you with the impression that you are obligated to satisfying her every need. So Victor was just lingering along in his curiosity to see what soul-stirring move was next. After all, she was "paying the cost to be the boss." So the least he could do, to be disruptive, would probably be appreciative. Meanwhile, the suggested rabbit delicacy was uttered from Victor's lips to the waiter.

"Will I be happy or surprised about this secret of yours Angela?"

"I hope so, Victor."

"Well, which one"?

"Which one what Victor?"

"Happy or surprised?"

"Victor, why don't you give up trying to coax unwillingly answers out of me. Let me put it to you like this, you had better be happy."

"Is that a good clue?"

"Maybe Victor."

"Angela, I could get happy over a lot of things."

"That is true, I had not thought of that Victor."

"I will be very pleased to hear this, right, Angela."

"You are getting warmer Victor."

"Angela, you aren't going to tell me, are you?"

"It is nine o'clock now Victor, you will know before twelve."

"That's three hours away Angela!"

"How fascinating Victor, you can count."

"I'll make a deal with you Angela. I promised to spend the weekend with you. If you tell me now; we'll spend the entire week in this lovely oasis at my expense."

"Victor, you are so wonderful."

"Okay, what is it?"

"Victor, I am not telling you; you will just have to wait. This is going to be the loveliest week we have had in some time."

"Angela, that's not the agreement, you didn't tell me anything."

"Yes, but you would not have brought it up if you did not want to remain here."

"Angela, that's not fair."

"As they say, "all is fair in love and war". And this my sweet Victor is love. It is now 9:30; you have no more than two and one-half yours to wait."

"I just remembered Angela, I cannot stay this week anyway, I have to go out of town Monday evening for two days. Could we put this place on our front burner for a return visit. I love everything about the place so far; and can hardly wait to get back to the queen's suite."

"Now Victor, you have me getting all anxious."

They finished eating and retired to the room after another brief walk around the place. As it turned out, Angela enjoyed the rabbit and ate practically all of it. This had been a remarkable evening; it was happiness redefined. Angela had never been this exuberant before. Angela's vitality had a lot to do with being stowed away. There is something about disappearing from the masses of people you know, that dictate coping with the true-self or the real sub-conscious you. Angela apparently wanted two pulses—Victor's and hers. They were probably beating as one because of their closeness—coexist—would be more descriptive. Angela had not let Victor out of her clutch since their arrival. Even during dinner, she was ambitiously rubbing his innermost thigh. It appeared that their true-selves were gradually changing into uninhibited barbarians as the touching persisted.

"If we're going to spend the weekend, we'll need some extra clothes Angela. Maybe tomorrow, we can go to the mall."

"I do not think that will be necessary Victor; we are leaving Sunday. And tomorrow, I am not letting you out of my sight—in the suite. We will not need any clothes."

"Angela, I'm not going to be parading around in the nude, an entire day."

"Well Victor, they have robes in here, you can put one of those on. Now that we are in this suite, you are not leaving; there is nothing arduous about not having garments upon one's skin."

Angela had ushered Victor into her guard house and was insistent that no clothes would be tolerated. She was also adamant about them not leaving the suite.

Angela ordered breakfast as soon as they finished making love. And that was on top of making love all during the night. They had not made love this much since grandma went out of town. After eating, Angela had to have her favorite massages. So Victor dutifully obliged, what is never easy to do without getting horny. Angela can always predict that much. Now they are making love all over again. Then you guessed it; Angela is ordering lunch. Victor was hoping for some stillness, but Angela's impending love train is about to be in motion again.

Angela has this bright idea, they should feed each other, since

Victor was her prisoner. She insisted he feed her first. That was pretty standard, and pretty much resemble the giving of food to any delightful infant. Victor really enjoyed waiting on Angela. Now it was his turn to eat. Instead of what he thought to be conspicuously routine, turned out to be erotic. Angela started by taking the cherry from the lemonade. In order to get it, he had to kiss her, removing it from her luscious lips. Now the imaginable becomes real—that coconut cream pie could really get sadistic; but a ham and cheese sandwich has to be consuetude.

"Angela, are you thinking what I perceive you to be thinking?"

"You are my prisoner, Victor."

She lavishly crown each breast with the pie's cream filling. Then she commence to break the ham and cheese apart. Now Angela placed pieces of cheese on one side of her stomach, and ham on the other side; all the way down to the middle of her thighs. This is very uncharacteristic of Angela, but Victor's admiring her for it.

"Okay, what about the bread Angela?"

She smiles and placed the bread in the center of her stomach, inch by inch until she is completely out of space. Angela is now laughing mischievously as she lays back on her pillow.

"Will you please start with the dessert, oh captive one."

Angela does not know it, but the last laugh will be on her. This could be at least a one hour sumptuous meal. Victor's appetite for her is sizzling. Angela is sprawled on the bed, where her body is perfectly positioned for a digestible feast. Victor thought; "I'll be slow and deliberate; as I devour my fill or filling of dessert." Angela begins to squirm as Victor cup each breast in his palms and politely roll his tongue over each nipple. "This works out pretty good," thought Victor, "because the filling is sweet, and Angela is really beginning to enjoy herself."

"Do not forget the ham and cheese, and please eat all of the bread, my captive one."

"Oh, don't worry Angela".

Angela is having the time of her life as she encourages victor to move on. Instead of skipping to the ham, cheese and bread as Angela had intended; Victor decided to teach her a lesson and give her a tongue bath. He slithered between each piece of ham

and cheese before grasping it. Angela's disposition started changing, causing a performance of loud breathing and whispering
sounds.Oh yes, sweet Angela is no longer vocalizing any more
orders.

Victor is taking his own time as he slowly search for other hidden treasures. After about twenty minutes, he is halfway of her
stomach. Angela is squirming vigorously, with her hands pushing
on his head. But he wanted to tease Angela ever so much for playing this captive game. So he goes back for some more dessert. Her
nipples are hard and red as a beet. "The good thing about this,"
Victor thought, "it's not hard to torture Angela, because she is ever
so beautiful." The imperfections on her body goes unnoticed.

Victor laughed to himself as Angela has thrown her legs around
him and grabbed the head of the bed in her eagerness for something to happen. Pushing her legs out of the way, Victor goes back
to the stomach to finish his ham and cheese, oh yes, and bread. Of
course, by now, most of it has fallen off, but Angela does not know
it. And no doubt, at this point could probably care less. Her
expectations of captivity has slowly drifted away. These tongue
baths take time, and it appears that Angela does not have time on
her side. She is now screaming for Victor to do something.

Victor pretends like he does not hear her and proceeds with his
exploring. Angela is now having fits. She is bucking furiously, but
Victor latch his hands around her buttocks and holds on. It's like
that rabbit has come alive. He continues his slow and deliberate
pace as Angela is still screaming for him to do something. She
grabs Victor's head pulling him forward, but he is not far enough.
Then she pushes him downward as he continues to bathe her gorgeous body. Finally, Angela can take no more and climax. Victor
must admit he is pretty horny by this time, but he had fun being
Angela's prisoner.

When Angela caught her breath, they made love again; out of
captivity. Nobody ordered dinner. Angela was completely
exhausted and was snoring like a wild captive tigress. And Victor,
well, he had his fill of ham, cheese and bread for the weekend.
They were both saturated with an overdose of love. Angela was
right after all; they did not need any clothes. Victor must learn to
listen more. Oh,——somewhere——on Saturday, Angela told Victor

they were having a baby.

This weekend was comparable to the cruise, Helen and Victor took; but was far more imaginative. Never in Victor's wildest dreams of Angela, would he have had such a fantasy. Angela had provided the excitement and adventure of a long vacation, without leaving the city limits. A most enjoyable, satisfying, and relaxing weekend. There was no friction, no emotional breakdowns, no surprise depressions, and no moments of despair.

Victor thought: "I experienced a weekend of happiness and a renewed faith in mankind—I mean womankind. One, sometimes wonders, if life can be smooth and carefree, in such a hectic breakneck world. But, when I'm with Angela, it's like she dreams all the troubles away."

Angela started the weekend with two highly-polished ingredients——diplomacy and cooperation; and ended it with the same two, plus fulfillment. She has the maturity of a grandma; and that is probably where it is coming from. She could have informed Victor of her status—the new arrival—over the phone or sitting in the living room, but not Angela; she chose the enchantment of a quaint hide-a-way; the solitude and quietness of an Elizabethan suite; the warmth and coziness of a French restaurant—all packaged into a pulsating, glamourous weekend——in one place.

Angela indeed had made a powerful statement. One with today's actions and tomorrow's vision; one presently achieved with future implications. Yes, Angela had just buried a time capsule. "The lady's actions not only impact the body," thought Victor, "but also the thought process—like——hmmm—what if! What if we're together every day for a lifetime."

Tiffani could tell, Victor had had a hell of a weekend or something awfully good that morning. She was correct on both counts, for Angela had prepared him a large breakfast in the mansion to give him a good two day send off. Anytime, Victor comes down the hall whistling, he was happy. Always.

"Good morning Tiffani."

"Good morning Victor, happy huh, what's up?"

"Oh, several things really; have you ever stayed at the Dorchester Hotel; I spent the weekend there."

"Do you mean the quaint looking place down on Joplin,

Victor?"

"Yeah, that's it Tiffani; so you have stayed there."

"No, but, a girlfriend of mine spent her first honeymoon night there last month; she said they would have stayed longer than the one night paid for, but it was booked solid. It was described by her as utopia and as being on a trip, out of town. I hear it is extremely expensive though. Tell me Victor, who was fortunate enough to get those kind of honors?"

"Angela; it was Angela, Tiffani, and she treated me, mind you....utopia is the word I have been searching for all morning."

"Do not look now Victor, but I believe Angela has great future plans for you."

Victor suddenly remembered the second chapter of the weekend story; the baby and all. And not that it was a secret or anything, but he decided not to mention it to Tiffani at this moment; "her comments," he thought, "might taint his today's spirit a bit."

"Yeah, maybe so; you could be right Tiffani; oh, how are the reservations for the trip coming?"

"You are all fixed up Victor; your flight leaves for Atlanta at eight this evening and returns at nine in the evening on Wednesday. Why did you want such late flights?"

"Oh, just milking the clock, I guess Tiffani; I really wish I could spend the entire week and weekend there, but the work load here is too heavy right now. Seeing a friend or two should be no problem though."

"Victor, I suppose there is nothing like going to your old home-town, huh?"

"Nothing like it Tiffani, except, this trip I will be somewhat limited, because of the brevity of my stay."

"You can always stay longer Victor; sometimes work is not as important as you think it is. Seems like, you could use the rest after that lovely weekend."

"So true——so very true Tiffani."

Victor was all smiles and Tiffani also was unusually happy. It was as if she was happy to see Victor leaving, which is only the partial truth. The other part had to do with Ralph, coming by this evening to get her budget in order. Victor was leaving an hour earlier to prepare for his flight; so Tiffani was excited. The budget was important, but Tiffani was excited about getting even with Ralph for torturing her; leading her on and deserting her. She felt he needed to be taught a lesson, and she was planning on doing so; starting today and going through the next two days. Tiffani, still could not believe the crazy thoughts in her mind; however, "its his fault," she says, "for making my temperature rise."

Tiffani knew Carolyn's tactic got Victor's attention; so she brought an extremely short skirt for that purpose. There was not very much material to the red garment, as it was folded neatly inside her handbag. She would change into it, the minute Victor left, and ready herself for Ralph arriving an hour later. Tiffani sensed, red did something to Ralph's demeanor, and had worn another pair of those bright red bikini panties; she noticed how Ralph had enjoyed them before. Victor finally got out of the office, thirty minutes before closing, which presented no problem; Tiffani still had ample time to freshen herself up in the bathroom. She pulled off her mid-thigh blue skirt and bikini panties, cramming the skirt in her handbag. Tiffani felt guilty as she slid the tight short red skirt over her round behind, for that is practically all it covered. Only a few hours ago, the red skirt had been the same length as the blue one in her handbag; that was before Tiffani kept cutting on it, for the right longness, until there was nothing to cut; so it was hemmed, with no place to restore its four inch split. "Victor," she thought, "would die, if he saw her in this skimpy outfit; twice the span of her hand."

The skirt had an affect upon Ralph with his first glance through the door, which Tiffani locked, leading him again to Victor's lounging area. Perspiration immediately surfaced on Ralph's forehead.

"Tiffani, could I have a glass of water with ice, before we get started?"

His eyes followed her to Victor's small thirty inch high refrigerator. An enthusiastic response filled his body when Tiffani reached, tipping, to get the glass on the overhead shelf, but Ralph went into hysterics when she bent to get the ice. The papers removed from his jacket's pocket fell to the floor; his eyes went goo-goo. Tiffani's entire nude behind was exposed, along with her soft furry furrow, and she could feel his eyes glued to her; which is one reason she lingered in that position, inquiring.

"Ralph, do you just want water or would a Pepsi work better?"

"For now—just water—Tiffani—but maybe—later—."

Tiffani began to feel good, when she heard his voice breaking up; "the torture was going to be reversed today," she thought, "if I have to squat my furry furrow in his face." Turning her behind a bit, which he had enjoyed, while she washed the tub, gave Tiffani even more satisfaction. Sweet little Tiffani; who would ever believe this? The glass table between them, again, saw reflections of a truly fine soft furry object as Tiffani sat before Ralph; there was absolutely nothing to cover this digestible object with, but her hands, and unfortunate for Ralph, one of Tiffani's hands was on her knee, and the other rested, gratifyingly on the chair's arm. Tiffani saw no need to cross her legs as before, for fear of hiding what Ralph's eyes were glued upon, and what she admired, seeing him watch.

"Can I get you something else Ralph before I get too comfortable?"

"No, I am fine Tiffani." Ralph leans down picking up his papers, but still observing her exposed softness; returning them next to a red piece of cloth on the glass table.

"So you think I can make some money, investing, huh Ralph?"

"You certainly can Tiffani; take a good look at this statement!"

"There must be a mistake Ralph; this statement has my name on it, and ten thousand dollars worth of stock in it."

While Tiffani, in her amazement, was looking at the finer points of the statement, Ralph had turned his affection to the red bikini panties; holding them in his hand. He remembered them from the last time and had wondered how they felt and—well, by that time had raised them slyly before his face, inhaling a large breath. A brightness came into his eyes as he seemingly inhaled twice more without letting go of a single breath.

"There is no mistake Tiffani; good investments pay off."

"But I have not invested anything Ralph!"

"Sure you have; your time and interest; oh my," looking at his watch. "I must go Tiffani, see you tomorrow."

Ralph does not realize the red panties are still in his hands, until he reaches the locked door.

"I want these Tiffani; can I have these?"

"What!—yes—why not—Ralph."

The puzzled Tiffani is again left holding the bag, well——in this case, her ten thousand dollar statement. She says out loud, "Ain't that the darndest thing you ever want to see; I delivered my furry furrow to that man on a silver platter and he turned me down cold. To hell with tomorrow, I am out of ideas; that joker must be –oh well, he did say he would see me tomorrow. Maybe, I will think of something else sexy before morning."

Well, morning came, day came, and Tuesday evening came. Tiffani had thought all day, and an idea finally hit her. "It was obvious," she thought, "Ralph like to see me exposed; and for ten thousand big ones, he deserves the finest exposure I can give him." Who would ever believe Ralph and Tiffani?

When Tiffani met Ralph at the door and locked it behind him; the smile upon his face told the whole story; he was pleased to see Tiffani in the bath robe. Neither of them said a word as she led him into her bathroom, where she pulled off the robe and immediately got into the glass-door shower. Ralph watched intently as Tiffani exposed every inch of her gorgeous body. Tiffani thought, "I wish I could think of something sadistic to do in this shower, but Lord knows, if I tried anything cute, I would probably slip and bust my butt." So Tiffani showered as she would normally, while Ralph alertly looked on. Somewhere during this routine; however, Ralph left, for Tiffani looked through the glass, and he was no longer standing there.

Casually finishing up and dressing, Tiffani thought; "what is going through this man's mind." Then she thought of Helen and Carolyn and how Victor had gotten so excited being seduced by them as they revealed, for the most part, far less. Tiffani even thought how she had, silently, called the two, "little whores", for their antics upon Victor. "It was a shame," she had told herself, "for a woman to use vital parts of her body to entice men; and here she was doing far more than they ever thought of doing." And the whole point is, Tiffani does not even know why she is doing it; so she wanted a little revenge for him torturing her; not taking the sex, she had freely offered him. Tiffani thought, "if Victor ever finds out about this, he will surely kill me;" then she thought again; "knowing Victor, he would probably laugh, which would be even worse."

All dressed, Tiffani only had to clean the glass table, and she would be homeward bound. At first, the statement on the table looked like the one yesterday, until closer observation. Tiffani screamed real loud when she saw it; another five thousand dollars had been added; she was beaming because she had never had that much money at one time. A note on the back of the statement said; "thanks for being so kind and uninquisitive, see you tomorrow." Believe me, Tiffani got the message in a hurry. "Keep it up, don't ask questions." Tiffani knew she was doing something right and looked forward to tomorrow.

On Tiffani's drive home, she tried to feel guilty, but was unable to, because her faithful companion was happy and appreciative. "Sure the money was a large sum, but obviously Ralph could afford it," she thought; "otherwise, why would he give it to her; better her than some pick-up with no corresponding appreciation." "One day and hopefully soon, Ralph would tell her what this was all about;" Tiffani smiled, saying to herself; "until that day arrives, I will definitely keep on undressing and satisfying my man."

Tiffani would sleep fairly well tonight, she thought; "I no longer feel revengeful and the tingling of having sex is almost gone." She now looked at her new status as that of a performer. Ever since Tiffani was knee high to a duck, she wanted to be an entertainer of some kind, and make lots of people happy. Okay, so the big break was late in coming, and so what, if she was only entertaining one person; he was happy, and she was happy that he was happy. Plus, Tiffani thought, "I am enjoying stripping before a man; that's it, for tomorrow I will put a real strip tease show together for Ralph." Crawling out of bed, Tiffani looked in all her drawers to see what was available. There was nothing red, but there was a new bright sheer turquoise outfit. There were six pieces in all: a long sheer gown, a behind-length gown, a long and short pair of pants, bikini panties with no crouch, and a narrow excuse for a bra. Lying awake for hours, Tiffani finally figured what she would do; merely put everything on and simply methodically pull it off; thinking and smiling as she looked at the large opening on the bikini's front saying; "Ralph just might want to stick his head in there."

Ralph was right on time as usual, five after five, locking the door himself as he entered the office, smiling again at what he saw upon Tiffani. Tiffani led him to Victor's large leather high backed chair, and she proceeded to climb atop his desk. She merely sat on the desk, swiveling her legs around and standing up; Tiffani had not only practiced this move earlier today, but also how to move gracefully on the desk, while slowly removing a piece at a time. Ralph again looked engrossed as each piece was removed by Tiffani and thrown in his lap; except for the bikini. This was because Ralph stood, looking enrapturedly into the opening, which was precisely an inch or two from his lips; then without batting an eye, he pulled a statement from his pocket and inserted it to cover the large opening. Tiffani felt a tingle as the statement touched her; she wanted to remove it, and tell Ralph to replace it with something else, since his head was mouth level with the opening.

"I have enjoyed these past three days Tiffani; we will work on your budget and investment again, if that meets with your approval."

"Sure Ralph, anytime."

Ralph looked at his watch, it was only five thirty. "I will see you later; thank you so very-very much Tiffani."

Tiffani, looking like a tall gorgeous model, high on that desk, now felt helpless, as she watched her faithful companion walk out the door. She stood on the desk, with her hands on hips, for another five minutes; smiling solemnly, but smiling; as another ten thousand dollars had been added to her statement. In a way, she felt sorry for Ralph; and why; she did not know, because, again, he was happy and appreciative. Tiffani suddenly hollered out loud; "I want to give it up to you Ralph; I want to give it all up to you." Then she started crying.

Victor returned on Wednesday night excited about seeing old friends and also pretty excited about being a new papa; until he talked with Helen on late Wednesday night. The conversation surfaced on his late night there and went accordingly.

"Victor, I have some news for you; I am pregnant."

"Are you sure Helen?

"That is what my doctor said Victor."

Aren't you on the pill Helen?"

"Yes, but I forgot to pack them on our cruise. I started to tell you Victor, but you were having such a good time. I did not want to spoil it."

"Well, you just spoiled my day Helen, and the ruination is as inalterable now as it would have been then."

"Well—excuse me—you were the one wanting to screw every night Victor. If you don't want it, I will get an abortion."

"Oh, no you don't. It's just that, Angela is also pregnant; and I'm not ready for two babies Helen."

"Well Victor, that is your problem. What you and Angela do is your business. You are going around here having all this fun; I suggest you learn to keep your penis in your pants. You are screwing every woman in town and got the audacity to get mad at me. Man—you better wake up—and grow up."

"Helen, I'm sorry, it wasn't meant the way it sounded."

"Victor, you hurt my feelings. If you cannot be any more enthusiastic than that, please do not come around here any more."

"I told you I was sorry. What do you want me to do? I assure you Helen, my commitment to you is genuine. Just don't have an abortion; everything will work out fine."

"I want you to hold me Victor."

"Now-now, is that better——I'll even spend the night Helen."

Victor thought: "It's all my fault that I'm in this precarious condition. My best guess is that I've been overstimulated here lately. Now I'll have the unenviable task of dealing with, not one gravida but two. It's not the way one would plan a wholesome life. Angela, now Helen; it appears that they are fulfilling their own agenda. And you could say they're not leaving me out; I'm not only the assistant, but the victim as well. The word most applicable for my unhappiness at the moment would be——SPANKED. It's as if after doing something enjoyable, I've just been spanked for it. Spanked for putting my hand in the cookie jar and eating those desirous desserts."

CHAPTER TWENTY ONE

TATTLETALER

Talking about two heads buzzing, that is precisely what we have in the office this Thursday morning. Tiffani is still excited about her new role as an entertainer and Victor is excited about his new prospective role of being a father—twice. And it is that twice bit which has him reeling the most; Victor is still very much upset after Helen's disclosure last night. He wanted to get some relief by talking to Tiffani about it, but he did not know where to start, or even what to say; and would it be in the form of a statement or a question.

Tiffani, on the other hand was just as bad, wanting to discuss her three unusual evenings of imperturbability and ravishment with Victor; she was still trying to figure out how to approach him on those subjects and her new lucrative investment portfolio. Meanwhile, each sat in their individual offices, pretending to be very busy. In a sense they were somewhat occupied; Victor was drawing little stick-children on his desk cover. There was a bunch of them as they held hands and appeared to be dancing round and round some stick-trees and huge rocks; at least, a first glance made them out to be rocks, but probably they could have been small ponds. Overhead, a cluster of clouds were assembled, some, much higher than others; and all apparently, happy clouds at the moment, for no dark shades or raindrops had been drawn. It was difficult to tell by Victor's bland expression, whether or not a downpour would occur.

Tiffani had drawn a large circle on her desk pad, entering a dollar sign and the number, twenty five thousand; obviously signifying her new investment portfolio holdings, but within the circle was a conspicuous question mark. Tiffani thought of Carolyn and felt guilty for criticizing her in exposing her feminine assets to take advantage of Victor; she knew now, she must apologize to Victor; and she printed APOLOGIZE upon her desk pad and circled it. "Victor was due an apology," she thought, "because if he had seen her on his desk or in her bathroom shower; he would have demanded one." Tiffani smiled as she thought of how much she enjoyed stripteasing on the desk, while Ralph looked on; suddenly feeling a tingle, thinking how he could look into her furry furrow and not touch it. Tiffani thought, "maybe Ralph needed a little more encouragement" saying silently; "next time I will pull his head into me; I deserve it." The warmer Tiffani's body became, the faster she wrote, "love me, love me"; barely able to contain herself, and wishing for his presence until she felt miserably hot. If Victor had not been in his office, Tiffani would have screamed again and probably hit the showers again; this time for a cold one. She felt the extreme passion within and wrote it down; it spelled TORTURE. Ralph's lackadaisical attitude was definitely causing torture. "I must discuss this man with Victor," Tiffani said aloud and headed for his office.

"Victor, I need to talk with you for a moment; would you like a fresh cup of coffee.?"

"Now, isn't that funny, I was just thinking about how I needed to talk with you Tiffani."

Tiffani returned with the two cups of coffee and casually settling down in that famous chair in the lounging area; Victor remained seated at his desk.

"First Victor, I would like to apologize for all the raunchy things I said to you about Carolyn."

"Thank you Tiffani, that is one of your finer traits, apologizing when you find out you're wrong. What brought it on though; if you don't mind."

"Well Victor, I have been thinking about what she did to you, exposing herself and all to take advantage of your weakness. It was not right of me to come down on her, because when a woman does that, she generally has a very valid reason. Certainly, sex is part of it, and that is what made me so mad, but there is usually another deeper reason or ulterior motive, for clarification."

"You are absolutely correct Tiffani, and without discussing it, Carolyn did or does have a few problems. I probably thanked you earlier, but I want to really thank you Tiffani for being so concerned about me; it really means a lot to me. Maybe, I should have listened to you, because Helen is now pregnant."

"Oh my!"

"That was sort of my reaction Tiffani, when I found out last night; well, a milder version perhaps."

"So you were not expecting this pregnancy, huh?"

"Oh God no; on top of Angela's, are you kidding Tiffani?"

"Angela! You mean Angela is pregnant too Victor?"

"Yes, didn't you know Tiffani?"

"Oh sure Victor, the great mind reader that I am, I have been knowing that. How in the world am I going to know, if you or someone else does not tell me."

"I'm sorry Tiffani, I thought I told you; it happened, I mean Angela told me just before my trip to Atlanta, but that one was planned and expected. I was sure I told you; maybe I didn't; anyway, now I have two on the way."

"Bet you your last dime Victor, Helen's pregnancy happened on the cruise."

"That is what she said, how did you know Tiffani?"

"A girlfriend and her husband went on one Victor, she told me, when they were not eating, they were screwing." Laughing.

"We did a little bit more than that, but we did our share of love-making, or making babies, so it seems. Maybe it is a bit funny Tiffani."

"Look on the bright side Victor."

"What's that Tiffani?"

"Thank God, you can afford two coming at the same time. Huh, that is really something Victor. Do they both know of the other?"

"Well, not exactly, that is sort of why I need to talk, I guess

Tiffani; so I can get a feel for the situation."

"What do you mean Victor, "not exactly"; either they know or they do not know!"

"Helen knows about Angela, but Angela does not know about Helen; matter of fact, Angela does not even know I am dating another woman Tiffani, well, besides my wife."

"Victor, you mean sweet little Angela agrees with you screwing Samantha—your ex."

"Well, you see Tiffani, I sort of neglected to tell Angela, I was divorced; and then, things sort of just happened."

"You what? You mean, all this time, that sweet girl thinks you are married! So that is why she always sounds so apologetic when she calls. I hate to say this Victor, but you are one dirty dog; and all the time I thought those women were using you; man, you are just being greedy. And you know what, you deserve everything you are getting; I hope you have five babies each, and that includes Carolyn, for treating that poor Angela like this. If there is one person that loves you, it is Angela; you treat your love ones so bad Victor!"

"I'm glad you're giving it to me Tiffani, because its preparing me for when Angela finds out."

"You do mean, when you tell her and admit your stupid mistake, don't you Victor?"

"Now Tiffani, like I said, all these things sort of just happened, so I'm going to more or less play it by ear."

"If I was Angela, I would more or more, play it by your head; that would be a brick too; that poor little Angela. Man, you ought to be ashamed of yourself Victor. Don't you feel anything?"

"Well, yeah, but you know, things happen so fast nowadays!"

Tiffani suddenly thought, and felt the warm bottom of her chair, looking down to see herself in a short tight red skirt, showing Ralph her beautiful furry furrow. She saw Ralph sitting at the desk admiring everything she was deliberately exposing to him. Then, she saw herself in the shower, showing Ralph her nude body as he looked on intensely. And lastly, Tiffani saw Ralph approach her as she stripteased atop a desk down to her crouchless bikini, where she made him gently kiss her furry furrow; even making Ralph lay her backward on the desk when it seemed like he was inadequately serving themselves. Then she felt Ralph launch a delicate warm object into her furry furrow as she pulled his head in closer and closer; gripping it tighter and tighter, until both of them were happy.

"Okay, I forgive you Victor; things do sometimes happen fast, don't they? Do not worry Victor; I have a feeling things will work out for you."

"You are good to talk to Tiffani; you have eased some of my burdens; the music will be a little easier to face now. What else was it, that you had to tell me; I remember you saying, first."

"Without giving you any details Victor; what would you do if someone paid you, far more than the services you felt you rendered?"

"Did it happen more than once Tiffani?"

"Yes, three times Victor?"

"In that case, my opinion of course, and that is what you asked for; I would graciously accept the additional money, because it seems to me that this party is giving you what it's worth to them or trying to tell you, your services are invaluable. And in either case, if you even attempted to refund the difference, the party would feel ridiculed Tiffani."

"I wish I could tell you more Victor, but this is very confidential; and by the way, it is not illegal."

"Oh, I never thought that Tiffani, because anything of that sort would have been divulged by you quickly, I'm sure. I trust you!"

"To give you a little more relief Tiffani, men sometimes do that, but believe me, they always feel what they are getting or hope to get is worth every penny."

"How did you know it was a man Victor?"

"A simple guess Tiffani; women don't give women more–not money."

"One more question Victor; would you perform the services again?"

"Without knowing the specifics, that's a tough one to call Tiffani; you will have to give me more. Without that, my answer would simply be; if I enjoyed the work, I would continue."

"Thanks Victor, you have been quite helpful."

Well, let's hope things work out for Victor, because while he was playing things by ear; his daughter Stacy was playing things by running off at the mouth.

TATTLETALER
(Mine your own mind)

Think about the gossip
Let it slide with time
Keep it to yourself
And mine your own mind

What do you think
If you're not thinking at all
Can you control the thought
No matter how big or small

Just hear and not talk
Of everything you see
Or tell it on yourself
Don't tattletale on me

Don't mind boggle your brain
Thinking what they know
Elevate or eliminate the thought
And let the rumors go

Don't tell the thought
Waste not your precious time
Stay outta mind business
And mine-and-mine-and mine

Why not mind your thought
Then you cannot fail
Think about not thinking
And never tattletale

It's a thought to think
Bite the tongue each time
Think of your fellowman
And mine your own mind

Well it was pretty obvious that Stacy had never heard of, "Mine Your Own Mind." Here she was bugging Angela again.

"Hello Angela, I want you to know I'm holding you responsible for my parents divorce. You just couldn't leave well enough alone. You had to have everything."

"Stacy, what are you talking about?"

"Don't play me for a fool, you slut, you know damn well what I'm talking about."

"I swear Stacy, I did not know. When did this happen?"

"In March of last year. You know, your pretentious naiveness stinks Angela."

"No Stacy, I really did not know."

"Aren't you still dating him?"

"Well Stacy, yes, the last I heard——I was."

"Well honey, you're doing a piss-poor job of taking care of your man, because now he's running wild."

"What are you talking about Stacy?"

"You know how men react when they get divorced and women start chasing them. He's my dad, but somehow, men are all like my ex; they want to get it all. It's incredible, first they began thinking they're God's gift to the world and then they believe they're superstuds. Sounds like you're just one of the bunch now honey. That's exactly what your ass deserves, trying to steal my father. I just hope you can take what you've been dishing out."

"Stacy, I never meant to steal Victor from you; you know that."

"I don't know anything of the sort; you and all your sneaking around. But I do know you're in for a time of it now; because one of his girlfriends is also pregnant. I'm happy about that cause I always wanted a little sister or brother. My parents always put so much pressure on me to succeed. "To be somebody," they always said. If I'd had a sister or brother, maybe that wouldn't have happened; or at least there would have been someone to share it with."

"Stacy I understand what you are saying, but there is nothing wrong with wanting your child to be a bright spot in society. Of course, first we must prepare ourselves by getting the best education possible."

"Angela, you're beginning to sound like my mother; which you're not. At least, not yet anyway. I think you have your work cut out for you in that department. But since you know everything about getting ahead in society; you should have no difficulty beating the competition. We'll see how you fare in a competitive situation where you're on your own Angela. See if your grandma can buy you out of this one. You'll go running to her like always, I'm sure. Maybe she will buy the other ladies off, or; maybe you'll find everything and everybody won't respond to your treacherous wealth. It looks to me like it's pay-back time, honey; and I'd say Angela, you're entitled to any misery coming your way."

"Well Stacy, just how many women are you talking about?"

"There's at least two that I know of besides you Angela."

Angela, said "thanks" and slowly, dejectedly hangs up. Angela was stunned. It's like Stacy had hit her with a brick.

Angela talks aloud saying; "Why that Victor, he has been holding out on me. Here it is September, that is damn near eighteen months. He is up to something. This kind of news perturbs the shit out of me. But at least I have accomplished one thing; I am no longer a bitch, a whore, a slut, and the other foulmouthed words to Stacy. She finally started calling me Angela. That makes me feel good, although she is still angry with me."

While Angela wanted Stacy out of her affairs, she did appreciate the good gossip coming her way. Though the news was quite disturbing at first; Angela was interested in the affairs of Victor. It appears that his daughter, Stacy was going to be a valuable resource. She apparently was very knowledgeable of what was going on in his life. At least she knows more than Angela. Angela was willing to share Victor as a mistress, but this presents a different situation and calls for different strategy.

Angela thought: "I do know one thing, I am not going to give in to those women. They are out here like damn vultures. At one time, I was one of them; now they are shooting at me. I shared him once but I am not sure I want to share him again. I could give

Victor an ultimatum, but in most cases, they do not work to your advantage. Or I could just bow out of this scenario. Victor is having some sort of love fest. A pregnant woman competing with another pregnant woman; plus another broad. I want to believe it is a big lie, but Stacy sounded for-real."

Angela kept thinking saying to herself: "I wonder if I was putting too much pressure on Victor. Demanding a baby could have set him off. Because as I recall, he reluctantly consented. I should have known better than to date a married man in the first place. Stacy was initially trying to break me and her father up, but I will never give her the satisfaction. It does appear now, that things are a bit out of control on Victor's part. We will just see what transpires. Grandmother always said that "some decisions, though bad at the time, turn out to be good later on." I started out a mistress, and now; I do not know what I am, but I am certainly no worse off."

It had been a while since Angela had this many thoughts concerning Victor: "Victor must be having a tough time. I would hate to try and satisfy, one woman. Most of us are too fickle. I will not be divisive; I'll just play things by ear. Of course, I am not going to make it any easier for Victor. Every spare moment I get, he is going to love me. I am going to be loyal to him and screw him into misery. His abundant delicacies of flesh will cause his body irreparable damage. I will be more accessible but he will still have his undisturbed spaces. Call it my revenge, if you will. I will not let on about the other women. If he loves me and want me to know, he will eventually tell me. But I must know why he did not tell me of his divorce. There must be a plausible explanation."

Angela, after contemplating the inevitable and charting her future course of actions; quietly went back to her readings. She had been biding her time between novels by William Wells Brown and Harriet E. Wilson; supposedly the first ones written by a Black male and female, respectively. Angela was all too consumed in their ability to tell a story; and found that wealth of knowledge simmering within their brains, had made its way to pages for the world to laud. Of equal importance were works by Frances Ellen Harper, James Howard and Charles Waddell Chesnutt. These nineteenth century Black writers all had one thing in common—a desire and talent to uplift their race. Angela had found new heroes and heroines to seek a reading refuge. With each drink of her heritage, she became proud of her ancestors; and prouder still that she was one of them.

Their works had become dynamism to Angela. She had not only read the authors works, but was beginning to study each one's background. Her interest was growing deeper and deeper into those who had tried to make a difference. The libraries and bookstores were Angela's constant companions She scoured everyone of them she could find. And it soon became evident; when you look for something hard enough, you'll find it. Angela had located voluminous sources of Black literature; most of which, she never knew existed. Ann Petry and "The Street" was one of them; Arna Bontemps and "Chariot In the Sky" was another; as was Emma Kelly-Hawkins and "Four Girls at Cottage City." She couldn't help but think of a deliberate effort on our educational system, from elementary through college to suppress these great writers.

It is little wonder, Angela had time for anything else, except her new-found literary fortune. But she was still very much focused on Victor and the reading of his lines. And thanks to Stacy, brother Victor's chapters were unfolding.

CHAPTER TWENTY TWO

AN EXPLANATION

Angela was sitting at her desk at work when it seems, the aftermath of Stacy's call really struck her: Victor is divorced, Victor has another woman pregnant; Victor has yet another woman. Those words were now falling on her like an avalanche of rocks, hitting her one by one; each saying,"Victor is divorced, Victor has another woman pregnant, Victor has yet another woman." Angela's primary thoughts had soothed Victor's actions over with reasonable justifications. Now, she thought, "why am I making excuses and justifying this man's numskull behavior; that is his role; to explain what has happened."

Angela looked about the room and the dark brown paneled walls seem to brighten up and expand outward. This only meant, her battlefield for life had magnified from mere problems in the workplace to a greater plateau; personal conflicts, deep inside her body; pretty soon there would be kicks against the walls of her stomach. Angela up to this point, had been looking forward to a smooth carrying and delivery of this new life, and now it appeared, the falling rocks were beginning to block that smooth road to happiness. She wanted to cry, but remembered a statement spoken by grandmother once; "you can't fight with tears in your eyes". Not shedding any tears in no way eliminated the hurt, because Angela felt, real bad.

Angela needed to hear from Victor; there were things she needed to hear and know. She thought; "I need to hear Victor say, I love you and I need to know if he means it; he must communicate this to me; not at once, but he must start." Angela made her mind up, to be firm with Victor, with a bit of leniency; even to the point of being conciliatory, if that is what it took. Angela had a new determination to fight for Victor; she now knew he was free and was hers to win or lose. There was no way Victor was going to slide through her fingers into the arms of another woman without a fight. Grandmother had told Angela how to sexually keep a man hanging around, but it was now obvious, another woman, apparently had the same grandmother, because both of them were pregnant. Angela realized she had a real fight on her hands and there had to be other punches thrown; if she was to keep her man; conceding, the other woman, whoever she was, to be as smart as she was, and it might just come down to a simple tactic—Angela promised herself, there would be no frustration and bitterness toward Victor or the other women in an endeavor to obtain what was rightfully hers.

Moving over to the window for warmth from the sunshine beaming through, did more than heat the coolness in Angela's feet, absorbed under her desk's breezeway, where air always thrived; the window gave her an inside view of an outside world. It was so interesting, Angela thought; looking at the riverwalk's bustling activity; people and more people, going about their business, and none seemingly aware of her, perched high above them; observing their every move. Many of their manners and actions seemed funny, because they were based in part on, no one seeing them from an upper angle. But the most interesting movement to Angela, came from three birds, chasing what looked to be a grasshopper. Two diligently pursued the insect as the other maneuvered ahead and waited patiently. While the grasshopper appeared to be winning out–maneuvering the two birds in hot pursuit, the third patient bird grabbed the grasshopper in its beak as it came nearby. Angela smiled saying, "now that is one, grandmother never told me about, maneuverability." She knew now, that could possibly be the simple tactic needed to hold onto her man. Angela walked near her desk and stood there, gazing at the telephone, trying to decide whether she felt like tackling this problem today or not; ultimately coming to the conclusion, to start today and forever be persistent. The call was made to Victor's office. Angela simply said to Tiffani: "Hello Tiffani, this is Angela; how are you this morning? Could you please tell Victor to come by when he leaves the office at five."

The little birdie had indeed taught Angela something; be decisive and maneuver. Normally, she quoted no times to Victor, but those days were over. From now on, she would tell Victor what time he was to be there, and what time, he was to leave for the evening, if at all. "Oh, Victor would have his space all right, just like the grasshopper, Angela thought, "I will give him just enough space for him to hop into my waiting grasp; and of course, he will spend the night, tonight." "Tonight," Angela thought, "would not only be one for testing her maneuverability, but one of celebration." Yes, celebration; Angela would celebrate Victor's divorce and her new found freedom; the freedom she needed to pursue Victor to the bitter end, at all cost. Certainly not at the cost of buying him as Stacy had mentioned earlier, but to the point of being firm, nice, and having lots of patience. Angela wondered what Victor would say, if he knew his daughter, was inadvertently keeping her informed of his gallantry. She smiled as she thought of other ways to clip the grasshopper's wings.

It was evident later on, that Victor had received the message from his efficient secretary, Tiffani, because shortly after five he was ringing the door bell of the mansion. It would take a while for the door to be answered, as grandma was gone for the week, and Angela was busy, testing her patience, by lying on the sofa, listening at the pleasant sounding chimes. She reasoned to herself, it was fine to make Victor wait; after all, it appeared, he had the perfect wait attitude: Waiting to tell her of his divorce; waiting to tell her of the other pregnant woman; waiting to tell her of yet another woman. "Maybe, I will make him wait as long as I have waited or maybe, I should not answer the door at all," thought Angela. Angela tried to keep from fuming, but she could not help herself, thinking the cruelest thought of Victor all day; "he is playing me for a fool and should be punished." Victor on second thought, "did not deserve any nice and patient treatment; to hell with that, kill him with kindness stuff; let him stand there, let him be anxious about me."

Angela felt like crying again and she began to feel the hurt again; so she laid back on the sofa and closed her eyes, for fear of seeing a teardrop fall. The bell continued to chime; Angela knew Victor was not going to leave as he probably assumed she was in a remote part of the large mansion, so she could take her time and relax. Now, as relaxation crept into her tension filled body, Angela could see, she and Victor playing with four tiny children, two boys and two girls. They all were so happy; everyone was laughing; it appeared that each one of them was enjoying musical chimes. A smile came to Angela's face and suddenly she realized that Victor was still ringing the bell. Quickly, she ran to the door, still carrying that lovely smile, she looked so radiant and beautiful. So gorgeous and charming indeed, that Victor even forgot he had been standing there for ten minutes.

"Come in Victor; what would you like to eat this evening?"

A large smile came upon Victor's face as soon as he saw, the lovely glowing Angela. Victor loved the brightness showing in those black eyes of hers; it was always those marble black eyes which had the greatest effect upon him. One look and he was prepared to do anything Angela told him to do He became a weakling, and Angela could feel this weakness; it showed on his face and it came out in his; otherwise, strong voice.

"Oh, it does not matter Angela, just whatever you put before me."

Angela immediately looked at the sofa and was reminded of the night they first made love; the night she made Victor bow down on his knees, before her. That same passion was filling the room; Angela felt her body moving and Victor's nostrils got a whiff of Angela's sensuous scent. There was no more hesitating as both of them quickly removed everything that concealed their nudeness. Angela whispered the softest, "I need you to obey me Victor", command in his ear. Then she sat down upon the sofa and beckoned for Victor to assume his rightful obedient position. Victor, feeling as helpless as one could be, under a spell, slowly kneeled down upon his knees, bowing before her, the same as that historical–virgin irreclaimable night.

Victor's mind told him to be gentle and he could hear Angela telling him to take his time. Victor could feel Angela's soft hands pull his head upon her curly cavern as she laid back. Only sweet sounds of purrs and swishes were heard as Victor held Angela's behind firmly in his hands and bowed faithfully as commanded by Angela. Victor could hear his queen telling him the directions to take and he quickly obeyed. The enjoyment Angela was feeling far exceeded that first night, and she would make it last as long as her patience could stand it. She would make it last as long as she felt Victor deserved to wait. Angela knew, the longer she made Victor keep his taste-tester inside of her, the more his body would throb for an ultimate satisfaction. When it appeared she was losing control, she directed Victor to back away and he politely did so, like any powerless man would.

Angela thought of how Victor was making a fool out of her and she wanted to become abusive, so she locked her legs around his head, squeezing her thighs against his ears as forcefully as she possibly could. Angela could hear Victor gasping for air, struggling to free himself, but her grip was too powerful. She did not want him to suffer, but she said to herself: "Here's to you Victor for waiting to tell me of your divorce; here's to you Victor for waiting to tell me of the other pregnant woman; here's to you Victor for waiting to tell me of yet another woman." The more he gasped the more she felt his tongue surge deeper and deeper inside of her curly cavern, until suddenly she felt like celebrating; saying inwardly; "here's to your divorce Victor, and my freedom; my freedom to love you as my very own." Angela slowly removed her chokehold and commanded Victor to love her, the way he knew how. She spoke out loud, practically screaming, saying; "we are both free Victor, love me freely." Angela could now feel Victor's gentleness; she could feel herself giving way; she could feel Victor unleashing a smooth relentless tongue attack upon her curly cavern; she could feel gratification oozing to the surface; she could hear Victor's throat gurgling sounds; she could feel freedom gushing with every gurgle; she could feel Victor also tasting that same freedom, she was now enjoying.

Yes, this had been a bitter-sweet evening for Angela, but she was all smiles as she laid back, propping her feet upon the sofa.

Victor had not been given a new command, so he remained upon his knees, bowed before her. Angela wanted Victor to reap all the rewards of her freedom; she wanted him to understand, what consuming her time and freedom really meant. Angela flinched a bit giving out a loud sigh as Victor's swishes played a final freedom tune upon her curly cavern. She faintly heard Victor say; "did I obey enough?" Angela knew he was looking for a new command, but she pretended, she did not hear, because she wanted to make his body throb as he waited. She wanted to have his body continue throbbing as she waited to hear him explain what happened. She wanted Victor's body to throb until she heard him say, "I love you." She wanted his body to throb as she waited to hear him tell her of his divorce; throb as she waited for him to tell her about the other pregnant woman; throb as she waited to hear him tell her of yet another woman. Angela would make Victor continue to kneel upon his knees, bowing before her, as she listened to his explanation.

Victor, why didn't you tell me you were divorced?"

"I was going to Angela, and changed my mind."

"Why?"

"Because Angela I didn't want to further complicate my brain. You see, I believed I love you, but wanted to be sure it was not a bad case of loneliness. I had been married twenty odd years, but it didn't seem like it. It's amazing how fast time flies. Samantha and I had been classmates since the first grade and that's all we knew. Somehow, it just didn't seem fair. Even when we went to college; her family selected Spelman, and mine, of course, selected nearby Morehouse in our hometown of Atlanta, Georgia. It was one of prestigious tradition. We later discovered that our parents had controlled our lives completely."

"Our parents had made it, so to speak, and they didn't want no, so called "no good" Black marrying into their family. In their minds, they knew all about the uplifting of our race; and in their hearts, they weren't willing to take a chance on romance involving poor kids several blocks away. Papa use to tell me all the time; boy—I don't want you messin around wid that Davis girl."

"Maxine Davis was a neighborhood classmate of mine. We were often, together, as our house was the closest to the school. We were only walking to and from school; why all the fuss. I was grown before I knew the meaning of what papa was constantly telling me. In the days in our community, it was common practice for a pregnant girl to have to marry the boy. And mama and papa didn't want their back-breaking bourgeoisie status broken down by no poor class like old man Davis and his kind."

"He and mama had struggled so hard to represent what was good about our people. But there was only one problem; we were still Black and we still had to go to school with all the "poor Black kids." I didn't see any difference in us and would fault them for it later in life. Classism hurts a child as much as discrimination. Of course, our elders would never have subscribed to that logic. Parents, I think, make decisions for their children based upon their childhood; rather than what actually works. They couldn't understand that Maxine and I were classmates and friends. She didn't care about no status of my folks; and I didn't know what "old man Davis and his kind", had to do with me and my friend."

"Maxine went on to become a college history professor. How is that for judging a book by its cover. Maxine and I don't laugh at the ignorance of papa, today, because it wasn't ever funny. We both understand, he thought his way was right. We must understand as parents that each child, given the same opportunity can learn the same thing and excel together. And who knows, if it wasn't for mama and papa, I could have ended up married to that "Davis girl".

"Tell me more about the Samantha story, Victor."

"Well, it's not that Samantha and I didn't admire and respect each other, but there was that missing ingredient. We are what you would call good friends; but to be specific, we're more like sister and brother. We were not even childhood sweethearts. Our parents always put us together and we never rebelled. On our wedding night, we couldn't even make love, because our bodies wouldn't respond. We apologized to each other and went on to sleep. We discussed it briefly the next morning and decided, it was what our parents wanted; and we would have to make it work. Society sometimes has a way of playing tricks on you. This was that old Black Bourgeoisie of Atlanta at work."

"We were given a head start in life. A small two-bedroom

house, a modest bank account, and a 1954 Studebaker with a lecture not to ever get rid of it. Our parents told us that 1954 was a significant year for the history of Black people. What they had reference to was, on May 17, 1954, the Supreme Court of the United States unanimously outlawed racial segregation in the public schools; setting aside the "separate but equal doctrine". That was indeed the turning point for so many other good things to happen to our Black race of people. It was not just a step; it was a giant step forward. That case argued before the Supreme Court in 1954 was Brown vs. Board of Education of Topeka, Kansas. Our parents knew it was historical, but only time would bear out the impact it made. It's ironic that Thurgood Marshall, one of the many black attorneys that worked on the case; would eventually become the first black to be appointed as a United States Supreme Court Justice."

"Yeah, my parents were prouder people in 1954 because they felt our people would finally get a quality education. The struggle had been long and hard for an equal opportunity at learning. Just think, they would say, "no mo used books wid those other folks names in dem." Of course that change was too late for us; we had already made it through."

"Used books and all; they read just like the new ones. Dirty and soiled books should never be a handicap to learning. We were encouraged to buckle down and study; and we would learn just the same. And as you see, it worked; we both turned out quite well. As a result, today, I'm so proud of those black schools and teachers. They did more with less then, and our Black colleges are still having to do the same thing today. Papa would always say; "if you start behind, and run harder and faster than the next, you bound to win every time." Papa knew we had to work harder to make it; and make it, we did, all the way, including following their allurement to the altar."

"As I was saying, it was a large happy wedding. All their Bourgeois friends were there. We received presents galore. Fine silver, china, crystal, linen. So much in fact; when our daughter got married, we told her to take whatever she wanted; little good that did for the brevity of her marriage, but that is another story."

"Now the happiest moment of our lives, was when our daughter

Stacy went off to college. Happy because we both knew we had stayed together because of her. Happier because we had made it work. Happiest, because we were now free. We actually cried like babies when we parted, and for the first week; we called and visited each other every day. For a while I thought Samantha wouldn't make it; and she confided in me later, she thought I wouldn't make it. Our parents were now deceased; our daughter was gone, and we could now see what else there was to life."

"We never suffered for any money or material goods. And we always looked happy to our friends. They branded us the ideal couple. And to be honest with you, we were happy to a degree. We took our marriage vows and we almost kept them. We made more vows when we divorced. They were, "if we ever needed the other, no matter what, we would be there." These I know we'll keep. Because these are vows made from where they're suppose to be made—from the heart. Samantha even told me she loves me, and I told her the same—and we both truly meant it. But the time had come for us to go our separate ways. We wished each other good luck, the best in the world, and that we would stay in touch."

"Anyway, how did you find out Angela?"

"A little birdie told me Victor."

Victor thought: "My five against her hundred that it was the old birdie——her grandma. Grandma was a nice lady, but knew everything going on in this town. Keeping a secret from her would have meant the loss of a complete Intelligence Corps. Grandma has a network of spy antennae, and usually received reliable information. Her good gossip sources usually exceed the third-line edition of rumors. The only surprise here is, why did it take granny so long to tell her."

"Victor, I do not see anything so difficult about wanting some time to think, after the termination of a long relationship. Any sensible person could see that you really need some fresh air. Well, are you getting enough now; fresh air, I mean?"

"I think so, Angela, but I can't say that it's working out any better. Let's put it like this Angela; life throws complex challenges at you daily."

"What do you mean Victor?"

"I'll tell you later. Anyway, I'm sure now, that I love you. Will you please remember that Angela."

Angela looked down at Victor when he finished talking; he looked so pitiful kneeling before her, with his head resting on her thigh. She on the other hand, felt so much better, because Victor had told her, he loved her; and whether he meant it or not, the words sounded real good. Angela also felt good, because Victor had told her of his divorce and a bit of his life's history, including the status of his ex-wife, Samantha. Victor; however, did not explain the details of Samantha's needs, which included loving her delicious dessert. It was only after the divorce that Samantha really enjoyed making Victor get his fill of her delicious dessert. He too had come to enjoy spending this needed time with Samantha, dining on her delicious dessert; for in his own words; "Samantha's dessert was sweeter than all of the others combined. Anyway, Angela smiled at Victor, although she had heard nothing of the other pregnant woman; Angel smiled, although she had heard nothing of yet another woman. Victor had made a statement about the complexity of some things; and would tell her of them later; that, Angela thought, included the additional explanation. Suddenly, she thought of being nice and having patience with Victor again; her curly cavern instantly felt the warmth of his breath. Angela, then told Victor to kiss her tenderly, and moments later, they retired to the Queen's suite, upstairs, for the night.

Victor thought: "I want to tell Angela what's going on, but this just isn't the appropriate time. And I can't say, if there is an appropriate time to deliver immoral and untrustworthy news. It doesn't seem so bad, when I'm not getting all sentimental over it. Maybe, after the baby is born, she won't take it so hard and it won't be as difficult for me to say. Getting into precarious predicaments are so easy. I'm really not sure how all this happened myself. Somehow, I shouldn't feel guilty, but every time I think of Angela, I feel so bad."

CHAPTER TWENTY THREE

BETWIXT AND BETWEEN

"Victor you look as though you are dragging this morning."

"Tiffani, let me tell you. I didn't plan this entire enriching experience, and for the life of me; when it's over, I'm going to sleep for weeks. Why is it that women today, have so many more problems when they're pregnant. Samantha never had all these cramps and nagging aches. Women accessibility to the good life has made them more delicate these days."

"You are right Victor, but I do not see anything wrong with that."

"Look Tiffani, my mother told me she only stopped working for a week when she had me; and her mother Mattie Hudson, who had babies as fast as she could get pregnant, never stopped working the fields. There were twelve of them in all. The stories told on my poor grandmother was enough to quiet me down for hours. Although our paths never crossed, I feel as though I knew her personally. Any woman who bore or raised half that many children should be admired. Mama said it was the childbirth and not the child rearing that done her in. The last one, a fourteen pound baby boy, never allowed her to recuperate. "She just wasn't no mo good after the birth of jumbo Chris," mama would say; "Neva got aroun much no mo." Well, for sure, Angela and Helen don't come close to being no Grandma Hudson."

Victor was spending practically all of his spare time either at Angela's house or at Helen's house. Both wanted constant vigilance. In order to satisfy them both and keep both unruffled; he agreed to spend every other night with them. This worked out pretty good, except for the time Carolyn needed him. Victor only went home to get his mail. In other words, half of his clothes were at each house. He had transformed himself into a modern day nomad. There was a passing thought of moving them both in with him. Seems he thought; it would have been less strenuous on his body to unify the pair; but on the other hand, Angela and Helen might have needed more space. Well–it was—just a thought or a tasteless gesture on his part.

"Victor, the pregnant women are only part of your problem. The real problem is you, trying to be all things to all people, or four women in your case; and not knowing how to say no. You cannot do that Victor. Carolyn has been calling here regularly lately, so I know you are servicing her damn near daily. Is her stuff that good man? I do not want an answer Victor. And the fact that you say she is having a few problems does not warrant you screwing her everyday or every time she calls for you. I wish I could be inside of your skin for an hour; I would straighten that chick out. Then there is Samantha, does she know about Helen and Carolyn yet?"

"Not that I know of Tiffani."

"So you see, that is part of your problem Victor; if Samantha knew about them, she might bow out. I doubt it, but she just might."

Tiffani was right on all counts; Victor did not know how to say no. That is because each woman came at him from a need point of view and Victor was definitely a sucker for helping a pretty woman in need or "a mistress in distress". Of course, that was only half of it; for some reason Victor himself got hornier when these two got pregnant. Some of that was attributed to the fact that Helen did not want to do anything and didn't. She only wanted Victor to be there near her; his companionship meant more to Helen than anything. And her friend Carolyn knew this. And speaking of Carolyn.

"You are probably right Tiffani, but—hello Carolyn."

Victor speaks and heads for his office, because he knows she is there to see him. Simple deduction, Carolyn has never come to visit with Tiffani.

"Hello Victor, hi Tiff!" Pausing long enough at Tiffani's desk to softly say; "Ralph told me to tell you hello." Winking her eye in the process.

"Thanks Carolyn."

Tiffani watches Carolyn as she heads for Victor's office thinking to herself: "I can see why Victor likes Carolyn, she is one more well dressed, well groomed lady; everything about her is in order. And look at that body she is built so nice. It is obvious, she is up to something though; she does not wear her skirts that short unless she is; probably wearing no underwear. Victor is in for more trouble, I am sure." By that time, Carolyn had made it to Victor's door and was slowly closing it as she entered; sitting down in the famous chair.

"Victor, I have been thinking and have decided to move in with you."

"You what!"

"Oh, do not get so excited Victor, it is only temporary. Helen and I have been talking; she only needs your presence while the baby is coming, but I need quite a bit more."

"I'm afraid that is totally impossible, Carolyn; I'm hardly ever at home; you know my situation."

"That is my point Victor, but you do go home, don't you?"

"Sure Carolyn, it is my house, you know! What are you saying?"

"Calm down Victor, listen for a minute. Why do you go home? I mean, other than the fact, you live there."

"Well Carolyn, I have to get my mail from the box, keep my newspapers from piling up in the yard, and remove those solicitations from the door."

"You go home everyday, just to do that, except for the day you see Helen. Most of those days, you hang around for several hours before going by Helen's later on. What I am proposing Victor is to be your housekeeper for a few months, or more specifically, until the girls have their baby."

"And what comes with that Carolyn?"

Carolyn crossed her legs, looking at Victor one-sided. Victor's eyes followed her legs as if his eyes were steel, drawn by a magnet. As far as his eyes could see, Victor saw nothing but long precious thighs. He remembered the first time she sat there and how it had affected him; how he wanted to kiss what was before him. That was when he was trying to hold out on loving Carolyn and she foiled his brain by displaying her woolly center; that had been months ago. He had loved her many times since, but that spontaneous showing of artwork was one of the most magnificent breathtaking pieces he had ever seen. Victor knew if he was too slow in responding, Carolyn would probably do something similar, and he did not want to be looking glassy-eyed in the front of Tiffani, the rest of the day.

"Never mind Carolyn, I agree; I suppose this means you'll come over today."

"If you want me to Victor, I will pack some items at noon and follow you home after work." Using her sexiest voice. "But to answer your question, I don't do cooking; for everything else though, you have the perfect housekeeper Victor."

Carolyn got up to leave; Victor could not help getting excited, just looking at her fine body. "Man," he thought; "that girl is too fine." She started out, for a step or two, but quickly turned back saying:

"Oh, I almost forgot Victor, here is a set of keys to my place; it is close by, you know. On the days you go see Angela, use it; I would not want to interfere with anything she has planned for you. We can talk more about it tonight, if you like."

Carolyn opened the door and was on her way, casually and smoothly strolling, the same as she had entered. Victor thought, "there is not anyway I could ever resist that woman." Carolyn looks at Tiffani saying:

"Girl, we gonna have to talk sometimes!"

"Lemme know girl; maybe we could do lunch!"

"You got it girl, how's next week!"

"You're on; gimme a call girl!"

"See ya, Tiff!" winking her eye again.

"Luv ya perfume girl!" winking back.

Carolyn started her conversation with Tiffani when she opened

Victor's door and ended it as she was exiting the door to the hall-way. She never faltered in that smooth stride she had. Tiffani, watched enviously, again thinking, "those clothes, that stroll, that body." She could only shake her head when the door finally closed. Tiffani had been sitting at her desk wondering what Carolyn was talking to Victor about, but she had wondered more so; what the hello from Ralph meant. She wondered if Carolyn knew about she and Ralph, and if Ralph had told her about how she had shown Ralph everything. If Carolyn did, maybe she could give her the scoop on Ralph. Victor made his way to the coffee pot for a refill.

"Why were you shaking your head Tiffani?"

"Oh, just thinking about Carolyn; she is so calm, so cool, so smooth, so fine. I would hate to be you or any man around that woman. Do you think it is her height Victor?"

"I don't know; isn't that the same chick you were going to straighten out in an hour Tiffani?"

"I am sorry Victor; well, what did you agree to this time?"

"That fine lady you just observed Tiffani, is my new house-keeper. Reaching up and patting himself on the back. It was tough, but I finally talked her into it." Laughing.

"Yeah, I just bet Victor; probably the other way around; and after you took one look at those juicy thighs, you no doubt caved in." Laughing even harder than Victor. "Oh, so when does all this take place?"

"I talked Carolyn into starting today if it met with her approval." Still smiling.

"What is the pay for this lofty title Victor?" Smiling right along with Victor.

"We did not get around to discussing compensation Tiffani, but it will be commensurate with Carolyn's ability."

"You are laughing now Victor, but it is not going to be too funny when you drag in here worse than you did this morning. What about Samantha Victor?"

"I'll manage; to use your phraseology Tiffani, she only needs servicing about once a month."

"That will be just enough Victor to send you to your grave."

Victor laughs as he walks back to his office. He had become

much hornier since Helen and Angela were pregnant, so loving Carolyn more was really going to work out. After all, he was not getting anything from Helen; to make himself look like a real stud, he would never tell Tiffani that important fact. Victor did have a problem with his ego at times; Tiffani never beat him over the head with that. He sat at his desk thinking about tonight and Carolyn; becoming more and more excited as he thought. Carolyn was versatile when it came to making love; their last session had been on the plush carpet, with nothing but a small sofa pillow as their accomplice. Victor loved the way Carolyn propped the small pillow under her curvaceous behind. Talking about small pillow talk, that night he experienced the true meaning of it. He wondered what she would come up with tonight. It really did not matter, he would wait and follow her lead as he usually did.

Carolyn went back to her office, realizing after Tiffani complimented her on her perfume, she used the last of it this morning. During lunch, she would shop for a bottle to carry over to Victor's. She would put it with the rest of her items, already packed in the trunk of her car. Carolyn knows, she told Victor, she would pack at lunch, but she really believed in women having some secrets from men. She too, sat and thought of how they would make love tonight; trying to think of something to send him reeling and rocking. She could still feel the carpet burns on her elbows where she lowered Victor's head into her woolly center and held on as his tastetester performed those versatile intricate movements. Carolyn was getting excited thinking about Victor and looked forward to spending all those months at his place. "Maybe it will keep my mind off Sharonda," she thought; "maybe it will take my mind off my parents." Carolyn spoke to herself saying: "Anything would be worth a try; my life is falling apart, unraveling where there are no seams, and I just cannot go on like this. Being around Victor soothes me especially when we are making love. Loving him every other day should really take my mind off things; his bigness always-always relieves my stress for several hours. Then, maybe we could talk about me; I feel I can talk to Victor, but I do not seem to have the strength."

Of course, that evening Carolyn did have strength to make love. She hurriedly found her way to the shower in an attempt to locate another special spot for making love in Victor's house. And after a short search, she accidentally discovered an armed cushion rocker that swiveled. Talking about reeling and rocking, Carolyn spun around in the chair and rocked back, spreading her large nude thighs upon the chair's arms. The surprise on Victor's face when he emerged from the showers and entered his family room was pleasant indeed. There was no question what Carolyn had in mind as her woolly center had an open invitation. They both enjoyed the chair immensely as it seems to have made the whole process so much easier. With Victor bowed upon Carolyn's woolly center, she merely placed her hands lightly on his head and lovingly swiv-elled and rocked; then as Victor stood over her, she again lovingly swivelled and rocked his bigness down deeper and deeper. However, during today's stay and during the entire months of reel-ing and rocking, Carolyn never found the strength to talk with Victor about her problem. Meanwhile, her nightly drinks grew heavier and heavier; when Victor left for Helen's later on in the night, she drank out of the bottle and on the alternate night when Victor visited Angela, she again drank, out of the bottle.

Angela was surprisingly lenient with Victor's comings and goings. It was almost to the point of having sympathy for him. And of course that made him feel even worse. Angela was acting as though she was inside of him. Only minor irritations from being pregnant distracted her attention from caring about Victor. He was there to help her, but a spectator would have thought the opposite. She took advantage of her days to pamper him. Maybe this was her way of showing Victor her appreciation for allowing her to have their child . Whatever the reason, he could not ask for more equanimity.

Helen had been accepted and was attending a local Med school. Plus she was still doing all that non-compulsory volunteer work. So most of the time spent with her was after nine or ten at night. The good thing about this moving around was getting those home cooked meals again—at least half the time. Angela, was that half, practicing her experiments on him; and lucky for Victor, she was getting grandma's recipes down exceptionally well. His stom-ach was always eager for her day to roll around.

Helen never had time to cook before pregnancy, and of course that did not change. Victor asked her one day, what their child was going to eat. She acted pretty surprised, like—you mean, they have to eat.

"Victor, I had not really thought about that. But I suppose we will work something out."

Victor sort of gathered that the "we" meant; he would work it out.

Of course, Helen really wanted this baby, but for now, it was school and volunteer work as usual. Victor wanted to complain and did when he saw her imperceptibly running out of steam. Otherwise, it was no use; that girl was just meant to be on the go. The only thing helping her was Victor making her quit work altogether. At first, she was still working part-time.

Helen did not cook and all that, but when she came home, the room always lit up. She was by far the most radiant individual Victor had ever known. You wanted to make her comfortable. And Victor always found himself asking her, if there was something she wanted done. Helen's presence could conquer a frown, a tired body, or any other ailment you possessed. Victor always—mind you—always delighted himself, looking forward to Helen coming home. It was not hard to explain that something special——that something extra she had—that bubbly smile which made your body become crisp.

Victor had agreed to the natural births with Angela and Helen; and was one happy soul when that happened. Victor felt so relieved the morning after a beautiful bouncing baby girl oozed out of Angela. Angela, he thought had really been lenient with him. She had been loving him abusively, which he enjoyed, but could never let on, because of Angela's displeasure at the time. He wanted to admit to Angela several times during these assaults, that her curly cavern was getting better and better and sweeter and sweeter. Victor had learned a lot about Angela during their almost daily contact, but what he learned the most was Angela's correct instincts about other women. Between the young Angela and Tiffani, Victor come to realize their counsel was worth listening to. And Angela's counsel of "letting things run their course", was definitely among the best he had heard lately. Giving it a try though, did not come easy for Victor, because it seemed to him, "your life was an opened book"; it meant to him acknowledging pieces of one's life, to others who really loved you. To Victor, this was especially hard, for it meant telling secrets, it seemed.

Anyway, during Victor's joyful moments this morning, he called Samantha to tell her of the good news. She was happier than he was, it seemed and came right over to the hospital. The beautiful baby girl looked exactly like Grandma, to include those marble black eyes. Grandma and Samantha suggested the name Hattia, because Hattie sounded too country, and Angela and of course Victor agreed. This was indeed a proud moment for Hattie Lincoln. (Grandmother). Today, however was more than the beginning of a new life for Hattia, it was the beginning of a warm and cordial relationship between Angela and Samantha. Samantha had been wanting to meet Angela since Victor told her of those dreams he was having, and later, after really discovering that such a person could be real; she had lived for this day for months. She took to Angela as if she was her own daughter; even taking time away from work to be with Angela during the day, waiting on Angela and Hattia, hand and foot. Grandmother and Samantha exchanged the chores; one looked after Angela while the other cared for Hattia; Samantha even claimed her half of the grandchild.

Initially, Angela felt uneasy, because of feeling that she had stolen Victor away from Samantha; that all happened because of Victor's failure to tell Angela, he and Samantha was already in the process of getting a divorce. Once Angela accepted the fact, she had nothing to do with their breakup, she and Samantha became intimate friends, even sharing a few stories on Victor. Samantha explained she and Victor's relationship to Angela, as the closest of friends, saying; "Victor is always there when I need him." Angela felt a touch of herself, inside Samantha, when the words "I need him" was softly and solemnly spoken by this woman. No details were provided by Samantha on all of those needs, nor was any asked for by Angela. Somehow, Angela's good instincts on women told her what they were. Their eyes met and that one need became as clear as if a picture had been drawn; they smiled and embraced each other tightly to fortify their unique bond. Angela, thought to herself, "a woman as honest and warm as Samantha deserves to have all of her needs fully satisfied by her life long friend." Somehow, Angela felt Samantha would also be her life long friend. They held hands, squeezing them at intervals, long after their embrace had ended; obtaining a silent, but perfect understanding of the others sentiment.

Grandmother, Samantha, and Angela did those baby shopping sprees together. Grandmother was equally impressed with Samantha; inviting her to spend the night on several occasions. Samantha simply told her; "I would love to, but Angela and Victor need their space." That only strengthend the relationship between grandmother and Samantha; their weekday lunches and weekend outings became commonplace. Of course, when you have a beautiful cooing Hattia, between you, it makes for a splendid way to spend time together. The two women had facial features with those same smiling lines around their mouths; happy lines which told one, a new baby was nearby. Even when baby Hattia was asleep, these lines were still on their faces, just watching. These two even shared conversations which bonded them closer together. It was surprising how much they had in common; it was that bond of motherhood and watching your child grow up. Grandmother shared her closest secrets with Samantha, and afterwards, their lips were again sealed. One day, grandmother would tell all to everyone concerned, but the appropriate time, in her opinion, had not yet arrived. She too was like Angela, letting things run their course. Like Angela, but we all know, the reverse is true, as Angela's most profound and immeasurable habits come from grandmother.

Angela had a girl and the following month; Helen had a boy. The babies were actually three weeks apart. Victor was happy for the both of them and for himself. His daughter, Stacy was happy now that she had a sister and a brother. As a matter of fact she was more excited than anyone. For some reason, Stacy took to the boy and coaxed Helen into staying with her to help out. That did not take much, because Helen enjoyed Stacy's company. The rapport between Helen and Stacy was like that of mother and daughter.

Angela was relieved as well as happy. But grandma was all smiles. She actually took the baby for hers. Just from the outset, it was obvious to Victor, he would have two more spoiled children on his hands. He did not relish that idea; and would have to think of something before long. Grandma kept the girl and Mrs. Edna Garley, yes the lady at the Senior Sitizens Senter. Except now, she was not at the Senter. Mrs. Garley or Edna as she preferred, had gotten her life back together, thanks to Helen; and had volunteered her services to keep the boy. Edna stated that she loved children, but Helen's boy meant something extraordinary to her.

Victor and Helen offered to pay Mrs. Garley, but she would not accept it. They even tried leaving money on her table, but she always returned it. "I do not need any money and I would appreciate it, if you will stop pestering me with such." She said.

One evening Mrs. Garley made them sit down and listen to her: "Life, whether you two youngsters know it or not is a two way street; a give and take affair at best—not they have when you have and you have not when they have. It is about recognizing a real friend."

"A real friend is someone who treat you the good ways they wish to be treated; who gives you the things they want, not garbage and indifference; but love and devotion." "And your wife," as she referred to Helen around Victor, "has been just that to me. Now, some people cannot tell the difference from the real and the so-called friends; which makes them stupid, and they deserve each other or whatever they get. But they will wake up eventually; believe me they will, because no one is a fool forever—at least to the same person."

"I find it best to stay away from people who deliberately intend to harm or mislead you. This applies to your enemies but applies doubly to your so-call friends. For instance they tell you one thing and do the exact opposite; or they conveniently borrow something and never pay it back, let alone mention it. And believe me, you can tell when they actually forgot or are just using you. Most of the users are pretty consistent—always steady socking it to you, for their gain every chance they get. Constantly having excuse after excuse for not living up to their part of the bargain and avoiding you when there is a real need for a friend."

"Friends like this, you don't want and sure as hell don't need. Discard them from your collection, cause when the ship sinks, you will be the one who drowns. Your wife, I found, will never let me drown and I will never jump off her ship. Please excuse me for getting carried away, but that was on my chest and I just had to tell it."

Mrs. Garley had a good sound philosophy and Victor thanked her for her gracious words of wisdom and the compliments of his wife—I mean Helen. Anyway, she was proud of that boy. She said it made her life worth living. Of all the things, real people do; she took one of her bedrooms and transformed it into a nursery. It was the most gorgeous nursery Victor and Helen had ever seen; all beautifully decorated with Disney characters. The boy has his paradise, right in Mrs. Garley's home.

To be honest, Victor believed he received better treatment there than he did at home. Mrs. Garley is like a "spring chicken" or a "new born calf", to use a few country terms for descriptions. "That boy is my heart," she stated, "and I am going to stay around here and watch him grow up." Of course that was fine with Victor and Helen, but they felt so guilty with Mrs. Garley, not taking any money for her services. So Helen and Victor were constantly discussing things to do in return.

The good thing about Helen having a small child was the elimination of volunteer work. There was now only time for Med school and the baby.

The bad thing about the babies coming was; it did not give Victor the relief he expected. He was now immersed in baby care and women attention. But thanks to grandma and Stacy; he had moved back home. However he was still floating to and fro.

CHAPTER TWENTY FOUR

CONFESSION

Months and months later as all during the pregnancies, Tiffani's rendezvous with Ralph had continued and she was no closer to solving his mystery than the day it all started. Her curiosity level, of course, had decreased and it pretty much did not matter as to what his conceptualization was, because Tiffani's investment portfolio was now in the six figures, standing at one hundred eighty five thousand dollars. Tiffani was proud of Ralph; he had shown her how to eliminate all of her debt and to remain debt free. A great portion of the increase for her portfolio was from Tiffani's own ability; she was saving practically her entire check and making wise investments, studying stock market reports. There was no way she was ever going to be able to repay Ralph for his generosity and investment counseling.

Their sessions had now taken on a more structured twist, with twice a month meetings, still after work in the office. Tiffani never had to brainstorm anymore as to what she was going to wear, because Ralph provided her with the finest in lingerie, bringing it with him, but always taking the used panties or bottom strip with him. Her curiosity now focused on what style and color the evening's lingerie would be. The sessions generally lasted two hours, split evenly; the first hour was all about budgeting and investments, and the last hour was reserved for entertainment. Tiffani was enjoying the sessions more and more, even climaxing a few times as she brushed her furry furrow into Ralph's face for an extended period, while trying to get him to respond with a taste or two. She had tried everything, short of pulling his head forward and choking him, to get that tongue jutting, where the evening sessions would have been more pleasurable. The session this evening would be another one of Tiffani's attempts to get a more open and touching response from Ralph.

The lingerie for today was not only sheer, but was skimpy; matter of fact, it was the boldest ever, consisting of only two pieces; a pencil thin bra string which merely went underneath the breast and around the neck, and a corresponding string on the bottom which slid intimately into her furry furrow and behind; hiding nothing. At first these bright yellow strings were uncomfortable for Tiffani until she starting dancing around. Ralph watched enthusiastically as he sat in her swivelling secretarial chair. The four inch heels concealed in Tiffani's bag elevated the yellow crouch string on a level with his broad nose that seem to be sniffing her sweet furry furrow's aroma. Tiffani was only moments away from delivering this used string to Ralph when she executed her new plan to get him to be a bit more participatory; sliding her fingers along the deep route of the string; rubbing the sweet moisture onto Ralph's nose and lips. Tiffani watched Ralph's eyes brighten and she paused, knowing it would not be long before that long tongue of his came forward, to at least remove her sweet wetness from his lips, and boom, then she would have him. She got excited as Ralph's nose twitched; again Tiffani slid her fingers through her furry furrow depositing another round of sweet fluids to his nose and lips.

This would be Tiffani's evening, she thought, as Ralph's nose continued to twitch, and now his closed lips were puffing up; it would be only a matter of time before that tongue was wagging all inside of her. Tiffani's hands continued to move behind the yellow string in case Ralph needed another extra dose to get him going; rubbing slowly, then vigorously as a climax occurred. Ralph's eyes widened even further when Tiffani, in ecstatic frustration rubbed even sweeter juices onto his nose and lips, and with a steady abundant flowing supply, rubbed it irritatingly all over his face, hoping for a positive response. She did this, totally saturating Ralph's entire face until several more climaxes weakened her to finally sit down. Ralph's anticipated tongue never left the confines of his closed jaws as he rose and walked out, leaving for the first time without the panties or string in this case. Tiffani had never felt so miserable and so good at the same time. She smiled because she knew it was getting closer and closer to the session where Ralph would be swishing his tastetester into her furry furrow. She wondered again where he rushed off to so quickly after seemingly been ready to thrust every inch of himself inside of her.

Of course their silent agreement to ask no questions left Tiffani shaking her head, but laughing now, as she noted her chair completely saturated with her wetness. She thought, "that Ralph does not know what good stuff he is missing; anyway, I feel good," she said, relaxing and temporarily forgetting about her cleanup; smiling, thinking how surprised it was to so easily satisfy herself. Tiffani was also surprised the next day, while sitting at her desk, to find that a whopping fifty thousand dollars had been invested in her account. This represented by far the highest single total to date, and if she read it correctly, it meant that Ralph was pleased, extremely pleased with yesterday's results. Whenever he gave her a hefty increase, it usually also meant, he wanted more of the same; and Tiffani thought, "I will give Ralph much, much more of what he got."

Tiffani remembered how guilty she felt when Ralph first gave her a large chunk of portfolio dollars. She actually felt as though she was taking candy from a baby and was not earning her keep; that was a long time ago. After the excitement of the big dollars wore off, Tiffani simply said; "where else could I satisfy myself and someone else so rewardingly; thinking, one day Ralph would benefit most by satisfying she and himself by succumbing to her urges." By the time their next session date rolled around, Tiffani promised, there would be enough liquid available for Ralph to wash his face in a kitchen sink; if that was what he wanted.

Tiffani spoke lowly to herself saying; "I almost confessed to Carolyn about me and Ralph's secret." She and Carolyn had gotten quite chummy over those lunches; which now as she recalls, the conversation always came up about she and Ralph. Carolyn really thought she and Ralph had a thing going on, but Tiffani insisted their relationship was dealing with investments only; and she was right to a certain extent. Okay, so what, if Tiffani entertained a little for some of those investments. One day, in order to convince Carolyn, Tiffani almost showed her the investment account statement. Now that would have been a mistake. In an effort to get Tiffani to tell more and satisfy her suspicion of Tiffani and Ralph, Carolyn said she could have had Ralph if she really wanted him. Get a little information by giving a little; not bad if it works. Tiffani was on to Carolyn by now and was much smarter than Carolyn gave her credit for. Carolyn would probably doubt a story like she and Ralph's anyway, and want more, which she would be unable to tell.

Also during their many luncheon outings, Tiffani noted Carolyn's increase in consumption of cocktails. From the beginning, Carolyn always had one drink, and here lately, it had increased to three and four for that hour to hour and a half period. The drinks stood out, becoming very evident when most of Carolyn's food was remaining on the table. Tiffani even mentioned several times to Carolyn; "you have not touched your food;" and of course her replies were the same; "It is not very good today or I am not as hungry as I thought I was." One thing, thought Tiffani, "not eating did not appear to be affecting Carolyn, because she still had that fine body." She wondered if eating or in this case, not eating was one of the problems Victor was helping Carolyn with.

Tiffani was proud of herself for refusing to disclose Ralph's confidentiality and her secret. She was proud because this was the first time she had been able to retain a secret on herself. Carolyn was persistent though; Tiffani reasoned if she had been a man, the secret would have been disclosed a long time ago. Then on second thought; Tiffani thought of Ralph and how he had held out for a year; even walking out on her with sweet stuff smeared all over his face. "That," she thought, "is not a weak man; a man with that type of strength could avoid even a fine lady like Carolyn." Carolyn in her persistent effort even introduced Tiffani to Gerald's Boutique and those fine expensive clothes she wore.

However, Tiffani thought, "Carolyn seemed a bit jealous when she paid for everything with a personal check;" even commenting that "Ralph's investments must be paying off." Tiffani could only smile at remarks like these, because Ralph in her opinion had been the best thing that happened to her, since getting a job and having Victor for her boss.

Tiffani thought of these two men and how much she owed the both of them, saying; "there is nothing I would not do if they asked." Obviously, Tiffani figured, Victor would never ask for sex because they did not have that type of relationship, but for Ralph, she would screw him in a quick minute without even hesitating. Tiffani wanted Ralph's love so bad, she could taste it; and she wanted to tell him in words instead of actions. Her actions with Ralph definitely did not speak louder, and just maybe she thought, the next time, a few words might not hurt. Tiffani wanted to make love so bad, but had made her mind up, it had to be this man; this man that refused to touch her; this man that continuously gave her thousands of dollars; this man that tortured her into misery, making her love and satisfy herself. Tiffani reasoned; no woman had ever been presented such a challenge.

Tiffani smiled when she thought how lucky his wife must be, to have a man like Ralph around the house everyday, and she was getting hornier and hornier just thinking about their next session. Tiffani had decided in her mind; words with more force would be used on Ralph to generate a positive response, in her favor. She also thought of confessing to Victor on what had been happening, to see if he might have some ideas about getting Ralph to respond.

And speaking of confession, Victor was coming to Tiffani just now, for some more of her good free counsel to cap off a wonderful afternoon.

"Tiffani, do you think I should tell Angela, I am seeing two other women.?"

"I would Victor, because she probably knows anyway; and the stress and hardship is really hurting only you."

"You really think women know these sort of things, huh! You are not giving yourself, too much credit, are you Tiffani?"

"No, not at all Victor, and please do not ask me how she knows; but believe me, she does. Those are some of our strongest instincts, Victor. Look at it this way Victor, the worse that can happen to you is for Angela to possibly get angry for a day or so, because if she had wanted to leave or do something else, it would have already been done."

Tiffani almost screamed at Victor; asking him how could she get Ralph to screw her, but the words would not come out; even though the timing was right. She knew Victor could help her, but she worried about breaking Ralph's trust in her. Maybe later, she thought.

"Tiffani, you are always right, so this evening when I go over there, I will tell Angela about Carolyn and Helen."

And that is exactly what Victor did, as soon as he felt comfortable.

"Angela, I don't know where to start; other than I've been unfair with you in my opinion."

"Victor, I have been waiting on this moment."

"What do you mean Angela?"

"Go on with your story Victor."

"Well, I've been dating two other women since my divorce Angela."

"Yes I know—Carolyn and Helen."

"How did you know that? And why didn't you tell me Angela, you knew?"

"To answer your questions, first it was pretty unsettling when I found out what you were doing. And like the divorce bit, I figured you had a good reason for not telling me; other than the fact, you were going to the dogs. I was hurt Victor, but decided to ride it out."

"You were carrying our baby Angela, and could have had problems because of worrying."

"Oh, I was hurt Victor, not worrying. You told me you love me; so I knew there was something peculiar to this story. Plus I am not letting you go, it is as simple as that. As to who told me, that is my secret."

"But you're taking it so calmly Angela."

"Not really Victor, I have had time to think about this, and simmer down. I truly value our relationship and obviously you do to. Otherwise, you would not have told me about your other women.

It is true; I feel you should have told me sooner Victor."

"Why is that Angela?"

"Because Every time we were together, you were in agony. I could tell you were wrestling with something painful. I knew what it was Victor, but you are accountable for your own actions; so the discomfort was yours to weather. Most times, Victor, as you have told me about my boss, people do not always communicate as effectively as they should. This holds true, especially when they are trying to conceal an uncongenial act or remark from you. Although you are now looking puzzled, Victor, you are certainly looking better."

"What do you mean Angela?"

"You should have seen yourself—your forehead had tight wrinkles, from having to squint your eyes in that sneaky downward position. You were living a lie around someone you felt truly, did not deserve it, and you did not know how to express or expose the truth. You took a long conscience whipping Victor; and it had beat the cheerfulness out of you. I was glad to see you somewhat dispirited because that told me in no uncertain terms, where your mixed up heart longed to be."

"These things happen when you are vulnerable and weak, Victor. Remember, it happened several years ago with me. I was a weak virgin when you came along. And you overwhelmed me. Now, two strong experienced, good-looking sisters come along and because you are weak and indecisive; they overwhelm you. Your capability for self-restraint was nullified by their sexuality."

"You make it sound so simple Angela."

"That is the way it is Victor, but they do not love you like I do. And I am not saying they do not love you. What is happening; they are merely using you for their own satisfaction. You are their sexual god. And I am not saying, all they want you for is sex, but that ostensibly, the controlling factor. They might not want sex that often and you might not screw them but once a year, but that is the clincher. You are convenient. You are their safety valve."

"But Victor, I am going to be as patient as the circumstances will allow me; knowing that even safety valves, sooner or later are not needed. I am being patient because I know you are entangled and must work your own way out. In a way I feel sorry for you,

Victor; but I am not going to waste an abundance of sympathy brooding over your weak childish mistakes. You will learn from your weakness and I just hope and pray, it does not destroy what we have or could have. I would hate to think our relationship was destroyed by three lame brains."

Angela's description of Victor having crippled intelligence was seriously intended and probably deservedly so. There is nothing that he can say to counter her opinion. Listening to whatever else is on her mind, most likely would be his best move. Beneficial in the sense, Angela remains as calm as possible, ensuring a soft approach toward him. Angela will not have to worry about hearing any words that might antagonize her. No one has to tell Victor to be cool in a volatile situation.

"If I was the bitch I should be, I would cuss those heifers out, and give you an ultimatum Victor. If that did not work, I would do something else foolish, like not ever letting you see our child. But all those things will only serve to make matters worse. Which is not to say, I am going to be easy and over compromising on you. I am going to merely demand and dictate my rights to you on a daily basis. If you can deal with that Victor, that is fine. If they can deal with that, it is also fine. But Victor, I am telling you now, I will not be taking no back seat to two scheming, conniving, women passionately using my man. You have been entrapped. And things could get worse for you, before they get better."

"What do you mean Angela?"

"Why Victor, they could get real selfish and want to marry you; although they do not sound like the marrying kind. Or you could act stupid and feel you are so in love with one of them, that you want to marry."

"Angela, you appear to have more insight into this than I do. What do you suggest I do?"

"I am a young woman, but a woman Victor. I am just using a woman's mind. These women will share you, until they get tired of you. They will squeeze you until there is nothing left. Look at that Helen; she is using you to the max. Now she is making you have the children she wants."

"We only have one child Angela, and that was a mistake."

"That is what she told you Victor; can't you men do any thinking for yourself. When she gets ready for another one, you will be the father of it. And do not be surprised Victor, if she is not pregnant right now. Do not get me wrong Victor. I do not want you to be nasty to these women. You were free game and they took advantage of it. And I do not blame them. If I am to throw any blame, it is going to be on you for letting yourself get trapped. Grandmother would probably tell me to let it run its course. So that is what I suggest you do. You can be nice to them and do for them, what you feel is the right thing in your heart. You are my alpha-omega for love Victor. And do not ever forget that. There is one thing I am going to ask you."

"What's that Angela?"

"Let the other women know that I am number one Victor. Will you do that?"

"Sure Angela, is that all?"

"No Victor, not really. I am going to demand most of your time and expect to receive it. They can scramble for what is left."

What Angela had just asked of Victor seemed more reasonable than practical. Carolyn and Helen knew where they stood——at least they did initially. Now, Victor is not so sure; those take for granted positions do have a way of changing. "Helen," Victor thought, "sure feels, with the new arrival; her position has been strengthened." And Carolyn's disposition is already telling Victor to run to her whenever she calls. So, to be secondarily accommodating to these two might be easier said than done. "Each," Victor thought, "sure feels a certain amount of weight to unerringly impose upon him."

"A woman, Victor, wants companionship but a woman in heat has to have sex. That is the function you are serving. They probably came around you at one of those moments. You took one sniff, like a little puppy, and was hooked."

"Angela, how do you know all of this?"

"Because Victor, I did the same with you. You fought it until you were sure of getting your divorce, then you caved in."

"How did you know that Angela?"

"I sort of figured it out later Victor. For a while though, you had me worried. I was beginning to think you were some kind of queer."

"Is that right?"

"It is true Victor, I even mentioned it to grandmother."

"And——what did she have to say?"

"She said, to give you some time. But I never lightened up, because I was curious to know what it was all about. So you see Victor, you have good morals, but in your strongest moment; a heated woman can take advantage of you. The key is to stay away from them during those perfervid times. Especially in those enclosed areas, where you are alone, otherwise it is all over. Victor, you still stand tall in my heart. Having believed you have learned your lesson, I have no reason not to trust you. The first tide, I rode out for me; the next tide, I will ride out for you."

"Angela, I owe you one——I will never forget."

Victor had been afraid to confess to Angela, but she handled herself and him so well. Of course, Victor is more miserable now, than if she had cursed him out and left him forever. Her understanding is whipping Victor, and her straightforwardness is making him feel even worse. Angela had cast those black eyes upon Victor; he read into them, words which said; "Victor, I am trusting in you, please do not let that tide swallow me."

CONFESSION

Confession time, how hard it is
Worse than swallowing a bitter pill
Careless actions from the start
Caused problems hurting the heart

Love ones, it hurt even more
Can they trust you, as before
If ever out, of this ordeal
...be trustworthy, long as I live

CHAPTER TWENTY FIVE

CRISIS CONTINUED

"Victor, you mentioned the other day, you were helping Carolyn with some problems. And speaking of problems; what is the story on Carolyn's lack of an appetite; she hardly eats anything at lunch these days."

"It's not the eating part that bothers me Tiffani, Carolyn could actually stand the loss of a few pounds; it's the substitute she uses for food."

"You mean the alcohol Victor."

"Exactly Tiffani, Carolyn has been hitting the booze constantly, since the loss of her daughter, Sharonda. At first, it was a drink or two, but now, she drinks it as if she thinks someone is going to steal it."

"Why didn't she mention her daughter when I brought up her not eating? I could easily have understood that Victor."

"Carolyn does not like to be reminded of Sharonda, Tiffani."

"Could there be something else bothering her Victor?"

"What do you mean? Other than the death of her daughter...that would be enough for me Tiffani."

"Well Victor, sometimes people drink for an obvious reason, but it really is to conceal something else, they are trying to forget or not focus on. Do you know of any other reason, why Carolyn would act this way?"

Victor thought, "it is probably Carolyn's recurring thoughts of her former old man slapping her around; maybe it takes a while for some women to get over these beatings by their ex-husbands."

"No Tiffani, but then I have not inquired either."

"Oh, I would not ask her Victor, if she does not want to talk about it. If you are around her enough, she either will volunteer and tell you or it will accidentally slip out from too much booze."

"Well, I have been around Carolyn a lot lately and neither one of those has happened yet Tiffani. At the rate she's going, she'll be an alcoholic in six months or less."

"Or dead; alcohol kills too, you know Victor."

"Yeah, I had not thought of that; so this could be more serious than I ever imagined; huh! Maybe you could coax something out of her over lunch Tiffani."

Tiffani thought, "yeah, maybe I could exchange some of my strip tease stories, about Ralph for what really ails her. The way Carolyn had been trying to find out about she and Ralph, it would probably work." Tiffani thought again; "then I will be the one with a drinking problem."

"Maybe so Victor, maybe so, we will see. It is getting harder and harder to catch her, you know; coming to work is not one of her strong suits these days."

"Buy her lunch if you have to Tiffani, and complain like hell when Carolyn does not eat it. Don't worry about the money, bring me both tabs."

"You really care for Carolyn a lot, don't you Victor? I believe you care more for her than she ever cared for you."

"You must remember Tiffani, people care for each other for various reasons."

"Yeah Victor, selfish reasons should not be allowed to count though. Carolyn's caring has always been strictly for Carolyn!"

"Seems like, we have been through this before Tiffani!"

"Oh, I am sorry Victor, that Carolyn is nice, but sometimes, just thinking of her using you, irks the hell out of me. I promise, from now on I will restrain myself and be exceptionally nice in my thoughts of the two of you."

"Now, that Tiffani, is a very good idea."

Victor thought: "Life throws one so many curves. At times it seems unfair, especially if it's toward you or someone close to you. Carolyn was still having problems dealing with Sharonda's death. She had been on and off work since that time, but here lately, mostly off. I can say I understand, knowing full well, there's no hurt in my heart. I haven't had to deal with the loneliness and the void that must be there. I haven't had to deal with the sweet memories that crashed on that otherwise calm night. I only have to deal with the sympathy for Carolyn. I thought she was going to be all right; and when you talk to her she tells you she's okay. However actions speaks louder than words. And half coming to work for no other obvious reason is a lots of action. Carolyn was a seven to seven kind of worker, so this is quite unusual."

What Carolyn needed most was time to saturate the truth. She needed time to absorb reality; the question was, how much time. More than a year had gone by and Carolyn was visibly having a rough time. Victor often had lunch with Carolyn before; but lately her office was becoming the perfect silent refuge. The office was unilluminated as it was when he occasionally dropped by on a long work day. Except, it appeared much darker. Darker because, he knew of the shadows in her life; darker, because a light had gone out in Carolyn's heart; darker still, because she could not find the switch to turn it on again.

Talking with Carolyn earlier as Victor was constantly doing, she assured him she was tired and needed time off to think. That remark bothered Victor the more he thought about it. "Tired and time off to think", not tired and time off to rest. So after lunch he took the rest of the evening off to check on Carolyn.

Carolyn lived in a ritzy area befitting a successful corporate attorney, only a block or so away. The bell rang for a while, but Victor was determined to make somebody home. Carolyn finally shows up in the doorway, in her house robe.

"Did I wake you Carolyn?"

"Oh, hi Victor, come on in. What are you doing here?"

"I believe you're stealing my lines Carolyn. What are you doing here? I understand you've been missing a lot of days lately."

"Oh, I am okay Victor; how about making love;" as she unrobes to a naked body."

"I didn't come over here to make love Carolyn."

"Victor, I do not care—why you came here." Carolyn was now getting voluble. "I want to make love;" embracing and pulling him to the floor. As Carolyn pulls on Victor's clothes, he realizes she is inebriated.

"You're in no position to make love Carolyn. What have you been drinking?"

"Why? Do you want a drink?" Her head bobbing and weaving like an out of control kite.

"Carolyn, you should be ashamed of yourself."

"Well, I am not. And who are you Victor to tell me about being ashamed. Let's make love, damn it."

"Okay, simmer down Carolyn. First let's take a shower."

Carolyn is a large woman, but Victor did not realize how strong she really was until, she unleashed that grip. It was like letting Victor's belt out another notch after a humongous meal. They got in the shower and Victor lathered her beautiful body all over. It is hard to keep his composure as the soap foams, lace Carolyn's shapely brown body. Her breast peers through like, two heads looking out a window. Victor continues to rub his hands and eyes over what has to be the most magnificent body in the world. The wrong head is trying to do the thinking as he is horny and hard as a brick; until he flipped off the hot water.

Carolyn screams saying; "what the hell are you doing?" Victor held her under the cold shower until they both have their composure and senses.

"It's no question, Carolyn needs attention and a good screwing now, would probably help us both; but it's just not the answer," thought Victor. Her inability to cope with the loss of Sharonda is inducing her to drinking more and more. Drinking when there is no party; drinking when there is no celebration; and drinking when it is not sociably, spells problems. To be drunk, in the middle of the day, all alone,—yes—that spells problems. Victor loves Angela, but he can not just throw Carolyn in the trash pile. To cast her aside now would go against all mama and papa's home training. Not to mention, having a difficult time living with himself if something disastrous happened to her.

"Are we, ready to talk now, Carolyn?"

Carolyn starts crying. "I miss my daughter Victor. Sometimes it seems like I just cannot go on. It's all my fault."

"Carolyn, you weren't driving the car."

"I know, but she talked me into going to that party; when I originally said no. If I had stuck to my no she would still be alive. It was stupid of me Victor, to bow to a teenager. I was always weak in giving in to Sharonda."

It is amazing, the things you find out after the fact. Carolyn had gotten pregnant, and had this child as a senior in high school. Carolyn's parents had been very strict; not letting her roam like her girl friends.

"Victor, I was more than sheltered. I went to no basketball games, no football games, no dances and no proms."

Carolyn was determined to get even with her parents. So she made a hotel out of the family home each evening after school. She confided in Victor that she screwed boys just for the hell of it. Sometimes inviting two or three at a time. So when she got pregnant, she got a beating for doing so; and got another beating for not telling whose it was. What her parents did not know; Carolyn really did not know whose baby it was. That would have been a triple beating if they had known she was taking on multiple partners. So her daughter, Sharonda, died not knowing who her father was.

Carolyn had promised herself, she would not make the same mistake her parents made by sheltering Sharonda. She let her daughter go all the time; even when punished, Carolyn always gave in, as she did that fateful night; and let her go. Now, Carolyn was blaming herself for Sharonda's death. Trying to explain to Carolyn that she was not responsible; consoled her for the moment, but somehow, Victor got the feeling it had not really solved the problem.

This was Monday, so Victor stayed the rest of the week and again chauffeured Carolyn to and from work. Carolyn was so relaxed while he was with her, and that made Victor feel good. Good in the sense, he might be helping Carolyn to forget the past, or at least learn how to deal with it. Listening to her tell all, had to relieve some of the pressure. Victor gave Carolyn his complete ear and encouraged her to talk as long as she felt like it.

They both were coping the only way they knew how; spilling the gut and getting an ear full. Carolyn sang a tune and Victor hummed along. A pat of the foot and a nod of the head, could not have signified a more harmonious chord of inaction on Victor's part. Deep inside, Victor felt, there was more to do than unclog the ears. But WHAT!

Victor thought, "Tiffani was right, there was an underlying reason for Carolyn's drinking problem." He had the least idea it could have been for having a child out of wedlock; thinking all the time, it was those beatings her ex-husband put on her. With this new information, Victor felt better prepared to help Carolyn. He did not know what he was going to do, but maybe his genius of a secretary knew, or maybe Samantha could help; After all, she was one of those psycho doctors. "Pursuing all avenues was the thing to do," thought Victor. Tiffani had calmly spelled out the serious nature of drinking and he certainly did not want that for Carolyn. Victor was hopeful of finding a solution for Carolyn's problem as soon as possible.

Victor's time was limited more than ever; when he was not visiting Angela or Helen, he was going to the store picking up some of those urgent baby items; and this was with help from Stacy assisting Helen. His sexual life was all but shot; we are talking about far, few, and many in between sessions. Even Carolyn was down to once a week. Victor thought of asking Carolyn to move back in, for his sake; he had not realized how much he missed her, until his sexual appetite stayed hungry all the time. It had been a long time ago, but he could not remember Samantha taking up as much time with Stacy as Helen and Angela was doing. All of their time and spare time was consumed in caring for these babies. Victor thought, "if he had known, he was going to be the forgotten man, then he would not have gotten these two pregnant." This told him, he would have to be much more careful in the future. "Even with the hustle and bustle," Victor thought, "his problems were minor when compared to Carolyn's."

Victor's approach to new days were fairly simple; he looked for new ideas to solve old problems. And this morning was no different, he expected Tiffani to solve Carolyn's problem, once he told her of the new developments. Pouring his large coffee cup to the brim and standing there, gave Tiffani an indication that Victor was looking for conversation, looking for answers.

"Tiffani, you were right about Carolyn; her additional problem stems from the mere fact that she had a child, Sharonda, out of wedlock."

"There is nothing "mere" about having a child Victor, out of wedlock. All types of circumstances and questions come into play, such as; where the father is, the idea of letting her parents down, what the parents think, and a whole host of other things."

"Well, I didn't mean to make it sound so routine Tiffani, but you're correct. You know, she did mention something about the father; it was not her ex-husband, I know that, but I can't remember if there was anything said that would cause her current conditions or state of mind."

"Victor, did you not tell me one time, that men listened better than women?"

"Well Tiffani, when I found out about Carolyn having a baby while still in high school and no husband, I figured you would be able to solve the problem from there."

"See there Victor, you were listening; she had the baby in high school; which means some of those same questions appears, but probably with more seriousness. If you concentrate hard, I bet you can come up with something else, Carolyn told you."

"That could be true Tiffani, but my mind automatically leaped to you and probably, Samantha, solving this thing."

"Thanks Victor, for having confidence in us; I will put on my best thinking cap. Oh, speaking of Samantha, she called earlier, and wants you to come by after work."

CHAPTER TWENTY SIX

SAMANTHA BELIEVES HER EX - CRAZY

Victor says to himself: "Samantha wants me to stop by. I know it's important; at least something other than a friendly chat. She didn't sound very amusing. Samantha, since our divorce, always believed nothing of real importance should be discussed over Ma Bell."

"Stacy was by here yesterday Victor."

"Who?"

"Stacy Previtt, our only child; you remember her, don't you Victor?"

"Oh–yes, was anything wrong?"

"She is all right. It is you I am worried about Victor. She had a baby with her and said it was her new brother. I have never seen her so excited. It is that brother she always wanted while growing up. I just naturally thought it was Angela's, but she tells me it is Helen's. Who is Helen?"

Samantha was not giving Victor any time to answer, because she did not want an answer until she gave him his turn.

"Man, are you going crazy; that is two babies in two years, by two different people! She also says you are dating another lady named Carolyn on a regular basis. I do not mean to interfere in your personal life Victor, but have you turned into a sexual maniac. I guess next year, we can expect a baby by Carolyn!"

"No Samantha, Carolyn can't have anymore children."

"You mean—"

"No, don't get excited Carolyn, she had two already by her first husband."

Victor had no idea Samantha would be so upset—maybe concerned is the appropriate term. Of course her voice was a trumpet sound higher, which might have led to his first assessment. This high soprano had never shown this much range, in their twenty plus years of marriage. She sounded as if a scorpion had just been found in her underwear. The more Samantha found out about Victor and his clan, the louder she had become. Expressing hisses of disbelief, Samantha plops down on the sofa. Victor knew what that meant—he was now stuck here for a while—like until she is completely satisfied. It was explanation time until Samantha no longer had an appetite or thirst for information. The only time Samantha had come near been this aroused was when Stacy first left college and declared her authority on not returning.

Yes, that was the day the roof wanted to leave the house. The day Victor had to calm Samantha down for fear his heart would not survive. The day Stacy tuned her out for good. Victor heard every blistering word, which came in explosions and repeated themselves, over and over again every few minutes. You would have thought Stacy had ear plugs, she was so calm. That is also the day he discovered his tuning out ability was gone. When he was a kid, he was as adept as Stacy in tuning his parents out.

"So Victor, you now have three wives and four children."

"Don't blow things out of proportion Samantha——I'm not married."

"You might as well be Victor, this is a common law state you know. I understand Carolyn is an attorney. She will probably sue you for everything you've got. And deservedly so."

"I hadn't thought of that nor do I worry about such an ordeal Samantha. You see Samantha, I am not their master. These are free women, with their own thoughts, their own words, their own deeds. They do what they wish, and I love them for it. If anything, I complement their lives. They are truly independent women with their careers, who knows what life is all about, and where they are headed."

"That is good Victor, but do you know where you are headed? Because it sounds to me like you are playing with fire. I love you Victor and I do not want to see you get hurt."

"I believe I will be all right Samantha. Although I'd be the first to admit it——life can be complicated if you make it so; but it can be simple if you let it."

Victor thought: "Now, I don't know how I made that remark; I had gotten into this predicament sort of before one could safely be cognizant of his encirclement. And believe me, that was my status; encircled by three beautiful sisters. Angela's term is entrapment; Samantha's term is, a lunatic. Whatever the term, it's life's ups and downs, happening simultaneously, and I've got to deal with it the way my advisor, Angela suggested—until it runs its course."

"Samantha, each woman knows that I will do anything for her. There's more here than just sex. I enjoy their sex and they enjoy mine, but we enjoy each other as an individual."

"Victor, do these women know each other?"

"Let's say they found out about each other. Helen knew about Carolyn and Angela initially and readily accepts them. Carolyn knew about Angela, initially and found out about Helen. Carolyn tolerates Angela whom you love, and is now a very good friend of Helen. Angela tolerates Carolyn, but she despises Helen. Angela has also threatened in a sultry sort of way to terminate our relationship ever since I told her what was going on. That's a very involving discussion and you don't have time for it tonight."

"Continue Victor—let me worry about that."

"Well Samantha, it's generally when Angela is horny or the child is acting up; which is sometimes daily and continuous. And as a result, I spend more time with Angela. I don't believe Angela is that jealous, but is extremely selfish. And between the two of us, Angela does cause me problems because of her demand for attention. But she has always been like that. She'll never change—I don't really want her to change. She's the youngest. She knows it, and she's acting the part."

"Which one of these women do you love the most Victor? I do not mean to ask you such tough questions, but I am curious.

You do not have to answer Victor?"

"No, Samantha, it's really not a tough question. I love them all. I can't say I love them all the same or one much more than the other, because I never think of it that way. What I'm saying is, they do everything different, with each having, good and fascinating qualities not found in the other.

"If you had to make a decision Victor, for only one; which would it be?"

"I don't know Samantha, I just don't know. Samantha, you must remember, I did not plan to do this. As time revolved, it just happened. I met Angela and the other two met me. Each think they are the missing piece to the puzzle and the strong link in the chain. I believe as they believe. Sometimes, it's difficult, but that's life. Because just as I feel you and I are friends; those three are my friends. I think you would have to consider yourself God-blessed to have four friends. Most people are lucky to have one Samantha."

"Yeah Victor, I am not so sure you would not be better off with just one friend—me. Because at the rate you are going, someone is going to get hurt. And I do not mean hurt, where you live to suffer to tell others of your misfortune. Angela seems harmless enough, but promise me you will be careful. It would be a shame Victor, to have so many fatherless children in the world."

"I can relate to that Samantha."

"Victor, I do not want to keep you all night; but as a friend and sociologist/psychologist, I want to discuss this with you further. This is by far the most amazing case I have ever seen. And to be honest; if I had not been married to you for such a long time, I would say you are crazy as hell. Nowhere else can this be found, but in a story book. I would love to meet Helen and Carolyn, whom I vaguely remember."

Samantha had already met Angela and sized her up. She adored Angela and looked at her as her daughter. She wanted their daughter, Stacy to get a college education like Angela. Of course that only made Stacy hate Angela even more.

In other words, Angela could do no wrong. They even went shopping together; and Samantha shopped all the time for that little girl of Angela's and Victor's. Sometimes it worried Victor, they were so close. He never questioned them about it, because, he knew, when people close to you are happy; you don't ask dumb questions. Samantha was the psychologist, but Victor did know a little about human behavior, to leave well enough alone. As his father said, "don't disturb a hornets nest and you'll never get stung."

Samantha had first wanted to meet Angela, after Victor telling her about that dream. She had thought it unreal and wanted to meet the subject. She found the whole scenario to be fascinating. Samantha had earned a Doctorate in Sociology/Psychology and refused to let a good case escape her. She had long stopped studying Angela because of the personal interest. But this new incredible information concerning Carolyn and Helen has undoubtedly put her back on Victor's case. Samantha was good at her work. People willingly volunteered information to her.

Samantha was held in the highest esteem of everyone she came into contact with. She was down to earth and had no problems conversing with anyone. This of course did not apply to the rebellious Stacy. Samantha met no strangers and made clients and prospective clients feel at ease. She enjoyed her work and knew exactly what she was doing at all times. Her work was taken very seriously, but it was in a manner in which people were not alienated. She was never accused of making offensive remarks and was a pleasure to work with.

A case was always on her mind. Even at social functions, Samantha studied people. Victor had grown use to it over the years and it did not necessarily bother him. And times he relished the opportunity of seeing her in action——so smooth, so suave. So when Samantha asked to meet someone; he knew she wanted to study them. Samantha had written two books from her research and pretty much knew what she was talking about. She had logged thousands of miles in this effort traveling the countryside.

Her first book entitled "Attitudinal Problems of the Northern Black". This book dealt with the problems faced by the second generation of the original migratory workers from the South. One case in particular that caught Victor's attention was that of a young man. This young man, Clarence, we'll call him; had done everything it takes to succeed in this world. His parents saw to it that he was educated with the finest in the country. Clarence, the eldest of six children would be the first of his family to ever set foot in college. He knew the importance of this and was determined not to let his parents down. So Clarence studied hard and graduated among the top students in his class.His family was happy to see their hard work and struggles to keep Clarence in school had paid off. He could now assume his place in society and help put the other siblings through college. This generation would be able to rise above poverty and achieve heights only reached by the affluent.

Clarence was armed with a BA Degree as he sought employment. He was happy in his new suit his parents had sacrificed to get. Appropriately attired, he hit the trail. Well, after many days, weeks, and months of applying for positions with no success, he became unhappy. Clarence was discouraged and his parents were also discouraged. They put additional pressure on Clarence, telling, him he was not trying hard enough or it is something you are not doing. "You're well educated" his parents would say and "you're dressed in the finest suit" they bemoaned. Clarence tried harder, because he knew the family's burden was on his shoulder.

His new suit was not so new no more, but he pressed it each night and continued his search. Day in and day out Clarence went about this ritual. Gloom was beginning to show in the wrinkled lines of his parents faces. He looked into his sisters eyes with the same dismal expression each day. His attitude was full of anguish gravitating into the once admiration from his brothers. "I must, I must", Clarence often said to himself. And after eleven months of looking, he finally landed a job at the Post Office delivering mail.

Not to be out done; on every off day, Clarence continued his search. Every ad he applied for, either had just been filled or "we decided not to fill that position." The closest Clarence came to getting a job referencing his degree was "your educational background looks very good for the opening; come back tomorrow to interview with the manager in that department."

Clarence was full of joy and hope. Maybe the time had come. At last he would be able to show what he could do. He would be able to show the world what a well equipped college grad could do. His attitude brightened.

The next day, Clarence arose to hear birds singing. He was even whistling a tune. The manager upon seeing Clarence realized the position, like all the others "wouldn't be filled at this time." Again Clarence was discouraged. But this time he became despondent. That night about midnight; Clarence took the gasoline can he had obtained and poured gas throughout the house. He set it afire and walked out. The house burned like a paper box. Clarence stated at his hearing that nobody screamed, so nobody suffered.

Samantha asked three questions after this case:

Where was liberty and justice?

Is morality racially motivated?

Can society save the prepared generations?

Samantha's second book was entitled "Southern Sisters". This book was comprised of cases concerning the work ethics of the Black woman in the South; and coping with everyday problems. Victor's favorite story in this book had to do with a very young lady of nineteen, who at that tender age already had three children. The young lady named Dora, was only eleven years younger than her mother, Debra, whom she still lived with. Also in the house was four other children by her mother; one of which was younger than Dora's oldest, a six year old girl. It is not clear which children had the same father, if any.

This however, was not a case of incest or even promiscuity. It was a case as Samantha surmised; one due to a lack of education, lack of sexual education, and poverty. The other females in the house consisted of Dora's sixteen year old sister and Dora's youngest daughter of two months. In case you have lost count as Victor did; there were a total of eight children, including Dora; four of which were females.

The ages of the children are spaced far enough apart to indicate; and the facts, not mentioned here, bear out; both mother and daughter had been victims of smooth talking imposing men who promised the world. They of course sweet-talked the women into bed each time; hence, a pregnancy and a disappearing act followed. Currently, neither Debra nor Dora had a male companion. Also, neither is on welfare, but, both work below the poverty level.

Samantha's questions following this case had become longer and more detailed:

What is the primary solution to solve the families problem? Discuss reason.

> Education
>
> Sexual education
>
> Birth control
>
> Other

If you were Debra, what advice would you give Dora?

If you were Dora, what advice would you give Debra?

The family lives in a three bedroom apartment. Without any additional information—how would you assign the sleeping quarters? (One can sleep in the living room).

> Discuss in detail and why.

Can the cycle of teenage pregnancy be broken?

> Give at least three reasons.
>
>> Of the reasons given, which is the most effective?
>>
>> Of the reasons given, which is the most practical?

Whose responsibility is it to inform the sixteen year old of sexual education? Discuss reason.

Debra

Dora

Debra and Dora

Other

Samantha has a knack for solving difficult and complicated cases in her actual casework. I hope you are as successful in solving this one, as she was.

Victor could just see Samantha's third book entitled: Crazy Victor's Harem and their Behavior Patterns. Anyway, she wanted to meet Helen and Carolyn. Her casework was a case load, and should prove interesting when that time comes around.

"From the looks of it Victor, it appears you might be in the midst of three unyielding bronze; yes three sisters who are not going to relinquish any part of their hold on you, until they are ready to do so. And if I were you, I would not look for anything like that anytime soon. You can believe me too, Victor, because I am talking from personal experience."

"So what do you suggest Samantha?"

"Until I talk to Carolyn and Helen and get a better feel, I suggest allowing these entrenched holds to run their course."

"There, there goes those words again," thought Victor, "run their course; I wonder what's the real essence of those words."

"What exactly do you mean Samantha?"

"Well, generally Victor, it covers two major categories; one is when a person cares or actually loves you, and the other deals with a person depending on you for some want or need."

"How can you distinguish the two Samantha? In my case, everything to me, looks like a need, and feels like love."

"You are no different from most men Victor, who allows two heads to do their thinking; and what you are really talking about is loving, not love. But to answer your question, it is sometimes difficult, because a "want" might develop into a "need" to love. That is why it is best to let these types of things, run their course, where it is so hard to differentiate. Sooner or later though, you will know, because when this person's want, need, or love, no longer exist, they will quickly move on. In other words, Victor, the course has run out."

"If I follow you correctly Samantha; I will be rid of Angela, Helen and Carolyn when their course runs out."

"That is correct Victor!"

"Tell me Samantha, what happens if their course does not run out?"

"Simply and personally put Victor, you have a problem, for you will truly be overloaded. I can tell you now about Angela; she is in love with you, and is not going anywhere. I love that girl too; you know Victor, for a young lady, she is so smart."

"Yeah, probably all that coaching she is getting from that grandma of hers Samantha."

"She is doing no more nor less than what she should be doing Victor; no need for you to sound edgy, you dreamed her up." Laughing.

"If I follow you correctly Samantha, I am stuck with Angela, huh?"

"Look happy Victor, Angela is really nice, if I have to say so myself. And for your information, you just might be stuck with us all." Laughing.

"I would laugh with you Samantha, but at this stage, two new babies and Lord knows, what else, even my ego has started dwindling."

"You really do not have any problems as far as those kids are concerned, we are all helping out; psychologically there may be a problem or two, but you will get over that. Talking about a case study Victor, you are really a case study; I am so glad, we are the best of friends." Laughing again.

"Thanks Samantha, is that a case study like, Victor and his Harem." Smiling.

Samantha, laughing even harder. "Now Victor, that is real funny; I was just having a little fun, but that is even funnier; of course that sounds more like a title for my new book. I am so glad you are taking my kidding around so good."

"Do I have a choice Samantha?"

"No, not really Victor, but I guess I had better lighten up while you are still in a good mood. I would not want anything to spoil your appetite for my delicious dessert tonight. Aren't you so glad I only need you sparingly?"

"I enjoy your dessert so much Samantha, you will never hear me complain. To be honest I can't seem to get enough."

"Speaking of not getting enough, I told Angela, I have already reserved you, for my fiftieth birthday celebration, next year; so there will not be any surprises on her part or worries on your part. So Victor, you can relax, even more so tonight and get yourself a good fill of this delicious delicacy before you. And Victor, dining and spending the night and dining again for breakfast is sort of what I had in mind for getting enough. I hope there are no objections on your part."

"How could I Samantha, it appears that the want, need, and love is all here!" Laughing.

"Perennial love Victor, perennial love!"

And with the perennial love on their minds, the night was filled with an enjoyment of delicious desserts. Samantha even showed her versatility with a hand held, mouth warming fill of his bigness. The early morning's breakfast was every bit as appetizing. Satisfaction beamed across their faces as they parted for their respective offices.

CHAPTER TWENTY SEVEN

DISAPPOINTMENT UPON
RETURNING TO WORK

No one expects life's bumps to always be against them. And Angela was no different. The rude awakening from her maternity leave defied all moral rights and human dignities. Angela found a reassignment within the department. A move that put her in a much inferior position. And the white guy who had been getting all the good assignments had now been promoted. Incensed was not the word to describe Angela. Her top blew like a fiery volcano as the molten lava rushed into the boss's office.

"What the hell do you think you are doing," states Angela.

Larry Trebor, a yellow and green tie, gray-eyed fellow, politely closes the door behind Angela.However it's to no avail, because Angela is still coming through the walls loud and clear.

"What do you mean Angela?" As he returns to his seat.

"You know damn well what I mean Trebor. I have been demoted and Mike has been given a promotion."

"He deserved one Angela. He has been working extremely hard of lately. Some of that work done was yours. And besides, your pay remains the same."

"You have no right to do what you are doing Trebor."

"That's where you're wrong Angela; I cleared it with personnel, and the president, Mr. Turpin approved it."

Why was something of this nature taken up with the president. Apparently there had been some discussion as to its lawfulness; and no one in the lower ranks wanted to put their neck in the noose. So, in steps the head honcho, Mr. Turpin to put his signature to it. Now there is no doubt as to who is in charge for actions or inactions; for morality or immorality; for right or wrong. The demotion while on maternity leave was probably a borderline illegality; but Turpin had no qualm with that.

"We are obligated to take you back more or less, but we do not have to give you the same job. Having a baby was your idea Angela, and has nothing to do with the company."

Trebor, in the same breath, had gone from being polite, to now attacking Angela personally. A degrading of the worst kind.

"What about my excellent job performance Trebor?"

"Angela, that was a year ago; things do change. You will have every right to gain your old job back and remain with the company; if your disposition improves."

His attitude was now, both cocky and repugnant.

"I am not being treated fairly Trebor, and you know it. What do you have against me?"

"Nothing Angela, you are a model employee. I have made you an appointment with the president at one p.m., if you care to discuss this any further. Now, excuse me, I have work to do."

Angela could not believe she was getting the shaft on this job, after all the long hard hours, she had put in. Angela had been having these problems with Trebor prior to leaving; but was uncertain as to the label on the indifference. Male chauvinism and racism, however was at the top of her list. Now, it seems, without any clear evidence, it has something to do with being inferior; whether it is the male superiority or racism, Angela still was not sure. The point of her excellent job performance signaled one or the other, or both. Angela's long and tireless hours had counted for nothing.

Angela opens and slams the door on her way out. It is only ten a.m. as Angela heads to her office and falls apart. Yes, this time, Angela would cry; there would be no holding back the tears. There would be no remembering grandmother's remarks about "not being able to fight with tears in your eyes." This time Angela wanted to cry; she wanted to shed some tears, because she knew afterward, she was going to be fine. She remembered from her own experience of seeing how grandmother's flowers were beaten into the ground after a heavy rainstorm and how they always stood straight and strong again when the sun appeared. Angela knew she had the sun, she had the sun and strength from reading about her heritage. She cries for some ten minutes before regaining her composure.

At no time during Angela's three month maternity leave did she figure on having such adverse conditions when she returned. She anticipated on assuming her upward mobility climb from her last stopping point, not from a lower rung on the ladder. If there was any satisfaction in this, Angela would gladly give it all up for a healthy baby by Victor. Little Hattia was doing fine as called for in the blessed prayers from Angela. Angela believed, no moments in history could exceed the job and happiness of seeing the birth of a healthy child. And while Angela felt having a child might not have been the greatest sacrifice a woman could make, it certainly was one of her greatest achievements. An achievement, in her opinion worth all the sacrifices in the world. When Angela saw the joyful exciting expression on Victor's face, during that special event, she knew, she would have to do this again, and soon; his disposition was an admitted approval. Victor's exhilaration decreased Angela's pain to no more than the feeling of a regular menstrual cycle and nature taking its course. So, doing this all over again, in her mind, should have double the effect; there would be no need to get another verbal approval from Victor.

Anyway, Angela's readings during her leave had gotten much–much deeper into her heritage. There was, The Life of Gustavus Vassa, the African, written by himself; Hagar's Daughter, by Pauline Hopkins; Wonderful Adventures of Mrs. Seacole in Many Lands, by Mary Seacole; Behind the Scenes, by Elizabeth Keckley; A Biography of the Slave Who Whipt Her Mistress and Gand her Freedom, by Silvia Dubois and Incidents in the Life of a Slave Girl, by Harriet A. Jacobs.

These readings had definitely prepared Angela for the insensitive, gutless slave owners mentality of Trebor and Turpin. A quick summation of this great literature told Angela, what Turpin would tell her. Oh, she knew he would go through the initial motion of being impartial, but that would quickly change. It was a shame, she thought, some formalities have to be attended to. But if nothing more, this could be an encounter for letting him know, she now knew where he and others like him, were coming from. It would be interesting, Angela mused, to see how old Turpin handled himself, from his already fixed position. She knew it mattered not, what her position or statement was; Turpin's make believe demeanor of her interest, would still quickly result in a denial of her American rights. Angela thought, "the statements made by Trebor had really expressed Turpin's point of view; if not, why else would Trebor be so eager to have her talk with him. Like to him, for someone else in a superior role, to quote his position, made it right to Trebor."

Trebor's arrogance this morning made him a star in his opinion as he boasted his chest out, far beyond that yellow and green polka dot tie and steps ahead of those greenish-blue plaid socks upon his feet. Angela could see Trebor's satisfaction behind that smirk upon his face, as he told her the things, really, that he and Turpin had already discussed. She could not believe, this was the same seemingly fair and impartial man who had hired her. "Goes to show," Angela thought, "why Trebor's face looked like the belly of a snake; this obviously was his crawling out party." Angela cleared away the remnants of her tears, saying silently; "why should I give Turpin more time to drum up more antics; I will go see him this minute."

Looking up the president's extension, she dials it; with his secretary saying, who shall I say is calling and getting Turpin on the line.

"Yes, Angela, may I help you?"

"Sure, I understand I have an appointment to see you."

"It is this evening Angela, but I am free now; come on up."

Angela pulled herself up, thinking about what could be said or done to rescue her from such a dreadful day. Her body felt like tons of steel. The weight upon her legs caused a dragging of the feet along the corridor to the elevator. Her arms could hardly reach the button and likewise the numbness in her fingers fumbled around before selecting the twenty fifth floor.

Angela was bounced between the elevator doors upon her departure, due to her ineptness to move with any conviction. "Why am I selected," she thought, "to have such cruelty passed upon. The system works, if you are in it," Angela continued to think. Yet, here she was, a well educated and diligent worker being treated like an outcast. "Who was the system for, if not for me," she thought.

"Good morning, Mr. Turpin."

"Come on in Angela. Now, what can I do for you?"

Angela could see the typical Texas redneck expression shining through. She had studied her Black heritage carefully, while on maternity leave. From slavery to our so called freedom; Angela had read enough to also see the old slave mentality shining through. But she did not dare make such an accusation. Not because it wouldn't have been accurate or because she was afraid of identifying a racist; but Angela wanted to be tactful and give Mr. Turpin the benefit of the doubt.

"Well, sir, you are probably familiar with my case, so to spare those details; I feel because of sexism, my rights have been denied."

Mr. Turpin, with his half-baldhead, leaned back in his high-backed chair, saying, what makes you think that?

"Well, Mike, my co-worker came at least six months after I did. I went on maternity leave for three months and he is promoted in that time. And I return to find my position is no longer the importance it once was. In other words, Mr. Turpin, in my opinion, I feel I have been demoted."

"My-my, we can't have you feeling like that." Rubbing that shining noggin. "I will look into this further and get back to you Angela. Thanks for coming by."

That was simple enough. Angela felt better; returned to her office thinking she had accomplished something. But by three p.m., all that had changed. Mr. Turpin called and informed her that he did not find anything wrong. She was told, "if you work harder, you will be back in your old position in no time". Angela knew that hard work had nothing to do with this conspiracy. Here she found herself having to catch up before moving forward again. Angela was disappointed, but her readings had prepared her for the band of togetherness often maintained by the slave masters and his overseer.

Poetic justice therefore reads:

STILL

To rear a child in this dreadful world
Strains a mother's strength indeed
No matter a black boy or a black girl
We're still slaves; haven't yet been freed

Slavery barbarity, in today's work place
Will it ever, leave this nation
Be ever black and of that race
Forever suffering, subjected to humiliation

Angela knew their African-American conference was around the corner and it could not have come at a better time. She thought, "this job discrimination is for real." Mr. Turpin had known what he was going to tell her all along, because he was in charge. Angela had no doubts now as to the reason for her reduction in rank.

Later on that evening, Angela found that Trebor's arrogance had even rubbed off on the white male, Mike, who had been given her promotion, when he asked:

"Angela, what is your new name going to be?"

"What do you mean—new name, Mike!"

"Well—I sort of thought—I mean—you are going to get married, aren't you? To give that child a name—I mean."

"For your information Mike, "THAT" child has a name! And for your additional information, please, do not ever, invite yourself into my personal affairs again."

Poor Mike turned another shade of red, but his silence meant that he had gotten the message. Angela thought, "this is what happens in corporations, when there is discrimination at the top; it filters down into everything below that level." Turpin's precedent gave Trebor his arrogance, and on to Mike, it went. Angela was learning more and more each day, of how the real world and its real people functions. Her two bosses had teamed together, against her, forming their mutual bond to keep things their way. She realized it had nothing to do with right or wrong, it was just the way it was. Be it feminism or racism, the end results were the same; the white patriarchal brute was winning. Trebor and Turpin had reinforced what Angela already knew; that bonding and sticking together was a winning formula. Now she knew she was on the right trail in organizing an African-American corporate group to work from within. A group low in numbers in comparison to the whole, but Angela and her members had a plan.

Having a child had even taught Angela something about life; she noticed that little Hattia had stuck her head out first, in order to begin the competition, and something had protected that poor defenseless head on its initial journey. Oh, there was Victor, grandmother, and the support from Samantha, but Angela became aware that a higher power had all the protection. We are talking about coming forth, head first and healthy; Angela had prayed for just a healthy baby. So when Angela saw a healthy infant with a head full of black hair ooze out of her curly cavern, she knew prayers worked. She promised herself, from then on, prayers would be a part of her beginning each day. Angela simply felt it gave her a head-up on the vultures of the world. "Just do your part," Angela says, "and it will work."

The formation of the African-American corporate organization was the new beginning for them. They were going to have to address their problems themselves, instead of sitting back, waiting on someone else, with no interest, to do it for them.Certainly, Trebor, Turpin and the like would not solve their inequities. How the group would solve their problems were yet to be determined exactly, but Angela believed whatever course they took, it would be successful, as long as they did their part.

There were not even any clues available when Angela looked out her office window; the riverwalk was quiet and peaceful. Oh, there was the usual crowd of people, but the bustle was not there; there appeared to be more strolling and casualness in everyone. The tree limbs shadowy presence flickered upon the water as it moved a riverboat effortlessly onward. Following the boat was a green leaf, twisting and turning, but nevertheless, following right along. Angela wondered if by chance, someone like Trebor or Turpin had yanked it, prematurely, off its branch and cast it evilly to its doom. These two now took on the image of evil doers who purposely attempted to destroy meaningful creatures. Angela felt, she had met these two people before; somewhere before in her heritage readings. She wondered if they expected her to use the same caution her forefathers used; singing those songs, with messages, or if they expected anything of her.

Victor had tried to tell her once that sometimes these attacks have no connotation other than being business as usual. "Maybe so," Angela thought, "but our group will make them aware of our presence; otherwise our dark faces will never appear as Corporate Executive Changes, as it is now, across America in the daily major newspapers." Angela reasoned as she saw that leaf float away; her chances of becoming an executive was nil, if she kept getting demoted and yanked off the main branches. She knew no African-American in her company would ever make the "Executive Change" section unless their organization moved forward with their plan.

CHAPTER TWENTY EIGHT

THE BIG CONFERENCE

"Well Victor, things have taken a turn for the worse on that conference we scheduled. At the eleventh hour, personnel notified us that we would not be able to hold a meeting in the cafeteria. The reason given was that the president felt it was not in the best interest of all our employees. And I say worse, Victor because of the defensive response we are getting from the corporation; but our registration has increased, and we will get almost one hundred percent participation. When word got out what the corporation had done in canceling that facility, it fortified practically all the Black workers. And thanks to you, Victor, we had already reserved a large conference room. How did you know we would have problems with the corporation? Were it not for you, we would be in total disarray."

"It is best Angela, to be prepared with your best weapons when going into battle. And the best weapon is not to underestimate your enemy. To be caught off guard cause much retreating and confusion. In our case we have come too far to turn back now. We cannot afford to face adversity; retreat and face that same adversity again on the same turf. We must constantly be moving forward, marking and meeting new challenges."

"Victor, you give me so much inspiration and courage. It is no wonder, you, like the struggle, is worth fighting for."

"Thanks Angela, please keep me informed; and promise that you'll stick to tactics, rather than revenge in preparing any plans. And be mindful of the spies among you."

Angela had worked long and hard to make their first corporate African-American conference a huge success. The initial obstacles to prevent their meeting had been noted and addressed. Victor had prepared them for the inevitable, and all attempts to deter their progress, had been met with the appropriate challenge; their response eliminated the frustrations that would surely have followed. The old adage "things happen for the best" was definitely true in these cases, because their forces were galvanized.

People who originally expressed only lukewarm interest, starting paying their registration fee immediately. And people who felt a conference would do no more than get a "bunch of sisters and brothers fired", changed that earlier disposition to putting their best foot forward, with the money, for registration. They ran out of registration forms, but made copies, and kept on processing disenchanted employees who said "enough is enough and fair is fair." They flocked to them in droves. It was like someone opened a flood gate, and the onslaught of enthusiasm, and optimism swept a pathway to their conference. They went into the conference charged up.

The conference, held on the following weekend, saw eight hundred twenty three of them present. The hotel on that Friday, Saturday, and Sunday, was full of all types of beautiful Black people—white, yellow, honeycomb, tan, light-brown, brown, dark-brown, chocolate, bronze, jet-black, coal-black, etc. They were all there, mixing it up for the same purpose. They were standing tall and proud. And dressed as only black folks know how to dress. They were "a sight for sore eyes", to borrow a saying.

It was the greatest blend of colors and the most beautiful bouquet Angela had ever seen. They were all smiles, because they had really surprised themselves on the attendance. They had encouraged workers to bring their wives and families to the beautiful city of San Antonio. And a number of them included a vacation for the prior week or remained for the following week, to the tune of 2,107 people. They immediately realized their clout, and put that on their agenda as a tool. Each worker was to give the finance committee a total of every dollar spent by them and members of their party, while in that fine city. They had worked so hard to make this conference a reality. So its fruition was a joy to all, especially the organizers.

The hotels, along the Riverwalk, provided the perfect setting. The serene and relaxing atmosphere provoked their thinking to an unrelenting end. Fresh thoughts oozed out after an evening's dinner cruise upon the winding waterway. Sweet Mexican lullaby's strummed by the guitarist on these treks, had composed a mental rhapsody to help them deal with the most important endeavor in most of their lives.They needed clear heads and uncluttered brains; and San Antonio with its world's competing atmosphere, generated the clarity moods for mind production. A conference of far greater magnitude could not have been held in a more charming place. The city, though void, historically of significant African-American presence; Black pioneers have not gone unnoticed, and they are not without some quality influence. However, they were not here to unearth and resurrect skeletal remains, but to preserve their ancestors gains, and to propel their offspring unto their rightful position before the turn of the century.

Friday was for registration only; with a come and go cocktail session from seven to ten p.m. On Saturday, the issues were presented. And smaller groups were formed to formulate detailed solutions. Late Saturday, the group leaders would meet to compare and finalize the solutions. Most issues were in the form of grievances, and most solutions were in the form of demands on the corporation. There was one exception.

The most grievances listed pertained to equal rights in the work place. Unequal pay led the list with bias promotional opportunities, a close second. The solution was to demand an affirmative action staff, headed by a Black; hopefully promoted from within their ranks. They also stipulated that their African-American group wanted input into the program.

One of their next demands was to be included immediately into the Management Training Program already in existence. About ten of them had applied, but no one had heard anything since. They knew the company was deliberately keeping Blacks out of this program. Their position was simple. They are doing the menial task with masterful qualifications. They could see the blatant discrimination, excluding highly qualified personnel. And they were not willing to compromise for a token Black for appeasement. When everyday, an inferior white was being trained to ride herd over them. So they would demand unequivocally that the ten applicants be approved.

The exception, referred to earlier had to do with a demand upon them as individuals. They were to, each be responsible for at least five hundred shares of corporate stock. Each member of their group was asked to join the corporate stock program immediately. Each member was also encouraged to buy corporate stock on the open market. They did not know if their demands would fall on deaf ears to the corporation; so they were putting themselves in position to get them presented to the Board of Directors. They knew if they could make an impact as owners and employees, their chance of being heard, became excellent, even more so.

Victor had put Angela on guard about spies among them. And in her reading, she became familiar with slaves who would tell on other slaves planning to runaway. This had been an apparent hindrance in some of their forefathers, not attempting to hit that great freedom trail; because one of their own had snitched on them, and they would be caught before getting started; only to be severely punished. So this inherent weakness had come down through history, and had brought with it, mistrusts among their own ranks.

In their early meetings, they put snitchers on notice as to what would happen to them when caught. Oh, they were not going to bodily harm, threaten their life, or anything like that. They would merely expose them in their newsletter. Then it would be their responsibility of how to deal with ostracism from their fellow African-American co-workers. To some it would not mean anything because after some African-Americans get to making a few dollars; they think they are one of them, or at the least, better than any other Black.

The newsletter was born, not solely to expose their traitors, but to actually report what was going on with the organization. It would report the good news as well as the bad news. It would serve to keep everyone informed. Do not get it wrong, it would not be the minutes of the meeting. But they decided in order to hold down the hostilities of secrecy; their meetings would be above board and open. In other words, you could miss a meeting and basically know what happened, pertaining to items of importance. So the snitch in this case, for the most part, lost his important standing and became a nobody. If the snitch could not tell them nothing; they do not need him, and their group obviously do not need him either. The newsletter would help to keep them focused on what they were doing and where they were going.

The purpose of their meetings were to make employment conditions better for them now, today, this minute; not tomorrow or promises for the future. Time was out for promises. Like the old love song of years gone by "if I ever needed love, I need it now". That is the way they are; if they ever need money, they need it now. No more procrastination and thinking about doing something later. If they take care of their needs today, and do what is necessary, the future will take care of itself. Again, do not get it wrong, their offspring will still have to keep the torch burning. So the newsletter would highlight items and help preserve the history to keep the flames going.

Somewhere along the lines they would have to make these people understand; they would no longer tolerate unfair treatment. On Sunday, their luncheon opened the floor for individual remarks on "fairness and what is just not enough". Person after person shouted his or her discourse:

"We are talking about being fair; fair wages, fair promotion, fair treatment. But we are our own worse enemy, because we are sitting back waiting on the man to be fair. In other words, waiting on him to give us something for being loyal."

"—After all those years of service. We have been the handyman and maid for thirty years, and we're waiting on him to be fair. We don't know what to expect, but we are waiting. We have raised fifteen children between us, and they all turned out fine. Three of which belong to him. Shouldn't we get a special token in the form of a check for at least raising his three. Especially since we were having to do it while cleaning the house, cleaning the baby, cooking the food; then cleaning the dishes."

"—We did this six days a week. Well, we did get most Sunday's off, so I guess we should be grateful. But we're waiting on him to be fair. We washed your dirty clothes; however, we did get to take the worn out sheets home with us. But we're waiting on you to be fair."

"—As handyman—my terminology—to you I was handy boy. I drove you to the market. I drove you to the office. I drove the kids to school; while you drove my body to the ground. And speaking of the ground; I often had to help with the gardening, mowing the lawn, and sweeping that big ass driveway. And we're waiting on you to be fair. Oh, I completely forgot; you gave me some old clothes and shoes. I'm still waiting on you to be fair. All of this is my fault, cause our parents taught us to never turn anything down; cause one day you would probably give us something worthwhile. We believed them, and we don't know why, cause you never gave them nothing. Well, besides, you know what."

"—We educated the twelve while you educated the three. Shouldn't we have gotten at least one full paid scholarship? How about a partial paid scholarship? Oh, what the hell, you did ask me how they were doing. This gave us the opportunity to pop out our chest and boast that five had graduated from college. We waited patiently for the next word;...send them to my corporation and I'll hire them with the other three. And we waited even more patiently for you to somehow say...if I can be of assistance in helping them get jobs, let me know. Yes, we're still waiting on you to be fair."

"—After fifty years, we had to retire. I use retire loosely, because there was no retirement party or pension benefits. Somehow, though, we managed to get some measly benefits from social security. And for this we should be very happy. It looks if though we're forever waiting on you to be fair."

"——Now, our sons and daughters are waiting on you to be fair. They are highly educated and as intelligent as any in the land. They are waiting to be hired. They are waiting to get promoted. They are just waiting on you to be fair. Being fair means having the same things your kids have; having the same things you want and enjoy. An equation would look like this for clearer and distinctive interpretation: FAIR = SAME THING. That is not too difficult for an intelligent being to understand."

"—But tell me, please tell me O' tireless warrior; whose fault is it that we wait?"

"—You see, we are suppose to be grateful for whatever the master gives us. We are not suppose to have what he has. The slave mentality is still there. That's why the white boy on the job has no problem getting his money. Most of the time it's at our expense. So in his opinion that's fair. When we demand fairness, and is willing to sacrifice for it, we will get it. Fairness will never be ours upon an expectation of fairness."

The fairness, unfairness segment wound down, and a new group started in on the second phase of remarks; "It's Not Enough".

"It's not enough for whites just to shake our hands and smile. That is not substance enough. To be friendly is nice, but if I am hungry, or cannot get that job, or promotion, because of covert racist tactics; you have not done anything. You only fooled yourself. And this is what we're seeing. A smile in the face or a pat on the back, but no money in my pocket."

"—It's not enough to pretend that things are right. If you take notice, the white gal beside me, got her increase and promotion with no problem. They didn't have to hassle you for it. And yes, even though they have been working here less time than me, they are making more money. And the first opportunity for promotion, it is given to the white, at our expense. You said, you were using job performance for the promotion; but when the time comes, your white friend gets it. And all of a sudden, there is something I didn't do or didn't learn, which eliminated me. However, just prior to that time, my performance and evaluations were excellent."

"—It's not enough to say I hire a lot of Blacks, but they always leave. If you notice, you are always hiring Blacks in the lowest paying jobs in the company. Whites hired at these levels are sent to seminars, workshops, and training programs; and soon find themselves moving on to the next level. All within a short period of time. And for Blacks, if we are hired in the file room, we die in the file room. If Blacks are hired in the mail and shipping department; we die in those departments. If Blacks are hired in the warehouse, we die in the warehouse. If Blacks are hired as maids and janitors; we die as maids and janitors."

"—It's not enough to hire one Black in every other department or one Black for every one hundred whites; just to say you are making a great effort to do what's right. And to pass the buck saying, I hired someone to implement a particular program, will no longer be considered satisfactory. You should not expect and will not be given praise for any token effort."

"—It's not enough to add "Equal Opportunity employer", to your want ad; when you either didn't mean it or didn't do it. Oh, I see, you hired ten Blacks this month. Let me guess, eight in clerical, one at another scummy or low paying job, and one professional worker. Not one in management—not even a trainee. Now look about you. The total percentage of Blacks with the company, including the ones just hired, now number a staggering 2.5%. The "Equal Opportunity Employer", wording is the biggest joke in America during the latter twentieth century. I hope it does not continue to be so into the twenty- first century."

"——It's not enough to say I have a Black friend, who by the way is vice-president of this or that; while as president, vice-president, manager or supervisor, you have no Black employees. In other words, don't try to hide behind having a Black friend, as I'm doing my part."

"——It's not enough to have good religion and Christianity on the Sabbath; when you defy all moral laws, for the new Fugitive Slave Law, the rest of the week. To pray for the wrong thing and receive it, gives temporary consolation, and is certainly not a passageway to where you want to go eternally or think you're going."

"—The dual system or double standard have been used much too long. If you think you're being fair and have been unfairly criticized; look around your company to see how many Blacks there are. And then note what capacity they're working. We are generally few in numbers and stand out in most cases, thanks to our beautiful darkness, so your count should be fairly accurate and quick. The real problem is; you spend so much time trying to keep the Black in his so-called place, that you don't have time to be fair.

Well, poetic justice describes "My Place".

MY PLACE

It's in the neighborhood
I choose to stay
It's in the country club
I choose to play

It's on any level
Education takes me
It's for any position
Based on my ability

For unlimited opportunity
My place is your place
Remove the artificial barrier
Caused by color and race

The total spent for the two week period came to 2.6 million dollars. Oh, they know the use of credit cards were heavy, but the city ultimately got the money. And they actually ended up spending more because they got charged with those high interest rates. This data was very important to them. It showed them the economic clout they had. Now it would be up to them to use this data to their advantage in the future.

Angela was very aggressive at this conference, and not even to her surprise, was elected its president. Yes, Angela of all people. That only meant she would get to meet with Mr. Turpin again; and listen to his conspiratory one liners; "I don't see anything wrong", or "Now, now, we can't have that". Presenting these grievances and demands to him would be the greatest enjoyment and challenge of Angela's life.

Angela was excited, not only about being named president of their organization, but about their accomplishments. The grievance committee was still giving Angela astounding financial reports. Besides the staggering funds spent by the families during the convention period, the most astonishing figures were being reported on the acquisition of company stock. Angela expresses this excitement to Victor as they sat around, playing with baby

Hattia. Victor does not appear to be listening, as he is really the one doing all the playing with Hattia.

"We only asked each employee to purchase five hundred shares and their response is continuing to be overwhelming Victor. Our daily reports shows this to be a tremendous success; Victor, did you hear me?"

"Uh huh Angela, the stock program is a big success, employees are buying the five hundred shares."

"Yes, and not only that Victor, they are exceeding that number of shares by far; most have purchased in excess of fifteen hundred shares. Did you hear me Victor?"

"Sure Angela, I am listening....you know, baby Hattia is going to be just as beautiful as you are."

"Well, what did I say Victor? You are not giving me your attention!"

"You said, the people are buying more than five hundred shares Angela. Don't be so irritable, I heard every word you said."

"Okay, how many more did I say they were purchasing Victor?"

"Most had at least fifteen hundred shares Angela; is that correct?"

"Yes, but, I want you to say something and look at me while I am talking Victor."

"Okay Hattia, promise me you won't get annoyed like mommy, if I don't look at you while you're talking to me". Victor laughing, directing his attention to Angela. "Are you a bit jealous Angela?"

"No Victor, I am not jealous, that is ridiculous."

Victor looks at Angela undereyed, puffing out his lips to show Angela how she is pouting, laughing at the same time.

"Well Victor, I may be a little jealous, but now that I have your attention, it does not matter;" Smiling. "Look at this report."

"Whoa, you are way over the five hundred mark for most people; look at all these three thousands Angela."

"Now you see why I am so excited, the over achiever represents sixty percent of the total Victor."

"And here's some six thousands and seven thousands; and who is this with ten thousand shares Angela!" Both looked at baby Hattia and smiled as she had fallen asleep. "She is representing the tolerance and relaxation part of me Angela." Smiling harder.

"Yeah, right; oh that is Darryl Strawsby, an accountant with the company; all of this was really his idea; his father is some type of financial consultant. Darryl is sharp though; he heads up the finance committee of our organization, plus——" obviously a pause at this point for baby Hattia is crying.

"Well Angela, it looks like the part of you in Hattia is coming out now." Laughing again.

"And from the smell, it is really coming out; since she loves your attention Victor, will you do the honors." Laughing.

"Come little one, let me clean up mommy's part of you." Looking and laughing with Angela.

Victor, of course was adept at changing Hattia, and could do it better and faster than Angela; so within a few minutes, their interruption was back to sleeping and they were back to their conversation.

"You were saying Angela, plus Darryl is something."

"Yes, plus, he is in charge of our organization's newsletter; I would like for you to meet Darryl, Victor. He gave us such a pep talk about taking advantage of our opportunities, telling us, "it was our own fault, we were depriving ourselves of ownership and America's mainstream." Darryl told us, "no one could stop us from buying company stock," saying, "they even encourage you, by matching a certain percentage." Practically, everyone felt like a fool when they realized they could not get fifteen percent on their money at the bank. Then we really felt bad, when he told us of the clout we would have if each one of us concentrated upon being owners of the company we worked for; "you will have more control of your own destiny," he said."

"Darryl is right Angela; he must be some kind of a talker, though, because this is a fantastic response. I would love to meet this young man."

"Well, he did sort of enforce it, with some charts and diagrams Victor."

"Still, Angela, this is some effective convincing."

"It worked on me too Victor; you see, I am the other one with ten thousand shares. What Darryl said made a lot of sense. Our goal is to obtain enough shares where we are no longer taken for granted by the majority. Darryl is right in saying we should help ourselves instead of sitting back making excuses as to why we always seem to come out on the short end."

"I agree with everything Darryl is saying; this is some kind of togetherness Angela."

"Victor, I am so glad to hear you say you agree, because I told grandmother about what we were doing; she said if you thought we had a good plan, she would help us out with an initial purchase of fifty thousand shares."

"Good—the plan is great; this is the greatest thing since the invention of the cotton gin Angela. There is no question you'll get results; the respect will be slow to come, but don't worry about that."

"What do you mean Victor, respect slow to come?"

"I will let you tell me later on Angela; what ever happens though, remember to remain calm."

Victor was right about respect coming slow; the Chamber of Commerce which usually has an excerpt in the paper about large conventions in town, totally ignored this one; the hotels though; several inquired about hosting one of their future conventions. Angela knew, the next one would be bigger and better, if she had anything to do with it.

"Thanks Victor, I will definitely keep that in mind. One quick question Victor, before we continue, do you think I am still too large?"

"What do you mean Angela, I never said you were too large."

"I know, but since the baby and all, my weight is up."

"That might be true Angela, but you'll never hear me complaining about your weight, as heavy as I am."

"Victor, I am not talking about complaining; just being honest, okay, what do you think?"

"In my honest to goodness opinion, you look better now than before; the little weight you have makes you protrude more, and I like that. You're even rounder." Laughing.

"You are making fun of me on a sly Victor, aren't you?"

"No—no—really I'm not, I love what I see; you look real good Angela."

"Okay Victor, now that I have heard your "honest to goodness opinion" on my weight gain; how about what I should do or say in my up and coming meeting with the president of the company, Mr. Turpin."

"Well, the main thing Angela, like I said earlier; remain calm. Remember you have a purpose for meeting with this man, so state your case clearly and concisely, and as brief as you possibly can. Let him know you are aware that his time is extremely valuable. Be business and tactful, but in all things, remain calm. Keep in mind; you might not be able to control the meeting, but you and you alone can control your mind and composure. And ultimately, whether in this meeting or another meeting, you are saying to yourself, you will be the victor——."

Angela laughing, "I believe I understand now Victor——be the victor——I like that."

Angela had gotten Victor's message. The wide smile across her still plumb-round face, from her pregnancy and her ever-glowing black eyes, melted Victor's business persona, back to that of being a loving father. And both their attentions were drawn back to little Hattia, working her pretty little mouth, as she continued to sleep soundly.

CHAPTER TWENTY NINE

MAKE MEMORIES SWEET

Tiffani's paid for lunches by Victor, with Carolyn had not been very successful in obtaining information. A stalemate had developed between the two; Carolyn would only talk about Victor, but in defense, would inquire of Ralph, when Tiffani tried to pin her down on questions concerning her personal life. Tiffani, still had not divulged a word about she and Ralph. So each luncheon generally ended with both of them being horny; Tiffani for Ralph and how she could make him do for her each session, what she was doing for herself; and Carolyn, horny for Victor.

Today's luncheon was not any different as far as Tiffani was concerned, but for Carolyn, she had made her mind up as they went back to the office; between what she wanted to do and the three drinks, courage entered her veins and flowed with the booze. Courage; much needed courage that she so desperately needed to tell Victor, more about her personal life. Their friendly casual stroll into the building ended with Carolyn telling Tiffani, "to tell Victor, she wanted him to come by her place immediately after work; that she wanted to talk." Carolyn knew, once she made the commitment to ask Tiffani to deliver such a message to Victor, her strength would remain, to deliver some more of her burden, off her mind. "She must talk to somebody," Carolyn thought, "she must talk to Victor today."

Tiffani sensed the urgency of the talk by the earnest expression on Carolyn's face. Her entry led her straight to Victor's office, saying:

"Victor, Carolyn wants you to come by her place immediately after work; she wants to talk. And for your information, it sounded pretty serious."

"Thanks Tiffani, thanks very much!"

Carolyn's plans had been made for the day; she would leave an hour earlier and prepare for Victor. When Victor rang the bell, Carolyn's voice over the intercom told him to use his own key, and to join her in the bedroom. He could smell her sensuous scent as he marched inside, to see Carolyn's imposing body lying upon the king-size bed's silvery-gray sheets. There were no pillows nor negligee to shield her voluptuous figure from view. Victor's eyes fell excitingly upon Carolyn's large desirous looking breast and her sumptuous looking woolly center. Victor's mouth flung open, but before he could respond, Carolyn pointed to the showers saying:

"First, I want to make love Victor, then I want to talk."

"No explanation could be more simple," thought Victor, and he was out of the water, after merely touching his most vital areas. He loved communicating with Carolyn, especially upon her favorite conversational piece, for it was here where he had truly engaged in her deepest subjects and obtained her greatest reactions. Of course, even the slightest of touches, upon another favorite conversational piece excited Carolyn, and she applauded Victor; telling him their communicable skills seem to gel real well. This really went without saying, because with Victor's lips attached and moving around and about upon this conversational piece, a separate language of its own was created. Victor loved the way Carolyn talked back to him whenever she made him communicate on her favorite piece. Yes, Carolyn had planned the evening's subject, and Victor moved swiftly to open his mouth and take part. He had welcomed this invitation, because Angela and Helen were still too busy most of the time with baby love. Even Samantha's needs had drastically decreased since she started spending all that time with grandma, Angela, and Hattia.

So the primary source of satisfying Victor's hungry appetite rested with the delightfully deliciousness of Carolyn. No sooner, this moment, had Carolyn's sweetness hit Victor's nostrils did his mouth water, as he hastily held her woolly center in a dining position. Carolyn's powerful hands gave him little time to savor this sweet aroma; pulling his head into her already moisture-filled and juicy woolly center. She could feel Victor's long warm tastetester glide inside of her as she slid happily about the spacious bed. Several moments of their intense friction-igniting sliding and gliding activities, had the two of them enjoying production and consumption. Victor was now use to the abundant supply of Carolyn's wetness; so the flood that preceded and the one that came after her long sigh, brought nothing but a treat to his diet. He patiently enjoyed himself, because he knew it would be over an hour before Carolyn moved her hands, giving him his original freedom.

Talking to this point was secondary to both Victor and Carolyn, but shortly before nine o'clock they finally managed to make intelligible sounds. Carolyn had been in no hurry to talk with Victor, because she was still trying to build up her courage. So, pressing his lips to her woolly center was another way of holding out for a little while longer. Carolyn knew what she wanted to say; the words were there, but so was the pain.

When the heart aches, it will ache until it is cleared of all that disturbs it. Carolyn was slowly removing all the pain from within. Victor recalled answering a phone call, from Carolyn's parents, after bringing her home from the hospital, after her daughter's death. And he had noticed, they were conspicuously absent from the funeral. Victor did not know why and to be honest, did not really give it a second thought. Carolyn was now expressing anger that her parents did not show up. The conversation on the parents end had gone like this; "Carolyn, I think you know we are not coming to the funeral". "Click." Carolyn had hung up briefly, without a word and without an expression.

The expressionless blank look was enough to tell a story. It told of a remembrance of things past; it told of a recollection of events; Carolyn was thinking way back. Her story told of thoughts that far preceded the present; thoughts which now seemed unreal; thoughts which Carolyn had been trying for years to erase from memory. Thoughts, though painful, only forged an expressionless stare.

Her parents were still holding a grudge after all those years. Of course with them it was a daily grudge.

"Victor, my parents told me that they would never consider Sharonda as their grandchild. And you know, for all those years, they never recognized her at Christmas or on her birthday. She never received a present from them for anything. It seems if though they were trying to punish me. I had to struggle with Sharonda and I am from a middle class home."

"They promised me they would pay for my education Victor, but would not spend a dime on that child, as they always called her. Matter of fact, when my daughter was born, they politely told me, I would have to move out."

"What did you do then Carolyn?"

"Well Victor, I was finishing high school, so I enrolled in college in order to get some money from them. Plus I had to get a part-time job to care for Sharonda."

"You're kidding!"

"Oh no Victor. So I decided, that I would stay in school until I knew, I could obtain a good salary. When I graduated from Law School, that was the happiest and most reliful day of my life."

"A day Victor, which meant no longer having to drag Sharonda all over town just to make ends meet. But Sharonda was always happy; it did not matter what. When it was raining, she walked in every puddle near her path. And in the cold, with the freezing wind jetting through her flimsy coat—she smiled and held tightly onto my hand. It was because of her cheerfulness and joyfulness that enabled me to halfway forget the heartless treatment of my parents."

"Then nine years later Victor, when my second girl was born, my parents wanted to shower her with gifts; but they would never send Sharonda anything. I was having to buy Sharonda presents, especially at Christmas; and pretend they were coming from her grandparents. Finally, after three years, my husband and I got sick and tired of it. We discussed it, and I called and told them, if they could not recognize both, don't recognize either. They thought I was kidding and sent presents, like before. But we started sending them right back. Finally, they stopped sending them."

"The return of those gifts troubled me then Victor; and I am still troubled, because it is like I was doing evil for evil. But I did not know any other way to respond when they refused to buy both the girls gifts. We could have kept pretending their grandparents were showering goodies upon them. But we were lying enough, as we concealed the real reason my daughters never visited them; and lied more so for the grandparents not visiting us. Many times I have wanted to wake up and discover, the whole charade was a huge nightmare. Victor, you just don't know the anguish I have been through." And she can no longer hold back her tears.

Victor consoled Carolyn as he often had to do in these circumstances. Victor held Carolyn snugly in his arms while his mind goes back to the time, a set of his grandparents and grandpa smiled upon him; and his thoughts were very deep and very long: "The summers spent with my grandparents were the best summers of my life. They watched me grow, with those reminiscent eyes of sweet memorable days, long since gone." And not to discriminate and show preference over either; Victor's thoughts told of them in joint and sweet memories:

"My grandparents were always eager to guide me in the direction, only they knew I should go. Their foresight was far greater than that of a parent. When they talk to you about being somebody, you're forced to listen. The stories I heard them tell seems unreal. One in particular that stood out; was how they worked all day for fifty cents. And that was from sunup to sundown. My grandparents stirred a curiosity in me. That curiosity was an awakening as to how they acquired the large acres of land and property on so little resources. How they had no money, but always managed to have tons of food on the table."

"But it was the good times that I remember the most. Like riding to town in the back of a pickup truck, loaded with freshly cut sugar cane, and newly picked beans, peas, squash, tomatoes, and watermelons. Grandfather sold or traded these items for things they needed back home; like flower, baking powder, and lard. I even got to get some store bought candy. And this was after eating all that sugar cane the day before. And this was after eating the hearts of many watermelons all week long."

"That was living at its best, because I helped grandpapa with everything. I'm sure now; I didn't do much, but he never fussed or screamed at me, like my parents did, when I screwed up. Grandpapa was always appreciative of what I did. And though I was small, I felt as if I was somebody; that I was really helping out. Grandpapa made me feel special, no matter what I did. Oh, they told me later that I sometimes acted like a little man."

"Grandparents are special people. They spoil the grandchildren; but the education obtained from them, more than offset any bad habits. My grandparents were farmers. And the education I obtained from them was invaluable; because I know potatoes, both Irish and sweet, along with peanuts grow in the ground; because I've helped grandpapa dig them. I know what a king snake looks like, and not to kill it, because it kills other harmful snakes. Grandpapa said, "that snake is your friend". I know that milk and butter comes from a cow; because I've helped milk them. And grandmama always let me churn for the butter. Grandmama always made me feel good, when she told me, "your butter make my cakes taste good." I know that chickens lay eggs and they're soft when they first come out, because I've felt them."

"It was really my grandparents that gave me my first lesson on being conservative. Oh, they never said, don't throw this away or save that. It was just natural for them to reuse everything. I helped grandmama tear up old shirts and dresses to make quilts. She also made dresses from the flour sacks. And grandpapa used old shoe leather to fix the straps on the plough-mules harness. And they used the cow manure for fertilizer."

"But the thing that helped me the most; right away, was how to listen. That's listening to them talk to each other, and the other old folks; the proper term is eavesdropping. One day I heard them say, "that boy is just like our daughter; and that boy is just like our son." My ears perked up because they were comparing me with my parents. That was mama and daddy being talked about. So when I got into trouble at home; I'd say "grandmama and grandpapa said I was just like you." That use to melt their hearts, and saved me a lot of beatings that I had coming. Parents, I found, take pride in their kids being like them. So when I was fixing to get the whipping of my life; I would politely say "grandmama or grandpapa said, I got that from you." It saved the day more than once."

"I can't help, but think of all the education and good times, Carolyn's daughters missed out on, by having stupid grandparents. And I cannot help but feel sorry for the grandparents, and the love they missed out on. Just think of never being able to hold your first grandchild and the others that follow. That alone would be enough to destroy one's soul. They should forever be ashamed of themselves. We must learn to forgive. To give up joy and peace for hatefulness, is not a fair exchange."

"I'm sure Carolyn's parents know it now, but they're still too proud to swallow that pride and ask her forgiveness. The girl, Sharonda is gone, and they're still holding on to a grudge, instead of precious memories. Memories that would be enough to heal a broken heart. Memories that would never cease to brighten a dreary day. Those everlasting memories which follow you around; making you smile at the darndest times."

"There is no replacement for sweet precious memories; and no recapturing of what, a foolish man neglected to grasp. And there is no better way for a grandmother to retrieve her beauty, other than through a precious granddaughter. A denial of any and all precious moments should cast a dark shadow on grandfather and grandmother's present days."

MAKE MEMORIES SWEET

We share a love
And then its gone
Sadness befalls us
And memories go on

Swallow your pride
Lose that grudge
Make memories sweet
Of a loss love

Noble to forgive
Indeed a gallant feat
Revive precious memories
And forever sweet

> *Days of reminiscent*
>   *Recollect happy times*
> *Make memories sweet*
>   *Leave antipathy behind*
>
> *Make memories sweet*
>   *Cast daily cheers*
> *Mend spiteful grain*
>   *With unregrettable tears*

It goes without saying anymore, that Victor was saddened by hearing of Carolyn's two girls, missing out on the love of their grandparents, and he was equally disappointed in the reaction of Carolyn's parents toward Carolyn and her children. Victor was also surprised that Carolyn's misery was not being caused by her ex-husband; he had been sure this "little green man" Carolyn spoke of, had something to do with him. Now it turns out, the little green man is really two little-hearted selfish black parents. Carolyn's love for her parents and their insensitiveness was causing her so much pain.

"Carolyn, don't you worry, don't you worry about a thing; sooner or later, your parents forgiveness will come forth; probably when you least expect it."

"Do you think there is anyway I can hasten it Victor?"

"I don't know, sometimes these things take time, because first, they have to admit to themselves that they are wrong. But believe me Carolyn, no one can be so bad that they continuously deny their love to their child and grandchildren. When the opportunity presents itself, I want to talk with your parents concerning this."

"Oh thank you Victor, I should have completely opened up to you a long time ago; now if I can just throw this ordeal out of my mind I could return to being normal." A smile lit up her face.

"Carolyn, do you mean, the loving I just received, was not normal, hmmm—may my lips forever be sealed."

"Victor, you know what I am talking about; try and deprive me of my favorite kisses man, and we will both have big problems.

I never told you this before Victor, but I love your responsiveness and effectiveness. You truly put yourself into your work, and despite me, really act like you love it."

"Carolyn, you cannot help, but to love something, when it is sooooo—good."

"Victor, you are sooooo—crazy! I hate to say this and I hope it does not spoil our evening, but I understand why Helen has fallen in love with you. If I was not so stupid, I would probably fall myself; excuse me for getting sentimental Victor, but you have met my needs and more. I know your situation Victor, but please, hang with me a little while longer."

"Carolyn, you make it sound like I'm abruptly going away!"

"Okay, let's clear our heads of all the sentiment and sorrow Victor and concentrate on deeper and bigger subjects."

"Now you're talking Carolyn."

They were both smiling; the evening at a quarter after twelve was still young. Carolyn grimaced in happiness as she held Victor tightly, clawing his back as his bigness found its way deeper and deeper into her woolly center. Such depth and enclosure gave Victor the warmth from Carolyn which he enjoyed the most. He was hoping that tonight's communication was at least a first step in solving all of Carolyn's problems. "It seems a shame," Victor thought, "for such a fine lady to experience such problems in his midst." Even without her asking, he had already made up his mind to do what he could; Victor too, felt the parents pain on Carolyn, first handed as Carolyn continue to claw and cut her powerful but powerless fingers into his back. Her hands were tied and bound with the loneliness of a dead child, but more so, from the stupidity and selfishness of her parents. Victor remembered how happy Carolyn looked when he mentioned talking to her parents; "this would be enough," he thought, "to stay by her side until all of her needs had been fulfilled." He vowed to make, talking, to those parents, his priority—his obsession; "deep down," he thought, "Carolyn's parents could be no different than the sweet and loving parents he had." Victor reasoned, whereas children must love their parents while they are with us; the reverse was true; and it was his belief that maybe, he could help Carolyn's parents realize, they must love their daughter. Maybe, just maybe, he could help them realize that they had to forgive and lose that grudge to make memories sweet.

CHAPTER THIRTY

MEETING MR. TURPIN

Prior to getting an appointment for them to meet with Mr. Turpin, Angela sent him a copy of their first released newsletter. Darryl Strawsby, the editor and writer of Angela's story had done a job on it. The headlines read "ANGELA WINS IN LAND-SLIDE". The story was on the 8x11 inch, second page, because Darryl took virtually the entire front cover for Angela's full length picture. He made her take a special picture in front of the corporate office with the logo showing. Here, Darryl said, "this makes you look like the owner of the company." Inside, nothing was spared. Darryl stated that, "this brilliant and magnificent businesswoman had faced the challenge of the male dominated convention and achieved victory as its leader." The article preceded as follows:

"She will be its first president," Darryl went on to say; "none was more beautiful and suited for the task than Angela. She won overwhelmingly on the first ballot in a field of eight males. Her nomination speech reflected the twentieth-first century. She stated that the hurricane wind stirring this decade would blow archaic methods and standards aside, as we neared the turn of the century. You would have thought Angela was the "her-ricane" as her speech received thunderous standing ovations time after time.

So many in fact that I lost count."

Darryl, continued saying, "I am glad to have been born during her time on earth; because she screams about moments forgotten, saying your forefathers would be proud of you now; and whispers about oncoming days as those of reckoning. She talked as if her course had been charted by some foreign breeze or mapped out by that unknown equation of which, only she had the formula. Somehow, we understood, though the distance did not seem near. She spoke at times like she was already at the top in the hierar-chy."

"There was no doubt, the voters knew, Angela knew where she was going, and that she wanted to take them with her. A dynamic lady and a born leader, if I had ever met one. She had my vote into the second sentence of her vibrant speech. Angela ended her speech saying; "It is so sad that battles have to be fought, before victory is won"."

Darryl ended by saying, "Madam President, when you need our help, do not look behind you, because we will be on your sides. We are ready to plunge our bodies into the depths of the discrim-inatory system, you speak of; and annihilate the treacherous enemy with deeds or with words."

Both Darryl and Angela, so genuine, so real, so mindful of today's duties. An awareness with the keenness of a well-bred hunting hound protracted into a finders point. Their thoughts and undertakings were too, straight forward unrelenting in the pursuit of job fairness. A chase of confidence, but with no assurance of achieving the desired goal. A very reachable, obtainable mark with seemingly only human obstacles standing in its path. However, Darryl and Angela knew they faced other barricades, with the for-mation of the African-American organization; yet perseverance was the only timeless tool. Pressing on for equality would be an obsession, unswayable by anyone, either in the organization or the corporation. They had been warned of the spies and had prepared their nullification. Now only the corporate unchanging powers stood in their way.

When Angela finished Darryl's story on her, she was a little teary-eyed; but she felt like a gallant knight, ready to charge and thrust her sword into the enemy. To know that the support is there was comforting. To know that those strong Black brothers of hers are there, makes the difference. And today three of them were with her as they strolled proudly into Mr. Turpin's office. There he sat in his favorite position, reared back in his high-backed chair.

"Good morning, Angela and fellows."

Angela introduced him to the fellows, as he called them. It was by design that each one of them had applied for the Management Training Program; because that would be their initial topic for today.

"I read that story on you Angela. You know that Darryl missed his calling on being an accountant. He should have been a writer. A very good piece indeed. Well, Angela, it looks like you have the support and respect of your co-workers. So what can I do for your group today."

"Mr. Turpin, we want to discuss the Management Training Program, of which we have all applied."

"Is that right," he muffled. "Well, now, I must look into that Angela. Tell you what, write all your names down here, and I will see that you enter the next session."

They almost fell out of their chairs. "Mr. Turpin gave in too quickly," they thought, "he must be up to something."

"Is there anything else, Angela?" As he glides a hand through a few remaining strands near the front of his shiny head.

"Well er, yes sir, there are others who have applied."

"Okay, send their names to me Angela and I will see about getting them in."

They were so in awe that Mr. Turpin was probably laughing to himself.

"Angela, this is a fine group you have here; I am going to enjoy working with you. I know you have other things you want to discuss. Please do come again. Just check with my secretary as to my availability."

They walked out looking shocked and bewildered as if lightning had hit somebody, like Mr. Turpin. They were ready to steam in, but he calmly stepped aside and let them through. He was up to something they thought. They would have to wait and see though.

Whatever the reason for Mr. Turpin's easy nature, they were certain, it would surface sooner or later. Now was no time for them to get complacent. Their next move was to get the Affirmative Action Program up and running. This was of prime importance, because that program would affect the majority of the workers. Their quartet along with several other African-American corporate members met to draft a letter to Mr. Turpin, outlining their demands for such a program, and the time frame expected.

In the letter was an overview of what they felt the program would include; and stressed the importance of the program to the corporation. They did not want to get too wordy, but merely to provide Mr. Turpin with an agenda of their next discussion. It also asked for a particular meeting date the following month.

In the meanwhile, things had begun to happen. And as evidenced in their next newsletter; which was more explosive than the initial copy. Darryl's headlines simply read "TEN IN". And again a picture captured the front cover. Darryl's imagination was at its best; displaying Mr. Turpin, surrounded by the ten African-Americans accepted into the Management Training Program. Darryl's story was also befitting. He pointed out that the ninety-six year old corporation, could not have chosen a better corps of men and women to lead it into the twentieth-first century. There were two other women besides Angela.

Darryl praised Mr. Turpin by saying; "our president, Mr. Turpin is to be commended for the outstanding group he has chosen for this task." Darryl went on to say, "this group is paving the way for others to closely follow in its footsteps. The burden is upon their shoulders; but they are prepared for the challenge and will do well. They are familiar with the weight of the world and the sacrificing of time and energy. Their education totals one hundred seventy six years; and their work experience with this corporation adds another seventy nine years to the coffer. Their qualifications are indeed impressive; but what is most impressive, is their attitude and dedication to making the corporation better in terms of profitability, as well as image."

Darryl continued by saying, "we will hear more from the dynamic ten, as they vigorously swim upstream to the spawning grounds. Characters will be tested, spirits will be broken; but successes will be in abundance. Again our hope is in their strength; and their strength lies in the support we will give them on a daily basis. We must remember, if the rope breaks, the bucket of water falls helplessly back into the well. So let up push and pull our brothers and sisters, and keep this dynamic ten rope from unraveling." Darryl concluded by saying; "a personal note to you from the editor, we feel the weight the greatest, because you are standing on our shoulders."

Darryl was truly an inspiration to them all; not only the dynamic ten, he so professionally coined, but the entire African-American organization. They could not wait for the next edition. The newsletter was printed monthly. Darry_ Strawsby, who hailed from Detroit, was a recent accounting graduate from Texas Southern University. Angela agreed with Mr. Turpin, saying, "he truly missed his calling. But being prepared in business is a way of the world; and nothing will be lost toward any other endeavor."

Darryl's insight into the corporate structure and the issues they faced, far exceeded, any professional in its respective arena. It was this kind of talent that they were fighting for. People who, if given the chance would respond to any challenge. No one was more in tune with them than Darryl; as further evidenced by his poem.

WEIGHT OF THE WORLD

The weight of the world
Don't let it get you down
Just keep swimming upstream
You'll reach the spawning ground

Others will follow closely
Endure and forget the pain
You're in the race for the Race
Stay focused on your aim

Problems: Gigantic but bearable
Burdens; heavier than steel
Don't! Let weight of the world
Break your back or will

Look not for fame or glory
Though it might unfurl
Eat adversity, never succumbing
To the weight of the world

Talking about coping, Angela was doing just that, and seem-ingly getting respect from Turpin; however, it was very much suspect at this point. Trebor's attitude toward her boiled con-stantly when he found out she had been accepted into the Management Training Program. An annual review which came up within days of that announcement was her worse ever by Trebor. The evaluation was so bad, it looked as if Angela had done absolutely nothing. Trebor deliberately used her absence during the maternity leave, to low rate Angela in every category. When he showed it to her, it came by way of being tossed on her desk, with Trebor leaning through the door, saying; "here's your review, sign it and give it back to me sometimes today." Angela took one look at the funky review, giving her a measly three percent. If it had not been for the Management Training Program, she would have cursed him out and quit; and that was with her knowing what his snaky motive was. She smiled to herself saying; "oh, how Trebor would love that." So Angela simply wrote a nice note dis-agreeing with the evaluation, signed it, and politely took it to his office, delivering it to his scaly white hands. She even surprised herself with the calmness displayed when she looked Trebor square in his treacherous lizard-eyelid eyes saying, "Here is your evaluation!"

Within moments of doing so, Trebor was leaning through Angela's door again, throwing her quarterly itinerary onto her desk. The schedule did not take into consideration the Management Training Program; now giving her those good travel locations out of town, she had bitched to him about getting for months and months. As a matter of fact, practically the entire itin-erary was travel. Angela thought it ironic, she would get her ideal travel schedule and more at this particular time. She smiled and headed for Trebor's office.

"Trebor, I believe your schedule is a bit off; you might want to give these assignments to your boy Mike."

"I know how to make out my quarter itinerary Angela; it will stand as it is. If you have a problem with traveling, you can always apply for another job."

"Thanks Trebor for your advice, but you apparently forgot about the Management Training Program; that was my inference; it strictly says, we are to be made available inside the office."

"Like I said Angela, I am fully aware of how to run this department; it is my understanding, my workload takes precedent over anything else."

"That might be true Trebor, your understanding; I mean, but other departments give priority to the program; you might want to check it out. Mr. Turpin, I am told, take these programs pretty seriously."

Trebor heard it; it, was that superior authority hanging over him, his small puckered kiss-kiss Turpin-backside mouth sucked inward. The thought of seeing Angela escape a round of his punishment, Trebor's sharp pointed tongue flapped onto his bottom lip as the gust of disgusted air left his body. Trebor's face turned a shade of red resembling a Texas plum in July. Words appeared which he never intended for Angela to hear:

"That damn Turpin, that damn Turpin!"

Angela's face showed no expression, but her inside rocked with pleasure, as she returned to her office. She wanted to laugh and rejoice right there in his presence, but she knew that was only one battle, and besides, her fight was no longer with Trebor. Their African-American organization had elevated the battlefield to higher ground; not that they had defeated the Trebor's in their path, but their kind had been seriously wounded. Yet Angela knew how a vicious heart could attack or retaliate, when provoked; so from now on she would stay out of Trebor's way; After all, he was never really running anything anyway. He merely carried out, what was handed down. Angela wanted to echo Trebor's words of "that damn Turpin", but for an entirely different reason, because she knew he was up to something; she could feel it. The days to come would tell that story.

Victor always accused Angela of getting that wise old counsel from grandma, but now, he was correct. Well; she had invested a lot of dollars in this company's stock, pursuing the African-American plan, so her interest was entirely personal. Now the three of them talked of the moves to be made, but grandma and Victor both agreed; the organization headed by Angela was going in the right direction. In other words, their contribution was favorably advisory. Angela and her gang, the new kids on the block, had it going on.

Angela liked this cohesiveness, coming together as a family, she thought, to get things done. With grandmother and Victor lending their ears and a comment or two as counsel; Angela had all the support she needed. This dynamic ten as Darryl called them were the front runners for the African- American corporate group, and anything added to their input was a definite plus. Successful implementation of the management training program would set a precedent for corporate recognition of utilizing all its employees talents. A tested and proven commodity is essential in its contin-ued usage; and that was what they were faced with. It should not have been necessary, but that seems to be the way it is sometimes. Ability alone should have been the corporation's initiative to move forward with all its employees, but Angela's readings had told her "tain't so."

Personal job satisfaction no longer interested Angela; oh, it was important, only secondary though. Her thoughts had graduated to the masses of African-American employees, not getting their just due, being deprived of opportunities, others were automatically getting. She had come to realize, "hoping in one hand and wish-ing in the other hand", was never going to accomplish anything. And that is exactly what had happened prior to the start up of their organization. Angela had noted several highly qualified-highly educated Black employees with seniority at this company; and all were at the end of the line, position wise. She found, she was not the only African-American getting three percent increases and expected to be happy or be gone. The more she thought of how this corporation was treating its precious Black human resources, she became angrier and angrier; and that much more determined to have an immediate correction.

"It was senseless," Angela thought, "for a company to use a race of people, without, just rewards;" and then she thought, saying to herself; "hang on children, help is on the way, help is on the way; we gonna help ourselves this time." Angela also smiled to herself, but she knew, traveling this new road at this company would not be easy. Opposition as Victor had told her, had a way of raising its ugly head. That ugly head today was that of old man Turpin; several members of the group called him sly-master, because they sensed he was always up to something. In other words, he could not be trusted to carry out his promised part, without some type of deviation. The group promised to watch Turpin very closely to counter any of his negative moves.

CHAPTER THIRTY ONE

PREGNANT AGAIN AND MISSING OUT

Helen and Angela acted if though they were racing in the baby department. Soon after the first was born, they were pregnant again. Except this time, Helen was a few months ahead of Angela. And regardless what Angela might think, Helen and Victor agreed on having this child. At least the final verdict was by mutual assent. Helen convinced Victor that a childhood environment was better, if there were two instead of one. He could not argue with that because he was in that category twice; once as a child and once as a parent. So it did not take a lot of coercing.

A sudden throwback to Victor's childhood days quickly sealed their positions as one. The most problems Victor faced was of loneliness. As long as he was in school with others, he functioned normally. Home. Going home was the most difficult part of his day. It had nothing to do with love for his parents; he just did not have anyone to play with. Oh, parents are fun, but they are not the same as a brother or sister or another child. You can argue, even fight, or spit on another child; but a parent, that is a no-no. So you see, the relationship is different, which calculates into less fun—your way.

So home presented being alone; playing with all the toys, any child would want. A missing playmate meant making-believe a lot;

talking to yourself; pretending to be two people, oftentimes more. Conversations went on like—it's your move; that's yours; give it back. "Mom and Dad," Victor thought, "had each other; and him, he had nobody." Alone. Soaking in the solitude of one's self. Being there—making one hand be the good guy and the other hand, the villain. Transposing a grumpy voice to the bad guy before returning to the all–American hero. A play of many characters and one actor is what Victor's childhood life was about.

Anyway, Victor had thought about it all night, Carolyn's situation was not getting better, but worse since she moved out. He had hoped the revealing of her parents problem to him would solve the alcohol intake. So during the night, as no sleep was going on, he thought; "why don't I ask Carolyn to move back in, like before, when Helen and Angela were pregnant." Victor was thinking about helping Carolyn, its true, but this was more a selfish move on his part; sexually, his body was suffering to the point, where he sometimes could not think straight. Being around that many gorgeous women without enjoying their greatest treasures could have an adverse effect on any man, no doubt. Large bags had begun to show under his eyes as noticed by Tiffani.

"Victor, that is your third cup of coffee, and look at the bags under those eyes; are you okay?"

"I certainly hope so, but who knows; I did not sleep at all last night Tiffani."

"Now, now, now, what is the matter with poor Victor; too many babies, I suppose." Smiling.

"Well, maybe, but I was thinking about Carolyn; she is not doing any better, you know. So I am going to ask her to move back in, so I can look after her again; she was doing quite well before. It is too bad too; I hate to see anyone destroy themselves, when obviously I could help."

"Victor, that is a great idea; apparently Carolyn is a good housekeeper, huh?"

"Well——yeah——she is not bad Tiffani, but her health is much more important; could you ask her to come down for a few minutes, when she's available."

"Okay Victor, I will call Carolyn right now."

"Victor, this is your lucky moment, Carolyn says, she will be here in a minute. Man, you sure have a sparkling effect on Carolyn, her voice perked up when I mentioned your name."

"You might say Tiffani, we understand each other, a bit more."

"Hi Tiff, good morning Victor!"

"Hello Carolyn, my, that was quick; are you sure you were not standing outside the door."

"Girl—Tiff, you are so crazy—I told you one minute—looks like I made it, huh!"

"Please hold my calls Tiffani!"

Even Victor was smiling as he closed his office door, behind the smiling Carolyn. She was looking good as usual, wearing an unusual long pleated black and gray skirt, made out of some kind of soft expensive fabric.

"Victor, you need to do something about those bags under your eyes, you look terrible; burning a little midnight oil for the company, I suppose."

"Well, that too, Carolyn."

"That too; sounds like you have a multitude of things going on Victor; is there anything I can help you with?"

"I hate to impose on you Carolyn—well, you know my situation; the girls are pregnant again——I was wondering if you could move back in."

"Oh—no—not on your life Victor—the inconvenience was just not worth it. And also, it seems like I stayed tired all the time; probably too much of your good loving, huh. Don't look so sad Victor; if it's more loving you want, you can always move in with me."

"Well, I thought of that Carolyn, but I would never have asked."

"There is no problem, I would love it; we could even walk to work together; you could use the extra exercise."

"Are you sure it is okay Carolyn?"

"Victor, I hate to say this, but you love me so much better when we are not rushed; and at my place, you will never be rushed. My body is already getting tingly for tonight Victor!"

"Carolyn, I was sort of thinking about tomorrow!"

"Tomorrow is fine too Victor, you can handle me back to back. A deal is a deal, Victor; you want more loving, you will get more loving, but I expect you tonight or the deal's off. Look at it like this Victor, you are real hungry, but me, I am starving for you—so I will see you tonight Big Boy. By the way, you can move in anytime, I do not care, but tonight—I need you; I was going to tell you to come by anyway. You have really made me feel good. And do not worry with ringing the door bell, use your key and come on in, I will be waiting."

Victor could only say okay, a weak one at that, but it did not matter to Carolyn, she was strolling out the door anyway. Carolyn indeed, had her claws in Victor, even when she did not touch him.

"Thanks for the call Tiff; that boss of yours is so sweet; see ya girl!"

It appeared as if Victor had not drank any of his coffee; at least the cup was still full, as he poured it out in the small sink.

"Did I make a bad batch of coffee Victor?"

"No Tiffani, it must have gotten cold, while I was talking to Carolyn. You know how she takes my attention away from everything."

"Yeah, everything but her Victor; well, did you get your housekeeper back? Carolyn looked awfully happy when she left; even said I had a sweet boss. What happened Victor?"

"Promise you wont laugh Tiffani! No I did not get my housekeeper back; I am sort of the new housekeeper."

"In your own home Victor, you were already that."

"Well, the rules reversed a little Tiffani; I am sort of taking up a new residence."

"Victor, don't tell me that; do you mean, you will be staying with Carolyn—at her house—for the next nine months?"

"It will not be quite that long Tiffani."

"Seven, eight, nine, what is the difference Victor; the point is, you will be living with Carolyn. Man, she really got a hold on you; and you say she needs help; I believe you might be the one needing the help. You told me Carolyn did not do cooking, but she is obviously feeding you something that must be pretty darn good. So when do you move in?"

"This evening—I mean, I'm going by there this evening. Who knows when I'll move in Tiffani."

"If I am correct Victor, Carolyn will probably let you know, if you do not do it soon. Victor, that is not even funny, but I certainly admire Carolyn, because she got, what I wish I had."

"And what is that Tiffani?"

"The ability to make a man do anything she wants; I envy that girl for that Victor."

Tiffani's mind suddenly had strayed off, onto Ralph and what she needed to do to get him to jumping like Victor. She was still trying to figure out how to make Ralph touch her affectionately, without forcing him. Tiffani was desperate enough now, that she had planned on sitting in his face the next session, if she could get him in a compromising position. Whatever; she knew she would have to be smooth about it and quick about it; almost to the point of doing something before she stripped. Because Ralph always ducked out on her, soon after she removed that bottom piece. She needed something by this evening too. Maybe, she thought, Victor could help her out. After all, Carolyn was making him do anything she wanted.

"What would I have to do Victor?"

"To do anything you want Tiffani; this is a loaded question. The answer though lies in the fellow himself, because guys respond to different things. Without getting specific Tiffani, you need to be aware of his likes and dislikes."

"Okay Victor, could I force a guy to do something, he does not like?"

"Oh, I suppose so, but generally you'll get no reaction or no satisfaction; if you follow me Tiffani."

"I follow you; thanks Victor, you have been a big help. Sorry I was fussy about Carolyn; I suppose down deep, I am a bit jealous, at how she seems to get whatever she wants."

"Well Tiffani, why don't you ask her how she does it, or what you want to know?"

"Oh—no—I could never do that Victor. Thanks, I believe you have told me enough to get me through the day."

"Another thing Tiffani; good communication helps!"

"Okay, thanks again Victor."

"Good communication," thought Tiffani, "that is out; Ralph and I only talk about investments; never none of that other stuff." "Maybe, that is it," she said softly, as she sat down at her desk.

"Tiffani, I will not be back after lunch; there are some things I need to do. If you need me after two o'clock, you can reach me at Carolyn's place."

"Okay, see you tomorrow Victor; and have a good evening." Smiling.

"Thanks Tiffani, I hope your plan works out." Smiling back.

Tiffani sat at her desk, making scratches on her note pad, saying "good communication—good communication." She had tried body communication and that did not work; "verbal communication might work," she thought, but said, "I doubt it; that Ralph needs some body communication put on him in the most forceful manner, and sitting in his face is the way to do it." That was her conclusion, but how would she do it, was the question. The evening went by quickly, and before Tiffani knew it, Ralph was there; and they were reviewing her portfolio, but in the middle of all that financial verbiage, Tiffani broke their unwritten rule saying:

"Ralph, do you like sex?"

He looked at her strangely, before answering, "yes". Then he gave her those same type of strings she had modeled the last time; this time they were a bright blue. Tiffani felt tingly as soon as she saw them, for it reminded her of how she climaxed the last session, from all of her own touches. "This time," she said to herself, "it will be different; Ralph will do the touches." Tiffani immediately stripped, removing that business attire as fast as she could. She took the two strings from Ralph, saying:

"Let me shower, I will be right out; if you like sex Ralph, you will love me when you respond to a wish of mine. Get your taste buds ready, Big Investment Portfolio Man, because you are going to make the biggest deposit so far, in my portfolio." Smiling.

Ralph just looked at Tiffani intently as she headed for her bathroom. Tiffani's nude body was smooth and exciting looking, but she was more exciting as she put an extra rush on to get through that shower in record time, She was so excited about finally getting Ralph to agree to exploring her furry furrow, that she forgot to put the strings on; Tiffani could feel Ralph's tastetester inside of her, and she rushed out to make him get right to it. But guess what, Ralph was gone. This was Tiffani's worse day of her life; not even self gratification would make her feel good today; she needed a man bad. Tiffani screamed out real loud saying:

"I need you Ralph—I need you real bad!"

And while Tiffani was having her problems screaming and later, lying awake because of her horniness, Victor had made his way into Carolyn's place, preparing a sumptuous meal for her arrival. His evening was smooth and enjoyable as he anticipated. Victor was doing what any friend would do to help a friend through the tough times; Well, so what, if he was servicing her as Tiffani labeled it, and getting a little servicing of his own. His action was proper and appropriate, if it worked and it appeared to be working, in his opinion. Victor looked forward to Carolyn's lovemaking surprises, and as expected, after the delicious evening's meal, Carolyn cornered him in the bathroom, following their shower; making him sit upon the commode, while she stood straddle him. Carolyn's large long thighs streamed upward, touching each side of Victor's cheeks. The excitement Carolyn generated in Victor, was really what he loved the most in their relationship; in other words, she kept him on edge; which exactly is where he is right now. The front edge of Victor's tastetester was loosely pressing and roving against the upper part of Carolyn's woolly center, massaging her clit as he often did. Victor held onto her gaping thighs until Carolyn filled his squashed cheeks with more than promises, and lowered herself where they both felt his bigness inside of her woolly center. Carolyn sat atop Victor comfortably, taking everything he had to offer, including his affectionate kisses upon her nipples as he held her breast. Needless to say, there was no lying awake, when Carolyn and Victor was done.

Tiffani heard Victor coming down the hall whistling, and she knew, his night had been wonderful.

"Well, I see the housekeeper is awfully cheerful this morning."

"Good morning Tiffani, how are we feeling this morning?"

"One part of "we" is feeling terrible and miserable while the other part is feeling deserted Victor."

"Huh, sounds like someone ran out on you Tiffani; anything you'd like to talk about?"

"Not today Victor, maybe tomorrow; I am just not in the mood for addressing anything of that nature today. I am trying to let my body settle back into its normal self. I take it, that Carolyn is doing okay."

"Uh huh, doing fine; Carolyn is fine as ever Tiffani."

"Victor, I am talking about her drinking problems, you know."

"Well, you know, its hard for me to say; seems okay to me though—doesn't drink when I'm around."

"That is good Victor, so you two have solved each others problem."

"I would like to think that we are both pleased Tiffani."

"Well Victor, while you are still excited, Angela called; she wants you to come by this evening."

CHAPTER THIRTY TWO

SURPRISES

Victor had asked Angela to keep him informed of her job situation, but she had not mentioned anything in a while. He never really liked to ask, for fear of agitating her more. This evening; however, Angela was in a very talkative mood. No sooner than Angela opened the door, her plump pregnant jaws were moving on a number of surprised developments in her workplace which had upset her. Why she waited until these things piled up on her before talking about them, Victor could never quite figure out. Anyway, Angela expected Victor to be all ears as she poured her heart out. Unfilled promises and agreements causes surprises. That is what happened to the management trainees. Angela expresses her concern to Victor:

"Victor, we entered the program with a one year training format. Now we are being informed the program is to last for two years. This means our wages will be frozen for that period of time and our advancement up the corporate ladder will be temporarily halted. It appears that our road to the breaking of the glass ceiling is taking a slow route. A route the dynamic ten did not particularly like."

"Mr. Turley it appears has thrown us another curve Victor. Here is the president of a major corporation, who in our opinion lacks integrity. And not only that, this man can not be trusted. His indecisiveness we found though, always pertained to the potent few of us who desired to be different, for our legitimate rights. Yes, it always pertained to employees of a different color; which incidently was the only difference. Our group met to determine what could be done and decide the appropriate action necessary. Then we met with Mr. Turley."

"Well, what was Turley's position on this issue, Angela."

"When we approached Mr. Turley on this issue, Victor, his explanation was; he did it for our benefit, because he did not want us to fail. Mr. Turley further stated that because of our backgrounds, it would probably take longer for us to grasp the management concept. He assured us the "small delay" did not reflect our ability to learn what was before us, but had more to do with inherent intangibles prior to entering the program. Intangibles, in our opinion, that existed only under terrible-Turley's turban."

"Angela, this Turley fellow sounds like he's full of a bunch of bull to me."

"Mr. Turley's explanation sounded like double talk to us too Victor. My interpretation to that garbage was; we were just some, dumb slow learning Black people. Why all of a sudden was this criteria being used. It had never been used with the white management trainees. And on top of that, the program was being temporarily suspended after our class. Prior to this point, it had been an on-going program. Talking about a setback for Blacks; Mr. Turley has done a job on us. The other qualified Blacks in the company waiting their turn have been dealt a devastating blow. We all felt betrayed, but not helpless. Thanks to you Victor warning us of rough and disturbing rides. Your words, though comforting, are still not enough to lift the bitterness I feel."

"Just don't forget your goals Angela."

"Goal Setting! Everything; everyone of us had in our minds and hearts Victor about goals in this corporation have been tested. Since being admitted to the Management Training Program, we have talked and developed plans where we wanted, or at least expected to be within a few years. Some had plans of staying with the corporation; others would move on and advance with different companies; while others expressed interest in becoming entrepreneurs, to work for themselves. Interestingly enough, none of the group felt their plans had been totally deterred by old Turley's unfavorable move. We still have the confidence that despite the counter-dealing, we will be the ultimate victor to the perfidious Mr. Turley. Here is a copy of our last newsletter Victor."

Darryl's headlines this time carried no picture; at least not of an individual or group. The picture was of a large question mark (?), and had in bold print, over it the word - WHEN. The size of the question mark itself proposed a question. Darryl opened his story with; "Madam President - do we have two years? Mr. Turley—— do you have two years? We know from past experience the formula 2x2x2 = infinity. So far that formula has not worked."

"The answer always comes out the same—wait a little while longer. Several days ago, when this news letter reported the acceptance of Angela and the others into the management training program; there was joy and job satisfaction for every African-American here. There was a feeling of accomplishment among us all. Our Richter scale hit a hundred."

"Now the reverse is true. The consensus among the African-American employees is clear, our current corporation officers cannot be trusted. It is not that they do not know what they are doing. And it is obvious, they are aware of our knowledge, of their stalling tactics. The question then is, why do they keep doing it? The consensus again among the African-American employees is clear, they have the power and they are utilizing it to their advantage. The final consensus among the employees, there is no guilty feeling among the corporate officials for discriminating against the Black workers. We had hoped to never experience the fact that some people have no conscience."

"In conclusion when will the WHEN——?——be answered equitably. The dynamic ten; however, is tough and the African-American organization is strong, and feel, they will bounce back."

"Well Angela, it seems if though you guys still have it together."

"Darryl is correct, the organization is strong. And thanks to Mr. Turley, we are getting stronger. He has become a galvanizing force for us again. Everyone recalled how he betrayed us on the cafeteria, promised us for our first organizational meeting. We would not forget his negative actions; they are making us stronger and binding us closer together. It will be difficult to do as you suggested Victor and not be revengeful. Your point was to stay the course and not forget our main purpose. Those points will not be forgotten in our next meeting."

"The calmer the better Angela."

"Anyway Victor, the group is constantly meeting now to determine new strategy from a position of strength. We have a number of options available; thanks to our being together. We told ourselves, it is old Turley against us ten, and that makes him in the minority and outnumbered. In our gatherings we voiced positive approaches to offset the negativism from our mutual antagonist. It has now come to the point that we, the dynamic ten will have to answer the WHEN question for ourselves; except it's WHEN are we going to get off our cans and really step forward."

"So what is your next likely move Angela?"

"Well Victor, since Mr. Turley was not addressing our needs, we needed a stronger voice to speak for us. We decided we could speak for us better than anyone—especially Mr. Turley who gave the white agenda priority. The decision on having all members to purchase company stock is about to pay off. We have as you are aware, amassed a substantial block of stock. And a surprise of all surprises for Mr. Turley, was when he found out, I had been elected to the corporate Board of Directors."

"I imagined that did take him by surprise Angela."

"With ownership rights Victor, we now have leverage and is using it. All of a sudden, I have become that new voice. Our purpose with this new voice is to show that the corporation would be more efficient with Black people included in management positions; and more effectively with a corporate affirmative action program in place."

"This seems to be going better than anticipated, huh, Angela."

"Hold on Victor, like any honeymoon, they are short-lived, and I do not expect anything different in my marriage to the lilly-white male dominated boardroom. The first meeting was cordial and informal with everyone exchanging pleasantries. I was congratulated as adding three first to the board. Not only am I the first Black and first female; I am also the youngest person to ever serve on the board. These first presented a challenge to me, because history had recorded a number of First and Last among us. I know there will be hard work ahead to prevent the Last and add to the First. There will be no time for me to rest on my laurels; my obligation to myself and the group has excelled that of a mere organization president."

"You are so right Angela."

"Check this out Victor; part of my introductory remarks went something like this; "while I do not wish to always appear feminist or pro-black, I will address those concerns." Those remarks popped opened no eyelids or brought no squirms in anyone's seat; but afterwards, the chairman, Jason Thorndew, questioned if there was an immediate urgency. Thorndew was a tall willowy fellow with green eyes. Along with his rustic complexion, he had no other captivating features. Here he stood towering over me with a concerned look on his face. The gate was open, and there was nothing to do, but express my feeling on the cancellation of the management training program and my disappointment with having to remain in the program for two years. Both grievances came as a surprise to Chairman Thorndew, who could not remember any recent changes by the board. "It could have been," he said; "I was not present at that meeting; I want to thank you for speaking your heart today."

"Seems like you might have found a listening set of ears huh, Angela."

"I sure did Victor, the following week, Mr. Turley informed me, the program had been restored to its originality. That gave me a sense of accomplishment. My voice—a conversation in the lobby—was already paying dividends. Mr. Turley's grin and stare said it all "we would have gotten away with it, if it had not been for you—you dirty black bitch." I could feel those words ripping through my body. I could see the pain in his silence darting within his soul."

"He caused his own pain, Angela."

"Funny Victor, but still sad when you think about it. Here was a program set up to maintain the operating efficiency of the corporation, being sabotaged by Mr. Turley and his racist buddies. A program mutilated and discontinued because of a few Black folks

wanting the same thing as the white employees. A program wiped
out because Mr. Turley felt it was not designed for the Black people of the World; and was willing to sacrifice his own people and
corporation if necessary. Though it hurts me, it's painless if I can
bring more pain on the downtrodden; seems to have been treachery—Turley's thinking."

"Now Angela, you understand more of what is going on in the
real-real world."

"So true Victor, we are talking about upward mobility and the
uplifting of a people. The irony of this situation is; you must first
get hired to even have a shot at the management training program. Compared to the total work force, our numbers are scarce.
So we have a dual problem. You cannot move up if you cannot
move in. That is why, getting the affirmative action program is so
important to us. Both programs are important; we cannot sacrifice
one for the other. No either—or will suffice this time around."

"I am real proud of you Angela."

"Thank you Victor for all of your support."

Angela knew where she was headed with this "new day", she
often spoke of. Her education had prepared her on the mechanics
of a corporation. In others, the system works for you, if you're in
the system. Angela had purchased an additional fifty thousand
shares of corporate stock in contemplation of her "new day" theory. Angela's short business career and experience with her racist
boss, Larry Trebor, and Mr. Turley has taught her; Black people
were not given a carte blanche into the system. Neither knew it,
but Angela was better off financially than either of them who was
discriminating against her.

It did not matter though, how much money, education, or experience you had; if your skin was black or you were identified with
the Black race; you simply were unwelcomed. Victor's introduc-
tion of Black heritage to Angela was changing her frustrations into
positive energy. Knowing about her people had brought with it,
the understanding of what the white man was continuing to do.
He still wanted servants, and wanted blacks to forever be inferior
to him. That is why blacks were continuing to get the lowest paying and powerless jobs. Nowhere did ability of a people or
fairness come in, to equate the scale.

Angela had made giant strives in such a short time. The new understanding of the struggles of her race had again made her live up to her mother's characterization—"the child is one track-minded." Angela had become unselfish in her struggle. She wanted to help uplift the whole Black race because, her words were; "if our Black race don't get respect, I'll never get respect as an individual—no matter my status." Angela knew she was in a unique position; she already had the financial resources, and realized, someone like her, had to take the challenge. The "new day" theory channeled resources where they did the most good——be it people voices or money.

Mr. Turley congratulated Angela on becoming a board member with parting words—"that organization of yours is doing a fine job." Mr. Turley was right, they had done a fine job. A fine job of pooling what little resources they had to gain leverage. Leverage that got them a new voice and a seat in the boardroom to make a showing. Angela thought; "A showing which says—I might not win, but I will be there to compete. In sports, you forfeit the game, if you do not show up—an automatic loss. We have been forfeiting our chances all these years because we either could not or did not get it together. This is a new day, and covert racism makes it mandatory, we use the leverage at our disposal. We will have to continue "doing a fine job"—whatever that connotes."

Though, there had been no confrontational meeting with Mr. Turley; they had grown tired of him leaning back in his high-backed chair, voicing his traditional "let me check into that." Then later, preceding with, it not being in the best interest of the company or presenting some of his favorite racist stalling tactics.Oh, he was always very nice in manner to them; almost to the point of being apologetic. But the result was always the same, he gave a little and held back a lot.

Holding back and taking back the gains they had made, was all too familiar. Angela's readings had cited many cases of that among her forefathers. Victor had spoken of it among his experience. Angela thought; "And in my generation it continues to happen. It appears that Ancestral Racism will never end. And it is all because of our Dark Skin. My message to the poor souls is clear:"

DON'T BE AFRAID OF DARK SKIN

My dark skin won't hurt you
Think of it as a tan
Remember how you bake in the sun
And come out looking so grand

Mine last a while longer
No need for the heating rays
...born this way you know
It'l last all my days

It won't rub off on you
No matter what the blend
We're just human beings
With beautiful darker skin

CHAPTER THIRTY THREE

FRIENDS CHATTING

For two who had become pretty good friends and who had so much in common, their time together in the last fourteen months had been limited to seeing each other at sorority meetings only. Oh, Carolyn and Helen did talk on the phone, but even that communication was down to no more than a call every two months or so. Having Victor as a common thread between them caused no problem, because initially, it was a competitive fun thing to seduce this fine man and have him provide them with their sexual needs. There was no jealousy among them as to who received the most, during those labors of lovemaking, and the same is pretty much true today. There is a bit of teasing which goes on between them, but animosity itself never surfaces. Today's rare meeting, as usual, found both of them in a pleasant mood, especially with Helen's pregnancy obviously showing.

"Helen, it is about time you came out of your cocoon and mingled with the regulars."

"I haven't been hiding Carolyn; girl, you wouldn't believe how busy I've been."

"That's what you say girl; look at that stomach of yours Helen; yeah, I'd say you have been plenty busy."

"You so crazy, I told you about this Carolyn."

"I know honey, but I just hadn't seen you; it becomes you Helen; you look so good. Somebody is taking care of you real good——I see."

"Uh huh, you know it too; you look real good too Carolyn. I see, having our friend around is not hurting you none."

"Girl, you are so right, I wouldn't take nothing for that man; praise the Lord I can't have another one of those things though. And you know Helen, if I could, I would, just to compete with you, chile."

"And I know you're not joking either girl, but Carolyn I wouldn't wish this on anybody; two times is enough for anybody."

"I heard that, girl, but with Victor being so fine, I'd have his baby for the hell of it, Helen. I seriously thought one time about getting these tubes untied; but I know down deep, I would only be trying to replace Sharonda, and that wouldn't work."

"Yeah, I'd say, leave well enough alone, honey. If I'm half as fine as you Carolyn after this baby, it is going to take an act of God to get me in this condition again. We both agreed, it was better for us as well as the first child to have another one."

"Girl, all you have to do is exercise a little bit, after you drop that load, and you'll be back fine before you know it. And with all that volunteer work you do, and that constant moving around, you should have no problem whatsoever. The thing really, Helen, is not to eat like a horse while you're pregnant; cause I know you're not getting very much exercise now."

"Exercise of any kind is the last thing I want to think about Carolyn. And you already know what I feel about sex; that is so crazy, but I just do not want any."

"Yeah chile; and I still don't understand that. When I was pregnant Helen, I screwed right up to the day. For some reason, those rascals moving around in me, made me want to do it honey."

"You just love to screw anyway Carolyn; has Victor moving in with you, helped any?"

"If you mean, the drinking Helen, it is better, but I still have my days. I really want to thank you Helen, because I know you are doing this for me; I have never met anyone as unselfish as you are."

Their sentimentality got the best of them, and they both

hugged each other and shed a tear; embracing, as two people who share so much in common should.

"You would do the same for me Carolyn; sisters as well as friends should help each other. You are really a good person yourself. And anyway, look at it like this, you are keeping my man in good shape for me."

"Yeah, I guess you are right Helen, because Angela does not want to do anything either—you two might be biological sisters and not even know it. Either that or you are afraid Victor will hurt the baby with all that bigness."

"That might be it Carolyn; all I can say is, you had better have your fun while you can; these several months will be over before you know it."

"I am definitely taking advantage of this opportunity Helen; there is not an inch of space in my place where Victor has not attempted to seduce me; somebody must have spoiled him."

"Knowing you Carolyn, I am sure it is the other way around."

"Yeah, so true, Helen, that man brings out the best in me; speaking of the best, how is that boy of yours doing?"

"I am glad you asked Carolyn; just happen to have a few pictures to show you, since you received the historical one."

"Uh huh, Helen, just happen to have a whole photo album, I bet."

"It is small, Carolyn!"

"I was just kidding Helen, but you really have a whole album."

"Well, it is my first child, you know, Carolyn; with the next one, I will have mellowed somewhat."

"Helen, he is far more handsome than that first picture I got; you must give me some of these. Gree is such a darling boy; it is too bad my girl is older or I would turn her on to this fine young stud to be; probably another Victor in the flesh. And that name, I meant to ask, where did you find that neat name?"

"Oh it is just a family name, I will tell you about it sometimes Carolyn; here, you can have these four pictures, they were taken last week."

"Last week, hmmm, aren't you something Helen, probably got some more on the way for this week, no doubt."

"How did you guess Carolyn?"

"It was a real wild guess; definitely a shot in the dark, Helen. I do not blame you though. When you get squared away this next time; I am going to start visiting you and keeping the kids, if that is okay with you."

"That is the best news I have heard all year, Carolyn; see, I told you; you are a good person."

"And while I am thinking about it Helen, how about taking a short three day cruise with me after the baby gets here? I mean, as soon as you get on your feet and all."

"That sounds wonderful, Victor can keep the children; I will need a short break before really resuming my hectic schedule. Just make sure the trip is no longer than three days Carolyn."

"Also, before we go, Helen, I am going to exercise with you, to help you get fine again, because I know Victor does not want a big fat slob around him."

"You are right Carolyn, but he would never admit it if I was. Of course, you can look at the women in his life; I understand, none of them are fat."

"You mean, none of us are fat, don't you Helen?"

"Uh huh, I had already included myself Carolyn. Maybe, you could help me work off those last ten extra pounds from Gree's birth; I would hate to think about doubling that, this time around. Victor or no Victor, that would be unacceptable to me. The bikini, I wore on the cruise with Victor is going to be my measuring stick."

"Helen, you are more serious than I thought you were; before both babies, huh."

"Well Carolyn, I have found, that is the only way to accomplish anything; get serious about it. Besides, my children deserve a fine—good looking moms around them. And let's face it Carolyn, I have to get serious just to keep up with you; I have always admired your body; you are so well proportioned. In other words, you are so fine; I really do envy you. The way you walk and carry yourself; strolling along, almost like you are gliding. One day, and I should not tell you, I even watched myself walk, in the mirror, to try and get that smooth stroll of yours down."

"Thanks very much Helen, you do not know how good that makes me feel, coming from you. Victor thinks, its my height; and that is probably close to the truth. To be honest, it has not always been this way; having a long tall lanky body that would glide. In elementary school, my teachers stayed on me all the time. They said such things as; walk tall Carolyn, straighten up Carolyn, walk with pride Carolyn, raise your head up Carolyn, shorten your steps Carolyn, walk like you are somebody Carolyn, and so many others. The one that I will never forget was told to me by my sixth grade teacher, Mrs. Helen Van Potter; even got your name Helen. Anyway, she told me, "God did not make trees tall, so they could bend over all the time; be proud, stand tall like the trees. God blessed you with height, be proud of it." So by the time I got to high school, I was one proud, tall, strolling sister, and have been that way every since. And believe me, even that has caused me some problems, but it was more from the attention I got from men, which I have always loved and quite frankly been able to handle. Even when the attention contributed to my getting pregnant in high school, I thought I was in control. Living through that ordeal was not easy, but I made it, at least I thought I had, until Sharonda's death. But now Helen, I know, that was my worse— mistake—"

"Now, now Carolyn, its okay to cry, we all make mistakes."

Helen and Carolyn are embraced again while a tear is again being shed. Carolyn is thinking of Sharonda, the daughter she can no longer feel, other than within her heart.

"I'm sorry Helen, but thanks for being here; you are truly the best friend I have in the world."

Before the day was over, the two had indeed reaffirmed their genuine friendship and mutual admiration for the other. There is nothing compulsory in life that says such has to be done, however, after months and months of abstinence, it certainly warms the heart to do so.

CHAPTER THIRTY FOUR

THE FAMILIES GROW

Why they really wanted the babies back-to-back was beyond Victor. Angela never mentioned anything about wanting another child; she just got pregnant and informed him afterward. "Some how, deep within," Victor thought, "I don't think either of them cared much of what I thought." Of course neither would ever admit it. They had a carbon copy of the first pregnancy. Helen had another boy and Angela had another girl. No one has to tell you, they were happy; but disappointed, because each wanted the opposite. Now the back-to-back pregnancies became somewhat clearer.

Victor's association with women has increased his knowledge of them to the extent, whereby they command his deepest respect. It is not that he did not respect them before, because he respects all individuals. The most interesting fact about women, he found, was their unyielding position. A position, without a doubt, is innate. There is just no other way to explain it. When they get something in their mind, they will stop at nothing until it is attempted, accomplished, or both. And in every case, they can give you a reason, why it has to be a certain thing or certain way. Now, here Victor was in the midst of a nursery, with two unyielding women. Both knew what they wanted, and was obsessed into an uncompromising state.

All in all, it was working out pretty good. The second baby in each case was getting some hand-me-downs. Not that they needed it, because Stacy, Grandma, and host of others were surprising them with something for them each week. And speaking of surprises, Angela sprang one on Victor, by naming the baby girl, Victoria, after him. That was quite an honor; and of course he was all smiles. Victoria looked like him; so that was very much appropriate. But she too, like the first baby, as well as Grandma and Mama Angela, had those shiny marble black eyes.

Eyes so piercing, yet so warm and melting, when coupled with a giggle and her genuine friendly smiles. Hopefully friendly, because grandma and Angela had some serious smiles that made those sharp black eyes cut right through you. You felt like a pin cushion with thousands of tiny stings biting and penetrating your skin. Either way, the shiny black balls had a conquering effect upon you. Victor had now come to the conclusion, this family had a patent on those eyes. He wondered, for how many generations could a birthmark continue. Stacy had no glaring marks of either himself or Samantha. Or is it that eyes of a striking nature always draws clearer attention.

There was one thing Victor knew, but would never admit to anyone; sweet Victoria was his favorite. It was the vibes he felt, when their eyes met. And early on, she gripped his fingers with her tiny hands. It was love at first sight. He felt the same with Stacy, but she was a first and only child, so he suppose that was different. Victoria made those burbling sounds, when he came around. It was like she was trying to tell Victor something. Angela too, had noted that she acted differently in his presence. Angela stated, "the exciting and comforting effect you have upon Victoria really makes me feel wonderful."

I suppose there are times in everyone's life, where they feel important. Well, that is the way Victoria had Victor feeling these days. Really useful, like he was the key to the door; or the last piece to the puzzle; or even greater, the only star in the Universe. Victor's imagination grows widest, when it comes to Victoria. He envisioned her telling him; she was the luckiest person in the world, and she was going to share all that luck with him. Victoria was the only child that made those burbling sounds, early on, looked at Victor assuredly and fell asleep in his arms. Needless to say, his life was complete.

Often times, Victor could not help but think of the reverse feelings, Carolyn was going through in the loss of her daughter, Sharonda. A child departs; a child is born; you can never equate the two. It will never be a fair exchange. Yet comparisons can be made, and justifications may be tolerated; but the gain/loss theory still creates a vacuum in the heart of the loser. No one knows more than Carolyn or Victor, though only partially, for having to see her go through such misery. The consoling nights spent there has given him new meaning to the word life. Life at times can be so complicated and mystified. We can put up a shield; but it will not guard us against the tragedies of death, nor will it stop nature from creating another beautiful flower, a singing bird or a burbling child.

WE MUST GO ON

A child is lost, a child is born
It leaves us sad or beaming
Either way, we must go on
For life, has a brand new meaning

Helen had some unexpected guest during this time; Hazel Gree and Ethyl Harre. The two sisters who had raised the orphaned Helen, surprised her with all kinds of gifts.These women were her only family besides Victor and the boys. There had been numerous phone calls from them since the first boy was born. Both women were of a gentle nature and pretty much seasoned in the winter, in terms of age. Helen had spoken of them often, so it is not like Victor was meeting strangers. They thought the sun set on Helen, and hung around for the greater portion of the month.

You see, the two boys were named after the two sisters; taking their last name and carving a first name for the boys. Their first son Gree, looked neither like Victor nor Helen, but exactly like Hazel. So to be named after Hazel was very appropriate. Victor did not know if he believed as Ethyl, that Hazel marked the child during Helen's pregnancy. It was however, one of her superstitions that merited some credit, because Gree had all of Hazel's facial features; even down to that coy grin of hers. Both Victor and Helen were dark, and the baby was a high "yaller", just like Hazel. Victor was pleased to see the likeness, because to be honest, he had been worried about that boy.

Harre, the second boy did not look like Ethyl, but to give honor to the people Helen, so dearly loved, it was only fitting. He looked exactly like Helen, but Victor was sure the both of them would have all his good traits. He thought he had better get that in before all the credit was passed out. The boys were as handsome as the girls were beautiful. They were also a handful of joy. And Hazel and Ethyl had the bundles of joy in their hands all the time during their stay.

They washed and pampered the boys and let them want for nothing. The boys were never wet and always full of food and care. Hazel and Ethel hummed the days through, talking that baby language; and passed the boys from one to the other. The boys were theirs for now and were treated as such. Two elderly women who had not forgotten the maternal instincts; busily and routinely doing the baby chores with a satisfying approach. One could tell from their expression, these moments reminded them of Helen's youth or the raising of their own children from years long since passed.

Helen let them do whatever they wanted; which meant she never got a chance to care for the boys during their stay. The three of them were constant chatter. You could hardly get a word in edge ways; so Victor limited his time in that arena. It's not like, he was going to be missed. The boys were getting their share of love from Hazel and Ethyl. Poetic justice reads as follows:

TWO WOMEN LOVING TWO BOYS

A reunion of sort, is what it was
Two more faces, two more new stars
There's no way, the boys could know
Two were strangers; it did not show

Each boy handled, with greatest of ease
No want of a kiss, neither a squeeze
Passed around constantly from arm to arm
Each woman extended that southern charm

One would think; the boys were theirs
With such motherly love and motherly cares
The real mother had, no hand at all
These two women, were having a ball

Boys were never wet or ever cried
Most unusual indeed; cannot be denied
Never ever hungry, eating right on time
Best love and care you'd ever find

Mother took a break, without a worry
Four loving other hands, never in a hurry
What would she do, when they left
The boys once again, all to herself

Oh well, lets enjoy, long as I can
It is so peaceful, this is so grand
In a way, I wish, they'd never leave
For bottles, pampers, I'll have to retrieve

One is one year, the other one month
From the two elderly women, never a grunt
Knew what to do, and when to do it
No baby tantrums, no woman fit

Love is easy, when it is done right
Children love it too, without a fight
No TV, toys and dolls, to entertain
Love and more love, was the refrain

CHAPTER THIRTY FIVE

SAMANTHA'S BIRTHDAY CELEBRATIONS

Victor had promised, and he would keep his promise; today was a special day for a celebration; Samantha was hitting the half century mark—yes the big 50. They had planned on a recognition of this event, whenever it occurred and regardless of the circumstances. Celebrate, "come hell or high water," was the way Samantha put it. This day had a special significance because Luella Mae Lundenberry made it to forty nine years and eleven months. So Samantha made Victor promise, if this time ever came in her life, he must honor the occasion for she and her belated mother. Samantha often said; the birthday party did not have to be anything big—just a pausing to recognize time well spent on this Godly earth; a party of two, she and Victor, was perfectly fine. This day; Samantha promised herself, would start out, the simplest of all days—"Lord I Thank You For This Day." And that is exactly how five a.m. found Samantha; sliding to her knees, off the satin sheets, she uttered; "I want to simply thank you, oh Heavenly Father, for this special gracious day...." This was unusual for Samantha because normally she prayed laying in bed, in the shower, going out the door, or down the freeway. Victor was to arrive later at seven a.m.; and Samantha's early start was to get all of her toiletries out of the way—her hair would even be completely fixed when he came through her doors.

"Good morning, Victor!" All smiles.

"Happy birthday, Samantha!" And they embrace, with Samantha wearing her sheer bright-red gown.

"You did not tell me anything Victor, so I sort of stayed undressed."

"That is good—I mean, we are going to be shopping all day— slide that fine body of yours into some old shorts, and let's roll; you got your hair fixed already."

Victor was in an extremely good mood, smiling as every syllable left his mouth. Samantha skipped to her bedroom and quickly returned, wearing loosely fitted blue shorts and an oversized San Antonio Spurs tee-shirt.

"Here, how is this, Victor?"

"You are looking good; how do you feel?"

"Good—I suppose—why do you ask?"

"Well, Samantha, they say if you look good, you should feel good!"

"Yes, Victor, but if you can remember that far back; it was you, who said I was looking good."

"You believe me, don't you?"

"Sure Victor——sure!"

When Samantha stepped outside, the first object appearing in her eyeballs, was a long-black limousine with black windows, with an equally impressive long tall lanky black man standing stiff-backed beside it. She turned and looked at the zestfully smiling Victor who said again:

"How do you feel?"

"I am beginning to feel good." And they both laugh.

The chauffeur opened the door, saying, "happy birthday ma'am." Samantha looked astonished; returned the greeting with a cool nod—thank you—and entered the spacious vehicle. The Today Show with Bryant Gumbel and Katie Couric was glaring on the television's screen. Samantha always watched them at least thirty minutes, before leaving for the office.

"How do you like your coffee ma'am?"

"I think you already—know!" Smiling.

Victor, in his best "Kingfish", rendition said:

"Well—I suppose—I do now, at dat!"

"What has got into you, George Stevans; you know—me and mama always take our coffee with cream and sugar!"

Samantha barely finished her Sapphire impression before they both were in stitches. They had not laughed this hard in years.

"Oh that Amos 'n' Andy was some show, wasn't it Samantha?"

"Well, it had its fine points and its drawbacks, Victor." Then apparently thinking of something, abruptly stopped laughing. "No, Victor, how about a change...black coffee—no sugar—no cream!" And she was all smiles again. "What did you tell the chauffeur?"

"Nothing, but today is my gorgeous lady's birthday."

"You did not tell him my age, did you Victor?"

"Oh—no—you know I would not do a thing like that." Looking undereyed and smiling. "One hot-black one, coming up—ma'am!" And Victor slowly pours Samantha's coffee; starting low, raising the pot, then lowering it again, stopping with a cup brimming full.

"Victor, you are so crazy! Where are we going now?"

"To breakfast, of course!"

"By this time, the chauffeur is pulling into a McDonald's.

"Victor, I know you are crazy now—I am not going to be seen in no limousine, eating at no Mickey D's."

Victor is holding his stomach, he is laughing so hard.

"Oh boy, your expression is that of a real sister; take your hands off your fine hips and straighten up that head girl. Nobody can see you in here."

"I am a real sister; you should know that by now."

"Ah—Samantha, you know what I mean!"

"This is my birthday and you are the one having a good time."

"Relax Samantha; remember we always said, neither status nor people would dictate where we ate."

"That is not quite how I remembered the statement Victor. I believe it was; neither status or people would dictate what we did."

"Same difference; I just detailed it; sort of refined the words——you know." Smiling and looking at Samantha with slightly puffed-out lips.

"Okay Victor." Smiling tenderly. "I will buy that; how about some pancakes and sausage with hash browns."

Turning some gadget; Victor tells Cleo, the chauffeur, to order: pancakes and sausage, egg bacon and cheese biscuit, two hash browns, and whatever he desired. While they sat waiting on the order, several of the workers were staring out the window, in hopes of verifying what one had said about a glimpse; "it is a good looking sister in there." Followed by remarks of: who is in town; man, I want an autograph; see if you can get us some free tickets girl; ask the chauffeur-man, who is in there girl; and finally, Mr. who is the fine sister you be driving around. Cleo was listening, having fun cracking his side; not even trying to reserve his composure. Then he told them real cool-like, slightly grinning, in his deep heavy voice, and sophisticated manner; "I am not at liberty to divulge my clients IDEN-TI-FI-CATION."

"What was all the commotion about, Cleo?"

"Oh, the usual curiosity, Mr. Previtt; especially wanting to know, who the fine sister is."

"Now, how do you feel, Samantha?"

"I feel pretty good, Victor; sort of like a celebrity!"

The chauffeur had his instructions as to which direction to pursue next, and continued his journey. Victor wanted this day to be something unforgettable to Samantha; or better still, every event, if possible to be memorable to her. In doing so, he had chosen a few items out of the norm; hoping to be different in some distinct and captivating way. Birthdays are birthdays, but let's face it, there is something unmistakably different about number fifty—the big five-0-the golden day of all humanity. Victor's idea was not to only have Samantha happy at the end of the day, but happy every moment during this entire day. Samantha was smiling as she tore into those juicy pancakes; which Victor had placed the sausage between the two, cut to comfortable bites, and poured over with that good maple syrup. He also had refilled her cup with hot-black coffee. Victor took a few bites of the biscuit sandwich and it was gone. Now he just sat back and watched Samantha handily devour the food; Samantha, only stopping to sip some coffee and occasionally gaze into Victor's joyful eyes.

"Victor, I cannot believe you have prepared me breakfast in a limousine; and I am cruising—down Broadway, it seems—eating it."

"How do you feel, Samantha?"

"I feel if though I want to cry—don't worry Victor—they are tears of great joy. You are making me so happy."

A few minutes and circular turns later; the vehicle came to a stop, and Cleo stood behind the opened door. The sudden bright sunlight made Samantha squint her eyes as Victor took her hand, as she landed a solid foot on the ground. Placing his right arm around Samantha's waist, Victor led her into a building where an attractive young Oriental looking woman greeted Victor.

"Oh, Mr. Previtt—we expect you—please have seat!" Motioning her hands toward the chairs in the far right section of the room.

Samantha leans against Victor on the way, whispering; "what are you up to now?"

"Oh my—did I not tell you—you get massage—today!"

Samantha could not help, but laugh, but recovered in time to say; "I do not want that young woman pawing all over my body."

"Do not worry—the young one—not paw over you—it will be her mother!"

By this time a nearby door open.

"Good morning Mr. Previtt, you right on time! Come—right this way!"

Somewhere midways in the corridor, they enter a small comfortable room; whereby Victor introduce Samantha and the elderly lady.

"Mrs. Chen, this is Samantha Previtt."

"So good to meet you—Mrs. Previtt—please call me Susan. Take off clothes—put on robe—I be right back!" Smiling at the both of them.

Samantha look nervously at Victor, who simply smiles and say real low:

"Take off clothes—put on robe—I be right back! In other words sister—git yo fine self outta dem clothes."

Samantha is laughing so hard, she can barely pull off her shorts. Victor tease her further as he helps, holding her up, as she remove, the other two garments. Mrs. Chen returns and say politely to Victor:

"Mr. Previtt—you stay—or you go—make decision now!"

"Samantha looks, confidently, smiling, at Victor and say:

"You go!"

"Okay, Samantha, I will be on the premises!"

For the next three hours, Mrs. Chen paws over Samantha's body. Her head, neck, feet, and toes are included. No sides of her go undiscovered—front—rear—left—right. Mrs. Chen's hands are magnificently gentle and effective. She had been highly recommended to Victor, and after conversing with her, early last week; there was no way, anyone else would put their hands on his true friend. The character and the exquisite different flavor portrayed were essential ingredients in selecting Mrs. Chen. If it was not for his shyness of having a woman, other than a sexual mate look at his nude body, Victor thought, he might have considered getting a massage himself. Victor had heard, these professional massages made the body and mind work a lot better afterward—whatever that meant. That certainly was not the reason for getting Samantha one; her mind functioned excellent and he definitely never had any problem with her body. Now, that Victor thinks about it, he says to himself; "this could be scary for me, what if she wants me two weeks at a time. Naw, impossible," he says.

Finally, Samantha emerges with a bright glow to her flesh; her large gorgeous thighs and legs are more gorgeous; her face and arms look so much smoother; and that smile of hers is certainly wider.

"Hello Victor, did you miss me?"

"Mr. Previtt; Mrs. Previtt—is lovely specimen—she easy to work with!"

"Sure, I missed—" Samantha has grabbed Victor and is giving him one of the juiciest kisses he has ever received. Mrs. Chen laugh saying:

"Massage—good—massage—already work!"

Yes, the masseuse had done her job well; Samantha was happier than she had been at any earlier point today. There had been bitter-sweet moments when Victor brought up Amos 'n' Andy; because that had been the only show her mother wanted on, even at her lowest ebb. Samantha remembered seeing her deathly sick mother, laying there, with her eyes closed; smiling, as those funny characters paraded across the old black and white television.

Luella Mae Lundenberry had grown up listening to this show on the radio and the sound was all the same to her—it lifted her heart on the light side. Since Samantha looked so much like her mother and had so many of her same ways; she had illusions of mother continuing her life inside of her from the fiftieth birthday, onward. But now, the solemnness of her mom was wearing off, and she seems prepared to get off into herself, by herself. One should use the past to propel them forward, she thought. Samantha now happily realizes that there was no stigma or superstition attached to her in her reach for fifty or the "magic age" as she sometimes put it. There had been no curse or limitation formed to prevent her from reaching her true maturity; and this was a blessed relief to Samantha. And crazy as it might sound, Samantha had not only worried about herself, but also her beautiful daughter, Stacy. It had been one of those silent suffering; neither Victor nor Stacy had seen the lining of her heart on that longevity question. That was then, this is now; Samantha's heart for the moment has definitely been lifted on the light side. A reality check.

"How do you feel, Samantha?"

"I feel good!"

That is what Victor wanted to hear all morning. There was no hesitancy, no pausing, no qualifications on "good." Simply—"I feel good." Victor sensed the change.

"Are you ready to cruise some more, Samantha?"

"Yes—yes."

And Samantha locks her arm into Victor's pulling him toward the exit. In the background, one could hear Mrs. Chen, laughing, saying "you come back, come back again, you have, happy birthday." Into the limousine and they were rolling again, except now, Samantha cannot keep her hands off of Victor. A new vitality.

"Victor, that massage was something else! My body feels alive, my mind feels fresh and open; they are both happy. For the first time ever, it feels like my body and mind are connected to one another. Each can feel the other's vibrations—tiny stinging pulsations going from one to the other. I feel good—I feel real good, Victor."

"Sounds like something rather penetrating to me, Samantha."

"That is true too, Victor; it makes you want to holler, you feel so good. Sort of like—shout and tell the world!"

"This is your day Samantha; if you feel like hollering—holler!"

"Yeah, but what about the chauffeur; he would think the fine sister had gone looney. Maybe, I'll just save it for later on Victor; it will still be good—don't you think?"

Samantha has now hopped into Victor's lap, stretching her big thighed legs across the spacious seat.

"I suppose that will have a lot to do with my status at the end of the day, Samantha."

"Do not worry Victor, your standing will always be good with me. Or put another way; even if there is a total letdown for the rest of the day, you will not be able to squirm out of this one. So get ready—massage good—your idea!"

Victor could feel the warmth of Samantha's bottom hot spot, upon him. She had ideas of Victor facing this hot spot, head on, while this sleek limousine cruised the Alamo City; but knew, later on was much more appropriate. Victor is happy that Samantha is happy; because she never for once let him forget, he was going to celebrate this day with her. He thinks to himself; how fortunate he is, to be able to entertain Samantha in this manner. Here it was, on Thursday morning, and he was off work, with pay for the week. His thoughts went back to his grandfather who would have loved to have received pay when it rained and he could not pick cotton, or when he got so sick, he could not work at all. Victor had already promised himself when he planned this day, he would not think of the countless thousands of less fortunate people. The thought of being so extravagant would have made his load too heavy to bear. However, if Victor had really known the real meaning of this day in Samantha's heart, the extravagance would have meant nothing.

"Victor, what would you say if I told you, I did not want to do any shopping as you have promised?"

"I would say you are probably losing it, in your old age Samantha."

"And what would you say, if I asked you to skip buying my birthday lunch and dinner, Victor?"

"Well Samantha, I would say, the old girl has totally flipped out."

"Victor, you might say I am stupid, but I feel like doing something freaky on my birthday; what would you say if we rode up and down Broadway, while you enjoyed my delicious dessert?"

"Samantha, I would say the old birthday girl has gotten her sense back and regained that youth."

Before Victor can tell Cleo their plans have changed, and he is to drive up and down Broadway, while they make love, Samantha has removed her shorts, exposing the most delicious dessert, Victor had seen today; continuing to remove her blouse and bra, flinging her nude body backward and curved upon the plush seats as they curved likewise in their most luxurious fashion. Samantha could see the sky out of the moonroof, but what was more apparent were the black utility lines slowly passing overhead; she felt alive, telling Victor that living until today was like living forever. She explained to Victor for the first time, what making fifty years of age meant to her; how she feared not making it; and to forget the sentiment and love her slow and easy. Victor understood as he pulled Carolyn's delicious dessert near his lips where he instantly began to smell its sweetness. Samantha looked beyond the sagging black wires into the heavens; hoping and praying her dear mother was enjoying the moments with her.

Samantha was comfortable, with her gorgeous thighs extended widely apart; she had spread her delicious dessert for Victor's appetizing pleasure. More preparation had gone into today's serving, fifty years to be exact, so it had to be especially good for his dining delight. Samantha wanted Victor to enjoy himself, but she really wanted her delicious dessert to be excellent for her sake, and also for the sake of Luella Mae Lundenberry; because it was a combination of her ingredients, which was making today so special. One reason, Victor always enjoyed Samantha's sweetstuff was because of its moisture, but now as he held her soft-wiry nicety in his hands and prepared to dine, it looked much-much larger. Its enormity was exciting to Victor's eyes, waking up saliva glands lying dormant for years. As he slowly put Samantha's delicious dessert into his mouth, he noticed it was much juicer than ever. Every spot his tongue touched seemed to manufacture buckets and buckets of sweet juices. Sweeter too than Victor had ever known. This mouth-watering delicacy of Samantha's was filling

Victor's throat with a digestible large portion that would soon began to fill his stomach. Today's edibles were so superb, even Victor wanted it to last, as he dined slower and slower, first around the edges, then inward, then outward, really savoring Samantha's extraordinary sweet flavor. The more Victor repeated this delicate process, the more Samantha's sweet juices flowed out, giving both of them a powerful urge to make this fiftieth birthday celebration last a long time. This told her, her preparation was more than adequate. To maintain her comfort, Samantha tightened her tender thighs a bit, pressing Victor's ears into silence of the smacking and lapping sounds from his mouth and tongue strokes.

Victor was deeply engrossed in Samantha's delicious dessert; so deep in fact, results were showing on his nose and three inches beyond his mouth. And the taste inside his mouth produced such satisfaction, he dreaded an end, begging Samantha for more. Samantha gladly gave Victor more of her sweet juiciness; and to make sure he got it, she pushed her delicious dessert forward as far as she could, giving him chunks and chunks of soft fluffy pieces upon his tongue. Samantha knew her delicious dessert was melting in Victor's mouth because he somehow managed to tell her; "Samantha, you are melting in my mouth, and I love it; this is by far the best you have ever given me." Then he braced himself for more of Samantha's generosity which he knew was on its way; holding her delicious dessert with both hands firmer than ever. Each serving Samantha gave Victor was warmer and juicer than the former. This made the moment in his opinion, that much more special, and he was glad to be part of it. Victor heard Samantha softly say, "happy fiftieth birthday mama." Then she whispered to Victor how she was beginning to feel, simultaneously sending a sweetness to Victor's lips which he had never before tasted; a sweetness which made him appreciate missing a shopping spree and two meals. Samantha felt Victor's appreciation as he slowly devoured her delicious dessert, relishing it so affectionately, she too felt like she was Heaven bound.

Victor knew this was a special day for Samantha, when she continuously sent gushes of sweetness his way. He stole a glance into her face and her expression even seemed as if this moment would last forever. Victor whispered to Samantha that they were going home and informed Cleo likewise. Noon turned to evening, and evening to night, and night to morning; when Victor awoke to find himself still cuddling Samantha within striking distance of his tongue. Victor's sweet tooth started acting up again as his sleepy eyes focused on the delicious dessert before him. Knowing Samantha and not hearing those loud frantic sounds, he knew she had apparently fallen asleep without giving him her last and best sweetness; he was puzzled though as to how she could hold out so long. His tastetester found its way upon her delicious dessert as he wondered. Within seconds, Samantha's tender thighs locked Victor's head like a vise, sending an abundant supply of sweetness into his mouth. Happy fiftieth, he told her later, and smoothly eased his bigness inside of her to climax a wonderful and exciting birthday celebration.

"Oh, Victor, think nothing of me missing your meals yesterday; I am sure, after today, Saturday and Sunday, I will not want to see any food for a long time. Isn't it nice of Tiffani to invite me to lunch today? By the way, Carolyn found out, and she is going to join us. I know you will not be there, but they want me to meet them in your office at eleven a.m. And Saturday, thanks to you, I will meet Helen, who has promised me another lunch. Then if that's not enough eating, Ms. Lincoln and Angela are taking me out to dinner Sunday. Victor, thanks to your talking up my fiftieth birthday, this will be the best one I have ever had."

"Give yourself the credit Samantha; after you made so much fuss about it, I just thought I would help it along a little."

"Thanks Victor, you are really a wonderful friend. This is so exciting."

And speaking of being excited; Tiffani loved preparing for special events. She had contacted her florist again for a birthday set up. So Victor's office had been decorated with two flower arrangements on the glass table, with birthday balloons attached. Between the arrangement was a three layered birthday cake; German Chocolate, Samantha's favorite. The cake had one candle in the center with writing upon the cake saying "Happy Half-Century Samantha." In partial view, underneath the table, but still very noticeable, were two small gift wrapped packages. This morning, Tiffani figured no one would be drinking much coffee, so only one pot was made, and it had yet to be touched; Tiffani obviously had been too busy with her cleaning and dusting. Victor had known better than to leave her with any assignments or projects for today. It was to be a short day anyway, as far as work was concerned, because Tiffani was taking this Friday evening off. Carolyn was doing the same; they had decided among themselves that the rest of the day would be theirs. In their opinion, rushing such an important occasion in one's life, would do irreparable damage.

At eleven o'clock, Carolyn strolled into the office, wearing a new purple suit, which buttoned to the neck, but it appears the extra material had been removed from the skirt, because it was tight and short; every bit of ten inches above her knees, and allowing a beautiful portion of her thighs to be exposed enough, to capture one's imagination on their entire magnificent beauty.

"Hello Tiff; how are you coming along with the preparation?"

"Hi Carolyn; my, don't you look good; it is a good thing Victor is not here today, because he would be all goo-goo eyes, but I am sure he will get a chance to see it, very soon."

"Now Tiff, you promised to be nice today, you are right though, I can hardly wait to hear what he thinks."

"Yeah, like you don't already know, Carolyn."

"I don't Tiff, but I have a general idea, he will think I look great. Are you saying I should not have worn this suit with Samantha coming down?"

"No, not really, but it is a bit sexy; Samantha might think you wear skirts that short all the time; when you and I both know, you only wear them like that, when you want something from Victor."

"So true Tiff, but there is nothing wrong with that, in my opinion, as long as it works; and since you are so observant, I believe you have noticed—it works—right!"

"Well—yeah—I guess so Carolyn, if you call playing on a man's weakness—working!"

"Plus, you must also remember Tiff, Samantha is sort of a competitor, you know."

"She is only his ex, and a friend, and you know that Carolyn."

"I do not know any such thing, for sure Tiff."

"Good morning Tiffani; and Carolyn, it is good to see you again, so soon. I love that suit; is that another one from that boutique, you were telling me about?"

"It sure is Samantha; Gerald's Boutique; I would never go to an important occasion, without wearing a piece or two from his shop.

"Or a piece and a half!"

"You must look over Tiff today Samantha; she is not in total agreement with my—two piece suit."

"Tiffani; why as young as you are, I would think you would love an outfit like that. Of course, Carolyn does have the perfect set of thighs."

"Yeah, but what about when you sit down, Samantha, you will darn near show everything else you have."

"Not if you know how to sit Tiffani; you should not show anything more, but the finer portion of your upper thigh. I am tempted, just looking at Samantha, to get me a few pieces like that, for my second half-century; I love that cake girls!"

"Oh, and it's your favorite too, Samantha!"

"Thanks Tiffani, you two, being around Victor, know so much more about me than I do you, that I almost feel at a disadvantage."

"Well, we have decided Samantha, you cannot cut it until we return from lunch; dessert should be last, you know."

"I am not going to argue with you there, Carolyn."

"But the gifts, you may open now, Samantha."

"Thanks Tiffani, is there any preference to which one first?"

"Sure, you can start with mine; here you go, Samantha."

"Sure, Samantha, open Tiff's first; we just made that fantastic decision!"

"I am glad you two get along so well together; okay Tiffani, here goes. I love to open presents fast; why don't I just rip this beautiful paper apart. Now, I will slowly open this box; there—Tiffani, this is a beautiful necklace—a diamond and emerald choker; Tiffani, you shouldn't have. This is so gorgeous, and it is far too expensive for a birthday present."

"Not if it's your fiftieth, Samantha; I am praying I make it that far, and look half as good as you. You are sophisticated enough to wear it well too. Here, let me help you put it on."

"Samantha, you are simply beautiful in that jewelry; green adds a radiance to your complexion."

"Thank you Carolyn, but that is probably those diamonds shining against my skin; oh Tiffani you shouldn't have."

"Ah, think nothing of it Samantha; it's also my way of saying, thank you, for getting me this job, working for Victor."

Samantha thinks of her mommy, who almost made it to fifty, and began to cry. Now, she is hugged by Tiffani and Carolyn, and one of them give her a tissue. She wipes the tears away saying:

"I promised myself, I would not cry today; please excuse me; maybe I shouldn't open the other present."

"There is nothing wrong with you crying Samantha, at a time like this; we are both aware of your loving mother. Here, you can open my gift now."

"Thank you Carolyn; this present is lighter than the last one; you two scare me—an envelope huh—a gift certificate; fifteen hundred dollars—"

"I know Samantha, I shouldn't have, but if you cry again, we are all going to be in tears and ruin this lovely cake."

Everybody started laughing and the birthday celebration was cheerful again.

"Thank you so much Carolyn; now I do not have an excuse to not visit Gerald's Boutique; maybe we can all go by there when we get through eating lunch. I am going to find a suit which will match this choker. Carolyn, Tiffani, you two are so wonderful; I am so glad we are cutting the cake later, because you two have absolutely taken my breath, and I couldn't blow out, even that one candle, right now."

"Good, Samantha, that means it is time to go eat; we will stop back by the office, blow out that candle, and head for Gerald's Boutique to do some big time shopping."

"Very well said Tiff, I could not have put it better myself."

"I know Carolyn; I had already figured that out!"

"Oh, come on you two funny bunnies, I am starving; and please don't tell anyone at the restaurant its my birthday celebration, and have them start singing, because I do not want to get sentimental again."

"We promise!" In unison yelled out loud by Carolyn and Tiffani.

Tiffani did all the honors of driving, mostly, because she was afraid of Carolyn having a drink or two, too many. But as it turned out, Carolyn did not even have a drink; as a matter of fact, none of them had any. Their conversations throughout lunch was nothing but wholesome and friendly with Tiffani and Carolyn taking occasional poppycock jokes at the other. And would you know it, Victor's name never came up. Each reminded the other to save room for a German Chocolate cake, and before long, they were back at the office, doing just that. Well, eating a slice each, but not before, Samantha made a wish and blew out the candle. They all disciplined themselves on one small piece of cake. Samantha boxed the remainder to take home to the waiting Victor, who she said, loved to eat her dessert. Samantha insinuated, she was too stuffed to go and try on some clothes, but it was said only in jest, to keep them all laughing. They were all in a very intoxicating mood, to not have had anything; they were a perfect threesome for having fun. Tiffani and Carolyn both admired Samantha for keeping herself with a shapely physique and looking youthful. And they were not pulling her leg; she really did look good; it appears, the burden of reaching fifty was off her shoulders, and so was about fifteen years. She looked no older than Carolyn, who was an excellent standard for measuring; her thirty plus years had the showing of a mature twenty nine year old. Carolyn, however, was no advocate of youth; she always wanted to appear older, for she felt it coincided more with her authoritative disposition.

Well, so much for age and youth, the three beautiful women, still chauffeured by Tiffani, headed for Gerald's Boutique. The intention was to use Samantha's gift certificate for an outfit which was appropriately designed to go with the diamond and emerald choker. It boiled down to two suits; one, green of course and one, black. Both suits had the proper neckline for showcasing her new exquisite gem and the proper tight fit, but there was something, according to Samantha, regardless of what Carolyn and Tiffani said, which was missing.

"Tiffani, Carolyn, I finally figured out what's not appealing to me about these suits; its the hemline. Even for my age, they are much too long. What is missing is, my thighs are not allowed to show; see, like yours Carolyn."

"I noticed that too Samantha, but I was not aware of how much sex appeal you wanted to come forth."

"As much as I can get ladies; afterall, I am single, you know."

"Well, start pulling it up Samantha, let's see what looks good; Higher—higher—higher—higher—higher—"

"Carolyn, that might be too high, its over halfway of my thigh; we need to leave stripteasing to some young whipper-snapper like Tiffani there."

"That's a laugh Samantha, Tiff is much too shy for anything of that sort; stripteasing would be more to my style of generating excitement."

"You are probably right Carolyn, but you should probably stick to speaking for yourself."

"Just thinking of your nerves Tiff; you don't appear to have the nerve to pull many pieces off, other than your shoes and jewelry. The thought of you stripping in the front of a man, in the light, is hilarious itself. I can see you now, using your hands to cover up those vital areas."

"Like I said Carolyn, speak for yourself; anyway, if you were a man, you would be beating down my door to get into my parlor."

"Now, now, girls, I only mentioned stripteasing in the fun of things; nobody in their right mind is going around stripteasing these days; least of all, you two professional workers. What do you think Gerald; what length suits you?"

"Well, both suits will take a large cut, halfway your thigh, and still look presentable; and on the other hand, your thighs are very lovely, and will look quite presentable. However, it is your taste and preference which counts the most Ms. Previtt."

"Decisions, decisions, decisions; very well put Gerald. I cannot decide which of the two to get, so I will get them both; one on sweet Carolyn and one on me. After all, I have two more birthday celebrations to attend. Gerald, you can keep all that extra material, please allow half of my thighs to be a new landmark.

"You will never regret this decision Ms. Previtt, I assure you; you really have one pair of fine thighs."

"You should not be flirting with customers I bring by Gerald!"

"Well, well, well, look who is getting jealous, Ms. Love train, herself; and Carolyn, she has not shown anything but her thighs——yet!"

"I am not addressing that issue anymore Tiff!"

"Sounds like it struck your last nerve to me, Carolyn!"

"You two are pitiful, do you carry on like this all the time?"

"Carolyn's competitive edginess is beginning to show Samantha."

"Tiff, that is not very nice!"

"Carolyn is right Tiffani, that is not very nice."

"Well, Samantha, she rubbed me the wrong way, talking about my stripping; I know, I am a darn good striptease artist."

"My, my, look who is getting so sensitive—and about a joke; Tiff, I was only teasing you and having a little fun."

"Well, Carolyn, who is it to say, I was not teasing you."

"I think both of you owe the other an apology; now I want both of you to hug and apologize—right now Tiffani, Carolyn!"

"I am sorry, Tiff, I was really only joking."

"I am sorry too Carolyn; and to show you that I mean it, I am going to buy both of us a suit, mid-thigh length."

"Wow, thanks Tiff, I should have spoken up sooner; just for that you deserve a kiss."

"Now, that's the way birthday celebrations should be; are you two about ready to go?"

"Sure Samantha, as soon as we get our suits; help us to pick one out."

"Tiffani, that was awfully nice of you, to apologize to Carolyn the way you did."

"Well, I did not want any lingering hard feelings, and bad taste left in our mouths. We joke all the time, but we did get a little too serious this time. I am just thankful you were here Samantha, to remind, us, we can irritate the other and still be friends. While I am thinking about it Samantha, the appointment I made for you at the masseuse; how did it turn out?"

"Tiffani, you will not believe the sensitive spots on your body which goes untouched. I was ready to make love before she got half way done with me. It was a feeling I had never experienced before; my body was totally rejuvenated."

"Do you think something like that would work on a man Samantha?"

"Tiffani, something like what I had would work on anybody

unless they're dead. That masseuse's hands were all over me. The best explanation; it gives you a feeling of immediately doing physical feats which you are probably not capable of, but will try anyway. Things with your mate, if you know what I mean."

"Uh huh, I gottcha, Samantha."

"Ms. Previtt, I will deliver your two suits at ten in the morning."

"Thanks Gerald, that will give me plenty of time to decide which one, I should wear to my luncheon."

Samantha found Victor resting in bed when she arrived home. She was still excited about today and her outing with Carolyn and Tiffani. Victor was unaware that Carolyn and Tiffani were buying such luxurious gifts, but he was very pleased when he saw how happy Samantha was. Good things always come unto him when Samantha was in a joyous mood. Victor's curiosity got the best of him, observing the unopened box. Samantha informed him that it was the remainder of her birthday cake; and for him to get ready to be served his dessert in bed.

Victor's tastebuds became extremely active as Samantha's delicious dessert passed over his tongue. He held her dessert with both hands, as usual, and tonight he really opened his mouth and went after it. Victor's mouth stayed full as Samantha smoothly stuffed her dessert into it. Victor was exceptionally pleased with the sweetness of Samantha's juicy dessert. The sweet juices flowed into his mouth and down his throat without any swallowing effort. Samantha was also very pleased when she saw the way Victor's tongue was lashing into her delicious dessert; it was the perfect climatic effect for a perfect day.

CHAPTER THIRTY SIX

SAMANTHA MEETS HELEN

Today, when the doorbell rang at nine in the morning, Samantha had just finished having a sumptuous breakfast in bed, prepared of course by Victor, who now was engrossed in his Wall Street Journal.

"Good morning Ms. Previtt, I know I am early, but I remembered, you said something about attending a luncheon; so I thought perhaps an earlier time might be beneficial."

"Good morning, Gerald, come in!"

"No ma'am, I must be on my way, but here is something from me for your birthday celebration."

"Oh, a red rose; Gerald, this is so nice of you, this means a lot to me."

"Thank you ma'am, enjoy these two suits, and have a very good day!"

Samantha closed the door, leaned against it, cuddling the rose, tightly to her chest, before her nose. Its sweet fragrance reminded her, as a child, when she use to cut one from her mommy's rose bushes, and take it to her. The smile upon Samantha's face just now, was the same delicate smile, her mommy wore. Samantha thought how blessed she was to make it to her fiftieth birthday, and she knew mommy was rejoicing with her, right now. She was still smiling and cuddling the rose when she went to the breakfast nook, to show Victor her suits.

"Well, my, you look wonderful Samantha; if I had known a rose would make you look that happy, I would have gotten you a whole dozen."

Samantha thought, a dozen red roses could never make her as happy as one. Because, she knew, if she had cut a dozen of mommy's roses, and taken it to her, she would still be picking thorns from her behind. Mommy always kissed her and told her how sweet she was, for the one, and it always made them both happy, which was always good enough.

"Thank you Victor, I would appreciate that very much."

"These must be the suits you were telling me about, huh! Oops, a card is falling from the rose, Samantha; Gerald's Boutique...Carolyn's favorite shop. These are really some lovely garments."

"Hold on, let me try them on for you, Victor, be right back."

Samantha rushed into the bedroom, throwing the clothes on the bed. Still lying out upon the dresser was the diamond and emerald choker, which she hastily clasped around her neck. She could hardly wait for Victor to see her; the green suit was quickly donned and she was standing before Victor, saying;

"Well, what do you think, Victor?"

"You look like a doll, Samantha, and look at those thighs; man, they never looked like that before; changing your image, huh! Looks good, looks real good."

"I take all of that Victor to mean, you approve."

"Well, yeah——I mean——I could get a little jealous if I'm not with you though." Smiling.

"Thanks Victor, that really is your better compliment; by the way, your friend Carolyn was more than a little jealous yesterday, when Gerald complimented me on my gorgeous thighs."

"You're kidding Samantha; Carolyn jealous!"

"Uh huh, that really made my day, Victor. That is when I also knew, I needed to do a little image swapping, because that was also truly a compliment, without being a compliment, if you know what I mean."

"I follow you, Samantha."

"If it's one thing Carolyn knows, Victor, it is clothes and what body looks good in them. Of course, she obviously has had a lot of practical experience; I hate to say this Victor, but Carolyn is the finest woman, I have ever seen, and she wears these expensive clothes, extremely well. I saw her in only her underwear; you cannot help, but admire a body like that. That girl would make anything look good."

"I agree with everything you're saying Samantha; now maybe, you can understand part of my problem."

"Indeed I do Victor, but Samantha did not drink a thing yesterday. Still, being jealous at the exposure of my bird legs, was a great compliment."

"Hey, wait a minute Samantha, you might not have Carolyn's tall structure, but your body is just as fine, and you do not have bird legs, plus your thighs are gorgeous as you mentioned earlier. And I can tell you this Samantha, there is not a woman in my life which has anything sweeter to offer—."

"Okay I am convinced Victor; I can see why all those women like you; you are a real softy, and that is a compliment, before you get started again; and save some of that lip service for my dessert tonight."

"Sorry, Samantha." Smiling.

"Hold that smile Victor while I change into the other suit."

Samantha even wore a smile as she put on the black suit, thinking how women get excited in the competitiveness of another woman. It is always reassuring to hear, whether from a man or woman, how good you look yourself, and Samantha had been told two days in a row, how good her thighs looked; by men—and women too, though loosely.

"There Victor, how do you like me?"

"Whoa, I love your new image, you have a great pair of legs, and your thighs are fantastic, Samantha!"

"Yeah, but how about the suit, Victor?"

"Oh, I forgot about the suit, it is great too, Samantha; those suits are tighter too, showing that shapely body of yours. You look so inviting; which one are you wearing to the luncheon to meet Helen?"

"That was going to be my next question to you, Victor. I really want to impress Helen. Hearing so much about her from Stacy, makes her seem so special; and for the first time ever Victor, I am sort of nervous about meeting someone."

"It's a toss up Samantha, either one will work, but since you're meeting a young woman today and a young and older woman tomorrow, my thinking says, go all glamour today and tomorrow, mix that glamour with the black sophistication you carry so well."

"Very well put Victor."

"And the choker looks real good with both suits, before you ask Samantha."

"Victor, that was my next question; you are definitely ahead of me today."

"Speaking of being ahead Samantha, you had better put a little pep in your step; the reservation is at noon, you know."

Victor had gotten Helen and Samantha a reservation at one of the city's swankiest restaurants; one of those reservations only, type of places. He did not say it, but he wanted to show the sisters off, in public; and though Victor would not be present, he knew the impression these fine ladies would have on the establishment and its ritzy clientele.

Helen was already there when Samantha arrived; and as expected by Victor, the stares Samantha received when she crossed that room, to Helen's table, were phenomenal. Helen stood to greet her, receiving an equal amount of stares, no sooner than she recognized what her description told her; "that sophisticated lady being led by the maitre d' in my direction is none other than Samantha Previtt." A bubbly smile came across her face puncturing her dimple deep into her cheek. When this happened, Samantha knew this beautiful coal-black complexioned lady was Helen. They embraced before they even spoke, and while still holding each other loosely, they looked into the other's face and spoke.

"Hello Helen!"

"Hello Samantha; happy birthday."

"Thank you Helen; you know, you are as lovely as Stacy said you were, and lovelier, I might add."

"And that snapshot I saw of you Samantha, does you no justice. You are so much younger looking than I ever envisioned; Stacy's portrayal was way off."

"Well, you know how children are Helen. most of the time you are only their moms."

"I am sure to learn about that Samantha; I love your suit and that length; when you were coming over, you looked like a walking mint, with a perfect set of legs."

"Thank you; Carolyn bought it for me yesterday."

"I also love that choker, it is really right for that suit."

"Thanks again Helen, I get no credit, but it matches by design, Victor's secretary, Tiffani, bought it for me; and she and Carolyn matched it with this suit."

"They did an excellent job of matching those items Samantha, but you do an excellent job of wearing them. Those pieces were made for you."

"Speaking of excellent, that was one excellent compliment Helen; we should have met years ago. Victor tried to get me to know you, but with so many people in that church, and different time schedules, and all, it's totally impossible to know everybody; and now that we are divorced, I don't even go there any more."

"I agree; talking about knowing people Samantha, I feel I know Tiffani, from talking to her on the phone, but I have never met her."

"She is a young lady, I recommended to Victor; she is a perfect match for him; always letting him know when he is out of line. Sometimes, or all the time, I should say, Tiffani is protective of him from other women, including myself; she loves that Victor."

"I sort of gathered that, but she appears to be real nice; sounds every bit as nice as Stacy. And speaking of Stacy, she is so proud of her brothers. All of her spare time is spent with them."

"Yes, I know, Helen, she brings them by often. They will be calling me grandma before long, I am sure. They are the sweetest and darling boys I have ever seen. Victor says, they got those traits from you, Helen."

"Oh, I would not take all the credit Samantha. Victor, is by far the sweetest man I have ever known. He is also kind and considerate. Of course, he was not always like that; at least not toward me. You could say I was one of those strained elements in his life, Samantha. Victor, really did not want to give me the time of day; but the timing was right and I knew it. You two had divorced, which meant, his eyes would now fall upon other women. Maybe only for a second's glance, and that is all I needed. Competition from other single women had never threatened me, because I was aware of my forceful capabilities and my superb womanly qualifications. Confidence, Samantha has never been one of my weaknesses; but in those days, I was downright cocky. Yes, poor Victor gave me several minutes of observation; which was far too many for him to recuperate. I am sure he would never admit it girl, but after that length of time, I could have hooked him with one of his eyes shut and the other half opened."

"When I forced myself on Victor, Samantha, it was for good clean sex, and to further my ambitious goals. I was very boisterous and selfish in those days also. At first he wanted absolutely nothing to do with me, but I am pretty persistent and persuasive at times. He is strong willed, but I finally melted him down. You might say, I sort of got him My Way. Little did I know how good Victor would be for me. There is not a man on this earth who has a bigger heart than Victor. You can talk about Victor all day and there is nothing but good things to say about him. He is a perfect father and he is perfect for me. I often wonder what would have happened with my life, had it not been for Victor. He has been my strongest supporter during the ebb moments."

"What started out as an arrangement Samantha, ended up a love affair. I have only seen Victor upset one time. That is when I told him I was pregnant. He was mad as hell. I had never seen anyone that angry before. Anyway we ironed it out. The baby came and Victor began to act different toward me. Because there were nothing but females in his life; the good Lord knew to send a boy. And thanks Heaven, that was good for us both. Immediately after that, we realized, we were in love."

"What about Angela and Carolyn—Helen?"

"Oh, I have never felt threatened by them, because I always knew about them. In other words, I was infringing on their turf. Other than Victor, Carolyn is now my best friend. When Victor is not around, we do things together—shopping, movies, or just talk on the phone. She lost one of her daughters a while back; and I believe the boys have been excellent therapy for her. Last year we went on a cruise together. Victor had to keep the boys, so everything works well for us."

"But that Angela; you are talking about something different Samantha. She has cursed me out on several occasions. Once was when Victor brought the girls over. They look like little dolls, and I love girls anyway. So I go shopping and buy each of them a dress and shoes. You know how it is, when you get to shopping for girls. Their clothes are so much prettier than boys. They just happened to wear them back home. Angela must have thought I was trying to tell her how to dress them. As soon as they arrived, she called and gave me a piece of her mind. I apologized and she slammed the phone down in my ear."

"One time Angela came by and picked them up Samantha. Victor had picked the girls up that Friday and dropped them home and left. He did that often, because we had agreed, it was good for them to know each other as brothers and sisters. Well, Angela called that Saturday morning looking for Victor. She knew the girls were here. She cursed me on the phone and said, get them ready, I am coming to get them. The visitation part has since been solved, but Angela still hates my guts. On several other occasions; more than I care to discuss, Angela has been nasty to me. In a way I can't blame her."

"Angela does not know it Samantha, but I admire and envy her so much. Maybe the envy, is because of those darling girls. I have always wanted a little girl. And because they are a part of Victor, I would gladly take them as my own any day. The admiration, goes for her patience. She gives one the feeling that she is in control of Victor and just biding time with others. Meeting Victor first, might account for her domineering of him. If I had been in her position, I wouldn't have been as lenient. I would have definitely told Victor, what to do and where to go."

"I know Angela is nasty to me because of my children Samantha; she probably feels, I am going to get the upper hand. I am sure that's it; but Victor spends as much time with her as he does with me—probably more. Angela has called here for one reason or the other, and he has left here and went to her. Either she is totally obsessive, maddeningly jealous, or extremely selfish, or maybe all three. Sometimes it burns me up, to think someone has the gumption to do something like that. I have suffered through that frustration many times. But, Samantha, the rewards, with Victor far outweigh the consequences."

"Tell me Helen, does your body ever run down? Victor tells me you are constantly on the go; that would be enough to wipe me out."

"Oh, Samantha, I get a little tired, but I think it is all in what you are doing. It is my firm belief, that most of us would be better off pursuing our talents. For in doing so, we could be happiest. And would probably contribute the most and everlasting good to society. These are generally the closest aspirations to our hearts; where there is much gratification. With those endeavors in mind and heart, we tend to work harder, as a result of much fulfillment. We get more things done in shorter periods of time, with less effort."

"The mood of the day is happier Samantha, making our surroundings one of enchantment. This is not to say everything will always go your way; but the successes will far outweigh the failures or temporary setbacks as I like to put them. The optimistic point of view becomes the norm; and the approach to life is reassuring. The rising of each sun becomes a joy; and the setting thereof becomes likewise, because of the accomplishments. Each day possesses exhilaration as it unwounds. This too, by no means, says we are getting great monetary rewards or wealthy, as we all are sure to dream. But the satisfaction obtained and the joy that it brings to us and others is wealth enough."

"Helen, your outlook on life is much different than most of the people I know. I am so glad Victor arranged this opportunity for us to meet. This chat and listening to you has given me a new consciousness for wanting to see tomorrow. It is a day I now eagerly await rather than one of work regrets; thanks to you Helen."

"Victor talks about you all the time Samantha; he calls you his right arm. And I think you are far more wonderful than Victor ever characterized you. I do not want to know Samantha, but I cannot understand why you ever let him go."

"I'll tell you about it sometimes, Helen, I have a feeling we're going to see a lot of one another. Maybe I can pick up my grand boys, when Stacy's not hogging them."

"Anytime, Samantha, just let me know; I really feel like I owe you something for being so gracious. My Way, worked on Victor, but you are blessed with a friend in him, Your Way, for the rest of your life."

MY WAY

Forced my way into his life
With my body and my voice
Once he looked and lushed
He had no chance, nor choice

Call it entrapment if you wish
But call his side for greed
Saw the flesh and he did want
With me I saw a need

We each got what we saw
Certainly, a tad bit more
Must use the tools you have
Figure that's what they're for

Though at first was tolerated
Now for sure, he loves me
Guilty of using female persuasion
But I offer no apology

Made him feel right for me
No more questions does he inquire
Responded well for us both
I'm glad he heeded my cry

There was a woman or two
But no ring did they carry
Obviously he's playing the field
Why else would he not marry

Staked my claim with others
Made him limit us to three
Safe sex, better than no sex
At least, it is to me

No intention to fall in love
No forecast for a child
No one predicts the future
If confronted, expect a denial

It took two, of course
The affair worked out okay
We are the better for it
True, everything went My Way

At the end of the two and a half hour luncheon, when the cake reading, Happy Birthday Samantha, with a number fifty and candle in the center was brought out; Helen presented Samantha with a gold cross and chain. Then she politely and calmly gave Samantha a handwritten birthday card, which read: May this birthday bring comfort and happiness to you always Samantha. God bless you forever. Love always, Helen Tafeel.

The day had been all happy smiles and joy until this point, when another form of happiness and joyfulness arrived with Samantha's tears. Before Samantha's watery eyes, the lone candle's flame seem to burn brighter as the two women embraced. It was Samantha's birthday celebration, but she asked Helen to also make a wish, and they blew out the bright flickering flame together. The two women again embraced when their time had come to an end, yet lingering, touching the others hands reverently, staring mistily into each others eyes. Even after Samantha departed, a tranquilness hung to her insides; she could actually feel Helen within her heart.

This time, Victor had Samantha's entire dessert when she arrived home. And again, her delicious dessert filled his mouth and fulfilled his hunger appetite. Samantha, still feeling sentimental could only watch in jubilancy, as Victor's tongue relished her luscious dessert triumphantly. Both, fell asleep later, feeling relaxed and satisfied, that the day had gone so well.

When morning came Samantha rose with the intentions of chilling out until her luncheon/dinner with Angela and Grandma. Then something came over her when she put on the gold cross to let Victor see it. Samantha began having these urges to attend church this beautiful Sunday morning. Before she knew it the black suit was on and she was merrily on her way to the ten a.m. services. Her subconscious had told her, this is where Luella Mae Lundenberry would have been. The dinner was not until three o'clock, so she was not pressed for time or anything like that.

The dinner with Ms. Lincoln and Angela was very jovial. Angela, with her youth appreciated the age distinction and Grandma, who had been there, had an even higher level of gratefulness. Their hearts were of the same warmth, when Samantha expressed her real significance for turning fifty. Ms. Lincoln, who knew best, made a toast, and they all saluted Luella Mae Lundenberry. Then the quick thinking Ms. Lincoln had another candle added to the large four-layered cake, which simply read, Happy Birthday Samantha. Samantha was tearful as she blew out the twin flames; a large smile formed upon her face as she made her wish, letting Angela and Ms. Lincoln know, these were tears of joy. These three women had a lot of talk in them; from Samantha's new image and hemline, to Angela's new baby, to Ms. Lincoln's wisdom of it all. Ms. Lincoln, during the course of the evening, out of the earshot of Angela, even told Samantha, she had made the decision to enroll in college; and of her dinner the coming week to inform Angela and Victor. In the absence of Angela, Samantha returned a toast to Ms. Lincoln for her willingness to face such a challenge.

The most astonishing occurrence during this dinner to Samantha, was the stares she received, making that lone trip across the room to the ladies room; they were phenomenal. The stares in Samantha's direction continued on her return trip. Those roving male eyes and the wild imagination Samantha read in their faces was exhilarating. If a new suit does this, she thought, what would a complete make over, do. Suddenly her mind leaped forward to a brand new life, the second half-century. "It could be fun, it will be fun," Samantha said to herself. Only three small pieces of cake was eaten, so Victor again, would have an abundance of Samantha's delicious dessert to himself.

As Victor readied himself to devour the last of Samantha's dessert; she lay still on her back, staring into the ceiling. Her body was relaxed with her legs apart, bent at the knees and propped upward. Samantha felt a relaxation and somberness which was new as her hands gently rubbed the cross around her neck. Her delicious dessert was positioned squarely in the front of Victor's face, and he never noticed Samantha's somber mood; he also never noticed her fine nude thighs. He was too overwhelmed by the multi-layers before him, with its smooth thick creamy surface. The sweet aroma penetrated his nose as the creaminess soaked through the layers; enticing his tongue to slowly slide into it. Sampling such a glistening moisture was definitely a prelude to nibbling Samantha's dessert. Samantha felt a soothing warmness upon her as she meditated. Victor's decision to clear away the delicious cream brought no opposition from the inspirational Samantha. When consumption started, Victor opened his mouth wide and crammed it full of Samantha's soft succulent dessert. Little or no chewing was necessary, but was performed slightly to embrace his dining pleasure. Samantha's movements upon the bed was consistent with the soothing movements upon her. Victor enjoyed Samantha's delicious dessert as he devoured layer after layer, lashing vigorously into it as it appeared to be tasting sweeter and sweeter. An abundance of sweet juices were flowing all about his mouth and down his throat as he dissolved Samantha's delicious dessert into a forceful stream of powerful sweetness. Samantha's meditative thought process came to an end when she realized her fiftieth had indeed come about, and her birthday celebrations were at a climax. Somehow, both Victor and Samantha knew, this was the final climax between them.

Turning fifty for some might not mean much, but for Samantha Lundenberry Previtt, it was a new beginning, a new lease on life. Her brand new image was causing rave reviews around town. Trading in her silver-streaked curly hairdo for the black smooth dual French rolls, accented with a left short forward bang, had removed another ten years of age, but had added ten years of sophistication and vitality. Carolyn and Tiffani had accidentally taught her buoyant dress, with those expensive suits from Gerald's Boutique, and exclusive pieces of jewelry appropriately worn. Funny, she had never noticed her beautiful legs and marvelous thighs before, but if they were enough to make Carolyn jealous, that was good enough for Samantha. And it's not like she did not have the body to match those other fine parts. That was by far, the greatest inadvertent compliment, she had ever received. Now she received intentional compliments from old and new acquaintances; most of which she thought was very genuine and flirtatious in nature. Such a twist had intervened in Samantha's life, she had already started writing her next book, entitled, "Fun Living—The Second Half-Century—Your Way". And ironically, Samantha no longer craved those special dependency needs from Victor, but their true friendship was even stronger. He is that brother, she never had; he is truly that friend of all friends; that someone she could trust and depend on as a real true friend.

CHAPTER THIRTY SEVEN

GRANDMA GOES TO COLLEGE

Carolyn welcomed her housekeeper back home on Monday morning. She smiled as he trudged his tired body through her front door.

"Welcome home Victor, you look awful; look at those bags under your eyes. Too much birthday celebration, huh?"

"Yeah, I suppose Carolyn; man, I'm glad I took two extra days off this week."

"Well, I suppose that ex drained you; huh, Victor?"

"Be nice Carolyn, I'm fine."

"Well, you certainly do not look like it; don't worry, I will give you two days to recuperate Victor; there is no need of me having a corpse on my hands. Get your rest today and tomorrow while you are off; and tomorrow night, prepare to touch me up a little bit, before I become a nervous wreck. Just between me and you, I have been horny and edgy ever since I found out about that damn birthday celebration."

"I understand Carolyn, thanks for your patience, but I will be ready for you after work, this evening. So hurry home!"

Victor was not trying to be macho or superhero or anything like that, but Carolyn built excitement in his body, he could not even fully understand. Of course, to be on the safe side, he took some of Carolyn's multiple vitamin tablets, and crawled into bed. Victor was not worried, because he knew Carolyn had a way of bringing you around to her way of thinking. When she came home at noon though, Victor's puzzled look told a different story.

"Victor, I could not think straight at work, so I took the afternoon off; I hope you do not mind. Being close to you, is all I care about today; I just want you to hold me. If you feel up to anything else, that is also fine."

Holding Carolyn, Victor had found, had always been a difficult stopping point. She stripped and slid into bed, next to Victor, placing his hand directly over her woolly center. Carolyn's fingers played atop Victor's fingers in a piano fashion, until his was doing the same upon her woolly center. Eventually, each of Victor's fingers were seemingly playing a note which Carolyn appreciated. These mechanics were new to both of them, especially for Victor, because he normally used his tastetester for such manipulation. Carolyn really wanted to be held, as she commenced to talk about what was really on her mind.

"Victor, I never told you before and I do not know, if I really knew myself, but I am a little bit jealous of your ex."

Victor wanted to tell Carolyn, there was no need to be jealous of Samantha, because she had moved on with her life; but Carolyn, he thought, deserved to suffer a little bit in this area, for a taste of her own medicine."

"Now Carolyn, that is a switch."

"I know, I know, but when you were gone, I could not help thinking of how Samantha was using you, for her so called fiftieth birthday celebration. I mean, the occasion sounds good, but I had the feeling she was putting more into it than what was really there, Victor."

"Blame me too Carolyn, because we agreed as friends to share that birthday together."

"I am not blaming anybody Victor, I am merely telling you of my jealousy; maybe it was the attention she was receiving from everybody, including you. People turn fifty everyday Victor, so what; it does not seem like any big deal to me."

"You are right Carolyn, but this one was extra special to Samantha. If it had been you, I would have done the same thing.

Maybe you are being too sensitive."

"Maybe so Victor or maybe I am just angry at you for leaving my house, for four days, to spend with another woman."

"Probably so Carolyn; if it had been someone else, you would probably be envious of them, also."

"That is real close to the truth Victor, especially if that person was another good looking female, like Samantha. I like Samantha too Victor, but I was so angry with her for stealing my man for four whole days. Please hold me tighter Victor."

Victor held her woolly center tighter, moving his fingers inside of it, as Carolyn grew silent and began to stir somewhat. Victor smiled to himself, because this was the first time Carolyn had really shown a jealous streak like a normal woman. He thought, Carolyn might just be a real human after all. Indeed, Carolyn was a real human as was evident from her immediate remarks:

"Victor, I am sorry, but I need more; I realize you are tired, so just lay here and relax, I'll take care of us."

Carolyn, this very moment, crawled atop Victor; her woolly center was spitting fire as her knees and long thighs straddled him; leaning back gently and gentler until Victor's entire bigness slowly made its way. Carolyn could feel the jealously and envy flow from her body as Victor's bigness continued its path into her woolly center. She took it all, to prove to him, she was still the best woman; then Carolyn adjusted her woolly center upon his bigness to the proper elevation. An elevation in which Victor could not stand very long, before he cried out. He cried out for more, he cried out for more and more, he cried out for more and more of the same. Carolyn knew her power over Victor and she was determined to reduplicate her dominion. She no longer cared about Samantha, she just wanted Victor to put his mind back on her, and Carolyn was succeeding, as her woolly center tightened its grip upon Victor's bigness, making him cry and beg. Carolyn loved hearing Victor cry and beg for her sweetness, because she too became more excited. She also loved Victor's bigness gyrating inside her woolly center as she revolved, round and round. And now as Carolyn slowly rotated, she could feel Victor's end was near; he gripped his hands firmly upon her behind and screamed, with those funny rhythmic jerks. At this point, Carolyn knew she had approximately ten seconds, to give Victor her most powerful grip, to force one last crying and begging from him, and to get in a crying and begging of her own. Carolyn no longer felt threatened by Samantha, as she felt Victor's bigness fall; she had reenforced her power as she felt that old sensuous vibrancy inside her woolly center. Victor was now asleep, and Carolyn felt bad for having made him miss lunch, but she would awaken him for dinner; here she would further establish her original position as she would make him cry and beg for more of her sweetness.

Even with all of Carolyn's sweetness, Victor still managed to call his office daily, for his messages; this is when he found out Angela had called and informed him, grandma expected him to dinner on Wednesday night. "It had to be something important," Victor said to himself, "because grandma rarely requested his presence." And as the three of them sat at the dinner table, grandma appears to be in control of the conversation.

"I know you two lovebirds are wondering why I called a formal dinner in the middle of the week."

"Well, grandmother; it does seem sort of odd."

"Not to me Angela, I attend these all the time."

"Victor, this is no joking matter, this could be serious; right grandmother?"

"It is for me Angela, but it is not something, we can't have a little fun with."

"I am really curious now grandmother; what is it?"

"Angela, you know, we must not forget our table manners; a prayer is always the proper thing before a meal."

"Okay grandmother, but I suggest a nice short one!"

"Since you feel that way young lady, why don't you do the honors."

"Okay grandmother; let us bow our heads. Lord we want to thank you for this special day, and we need not know grandmother's reason ahead of time for it to be so, because you made it special when you gave us our breath this morning. Father, I want to thank you for blessing me and staying with me, even though sometimes, I am not worthy of your grace; and dear Father I thank you for grandmother, and ask that you continue to bless her, that she will live a long life, to watch her great-granddaughters grow, with the strength you give them each day. And Father, please bless Victor, the man I so dearly love; guide him in the direction you would have him go, remove all obstacles and stumbling blocks from his path. And dear Heavenly Father, we want to thank You for this food, bless it, that we may grow stronger in Thy sight. And Father, we ask these and all things in the name of Your Son and our Savior, Jesus Christ; Amen.

"Thank you Angela; short huh!"

"Well grandmother—"

"Just teasing honey, that was nice."

"Thank you Angela."

"You are welcome Victor; okay grandmother, start talking!"

"Oh, I an not going to make a speech Angela; I only wanted to announce that I am going to college."

"Only, oh that is so wonderful grandmother; I am so happy; when do you get started? What are you majoring in? Oh, I have been wanting to hear those words for a long time; you will not regret—"

"Angela, I am only going to school, not into outer space."

"Yeah I know, but I am so excited grandmother."

"I am excited too, Ms. Lincoln, but I will relinquish my words to Angela."

"Victor!"

"Oh, just kidding Angela; Ms. Lincoln, this is not just a reason to be excited; it is a reason for a celebration. This dinner I might add is very appropriate. And since we have three glasses of crystal clear water before us, I propose a toast; up and to the center, everybody. Here's to Ms. Lincoln and a highly successful college career."

"Thank you Victor, but I will need all of you guys help."

"Ms. Lincoln; anything I can do, please feel free to call me anytime!"

"You know, you can count on me grandmother; oh, I am so happy!"

It appears, grandma felt, she had been talking about it long enough; and decided to enroll in college. The babysitting chores probably had worn the old nerves thin. Not that anyone can blame her, because even the best of babies need constant attention. One was not so bad, but the addition of Victoria really had her going. Changing those pampers and all that baby feeding can get pretty monotonous after a while. While grandma was talking about going to college; Angela was steady encouraging her. So the most exuberant person, of course was Angela, in hearing of the college-bound grandma. Yet it still came as somewhat of a surprise during this time, because grandma appeared to be having the time of her life caring for the girls. Surely, it had nothing to do with her affection for the little ones. The thought of raising two small children at her age would be enough to have any sensible person, choose a new career though.

Grandma probably felt the years sailing by more swiftly with another generation in the house. You could see the little ones growing before your very eyes. Grandma had noticed the rapid changes in her great-grandchildren, knowing college could be put aside no longer. Questions probably surfaced in her mind. What could she tell the new ones about school. What would be said when they asked how far she went and where did she go? Would she say I didn't have the opportunity. I didn't have the chance. Or would grandma do like so many of us who had squandered an opportunity; quickly change the subject or lie, that an education was not as important then as it is now. Whatever the rationalization, grandma had made a timely decision.

When Angela and Victor found out about the gigantic change, grandma had already selected a fine and reputable day care center for the little ones, and enrolled them in it. Grandma had also selected Business Administration as her field of interest. Victor had no doubt, she was going to do well, due to her daily readings and monitoring of the Business World. The Wall Street Journal and business magazines have been her constant companions, since Victor had known her. Their periodic discussions of corporate changes and decisions have been intriguing for sometimes.

Grandma was also very knowledgeable on all current events. For she not only read the local newspaper, but subscribed to and read the Sunday edition of the New York Times. Victor's most impressive and intellectual conversations have been with this woman. Grandma was able to discuss events of foreign interest as fluently as any local or national event. But business was her greatest love.

Grandma had a personal financial consultant, but as she would hastily say, "I know more than he does; and after all, it is my money." However, she further stated, "I do respect his judgment." She apparently had substantial investments in several corporations, because her knowledge of the stock market and certain companies was pretty keen. Now one can see where Angela got her tremendous business sense. Victor never inquired as to any specific personal details, and grandma never volunteered any. It was not his place anyway to mingle in her personal affairs, unless invited. It's not that nothing else was of great importance, but Angela's well being was in the superior category for grandma.

Her great-grandchildren were also very high on that list. Grandma told Victor not to worry about their education; it was already taken care of. Victor wanted to tell her, those were his girls and he could more than adequately provide for them. But, he realized, they too, were very much a big part of her life; and maybe he shouldn't intervene. Grandma was very much concerned about young people getting a good education. She had wanted Angela to remain in school until at least, she earned an MBA. On several occasions grandma even encouraged Victor to go back to school. He never questioned her as to why, and it was unclear during these urges, the significance for the highest plateau of learning. Victor thought, "I only wish, she knew Stacy, because that's someone who could use an effective lecture on higher learning." Samantha and Victor had tried for several years without success.

Victor thought; "If I were to take one guess on grandma's past; it would feature her growing up in a large poor family, where education was totally impossible. Because it was obvious, with her current desires; an earlier education was either, not affordable or due to circumstances, unobtainable. Maybe, they were sharecroppers moving from one undesirable place to the next; living in the shantiest conditions. Those more deplorable than any slave-house due to its temporary nature. Working by seasons, which never seemed to coincide with the school seasons. Always just five or six months off, from being right on time. So this little girl had to get her learning within the bounds of limited possibilities."

Victor continues; "I could see grandma, because of her bulky stout structure carrying the load of any bull, both in weight and temperament. Grandma had that book in her home-made pouch; and on every rest stop and every mid-day meal horn, she poured those black eyes at the crinkled pages. Pages worn but visible enough to beg for more reading. She took advantage of every opportunity, she had during each day, cause its end brought work to a halt, and no light remaining. No light to pull off those dirty, sweaty clothes. No light to wash her gritty, grimmy hair. No light to thumb through those precious pages; and no light to see the I's and T's, and other alphabets that danced across those pages."

Victor thought more; "Grandma had one book a season and she read it. She had two books a season and she read them. She read each book from cover to cover, over and over; until the next dictatorial word rang out, as the one before it faded into a predictable hush. The next word and next, and next, and next, all fighting for its individuality, that had long been lost, because of the reciting rapidity. Grandma now knew each sentence from memory, and read in the dark. She read from the dark corners of quoting that brilliant mind. Her memory needed no natural light for recitation; the visionary light was bright enough to thumb each page and read each line. After so many recitals, grandma was creating her own interpretations, giving new vitality and meaning to someone else's stale book. The books usefulness had played out in terms of knowledge, but continued to solidify grandma's educational foundation."

Victor reasoned that; "Grandma's mind was ready to travel; to move on to a higher plateau, but there was nowhere to go. She found herself hemmed inside a circle, and around and around she went. A circle whose rut grew deeper as she starved herself for yet another book. Grandma's thirst for knowledge exceeded the material at her fingertips. Her pouch didn't need to be any bigger, it just needed another book, and another, and another. Grandma's world was now bigger than the books she had read; it was now bigger than the next dusty town and its backward inhabitants she slaved for. She was trapped because that's all her parents knew. She was locked into a cycle that perpetuated the poor, the illiterate. A cycle that kept the downtrodden, down. Somehow, grandma knew she must break that cycle; someway, grandma knew she must get out.

BREAK THE CYCLE

Read a good book each day
Break the cycle of illiteracy
Work the mind and the hand
Break the cycle of poverty

Go to school with every chance
Break the cycle of the uneducated
History shouldn't repeat itself
Break the cycle of the ill-fated

No excuse smother tireless effort
Of unscholarly, impoverished, birth
Read On, Read On, Read On, PLEASE!
Break The Cycle; Break The Girth

Victor envisioned grandma's struggle and he envisioned grandma one day sinking all her energy and strength into that one step; leaping through the vicious cycle and into a new world of opportunity. Her mind could no longer be restrained within the confines of boundaries. The new world was without limits. There would be no perimeters; there would be no more reciting the overdone words.

Grandma's first year went pretty smoothly. She had some difficulty with the english and math, but managed to get through without failure. Other than comments about being a little tired, Victor never heard grandma complain. She looked forward to class each day. For her it was a rebirth. Grandma had begun to even look younger. Her makeup was different and earrings and necklaces were different.

The greatest change however was in dressing. She was now wearing designer jeans and sneakers for the most part. Grandma had become the hippest dresser sporting the latest. Her beautiful shoulder-length hair had been stretched backward into a ball on her head. The curly waves of black and gray gave an added sophisticated look; plus it gave her an even more youthful appearance.

Angela had tried to get her to dye it; but she refused, stating that she got more respect being herself; both from the students and professors. Angela hoped in her golden youth, she would be able to garner respect so simply.

The new generation had commenced to mark her era, in the wearing of wire-rimmed spectacles; so grandma was right on with the latest fashions in eyewear. She had now been accepted and was one of them in all the superficial sense. All the students admired Ms. Lincoln, as they called her; and drew upon her conviction and wisdom. They also benefitted from her advice and the historical value she possessed. There was nothing the students would not do for Ms. Lincoln. And she drew from them, that youthful vibrant energy.

Her strong features had lessened in her face and grandma appeared less intense and happier. Of course the helping of Molly, might have been the contributing factor in that endeavor. Molly was a young lady about nineteen, in grandma's history class. Molly was on the quiet side and generally only spoke to grandma upon returning a greeting. She caught grandma's attention, because she was very attractive, but always seemed to be sad or the least, to be a million miles away in thought.

One day nearing the end of the first semester; grandma found her with head and face down on her desk crying. At first grandma thought Molly to be merely resting her eyes or something, until she heard what sounded like a sniffle. Not being one to mettle into other folks business, grandma took a seat along side Molly as usual, and waited for class to start. During the class, Molly was her normal sharp and scholarly self. Apparently, she was very studious, because, not a lot of questions went unanswered in the class; Molly constantly had her hand in the air.

However, at the end of the class, Molly's eyes again were watering as they prepared to leave the classroom. The tears got the best of grandma as she inquired. "What is the matter, Molly; Is there something wrong?" Molly hesitated, but told grandma that, "because her father has lost his job, she would not be able to attend school, next semester." Grandma listened attentively and went through her normal spillage; that things would work out; and for her not to worry.

While grandma, believed in what she was saying, because those words had come to be part of her philosophy; she could not sleep soundly that night, for thinking of Molly. It was obvious to her that Molly was a fine student from a poor family. and it dawned on her. What if I help Molly the following semester. Grandma, thought, I'll just loan her the money, as she fell into an all night sleep.

It had never been grandma's idea, to help anyone financially other than Angela; but by the next morning, there was this wild and crazy thought on her brain. Don't loan Molly anything. Give it to her; and not only for the next semester, but for her entire college education. Grandma sort of smiled to herself and said, why not. Just the thought of helping someone in need, made grandma feel real good that morning. She went about her morning routine, singing and skipping around the house. It was the first time in years, that grandma felt like hop-scotch or jump-rope. A most unusual and happy day, she thought.

Upon talking to Molly the next class session; grandma found her to be from Waco, Texas; the first of three children in her family. When grandma informed Molly that she wanted to help her by adopting a student; Molly starting crying profusely. She grabbed grandma, crying, hugging, and squeezing her. Grandma was trying to control Molly, and she started crying; but these were all, tears of joy.

Grandma had never experienced anything like this before. Helping someone other than a relative had really made her feel pleasant toward life. She thought of how much happier Molly appeared. At first, grandma rationalized saying; Molly would have found a way and probably, have been back in school next semester or the least, by the following year. But the after thought that hit was more than enough to shake reality into its proper place. Why would you deliberately let someone suffer, when you could help. Thoughts of the glow in Molly's face and the tremendous excitement it had caused in both their lives; generated more positive echoes. Echoes which kept getting louder as their smiles grew wider.

Grandma was receiving treasures which she never knew existed. "How could one be so happy giving of themselves," she thought. Decades, she had lived as one of the fortunate few, and had never made an effort to uplift no one, but her own. "I can only hope this rarified pledge is the first of many to stir my heart," as grandma continues her thought process. A most joyous occasion for the both of them. When they regained their composure, grandma told Molly that she would foot the bill on the rest of her schooling. Molly thanked her again, and said, she couldn't wait to call home. Later, Molly had news, she would go home between semesters, and wanted grandma to go with her.

When Victor and Angela had first sat down to dinner, to hear grandma tell them of her plans to go to college, needless to say, they were both happy. And Victor had all of these puzzling questions he wanted to ask grandma, but somehow, with Angela present, he could not bring himself to ask any of them. Mostly because, Angela never talked of grandma's life very much. Oh, there were bits and pieces of little things, but nothing solid, nothing that you could sink your teeth into. There was so much, Victor wants to ask, but not knowing where to start, kept him as mum, as Angela did; nearly always being around. He certainly did not want to inquire while Angela was present because he had a feeling grandma's personal life was, pretty much, a closed subject in this large mansion. So Victor promised himself, when the time was right he would ask; he would ask all the pertinent questions; he would find out about grandma's personal life. And that time did come, only a few days later; it was as if both he and Ms. Lincoln had been waiting on the same opportunity; to be alone with each other.

CHAPTER THIRTY EIGHT

UNVEILING OF A SECRET

"Victor, I understand you love Angela and she truly loves you very much. There is something I must tell you—she is my daughter."

"She's what Ms. Lincoln!"

"That's correct. It is a rather lengthy story Victor, but I'll shorten it because you don't have all year. My life at forty six had sort of passed me by—no education—no decent job—just odd jobs here and there. And by some strange turn of events, I landed a job in this factory owned by J. B. Tankerstroke, the white Industrialist. He took to me, bought me a small frame house, with the understanding he could come by. Well I knew what that meant, but what damage could a sixty seven year old man do. That damage turned out to be a sweet and loving Angela."

"I was happy when Angela was born Victor, but embarrassed at her complexion. She was the whitest baby I had ever seen at birth. People told me she would get darker as she got older. Tankerstroke, even said, she'll get darker. She did, but not very much. With the exception of those black eyes and round hips from me; she is exactly like her father, Tankerstroke."

"Of course Victor, those shiny black eyes are what excited Tankerstroke the most. He'd often say, "that's what caught my attention when I first saw you. The most beautiful eyes in the world and now they're on our Angel." Angel, that's what Tankerstroke called her; and somehow I got the feeling, he was serious. Angela definitely was an angel to him, but the glow or halo hung over his head. Yes, Angela was a blessing to Tankerstroke and from his looks; his greatest gift ever."

"Tankerstroke was a good man Victor. He was married but had no children of his own; and melted at the sight of Angela. He swore me to secrecy and promised to provide for me and Angela's well being. Only his accountant knew the details of the millions left to us. Tankerstoke must have known his time was short - he died at seventy. The two years he spent with Angela were the two happiest years of his life. The gossip got too heavy in Ohio; and I had no reason to remain there, so I packed and headed for Texas."

"I had no idea Victor, what I'd find here or why Texas was chosen; other than I had heard it was a wide-open place, very large in size. Maybe my subconscious took over, since I was running away and trying to conceal my identity. And, I thought, the bigger the place the better. What I didn't realize was I couldn't run from myself."

"What about the grandma bit, Ms. Lincoln?"

"I'm coming to that Victor. Everywhere I went, people just assumed Angela was my grandchild. And to hold down on all the explaining, upon entering Texas; I was now a proud grandparent. And I must admit, I was still embarrassed over what I had done and that Angela hadn't darkened to my brown complexion. I often thought, that was God's way of putting a curse on me. San Antonio has been good for me; the people are wonderful, and I have a host of great friends. Of course it helps to be wealthy."

"Whoa, that's some story, but why did you tell me?"

"You are the man in her life, Victor; you are the father of her two girls—my darling grandchildren. I know, your life, like most of us is not perfect; but the Lord will make a way somehow. In certain ways, you remind me of Tankerstroke. Angela has no other family, so there's no immediate urgency to tell her."

"I don't know about that Ms. Lincoln—I believe you're aware of the identify crisis Angela has been going through. She's been studying about Black people in all of her spare time and mine."

"That is good for her Victor; we all need to know the history of our Black culture and heritage; now you can be more tolerate of Angela. I'll tell her in due time."

"Ms. Lincoln, how were you able to conceal this so long from Angela—didn't she ever ask questions?"

"No Victor, not really; I have managed it by keeping her busy, in school, in church, traveling and more traveling. We have traveled all over the World. So her fondest memories are of me and the good times we've had. And let's face it, I always treated her as my daughter."

"Ms. Lincoln, Angela is struggling now on that job and that's the real world."

"In growing up Victor, Angela has never suffered or experienced disappointments. She is well disciplined. I've taught her the value of a dollar, so there has never been any outrageous demands for material things. She knows no pain and misery. A little pain though is good for your soul—it makes you think. Angela has to learn how to cope with diverse situations. Would you have me tell her she's a multi-millionaire; and have her curse the bastards out. That will not do any good, Victor. A cursing will not change a racist heart—that's where prayer comes in."

"I don't know Ms. Lincoln, it seems like we've been praying long enough. What we need now is some more marching, boycotting, and ass kicking, to drive our point home a bit quicker. We don't have four hundred more years to be pussy-footing around with the man. We've taken one step forward and two backwards, now that affirmative action is dead."

"You got the message Victor, you just missed the point. Middle-age professional Blacks like yourself, and young Blacks like Angela, are going to have to map out an agenda with essentially the same ideas, for defeating racism in this country. But first, you must forget age differences and get together as Black people—no more old agenda for some and new agenda for others. You can't do nothing as long as you're divided. A lot of us old folks spend too much time taking the youngsters for granted. That must change. And on the other hand, the youngster think we're just old and stupid. So that must change. A meeting of the minds would help a lot, you know."

"Anyway, Victor, I understand what you're saying. I also understand Angela doing the Black studies thing—that's good for her. When the timing is right, she will know exactly who she is. Tankerstroke knew this would happen later on; and gathered personal information about himself. I don't even know what it is, because it is not to be released to us until Angela turns thirty. That's one of the reasons, I am in no hurry to tell Angela. I could only tell her, his name and how he was toward me. Not saying I'm right Victor; a decision had to be made, and that was my choice. We could both be wrong."

"Tankerstroke was a quiet sort of a fellow Victor, not talking very much, except about business; and never anything about himself. He was nice enough, but seemed to be a very lonely man. Sometimes he would just sit and stare into space, as if his mind was over a million miles away and on over a million things."

"Maybe Ms. Lincoln, he felt guilty of taking advantage of the po lil black girl."

"To the contrary, Victor, Tankerstroke was quite comfortable with me—it was like he yearned for good companionship. As far as sex goes, we only made love a few times; and after Angela was born, we never did anything."

"All his time and love Victor, was devoted to Angela. Tankerstroke wouldn't let me work after Angela. He came to see her everyday, and spent hours there; like that was his life's calling. And always for lunch, Tankerstroke was there. Red beans and ham hocks, chicken and dressing, chicken and dumplin, and neckbones and collard greens, were his favorite dishes. And for dessert, Tankerstroke could devour a whole sweet potato pie at one sitting. He had some appetite."

"One thing that seemed odd Victor, was his mixing of cornbread and sugar with buttermilk in a large glass. My parents use to eat like that; and here was this rich old white man doing the same thing. I'd smile and he'd only smile back, like we both had a guarded secret. Things were happening so fast, with the new baby and all; I didn't have nor devote time to being too curious or worrying about Tankerstroke's peculiar habits."

"While you're talking Ms. Lincoln, what about your background as a child?"

This, of course had been the question troubling Victor or most on his mind anyway.

"Well Victor, there's really not a lot to tell that's extraordinary. I'm a typical Black farm owner's daughter, from Georgia, like yourself. I was the youngest, by about six years, in a family of four brothers. Not knowing what a girl was suppose to be like, I always tried to keep up with them and do what they did. They looked out for me, but I must have been the biggest tomboy around."

"What about school, Ms. Lincoln?"

"Oh, I never set foot inside a school until I went to college, here recently. Victor, you're a city child; and there's quite a difference. When I said I was a farmer's daughter; I should have mentioned, this acreage of land was far into the backwoods. There was no such thing as neighbors next door and all that. And speaking of school, that wasn't a priority in our neck of the woods. Let's just say, you wouldn't have to worry about no Truant Officer coming by to get you."

"My father's primary goal Victor, was always getting out the next crop and getting ready for winter. So we're talking about hog-killing time and lots of canning from the crops. That's where I come in; I was mama's helper at canning time; along with the other numerous chores that had to be done. Don't get me wrong, I had fun back then, but the work was a priority and had to be done. I can't even say it was hard work, because it was so routine; and that is all we knew. That was just a way of life."

"You read all the time, Ms. Lincoln; how did you learn to read?"

"Ah Victor, I give that credit to mama. She knew papa's idea of women learning to read was out of the question. You see he felt that a woman would get married, and her husband would take it from there. A woman, he felt, needed to know how to cook, wash clothes, and everything else around the house. In other words, a woman's place was in the home seeing that her man was well fed. That didn't have nothing to do with no reading or writing. But somehow, my brothers knew how to read and write; so mama made them teach me. But we hardly had anything to read from. It was scarcely any books available; but somehow a dictionary turned up. I read that dictionary all the time."

"My mother didn't know how to read or write Victor, and she always felt at a disadvantage and inferior to papa, because he would talk about things she didn't know about. Mama told me, you'll learn to read if I have to beat it into you. I can remember, as if it was today, the surprised look on papa's face, when he started talking about something, he'd read in a newspaper from town; and mama started discussing it with him. How did you know about that, he said."

"Mama boasted out her chest Victor, and said; "my sweet Hattie read it to me. She reads to me everyday, while we're working." Papa couldn't do nothing but laugh, because he knew mama had pulled one over on him. He continued the joke for years; coming home in the evening, saying, "what's the latest news for today." You see, after that, papa always brought the old once a week newspaper straight to his baby girl. After supper he'd sat on the porch in that ole swing and let me read to him. Sometimes it was the same story, but papa just sat there and smiled. So you see, I'm sort of self-educated, but I had lots of help as a youth."

"As I got older Victor, I would read everything I could get my hands on. I knew I wasn't going to get married and become no farmer's wife. Those were not my plans. But there were no jobs back there for no uneducated Black woman that knew how to read. Of course, in our part of the country, there were no jobs for an educated Black man or woman. Victor, we were "sho nough" in the country."

"I told mama I wanted to leave home Victor and find some real work. She knew what I meant and helped me save some money. Actually, she saved it for me, on pennies and nickels, she managed to come by, here and there. I didn't know where I was going; but I knew it would be out of the South. Somewhere I saw Ohio, and a train ticket was purchased to Cleveland. Why there, I can't remember. It worked out, because during the war, women were working in factories, and that's how I got my first real job."

"That's also Victor, when I was having a good time. Having a job making my own money. I sent mama money every time I got paid. And here I was, a country girl in a big city, where there were real men. None of those country hicks in overalls. Talking about partying; you youngsters today can't never party the way we partied back there. Now, those were the good old days."

"I didn't think about tomorrow Victor, and pretty soon the war was over, and there was no job. But that was okay; men were plentiful and we could always find one to take care of a sweet chick. That lasted for awhile and then that played out. Times just got real hard all over again. I went from odd job to odd job; just anything I could find to get a meal. The one thing I was firm on though; and that was, there was no way I was going to give up and go back home. Beating around as I call it, must have lasted for twenty years; a decent job here, a bad one, and on and on. But all together, nothing good or permanent until I stumbled onto the job from Tankerstroke."

"Tankerstroke took one look at me Victor, and said, young lady you're hired. He didn't ask for no qualifications or nothing. He put me to work nailing shipping crates around cargo. That's all I had to do, other than let old Frank Tadford know, it was ready to go. Taking to the hammer all day seemed like a man's job, but my tomboy days had prepared me for that. Tankerstroke would come through every hour or so to see how, in his opinion, how I was coming along. I was a hard worker, and old man Tad, as they called him, had told me so. Little did I know, Tankerstroke had took a personal interest in me. Old man Tad told me one day, "the boss has set eyes on you girl." We joked about how this old white man, would probably die in his tracks, getting some hot soul stuff."

"Old man Tad was right Victor, cause one day, Tankerstroke came right out and said, "Hattie, you're a good worker, and I like you very much." I had been thinking, about what I would say and do if this old white dried up prune approached me. Now, that time was here, and all I could do was stand there—mute and motionless. He continued, saying; "you interested me, the first day, you showed up." Never, had I heard a man sound so sincere."

"Now, Victor, you're up to date."

Victor had guessed at Ms. Lincoln's life, and it looks like he was a bit off.

"Except, for one thing Victor, which I didn't quite understand. Before Tankerstroke died, he insisted that I see that Angela was well educated. He constantly labored on it and made me promise that I would see to it. I understood the importance of a good education, but I couldn't understand Tankerstroke's motive for harping on it."

"Maybe, Ms. Lincoln, its because he knew she would grow up as a Black girl and be denied certain rights that his white race enjoyed, otherwise."

"He also insisted Victor, that I go to school since, I didn't have to work. So going to college had been on my agenda for a long time. I'm having the time of my life, and the people I'm meeting are so wonderful."

Yes, Victor was a bit off in his summation of Ms. Lincoln's life, and certainly, without saying it, he was surprised at some of the things she said. Notably, that she was Angela's mother instead of grandmother, and that she had made love to an old white man. Surprised, mind you, not disturbed, because Ms. Lincoln had explained both situations fully and admittedly, satisfactorily, in his opinion. "What happened to Ms. Lincoln," he thought, "could have happened to anybody; she made what she thought was the best move at the time. And for her it worked, at least financially it did, but mentally, it has caused some scar tissue; it has caused her shame." Living with yourself, is what one must do, every second of every day; and one should be able to do so, without guilt or shame. And in the case of Ms. Lincoln, she has been unable to do so; the hardship and mental stress for her must be extremely tough. Just think, trying to hide the truth from your friends and love ones for thirty years, and the thought of them eventually finding out, you are not, who you are. This secret has burdened Ms. Lincoln for a long, long time, and in reality, is still a burden on her shoulder, because the most important person in her life, Angela, still does not know, grandma is ma. The shock and devastation this might cause Angela, undoubtedly had entered Ms. Lincoln's mind, and like she said, she made the decision, she thought best at the time; maybe, the right one from her point of view. Victor thought, "at least Ms. Lincoln had a plan; so what if it was a thirty year plan; it was still better than no disclosure plan at all."

A mild surprise to Victor was the telling of her secret to him first; but again, not disturbing, because she explained that perfect also. Victor would have considered himself, a victim of circumstance, if it had not been for Angela; she had fallen in love with him through no fault of her own. And for him, this dream come true, now had more of a special significance than previously thought; because now, when the "stuff" hits the fan, if needed, there would be a shoulder to cry on; and there would be two beautiful little girls to cushion the tears. Whatever; Ms. Lincoln had the faith, the vision, the fortitude, or the something, that things would eventually work out. For the wisdom she had displayed in his presence, Victor had confidence, things would also work out. And to be sure, Victor promised himself, he would be there, when this thirty year old secret was unveiled to Angela; he wanted that strong shoulder to lean on, to be his.

Victor felt good that Ms. Lincoln trusted him to share her burden, for the greatest love of her life. He reasoned, more than chance had played a part in his availability. Victor thought of a bunch of ifs which would have excluded him: If his dream of Angela had never occurred, if he had not gone to the market for flowers, if he and Samantha had not divorced, if Angela had not fallen in love with him, if, if, if.... "Fortunate for me," Victor thought, "none of those ifs happened, and his strong sense of positiveness told him, he was definitely in the right place at the right time." Because, there were no regrets when it came to Angela, and there was nothing, to date, that he would change. And thinking of his homegirl, Ms. Lincoln, Victor concluded, that was precisely what she was saying in her meeting of old man Tankerstroke. Now, Victor understood why Ms. Lincoln likened him to Tankerstroke in a certain way. Through it all, Angela had made them happy. "Angela," Victor thought, "was providing him with twice that amount of happiness in Hattia and Victoria, that she herself, provided a long time ago. Victor suddenly sensed a stronger bond in Ms. Lincoln; he realized her new trust in him was binding them closer and closer; theirs were a common bond, without question."

CHAPTER THIRTY NINE

LINCOLN AT THE CAPITAL

Molly was happier these days, and without saying, she and Ms. Lincoln were good friends. Ms. Lincoln had agreed to go home, to Waco, with Molly on one condition; they were to travel there in Ms. Lincoln's car. Ms Lincoln said, "I am going to start now, taking care of you." On their way home, they stopped in Austin, the Capital of Texas. Molly had visited the capitol while in high school, and wanted to show it to Ms. Lincoln; who though, having been to Austin, had never seen the House of Representatives or Senate in session. "A good time," she thought, "to see some of our taxpayers money at work."

This was the first highlight of the trip, as they watched the House of Representatives argue and state their positions on some bill. Ms. Lincoln was impressed, but became a little bored after an hour. Molly, meanwhile, was having a good time, telling Ms. Lincoln; "now that is what I want to do; only I am not going to stop here, I am going on to the Capitol in Washington, D.C.." Ms. Lincoln smiled at her and said; "if that's what you really want, you'll do it." Molly was a pre-law student and had ambitions to be a politician for her Country. It was nice to hear that patriotic ring in her voice. It is always refreshing to hear the words that spew out over an uncorrupted brain.

Ms. Lincoln was feeling somewhat weary after the first one hundred miles. Riding around on interstate highways was not the mode of transportation, she'd grown fond of in her accelerated years. She had thought it would be easier with Molly doing the chauffeuring; but when there's no restrooms available, an automobile trip—no matter the comfort—is still just another tiresome trip. Molly was patient in stopping anytime Ms. Lincoln wanted to vent her bladder.

Waco was about a hundred miles from Austin and reminded Ms. Lincoln of the small town she had left near Cleveland. Molly's house also reminded Ms. Lincoln of the one Tankerstroke bought for her in Ohio, except it had two bedrooms. It was one of those cozy little houses, sporting a new coat of white paint or lately painted anyway. And it was every bit as snug inside as it appeared on their arrival. Somehow, Ms. Lincoln could picture a swing on the porch, but it wasn't there. Molly was chirping more than usual, because there's no place like home and she was indeed proud of everything in sight. From the creaks in each step of the porch, to the worn out welcome mat, carefully centered in front of the doorway; all signs indicated a cordial and pleasing family within. Molly literally pushed Ms. Lincoln through the door to meet her parents and show her off.

They would spend two nights there; so Molly's father, Richard Cooper and mother, Sarah, volunteered their bedroom to Ms. Lincoln and Molly. Ms. Lincoln told them she didn't want to put them out; they insisted, and she unpacked. She had not been in a house this small in a long time; but to them it was home, and to her, it was very comfortable.

Oh, it didn't have all the new and fancy amenities, Ms. Lincoln had grown accustomed to in her later years, but it was indeed home sweet home. No unnecessary and wasted space could be found. She found out later, Richard and Sarah slept in the other bedroom; where the two kids slept on a pallet. That really took her back into another zone.

As a kid growing up, that's what Ms. Lincoln slept on when company came. They had tons of fun because some slept at the top, while others slept in reverse. They would tickle each others toes until they either got a whipping for too much noise or got exhausted and finally fell asleep.

Also, Ms. Lincoln use to make a pallet for Angela every day. Angela would crawl around on it, sometimes crawling to one side where Tankerstroke lay, and back to the other side, where she was. Tankerstroke often played opossum. When Angela crawled in to investigate, he'd grab at her, and Angela would scramble to her side. They played this game for hours everyday. It was like having two children in the house. Pretty soon they'd tire each other out and both would fall asleep. Angela always curled up in his arms. It was a ritual they both enjoyed. Each knew the final episode was resting together. Their minds and hearts were entwined. It was a perfect case of enjoying what you have today—they enjoyed each other. Even on cold days, Tankerstroke played with Angela on that pallet; she warmed his heart, more than the wood he chunked into that old pot bellied stove nearby.

Ms. Lincoln often wondered what would have happened had Tankerstroke been in good health and lived another ten or fifteen years. The question most in her mind was; would Tankerstroke have tried to take Angela to the Big House. It had been her experience, never to wholly trust white people. Just when you become comfortable with them, they would always sprang a surprise on you. These thoughts had kept her unnerved most of the time.

Believing in the Savior, Ms. Lincoln trusted the end would find her with the sweetest fruit. It was however, the between time that she was having the most difficulty with. Tankerstroke would cling to Angela at times, like she was all his. That made her happy, he devoted so much love and affection toward Angela; but she couldn't help but be worried about the greatest love of her life. Life had blessed Ms. Lincoln with a bundle of joy; a real treasure, and she was fearful of it slipping through her fingers.

Ms. Lincoln was not in love with Tankerstroke, because the relationship was not that type of affair. It was more like an employer-employee relationship; a master-servant, so to speak; and she never felt just real comfortable as far as Angela was concerned. She felt like she was always at his mercy. As they spent hours and hours together, she learned to respect Tankerstroke. Partly, because he was so intelligent. He seemed to know something about everything he spoke of. There's no question, he could have been anything, he wanted to be. But it appears Tankerstroke had spent a lifetime building a business empire, and that's what he stuck to. That big house he lived in was the envy of Ms. Lincoln's eye. She's sure that is her reason for having an enormous house today. Wanting to have what she thought happiness was, like we all often do. As Ms. Lincoln looked at Molly's parents; she realize you certainly don't need all that to be happy, nor do you need it to be comfortable.

Speaking of being happy, Tankerstroke was happiest in their midst. Ms. Lincoln don't know what went on in the big house; and she don't care to speculate. But, she did know, when his feet hit the steps of their small cottage, he was all smiles. People lives often get crossed up. It appears that life had dealt Tankerstroke and herself an odd hand; and through twist of fate, an ultimate winner with Angela. Their paths met at a time when there were desperate needs. Needs which, if gone unfilled, would have cast an uncultivatable position on their crops of life. Ms. Lincoln needed a steady job to get a decent meal, and he needed affection to feed whatever—ego, emptiness, loneliness.

Ms. Lincoln thought: "I have not always understood the WHY's of life, but it appears that certain people's paths cross for the betterment of mankind. It took all of these years for me to really realize that. It took Molly to cross my path to really put it together. Our paths crossed and my life changed. I am happier now, than I've ever been in my life; as happy as Tankerstroke looked when his feet touched the steps of our one room house."

"Coming to this small town and being the guest of honor in this small house is undoubtedly, my Savior's way of letting me reminisce on the past where I had doubt, and rejoice in my new found faith and happiness. The key, and secret point I always missed in being happy, was seeing someone else happy. Opening that lock is fairly simple, once you know. And that only occurs when you put your selfish ways aside and help someone in need. And when you see that smile as I saw in Molly; and those tears of joy as Molly displayed, you realize, there's no greater joy."

Ms. Lincoln almost didn't come to this small town, but she would have missed the pinnacle of her reward. Richard and Sarah Cooper are showering her with their appreciation. They don't have a lot, but they are sharing what they have—the giving of their bedroom, these sumptuous country meals, and the genuine friendly attitude toward her. Happiness coming from any other source besides sharing is only make believe.

The Cooper's bedroom, like the rest of the house had linoleum on the floor. The walls were covered with wallpaper. Not just any paper, but that of different colored birds, perched and flying about. There were red birds, yellow birds, black birds, blue birds, and birds of assorted colors. There was some significance to all this, but for Ms. Lincoln it spelled carefree and friendship. The pastel blue curtains hanging over the two, six-paned windows added to the beautiful colors and cheerfulness of the room. The warmness of the room bore out the heart-warm feeling upon meeting the Coopers. A charming couple with three lovely and mannerable children.

Molly and Ms. Lincoln got to know each other pretty well; sharing personal secrets like two real close friends—like mother and daughter. And for the first time since Ms. Lincoln's conversation with Victor; she was able to say, she has a daughter and two lovely granddaughters. Although Angela had not been told of her true status, Ms. Lincoln felt relieved to know, she wasn't living a lie to the rest of the World any longer. Just being able to talk freely without cover-ups, relaxed every muscle in her body.

Now, Ms. Lincoln couldn't wait until that proper time to tell Angela—she was really hers. Then she would be able to relax forever; she would be rid of this lie—a lie which had served its purpose, if there really was one; a lie which no longer had to be justified; a lie which ZIG-ZAGGED through her heart, keeping it apart; a lie which now seemed meaningless, to have ever gotten started in the first place. Ms. Lincoln was a new me, and she liked the reflection in the mirror. She was now a truthful happy woman, who cares for her fellowman.

Molly shared her dream of wanting to finish college and help her sister and brother do likewise. "Those are my ultimate goals; I do not want mommy and daddy to ever have to worry about them," she says. She thanked Ms. Lincoln again for helping her realize that dream. Here was a kid taking the weight of an adult on her shoulder—she was to be admired. A youngster willing to make a sacrifice for the betterment of her kin. She was willing to deny herself the luxuries of life to help someone. Molly, in Ms. Lincoln's opinion was already a good person from within, and had the makings of an outstanding humanitarian. If she continues that role of helping the needy; she will have a full and glorious life.

In Ms. Lincoln's wealthy days, she had forgotten what it was like to rub elbows with people. The closeness in this small kitchen took her back to her childhood. Here they were, six of them, seated around this small table for four. Passing the bread and other food to each other in this close family atmosphere, warmed her heart even more so. Nobody reaching across the table. Mr. Cooper squeezed in at the head of the table, led the charge with a blessed prayer over the food. He then paused for Ms. Lincoln to say a verse, followed by Mrs. Cooper and each child. The ringing of those verses around the table reminded her of the old values she use to have. The old values that kept families together. The old values that kept children out of trouble.

One of the things that stood out when Mr. Cooper said the blessing was "Lord we're thankful for our health, continue to bless us." For some reason, those words hung with Ms. Lincoln. Here was a poor unemployed man thanking God for health. What about getting me a job and getting me some money. But this family was already rich, in those old values. Mr. Cooper already knew, health was far more important than wealth. This family indeed, already knew what happiness was all about.

Happy? AND HAPPY.

Happy with jewels and diamonds
Glittering extravagantly during dinner
How about mink and fox furs
Proudly worn each cold winter

HAPPY as I awoke this morning
And heard a bird a singing
It was a HAPPY song indeed
On the ice capped branch, a clinging

Happy with mercedes and expensive cars
Styling ever graciously across town
What about stately exclusive homes
As you strut peacockishly around

HAPPY as I awoke this day
To see the sun a burning
It seemed to warm my heart within
And sent my blood a churning

Happy with all the riches acquired
Searching fruitlessly for missing peace
Never thankful for what you have
Taking goodness for granted, must cease

Materialistic things make you happy
It's only temporary and always end
Put something else into your life
Try God, make him your friend

Happy with a wealthy bank account
Resembling a lavish horn of plenty
Talk snobbishly with aristocratic job
Not held by the unfortunate many

HAPPY with my health today
Or blessed might be the cry
Feels good just to be here
I'm cruising on a spiritual high

This trip to Waco, Texas to visit the Coopers, was not only educational, but inspirational as well. And Ms. Lincoln found out from Molly later; there had been a swing on that porch. Mr. Cooper had removed it years ago because Molly and the gang kept abusing it. After it fell several times, he wisely took it down. Little did Ms. Lincoln know she would be traveling through Georgia and Ohio on the same weekend.

During the time Ms. Lincoln was gone, Victor and Angela had lots to talk and be excited about. They were pleased, she had adjusted to college so well. Victor was taking time off, and on this day, the two of them along with the two new ones, of course, were spending it on the grounds of the mansion. This they thought, being the perfect sunny day, was a good time for Hattia and Victoria to actually learn about the birds and the bees, because it was plenty of them in sight. Uncle Lonzo, the gardener, waved at them from the far north side of the lawn as he tended the myriads of flowers, which he considered his own. This early afternoon outing found Victor and Angela lying upon two of Grandma's quilts; the quilts had been her mother's, but after the birth of the little ones, Ms. Lincoln decided they must have one a piece, just to lie around on. So the quilts had been joined together, and Hattia and Victoria were lying in the center, with Angela and Victor on each outer edge. The spacious lounging area had been moved one time, as the shade from the large oak gave way to the revolving sun's brilliant light. Their plans were to absorb some of this warm sunlight for the education of some and its soothing effect for others, but the normal rays, as usual, always heat up and become a bit uncomfortable, after a while of sunbathing. Even the small wrens gave it up, after fluttering in the warm sand, in a nearby flowerbed for several minutes.

Angela and Victor rolled and sat one way, then another, but always on opposite sides; showing their natural protective instincts for the little girls. It was really unnecessary to be so careful, because the many bees flying around, only seemed interested in the nearby flowers. But there was an occasional ant which made its way onto the soft grass-cushioned quilts. And assumably, two darling little ones, would need protection from so fierce a monster, especially if it wanted something other than a bread crumb or two. And speaking of bread, there was quite a lot of it available to consume the tuna salad, insisted upon by Angela, who of course, was still concentrating on getting rid of what she called "extra baby fat." Victor had no comments, other than, "you look wonderful to me and I need at least five of those light tuna sandwiches." Angela ate no bread; so the lead ant, with minimal organizing, as what would surely have happened, could have camped on Victor's side for a hearty meal or carry out, as most of them are known for. Anyway, all ants were thumped back onto the grass as fast as one happen to wander in the direction of Hattia and Victoria.

Prior to Angela and Victor eating their packed basket lunch, Uncle Lonzo came over with a mixed bouquet of flowers, telling them, food was more digestible with pretty blooms on the table. Victor agreed with Uncle Lonzo, after his three sandwiches, three soft drinks, a large bag of potato chips, and a large box of fig Newtons, which Angela packed especially for him. The flowers, though pretty and digestibility creative, did attract a friend from the local community, as was apparent from the buzzing noise as it lit. Obviously, the harmless bee was accepting an extended invitation; Angela was less enthusiastic as she screamed and ran several feet away, yelling for Victor to get rid of the flowers. Well, so much for the protection for Hattia and Victoria; at least half of it anyway. Victor however, followed Angela's brave instructions and calmly lifted the bouquet, setting it in the nearby flowerbed. The girls who seemingly were quite amused, no doubt, never even saw one of nature's other winged-wonder. This being the excitement for the day; Angela became almost as excitable when an occasional fly buzzed near her, causing her to become less and less interested in remaining at this outside location. And within minutes, the inevitable happened; she informed Victor, it was time for them to break camp and move inside.

Victor laughed and teased Angela for her bravery and her solid support of him, when their camp was under siege. She jokingly thanked him for his keen observation of her. The family outing was near its end anyway; both Victor and Angela were full, and the little ones well, they had been educated enough in one day— about the birds and the bees. Half of Angela and Victor's evening, nevertheless, was consumed with both of them teasing and laugh-

ing with and at each other, for their eventful first annual lawn pic-
nic. Happiness was the tone and Victor did not want to spoil it.
Several times, he had to remind himself not to say anything to
Angela about grandma, not being her grandma, and then telling
her the better news. Victor had been tempted several times since
Ms. Lincoln divulged this secret to him, but he knew that was far
from being his responsibility, plus he did not want to betray the
trust Ms. Lincoln had shown, by telling him. Victor thought, to
himself; keeping your own secrets are so much easier than keeping those of someone else. Any number of times, he wanted to tell
it, and tell it all; just as he had heard it, of course.

Once, Angela bedded down Hattia and Victoria, she gave Victor
little time to think of anything else, but what was on her mind.
She always liked to take advantage of grandmother's leave of
absence, and parade around in the nude; insisting that Victor con-
form. Angela had told Victor, they should enjoy their leisure
outfits, while the children were still unaware of a more fitting
attire in the presence of company. Victor was easily influenced, as
this was the first time they had the house to themselves since
Victoria's birth. Angela, however, was still being lenient and toler-
able with Victor; she was determined to be firm in her
possessiveness of him, yet be patient and let nature take its
course, for she truly understood Victor's position. Angela realized
Victor was a family man that had somehow gotten himself
"involved with two families," and Carolyn, whom she was slowly
coming to resent as an outsider; one who should really have no
claim at all on Victor. Being patient, however, thought Angela,
was the key; Afterall it had worked in the case of Samantha.

Angela told Victor she wanted to use this opportunity to
reestablish her hold on him, and of course, he knew what she
meant; it was back to the old original sofa. Angela was the only
person he knew who enjoyed making love on the sofa, instead of
in the conforts of a bed. It probably had a lot to do with a psyche
sort of her domineering him in making him obey. Angela loved
making Victor obey her commands and—well, Victor loved playing along with her. Now, when she commanded him to bow, he
took several standing bows, before lowering himself upon his
knees, before her. Angela's curly cavern was now sweeter than

ever, since Samantha no longer needed Victor's servicing.

Angela's breast was more sensitive since the last baby, and she made Victor kiss them forever, at least, much longer than he wanted to. This was his only drawback in this servitude role, if you can call grasping two fine nipples in your mouth, a drawback. There was one advantage thought Victor, as Angela later commanded him to her curly cavern; it was already very much saturated with sweet juices. Angela always placed her feet, wide apart, on the edge of the sofa and scooted herself forward, enabling Victor to do precisely as she commanded. He obeyed her this evening as his tastetester examined an outer flowing stream, simultaneously caressing her moisture glittering surface. And as usual, Angela's curly cavern had an itching inside and she craved for him to be there; commanding him to do so. Angela loved the smooth manner in which Victor responded and obeyed her; slowly dipping and dapping his tongue onto her clit for a spontaneous rigorous tumbling motion of her behind. and always sending another stream to the surface. Normally, this was the beginning of the end as Victor's long tongue continued to press her clit as he surged it deep inside of her curly cavern; Angela felt the extremely warm object inside of her, and responded with another stream of warmness of her own; Victor loved this warn gush of sweetness. Victor did not have to hold on, because Angela curled both her palms around his head, pressing it tighter and tighter to her curly cavern, as he swallowed every ounce of Angela's sweetness. The night was complete as Victor carried her upstairs, placed her upon the queen-sized bed, where Angela enjoyed the bigness of the hour. Nature had indeed taken its course on today.

CHAPTER FORTY

MAYOR'S CONVENTION

Victor's week vacation with Angela had been a success; Tiffani could tell by his jovial disposition. Her time in the office had not been as cheerful; Ralph had called and wanted to come by, but she was still despondent over his last visit; putting him off to next week, when Victor's vacation would take him on a trip to Chicago with Helen. Tiffani had tired of thinking of ways to encourage Ralph to seduce her, and now would merely play things by ear.

"Good morning Tiff!"

"Hello Carolyn; hey—I see you are wearing that new suit I bought you; I sort of expected you last week; of course, I understand why, with Victor being gone."

"Oh really; well I was here Monday Tiff, but was not feeling so hot, so I took the rest of the week off; purely a coincident I suppose!"

"Yeah, I suppose; Victor's in, Carolyn; you need no announcement, and he is always available for you, so I guess you might as well barge on in. By the way, my suit looks good on you."

"Thanks Tiff, I knew you would like it; I wonder if Victor will like it?"

"I don't see how he can help liking what little there is of it; that skirt looks so much shorter than I remember it Carolyn."

"Oh, didn't I tell you! I had Gerald take another inch or so; he said the skirt could easily handle it, Tiff."

Oh, I was not exactly thinking of the skirt handling it Carolyn; it is Victor, who I was worrying about handling it."

"Tiff, you are getting crazier and crazier by the days; of course Victor can handle it. He can handle anything I put on him; at least he has been able to so far."

"Later Carolyn; talk to you, when you are through modeling!"

"Hi Victor, just came by to see how you like my suit."

"Like it, I love it; is it new?"

"Uh huh, Tiff bought it for me; she has excellent taste, doesn't she?"

"I'd say she does; it really looks good on you Carolyn."

"I missed you last week, Victor; I was wondering if you could stop by, for the evening, after work; a change of clothes is already there, you know."

"Sure Carolyn; be glad to."

"Oh; and Victor, you might want to talk about it later, but I want you to spend the week with me, when you return from your trip with Helen."

"Yeah Carolyn, we will talk about that later."

Carolyn pauses in Victor's doorway, saying softly; "see you after work Victor." And then turning her attention to Tiffani.

"Tiff, Victor really did like your selection; girl, you might get a big raise out of this choice. I will remind him tonight, you were responsible for me, looking so good to him, today."

"Will that be, before or after you remove it, Carolyn?"

"You are funny today Tiff; it does not matter honey, Victor has a very vivid memory, you know."

"When it comes to you Carolyn, I imagine so; it does not take a lot; you are either half-dressed or undressed."

"Keep talking like that Tiff, and I'll have to report you to Ms. Previtt, for an apology; I could use another suit, you know."

"Carolyn, you can forget that; there will be no more suits."

"Okay, I apologize Tiff, I can see you are upset; what are you so serious about today?"

"Oh Carolyn, I wish I could tell you, but you might laugh at me for being so immature."

"Young maybe, but immature, you are not Tiff! Friends should share things Tiff; I might be able to help you girl!"

"Yeah, probably so Carolyn. I am going to try and work it out on my own, a little longer, but I will definitely keep you in mind."

"Okay, now let's hug and kiss; Ms. Samantha Previtt would want that, you know."

"Okay Carolyn; now girl, get out of here—and thanks a lot!"

Tiffani nearly told Carolyn about Ralph, just now, but an idea came to her attention which prevented it. Gerald had taken up Carolyn's skirt another inch or so, and Victor had given it high marks; of course, she thought, Victor would give Carolyn high marks on anything, but it was worth a try. She would raise her new suit's skirt at least two inches or so, and see if it had any affect upon Ralph; it has to be the teasing that gets guys going; she said to herself. When Ralph shows up next week, Tiffani promised herself, she would be wearing her new hot blue suit, for their investment portfolio session. One more effort to convert Ralph to her way of thinking would be worth it, if it worked; certainly better, she thought, than having Carolyn find out, she really couldn't striptease; well, at least a striptease that worked in her favor. Being frustrated one more time was at least better than being ridiculed forever by Carolyn. And suddenly, Tiffani remembered, the skirt might work in other ways; she noted that no investments had been made in her account by Ralph after their last session, so its not like she was the only one disappointed; until last week, Ralph had not even called her.

"Tiffani, you have been awfully quiet today; I expected you to tease me when Carolyn left; are you okay?"

"Not really Victor; I am having men problems or a man problem, like you are having women problems, except my case is a complete reverse; whereas, you are getting everything, I am getting nothing. You probably remember, I inquired of you a few weeks ago, without giving you any details on this man. Well, I am still not prepared to give any details, but I am so darn frustrated, because I cannot get this man to make love to me. I am serious Victor, so please don't laugh; I have paraded nude before this man and even smeared my goodness upon his lips."

"What was his response then Tiffani?"

"No response whatsoever, Victor, he did not even lick them as I expected."

"Sounds like a pretty frigid dude to me Tiffani; that would be the ultimate turn on, for most men. Maybe, he does not like sex."

"Well, I asked him if he did and he told me yes, Victor."

"Huh, that's strange! You mentioned last time that he's paying you; is that for pulling your clothes off, Tiffani?"

"Well—yeah; man you sure put two and two together quick."

"Not really, Tiffani, that has been bugging me ever since you first mentioned it. I was going to ask you about it, in a few days, anyway. My best guess is, there is something wrong with this fellow, physically or mentally. And one thing I am not going to stand for, is some lunatic getting my secretary frustrated."

"Do not get riled up Victor; you have Carolyn tonight and the trip to Chicago, with Helen next week; we can talk more about it, after then. I am going to try one more time, and I will let you know what happens."

"I don't' know Tiffani, sometimes these kind of people can be dangerous; you had better be careful!"

"I will, I promise you Victor! What did you think of Carolyn's suit?"

"What suit Tiffani?"

"Victor!"

"Oh, just having fun; I understand you bought it Tiffani; I will reimburse you later. You have very good taste; and no reflections on your taste, but Carolyn makes me drool, regardless of what she's wearing."

"You are kidding Victor! I hardly noticed! Seriously though, what causes that?"

"Her fine body, Tiffani; my weak mind!"

"I figured that much on my own Victor; the weak mind part." Laughing.

"No, seriously Tiffani, I thought of that same question, long and hard, before I finally figured it out; it is my imagination. Imagination is the answer. Initially, it was her body and honestly still her body, but now its also wondering, what type of love antics, she'll have in store, when I go over. That drives my imagination absolutely crazy."

"Thanks Victor, maybe I'll see if I can hone in on my partner's imagination."

Helen, since graduating from Medical school, had been working at a local hospital. Here, she was doing research on the project nearest her heart—AIDS (Acquired immune deficiency syndrome). This dreaded disease, spreading out of proportion in the Black community, alarmed Helen even more so. As a nurse, she had seen the devastation it causes. The disease had long escaped the homosexual borders and was now plundering the lives of the general population. This meant a cure became paramount, since isolation among a given population was no longer a safe theory.

The disease leaped into the hetro-sexual community attacking the sexual promiscuous, killing them in their tracks. Promiscuity became a concern, not because the one getting AIDS was that way; but because of the unknowingly promiscuous habits of their partner. There were AIDS cases abounding—a loving wife on a one night stand or with a former boyfriend, infecting her family; a reckless husband infecting his wife, because he thought the use of a condom gave him the right to screw any hole in town. Helen knew of families being torn apart, and couldn't sit idly by and do nothing. She knew of sufferers and sufferers to be, if no cure was found.

She knew sex education was not enough. Sexual habits are hard to change after generations, especially if the attitude is—it can't happen to me. Young men and women were getting the disease because of that attitude. Teenagers were not immune, because they knew everything; and really knew nothing of the preventive facts—like—don't do it. All the cases involving AIDS touched Helen; but the ones affecting her the most, were the many children being born with AIDS. As Helen said, they never had a chance; they would never visit the Alamo or have fun running about Disney World. Can you, can anyone, she states, look them in the face and deny them that right.

As a doctor, Helen knew the continuance of her research for a cure, must be without short-sighted limits and tight pocketbooks.

She found herself working within budgets which didn't allow extensive research or provided inadequate materials and equipment. Helen had approached the hospital administrators on this problem; and though they were sympathetic, there was nothing they could do. Their answer was—the money is just not there. The now persistent Dr., refused to accept those tailored answers. Either they tired or Helen convinced them, she could do a better job in that area—she was chosen by the hospital to attend the Mayor's Convention.

Helen's motto, must have been, no dedicated person should have to give up their fight.

And being the fortunate person Victor was, Helen insisted he go with her to this convention. She stated Victor was her backbone, and she needed him for support. Victor didn't buy that, but when Helen wants something, she has a way of winning you over to her side. She will persist until you give in or give up—either of which, she's the ultimate winner. Of course, Helen only did that, if the matter was of extreme importance to her. Items of a trivial nature, went untold, hastily verbalized, or only slightly mentioned.

The July, Chicago conference was perfect for a mid-year break and body relaxer. Stacy consented to keep the boys for the week. The week was Victor's idea. It was his way of compromising with Helen for her one day presentation. Helen never took time off unless Victor insisted. Some things never change—and dedicated work—non stop, was it for Helen. How she found time for any other things in her life was amazing to Victor. But as Helen put it, you always have time for things that are important to you; and she illustrated that point to Victor.

"It is simple, Victor, budget your time like your money and it falls into place."

"That makes sense, Helen, but after serving time in the military, it appears the same—a bit regimented."

"When you look at life Victor, it is a regime—there is a time and place for everything. My time during the week breaks down to roughly six hours for sleep, twelve hours of work and volunteering, and six hours for our sons. The weekends are virtually reserved for me and the boys, and sometimes I volunteer a little."

"That's what I'm driving at Helen, you are totally consumed; I didn't hear about any time for me."

"What do you suggest, Victor—I thought you were getting enough already."

"Let's not be funny, Helen, you're killing yourself. That's the very reason we're taking the week off—your body is completely run down."

Little did Victor know, he was to be a working companion during the conference. Helen had prepared a slide and video presentation. She informed Victor of his duties the day before, which was being mechanically minded, like knowing which machine to turn on when directed. Victor was relieved to hear Helen was to do all the speech making. Victor thought of his friend Joseph, who had given his life to that dreadful disease; and wanted no part of another emotional speech.

Victor could never understand Helen's daily involvement with AIDS prevention and cures; and her calm disposition when it came to talking about it. Inside, he knew she was frustrated, but her outer shell was unbroken. In other words, she got serious, but, she never got out of control during presentations.

Helen woke up in a better than happy mood. Her large bubbly smile and glistening teeth were cast in Victor's direction.

"I take it, you feel good this morning Helen."

"After, virtually, just lying around for the past two days, Victor, I feel so relaxed."

"You look so much better, too Helen. Now you see what I've been telling you about getting your rest."

"I try Victor, it just does not work out the way it's planned."

"Tell me Helen, what was the big OK about in your sleep?"

"You mean I was talking last night, Victor!"

"You sure were. That was all you said, but it was the loudest enthusiastic OK, I have ever heard."

"That certainly makes sense Victor; it was more than likely, my answer to your question; when you asked me to marry you." And she falls out laughing.

"What's so funny Helen?"

"You should have seen the expression on your face, Victor—it was like, oh my, I opened the wrong can. Relax Victor, you're safe for now . I have not felt this good, since our cruise."

"Me neither Helen, the kids have sort of put a damper on our days alone; but it doesn't have to be that way; both Samantha and Stacy say they'll keep them."

"I know Victor, but boys those ages need their parents, especially their father. And look who's talking, you have only called home four times in two days Victor; don't you trust Stacy?"

"Well—yes, it's that Stacy hasn't had any children and...that does make a difference."

"Are you sure that's it Victor? Anyway it is comforting to know the boys are in such loving hands."

At the conference, Helen was still the same bubbly smiling person; a bit more cheerful than her normal self. She walked onto the stage with a hearty "Good Morning." The small response received, indicated the people were still sleep at nine a.m. or had their minds elsewhere. Some were talking while others were just milling around. Helen stood there smiling, waiting on everyone to settle down. No one appeared in any particular hurry for the morning program.

Helen leaned closely into the microphone shouting "AIDS— AIDS—AIDS." The room became silent. "At least one in five of you could test HIV positive." Their ears perked up like a stubborn jackass. Helen had their attention and was no longer smiling. Helen knew about tact and diplomacy—the delicacy which puts another's body at ease—but would hasten to seize the opportune time not to use it. She again said "Good Morning;" as the walls echoed the seemingly, in unison reply.

All eyes are now on Helen as she takes off:

"I see, by the time allotted this important subject; to you it is merely a side issue. Too many times, that is the case; too many times, life is taken for granted. To you, it might be just another item on the agenda; to occupy space between the good times on your trip. To you, it is not real. We are here today to tell and show you, it is very much real, and should be taken serious, as a small-pox or cholera epidemic. It should be taken serious as a bubonic plague; because the end result will be the same for us and our country, if AIDS is not given serious consideration. I am here today to talk about research for this deadly disease. There is a lot, we know about it, but there is more we don't know. And until there is a vaccine, or a cure is discovered, none of us are safe from AIDS.

Helen then directed Victor to run the video, and then the slide projector. Helen continued:

"The people you are watching (faces blocked) are regular people; people like you and me. These people are doctors, lawyers, teachers, businessmen and women; all outstanding citizens. And while none are mayors yet, they are friends and neighbors of yours. They also have one thing in common—each has AIDS. The other thing they have in common is acquiring AIDS through a freak source, such as a blood transfusion, an organ transplant, an oral surgery."

"I know you're probably saying, those are low risk groups; but what if it's your pregnant wife that needs that blood transfusion; and what if it's your husband who went to the dentist that day; or what if it's you, that had that kidney transplant. Low risk, but deathly, just the same. Your question to you is—do I want to be in that low risk group? And, my questions to you is—are you willing to take the chance, and bet your life, that your neighbor is A-OK? What I'm saying to you today is, this is no longer a side issue."

"You honorable men and women can help to make the difference. You can help to get what I'm appealing for today—money for research. We must have it, if we are going to defeat this monster. So please, I appeal to you—to make an appeal to your states. Appeal until they get tired and put some research funds in their budget. One of these days in the near future, I hope we find a cure. With your help, it is possible, and with your help, it will happen. Thank you for your time, thank you for your patience and thank you in advance for your funds."

Helen knew how to ask for research funds and felt if there were some available, she could pry it loose.

"Victor, I feel people understand the problem when I talk to them; or when they stop to listen. And that might just be the major problem; there is too few of us speaking and far-far too few of us who will listen."

"I wouldn't take it so personal, Helen; you can't solve the World's problems in a day."

"Yeah, Victor, but how about during my lifetime."

"I have my own theory on that Helen; what about other diseases such as sickle cell anemia?"

"I understand what you are saying Victor, in terms of the research dollars; but AIDS is a contagious disease, crossing racial lines."

"Sure, Helen, but throughout the Nation, it's affecting more countries where there's people of color. All I'm saying Helen, is the urgency does not appear to be there for a disease supposedly, racing across the Country like a wild fire. You're committed to a worthy cause Helen for a cure for all; I just don't want you to hurt yourself begging for research dollars which are just not there."

"The funds are there, Victor; it's the priority that's missing."

Helen had gotten her point across. The hospital administrators were proud of her; for they had received some additional funds. But as Helen said, "it wasn't enough." It is never enough states Helen, when there is research which must be put on hold. Helen wanted an unlimited budget to do her AIDS research, and AIDS research needed an unlimited budget to find a cure. No one was more aware than Helen, that time was running out for thousands of AIDS victims throughout the Country.

It mattered not whether you were unborn, the young and innocent, black or white; Helen believed everyone was entitled to an equal chance in life. A chance to be a mathematician; a chance to be an engineer; a chance to be an artist, a musician, an actress; a chance to be productive in the career of their choosing. Or the least, a chance to enjoy life without a lingering fear of what to touch or not touch; what is good or bad; and who is safe or not safe.

Helen is a fighter for the helpless, not wanting to let anybody down. She sacrifice her rest, punishing her body for another minutes research. Each project could be the one, she thought, as she plowed on. There was nothing more important in Helen's life than research; except maybe, asking for money to do more research. AIDS research consumed her life, despite her make believe budget of time for other things. When one is with you; but their mind is on something else, then you're, in essence—alone. Helen's self-imposed schedule was demanding of her time. She spoke for research and she researched for the spoken AIDS victims.

The Monday, while Victor was gone, found Tiffani in the office armed with her bright blue short-skirted suit. Victor had given her an idea on the imagination, and she was going to see if it worked on old cold—no touch me Ralph; any type of positive response would be a welcome relief. There had been no increases in her account lately, but hopefully, today, all of that would change. As they review their next investment moves, Tiffani notices Ralph straining his eyeballs to look under the remaining portion of the skirt, which covers not much more than the bottom itself. Tiffani was comfortable, crossing and uncrossing her legs, because her black pantyhose allowed nothing to be seen, other than complete darkness, where Ralph was looking, and having difficulty seeing. Into their second hour of reviews and nearing the end, Tiffani notices a bulge in the crouch of Ralph's pants; she was as surprised as she was excited. It appears she thought, Victor was right in his assessment of the imagination, but the question now was; where does she go from here? That was quickly answered when their review ended, and Ralph presented her with some of those familiar body strings, that covered nothing.

Tiffani took the fiery red strings, realizing once she had them on, Ralph's imagination would probably be gone. So to keep things going as smooth as they were, she merely told him; if you want to see me in this attire, you will have to help me get undressed, and also help me put these strings on. There was a twenty second hesitation by Ralph, followed by a nod, indicating his approval; to attempt the tedious task of removing only three pieces; a blouse, a skirt, and the pantyhose. Tiffani could feel Ralph's bigness as he unbuttoned her blouse, because she reached backward, grabbing his behind, pulling him tightly into her. When the blouse fell to the floor, her smoothly self-unfastened skirt fell on top of it, leaving her hands, holding Ralph's to assist him much more from here on. Still, backed against Ralph, Tiffani raised his hands onto her pointed firm breast; she would have to manipulate his fingers like a puppet on a string, but it was working. Ralph could not see anything, but Tiffani knew his imagination was still working, because she felt his bigness throbbing and pounding her behind. Slowly, and ever so slowly, Tiffani lowered Ralph's hands to assist the removal of her pantyhose from her waist, over her hips, and to the floor. To keep Ralph's sense of feel going and to maintain his high level of imagination, Tiffani pull his hands quickly upon her furry furrow and began to manipulate his fingers again. She could feel the reluctance in his fingers, but she could also feel the aggressiveness in Ralph's bigness as it was about to burst through his pants.

Tiffani thought, the response so far has been great and she did not want to spoil it by making any drastic moves, so she decided to continue manipulating Ralph's fingers; the reluctance was still there, but he cooperated fully, extending them upon, about, and within Tiffani's furry furrow. Now, the both of them were breathing hard. Tiffani had to do all of the work, but at least, she thought; I have the comforts of Ralph's long warm fingers. Finally Tiffani's intense moment hit, and she cupped Ralph's hands for them to fill with her sweet wetness. She had no idea if her next move would work, but for Ralph to eventually become the aggressor, he needed to know, exactly what he was missing; turning around to face Ralph, Tiffani lifted his cupped hands to his face, to his lips, saying very softly; "Ralph, my sweetness is good, you must find out for yourself; please relax, open up, and enjoy some of what you helped to produce; don't be shy, you may go as soon as you're finished, please open your—" And before Tiffani had finished her appeal, Ralph had quickly emptied his cupped hands as she wished, and fled out the door. Tiffani screamed out only two words today; "YES—YES!"

On Wednesday, a copy of Tiffani's investment account appeared on her desk, with a note attached, saying; "you are really sweet and good." Tiffani smiled, when she noted a whopping twenty five thousand dollar increase in her account; she was indeed happy, and could hardly wait to thank Victor, on Monday.

CHAPTER FORTY ONE

UNSETTLING

"Well Tiffani, did anything exciting happen while I was gone?"

"It sure did, thanks to you Victor; I got a pretty good response from that cold man; not exactly what I wanted, but I feel he is headed in the right direction."

"I am glad to hear it is working out for you Tiffani; the number one goal in life should be to be happy."

"Oh, talking about being happy; Carolyn visited with me on Friday; she says, she is so happy, now that you are an integral part of her life. You must have done something extra special to her before you left, she was really charged up over you."

"You mean, you didn't ask her Tiffani?"

"Well, I started to Victor, but I did not want to get to deep, into your personal affairs; that is, unless you volunteer and tell me."

"Oh, I see; well, there's nothing special that I know of. I did eventually agree to spend the week with her, but—"

"That must be it Victor, and I almost forgot; Carolyn told me to be sure and remind you of your visit with her this week. So she talked you into spending this week too, huh."

"Yeah, but I don't want to talk about that, Tiffani!"

"Okay; well, how was your trip Victor?"

"It was all right Tiffani; lots of work though. Some relaxation, but Helen even made that seem like work. She is practically, strictly business these days. Right now I don't know which is worse; getting nothing from Helen or too much from Carolyn."

"Since you re-opened the conversation on Carolyn, I would say from the smile on your face, when she comes in here, you prefer the worse of her."

"There is nothing wrong with being cordial, Tiffani."

"I know the meaning of cordial Victor, and that is not the expression on your face, when Carolyn is around; you look like jelly on a piece of hot toast."

"Carolyn is excellent at getting her point across, and maybe, we're leaning on each other, Tiffani; I promised to help with her problem, you know."

"Okay, Victor, you win, I suppose everyone needs a little help with their problems; Carolyn expects you this evening; by the way."

"That is the worse part, I was speaking of; Carolyn is so demanding; the other worse part is, she knows, I can't turn her down; and the last worse part is, I don't want to turn her down."

"Maybe, you are falling in love with Carolyn, and I hope that is not the case, Victor."

"Why is that Tiffani?"

"First of all, she is not your type; next, you mentioned it yourself, she demands. You need more control over a woman than that Victor, or one with much, much, less control over you; because, when your now powerful sex die down, you will resent being bossed around."

"We have not been talking about getting married, Tiffani!"

"Those things sometimes have a way of creeping up on you victor—like four children."

"Oh, I see what you mean, Tiffani."

"And, another thing Victor, while we are discussing Carolyn; the Friday, she came by last week, just happened to be her only day at work. So, while you are over there this time, you might want to mention her work habits. I understand, she just called in sick, each day."

"Thanks for telling me Tiffani; sometimes I get so wrapped up, in making love to Carolyn, I forget she still has a problem. It is so easy too, because she conceals all evidence of drinking when we are together. Matter of fact, I am sure she does not drink when we are together. How can she discipline herself so well when I'm around, Tiffani?"

"Hard to say Victor; either she respects you that much, or your presence is the cure. It looks like you might have to marry Carolyn, after all, Victor." Laughing.

"Funny—funny, Tiffani; like you said, Carolyn is not my type; although, between you and me, I don't know what I'd do if she asked me."

"I do Victor; I would be throwing rice upon you and Carolyn as you left the church."

"Think so, Tiffani?"

"Uh huh, Carolyn has your number, Victor. There is nothing to be ashamed of; it happens. But don't you worry about that ever happening; I would never let Carolyn marry you. And that, we need not discuss!"

"Thanks for looking out for me, Tiffani."

"Carolyn is my friend too Victor, and I want to see her problem solved. It appears to be on your shoulders Victor; you can help her more, because she respects you more."

"Why do you say that Tiffani?"

"It's obvious Victor; she drinks like a fish when we are alone, at lunch; yet, around you, you say there is no evidence of it. Her drinking really worries me; I care about her health in the worse way; that Carolyn does not kill herself on that booze. My suggestion to you Victor; get as serious about helping our friend quit drinking, as you are about helping to service her."

"Okay Tiffani, I will start tonight, and hopefully, by the end of this stay, we will notice some results."

Victor knew what he needed to do, and that was to talk to Carolyn's parents. This, he had been intending to do, but just like Tiffani had said; other things involving Carolyn had gotten in the way, or better still, received a greater priority. Of course, this was easier said than done, when matched with the dominance of Carolyn; she had a way of keeping your mind locked upon her gorgeous features.

Carolyn was still having her problems from the loss of her

daughter. For some reason she just could not shake it. Samantha had met and talked with her at great length. Samantha felt Carolyn's number one problem, besides blaming herself; was looking for sympathy. Not that Victor minded spending countless of hours with such a tall, smooth brown beauty. He always feels good in Carolyn's presence and always feels like he is making a contribution to uplifting her heart; her body; and well...okay his body.

So the question of, what it was going to take to get Carolyn back into the right gear, had long been asked. Samantha was solicited to obtain the illusive answer. Victor knew he could count on her expertise in getting at the bottom of a seemingly hopeless situation. His reasoning and talking to Carolyn had not done much good. Whenever he leaned too hard, a heated exchange was the norm. Carolyn, even with Victor's patience, resented him telling her of do's and don'ts. His sincere hope was to avoid facing a dilemma with her.

Friends stick by friends no matter what; but there are times when the friend in trouble borrow your shoulder too often, without once thinking of the others position. That is where Victor is with Carolyn, and it is becoming a bit hectic. Even a partial solution would be welcome. Anything to give him relief and assurance that Carolyn would remain safely and healthy on life's shelf. Desertion, though probable, had never seriously entered Victor's list of solutions. It did not appear to make sense to discard a beautiful brown flower because of one thorn. One must prepare to live with life's small irritants, until solace emerge.

Whenever Carolyn called Victor, sounding depressed, he would spend the week with her. To love Carolyn one night, never seems to suffice. It was only after an entire week, their sexual appetite ceased for each other, and then only slightly. Carolyn was experienced in the bedroom, bathroom, living room, kitchen, office, or wherever she decided love was to be made. That was the most exciting thing about being around Carolyn; you never knew when the urge would hit her; you only knew it would hit. That alone, was enough to make one's body pulsate just contemplating the inevitable.

Victor had never made love on so many pieces of furniture—chairs, sofas, footstools, tables, commodes, floors—Carolyn was an impromptu lover and made love where she was at the time. Carpet burns, back strains, and tired muscles, highlighted a week of staying with Carolyn. Neglecting the bed put the body in some pretty awkward love making positions. Detumescence, around Carolyn was always a problem. Those however, with Carolyn, are only pleasant complaints; Victor never had prolonged moments of dissatisfaction. Never was he aware those amorous feats were not solving her emotional depression. Seems funny, because he was always relieved of his emotional hardships.

Samantha concluded that Victor had become Carolyn's crutch, along with the alcohol. She stated, whenever, Carolyn becomes depressed, she relies on either Victor and his lovemaking or alcohol to get through it. According to Samantha, it really did not matter which; availability was the key. That explains why Carolyn was always sober when she called for him to come over; and why she was drunk as a skunk when he went by unannounced. She was leading Victor to believe, she was getting better. Victor told Samantha he would make more unannounced calls.

Samantha felt that might help, but "to be prepared to screw your life away." What she needed most, in Samantha's opinion, was sympathy—not from Victor—but from her mother and father; stating that Carolyn feels her parents let her down, and neither feel sorry for doing so. Now she is looking for an apology from them. Samantha continues, saying; and until Carolyn gets that apology or realize her daughter's death was not her fault; she will need her crutches forever.

Being a crutch for an extended indefinite period had never occurred to Victor. But he knew it was not good news for his already wearisome body. Victor could tell Samantha was serious in her evaluation and no doubt, just as accurate. Thoughts of Samantha's third book kept crossing his mind; "Victor's Life—— Screwed Up", kept jumping out as the title. There was hope, but that too, appeared to be fading with every empty whisky jug, hidden in the trash. In reality, Samantha and Victor were both looking for a happy ending to Carolyn's sad story.

Samantha's willingness to help, showed compassion and reinforced a conviction to stand by Victor if he needed a lift. Her statement was even more caring; "Victor, you did not cause the problem, you were just there when it happened." Comforting words, but they only served as a reminder of being in the wrong place at the wrong time. Maybe Victor was being too hard on himself for wading in troubled waters, which appeared to be getting worse or at the least, no closer to a calmness.

Samantha had no method for addressing her analysis, but felt since, Victor was Carolyn's closest friend, it should be him that initially tried to work something out. His body was wearing thin from that pleasant lovemaking. So something had to be done fairly soon, because either he would be drained dry or Carolyn would be an alcoholic, or both. The first thing that hit his mind, and what seemed like the simplest solution, was to talk to her dumb parents and explain the situation to them.

While the ideal contact with Carolyn's parents would have been in person; they lived on the East Coast in Silver Springs, Maryland. Knowing how they felt toward Carolyn, Victor's plan was to solicit a sympathy vote immediately; over the phone, if at all possible. Scaring them to believe Carolyn's life was in jeopardy might be enough to jolt her parents into that mood. For the first time ever, Victor wanted to be the carrier of bad news and make it sound worse. A fabrication of the truth would be worth it, if it worked.

Upon Victor's request, Carolyn's parents; Mr. George Lefholder and Mrs. Alice Lefholder were both on the phone:

"Mr. and Mrs. Lefholder, I'm calling to let you know, Carolyn is not doing very well. Since the death of her daughter, she has been emotionally and disoriently depressed. She rarely eats and has lost a tremendous amount of weight. She drinks two and three fifths of whisky a day, and only goes to work when she wants to. At the rate she's going, Carolyn will destroy herself within months."

Mrs. Lefholder speaking—"that's good for her; she deserves exactly what she's getting." Mr. Lefholder: "But Alice, maybe we should call her." "George, you stay out of this; that girl has caused us nothing but trouble. We tried to raise her right, and she done nothing but let us down. I washed my hands of her a long time ago. Now Mister, whoever, you said you were; as far as we are concerned, we do not have a daughter anymore. So please, do not bother us again."

"But, Mrs. Lefholder, I don't think you understand; we're talking about a person's life."

"No, it is you, who does not understand, Mister—our daughter died a long time ago."

Chills went through Victor's entire body, as he slowly put the phone down; saying, "I understand all right—that Mrs. Lefholder is a bitch; And old silent George is not a helluva lot better. She has thrust a double-dose of venom into the silent one, because he has the backbone of a snail."

Victor had no reason to doubt what Carolyn had told him about her parents; but he honestly did not think they would be this bad. The mildest assessment of their opinion toward Carolyn, would be—they hate her guts.

At least, that is the way arctic-Alice Lefholder felt. Somehow, Victor got the impression, spineless-George cared for his sweet Carolyn. What came shining through was an example of a henpecked husband. A man who shivers at the sound of his wife's voice; a man who can not make household decisions; a man who can not stand on his own two feet; a man who is a figment of a man. Mr. Lefholder is living a helpless life, while his daughter is helplessly holding on to life.

It appears, an apology for sympathy would not be forth coming from this direction any time soon. Two people so full of hate and in reality, are the one's that have ceased to live. Life to Victor is something vibrant and moving, sparkling and rolling with laughter, blossoming and springing forth. He did not see or hear any of that today. Today was like attending a wake; though not of someone you love, but pitied.

Samantha's family psychotherapy would have to wait. The solution for Carolyn's inability to cope with reality, now fell back into Victor's lap. And while he enjoyed Carolyn and would have been happy spending the rest of his life with her; he could not stay with her every night; and too, he could not cast her out like leftovers from a fine meal. Carolyn had become Victor's responsibility. If only there were two of him....well three would probably be more ideal at this point. Carolyn was leaning on Victor's shoulder for help; she was leaning on the whisky jug for help. It was now up to Victor to decide which would provide the most assistance.

Victor did not tell Carolyn of the unsuccessful attempt to reach her parents. He did not have the heart and the results probably would have made her even more depressed. After all, what would he have told her—your mother is stupid and your father has lost his individuality. Carolyn loved her parents very much; and just wanted them to show some compassion and understanding of what she was all about. But that one mistake of years gone by, had sealed Carolyn's fate; it seemed. It had extinguished the family communication lines. It had destroyed mama's sweet little girl image of her precious daughter. The bond of trust had been broken. And daddy's perfect little angel had gotten dirty.

Victor thought and quietly spoke to himself:

"I'm sure, Mrs. Lefholder felt her bourgeois circle could exclude her if she was found to be enjoying life with a bastard granddaughter. Those outside elements affecting the status quo had made her heart a festering sore. She wanted to hold her head up high without such a blemish. The ruthless woman had crawled into her shell of snobbery. And in her words, "Carolyn no longer existed," so her conscience, I suppose was clear. It is so easy to crush someone, when they can't defend themselves. Carolyn had been in a defenseless position, ever since her youth and the birth of the unwanted grandchild. Now the weight from all those years had become too heavy—much too heavy. I'm sad of the situation, but happy at the moment, despite my earlier disgust, Carolyn is my problem rather than society's."

CHAPTER FORTY TWO

THIRTY YEAR SECRET UNVEILED

It was Angela's thirtieth birthday. She was summoned, along with Victor to Ms. Lincoln's sitting room. Angela held Victor's hand, leading him all the way. They both knew about the document opening and they were as curious as Ms. Lincoln to review and learn of its findings. Victor being present was obvious to him; Ms. Lincoln did not want to face the music alone, when she unveiled a secret that had been bottled up in her for thirty years. Ms. Lincoln wasted no time; and without sitting down, glanced at victor; then looked Angela straight in the eyes and said;

"Honey, I'm your mother, not your grandmother."

Angela smiled at her saying, "yes, I know."

Ms. Lincoln looked directly at Victor as if he had let the cat out of the bag.

"How long have you known Angela?"

"Well mother, I have guessed it for about twenty years, but known it to be a fact only three. The curiosity got the best of me during black studies. I began to think I was adopted when there were no pictures in the house of my mother and father. Look around you, the only pictures displayed are those with you and me. Then I started rambling in your personal effects while you were gone. And mother, please forgive me for that."

"That is when I discovered a letter addressed to me from you mother, detailing and explaining the whole thing. Thanks to Victor for getting me off into black studies. There is no harm done and I hope you have no regrets; I loved you as my grandmother and I will love you more as my mother. I continued to go along with you because I did not want to spoil your revelation. I knew the proper time for you—would come—when your heart would sing that sweet verse—stuttering not—and being joyful in saying—Angela, I am your mother. At this moment, I am so proud of you—mother. You sang your verse so gracious, without hesitating, and with so much meaning. There was no way, I could have spoiled that for you."

Angela and Ms. Lincoln were now embraced, inseparable, smiling, and kissing each other like—well—like mother and daughter.

There's nothing more special than family reunions. People getting together again, after an absence, renewing old acquaintances; people meeting young love ones for the first time; but this was neither. These two people were around each other daily and probably knew the others traits as well as they knew their own. And here we were, having a thirty year reunion. It was a coming together of mother and daughter for the very first time. It was the coming together of a seek and truth. Angela's long search of her real heritage and Ms. Lincoln's refusal to acknowledge reality was now almost over. Each accepted their hurdles with the stimulation of a winner at the end of a race. Much relief—much jubilation.

"Mother, how about that packet?"

"Oh, my dear, I almost forgot, Angela!"

Ms. Lincoln opened it, and on top was an envelope addressed to Angela. Angela opened it and began to read:

Dear Angel, My Darling Daughter

    I only wish I could have lived to see you grow into womanhood. You are the most beautiful child, I've ever seen. My love for you is endless. All of my precious moments are spent with you. If there was ever a reason to live, it would belong to you. Your birth pumped vigor into my ageless veins—for you are my heart. Your tiny feet kicking me and those marble black eyes, spying upon me, directed me to divulge my troubling heart. I should not have you grow up in the dark as I have or as I have chosen to do.

Firstly, though, let me say that I love your mother Hattie; but current circumstances does not warrant my telling her so. She might have understood my plight, but I just couldn't take the chance. I lived in torture and pain until I met and loved Hattie. She is a good woman——a heavenly sent woman. She healed some of my wounds; the others, of deeper incisions will follow me to the grave.

Next, let me apologize for any and all trouble caused you in your growing up and livelihood. Also accept an apology from Hattie. I made her agree not to tell you who her father was until now. I know the ordeal has been tough on her; but there are, at times, some painful things, we must do in life, just to make it better.

Lastly, I ask for your forgiveness. I truly feel God has forgiven me, and the Kingdom will be mine. Hattie accepted me without question, because of my master image. I want you to accept me because of my love for you.

The facts of the dialogue are as such: My mother Matilda, was born a slave and later bought her freedom. Yes, I am a Black man. She had three children in all. I only know, my kin, were boys of the much darker species. She said it was best I did not know anything else. She died without parting her lips as to their where abouts. Not knowing where to search for my brothers has haunted me all these years. It has also hurt. I have lived a good life, but one of misery.

My mother also never told me about my father, other than that he was a white man. Pain showed in her face every time I inquired about me. I finally gave up. She made me promise that I would pass. This meant not ever seeing and calling me son again; but she was willing to make the sacrifice. As it turned out, I became wealthy and hired her to work for me. Those were the happiest days of her life. By the way Angela, you don't have any sisters or brothers.

I couldn't tell Hattie I was black, because I was afraid of losing her. I had longed to be around some of my people. Like I said earlier, she accepted me because I was the boss. Losing my wealth, status, and the hardships it would play on my family also prevented me revealing this secret. It was my mother's wish and I painfully obliged. One day, maybe in your life time, people will be able to be just people, and succeed regardless of their race.

Enclosed are pictures of Matilda and myself. She was a strong woman—a strong woman who departed this world with secrets on her chest—heavily imbedded within her heart. She rest in peace in the black cemetery in Bunkers Bottom. I'm sure we'll meet again on that great day.

Angela I know you will be successful because your mother and grandmother paid the price—not to mention those before them. Just, don't let us down. Be yourself and help somebody less fortunate along the way.

May God be with you until we meet again.

Your Loving Father,

J. B. Tankerstroke

Angela was crying, Ms. Lincoln was crying, and they were all dumbfounded. Angela's puzzle had now come together. By the way, they were all now sitting down. And Victor thought Ms. Lincoln's secret was something; this was incredible. There were several pictures of Tankerstroke, mostly when he was a young man. He was a fine looking fellow and Angela was of his likeness to a T.

Tankerstroke as well as Angela had Matilda's wide thick eyebrows. There, the resemblance ended; Matilda was beautiful, but dark, with all the African characteristics of the early arrivals. Matilda must have been a smart woman. At least she knew the pain and sufferings of her people. She made her son pass, to escape the hardships, she and possibly her other two sons bore.

Angela, smiling, said, "this is the happiest day of my life; Mother, what do you think?"

"I'm just glad it's over—the food, the solemn smiles, the comfort, the stares of Tankerstroke—now, all come together. I never dreamed he was a Black man."

"As to my not understanding or not telling his secret, he probably did the best thing. I was a bit daring and wild in those days and might have delighted myself in tearing down his Big House. And even if I had not told the world, I probably would have told old man Tad. We were pretty close, working together each day and all; so the secret would have been out. Old man Tad was not a big talker, but if he said something, folks believed every word of it."

"It seems as if Tankerstroke suffered a lot; and I can't say I blame him for doing what he did. I might have done the same; we do what we have to do. It soothes my heart to know I put some comfort in his life. And I thank God and ask his forgiveness at the same time, for sending Tankerstroke into our lives. My heart is lighter after finding out the truth."

Angela had clenched both her fists, shaking them in front of her breast; holding tightly onto that letter.

"Victor, this is by far the greatest Black studies class, I have ever taken. It is so good to know your heritage. I feel so good about myself. My father reinforced everything, I have been reading about."

Other material enclosed noted, her father's full assumed name was John Baron Tankerstroke; but his name at birth was John Fulton Baron. His mother was Matilda Faltaft Baron.

Ms. Lincoln was more relieved than happy. She had gotten two things off her chest. No longer would she have to live a lie to Angela as her grandmother. And no longer would she have to feel guilty of lowering her dignity in sleeping with a white man. She had been telling herself all these years, she did the right thing; but nothing in her heart would let her believe. The humiliation and embarrassment would not go away, until now.

Her philosophy, now true to form, was standing out; "some decisions, though bad at the time, turn out to be pretty good later on." Down deep, Ms. Lincoln must have known; she must have felt things would turn out right. At least she hoped and prayed for a better day and the clearing of her conscience.

Yes, this was a day for reunions. And if there's such a thing as heaven and earth rejoicing together, then today was one of those days. Matilda Faltaft Baron and John Baron Tankerstroke singing praises upon Angel and Ms. Lincoln. Angels and Angels of sort was the hymn of praise—a reverberation encompassing not only Angela and Ms. Lincoln; but all of the sisters and brothers who found the journey homeward rough.

Today, also was a day of reckoning for mother and daughter; woman to child; woman to woman. Angela, stood in the eyes of her mother, to have grown from a mere child to the maturity of a disciplined woman, within minutes. Ms. Lincoln could feel and see the growth as Tankerstroke's letter started, and finally made its way to its sweet ending. And there was no timing problem as Victor had feared there would be; Angela admitted as much when she spoke; her father's words had filled and heated her insides like the chunking of wood in that old pot bellied stove. Tankerstroke apologized, but he had the advantage; he had the advantage of wisdom; the wisdom of Matilda on his side. Angela graciously accepted the facts from her father's buried time capsule; his words further satisfied her hold onto her heritage, giving her the inner strength and peace she needed. Angela now realized the importance of not letting history down; "Just don't let us down", still echoed in her ears. And on top of that, Tankerstroke left his Angel with a challenge to help someone less fortunate along the way; and Angela promised, she would do just that. How could she do any different; Angela's blessings had grown so abundant in only minutes; a new mother and memories to cherish for a lifetime.

CHAPTER FORTY THREE

RECONCILIATION AND GROWING UP

Call it love for her father—Victor; an understanding of her mother, Samantha; isolation from her two new sisters, Hattia and Victoria; or the maturity of Stacy herself. Whatever the reason, Stacy had summoned Angela to her Mother's house for a meeting of the minds. Stacy wanted to settle a bitterness which had lasted for almost twelve years. A bitterness like all divisiveness, in the mind of the accuser, had a reason to exist. A bitterness though, that had run its course and now demanded a reconciliation. It is not easy to make up with anyone unless you first feel it in your heart. Stacy had wanted to for a while, but could not find the words to go with her courage.

If all of life's problems could be solved with only the passing of time, Stacy's solution was well in hand. But the time passes, and we see, no matter how lengthy; no malicious act by a performer can transcend the need for an expression of regret. Stacy's prior performance had been enough to cast spells upon witches. No one's feelings, no matter how tough could have gone unscathed. But the time had come to discard the frivolous malarkey. It was time to quit being evil.

Upon seeing each other they started smiling.

"Angela, I want to apologize to you for being such an idiot. You did not deserve the harsh treatment and foul language I used. It was silly of me to be mad at you for an indignation that happened years ago. I have thought about the majorette incident and realize how stupid I have been. I also want to apologize for the things I said to you concerning my father. You love him as much as I do, and I shouldn't be interfering with your right to happiness."

"I am sorry about the situation you're involved in with Helen and my father. That is so unique and I cannot interfere or help you there. I love Helen; she is like a mother to me, but much more, she's my best friend. I mean, she's a real friend and there's nothing I would not do for her. Maybe one day, you two will iron it out, and I wish both of you the best of luck."

"In the meantime, I don't want my little brothers and sisters growing up, not knowing each other. I want them to be able to play together and love each other as brothers and sisters. And maybe, just maybe, they will grow up unlike myself, not respecting others individual rights. As least they will have a head start with three others to keep them in line; reminding each other daily, there's other people living in their world."

"I guess what I'm saying now Angela is, I want to be able to see or pick them up on a regular basis, as a big sister. Call me selfish, but I also want them to know me. And in short, after all that; will you please forgive me?"

Angela and Stacy were now hugging and crying all over each other.

"Stacy, I not only forgive you, but accept your apology. It was just as much my fault as yours. Will you also forgive me for any hurt I have caused you. And as far as the girls are concerned; feel free to get them anytime."

The two had solved their differences and were now like two old hens——cackling all over the place.

Hattia had already made herself known to Stacy; crawling in and out of her lap. Doing so, as if she'd found a new play mate. The attention given her by Stacy was indeed that of a big sister; talking baby talk and sort of letting Hattia have her way. Finally, Hattia tired of all that climbing and fell asleep in Stacy's lap. Stacy had perfected her baby charming techniques on Helen's boys—her most adorable little brothers —and found it worked on beautiful little girls as well. None of this went unnoticed by Angela who was not as adept and patient in handling Hattia and Victoria.

For Angela, this was one of her happiest moments since the birth of her first daughter—Hattia. Ever since Stacy found out about Angela and Victor, a disagreeable fashion set in. Angela had been troubling herself on how to handle it. She had wanted to tell Victor about the cruel treatment being dished out by Stacy. Then Angela decided against it; and now feel proud of herself for exercising patience. Now the two of them could be friends. A reaction of, what a relief to have all this behind me.

And Stacy, well, she had to swallow a lot of pride to apologize. On top of everything else, Samantha had grown to like Angela, and pretty much treated her like the daughter she wanted—one who was going to go to college and graduate. Samantha and Stacy had argued about the comparison and Stacy despised Angela for it, until today. At least half of that was now solved; Samantha of course still had her educational hangup. This was a good day for Stacy, because the vision of her brothers and sisters playing together regularly, had come true. It took a big person to do what Stacy did and mean it. Her heart was truly in the right place today. She would never have to be rude and insensitive to Angela again.

Both young women realized what they had been depriving themselves of. Too many times, the young and fool-hearted take the first curtain-call for the VERY END. They must learn to expect, there might just be an encore; or if nothing more, someone might want to take a final bow. By acting in haste, the best part of the night's show could be missed. Angela and Stacy were learning that life's show could slip away as well. They had firmly learned the importance of patience.

Stacy had matured into a fine young lady over the past few years. Most of the credit should go to Helen, who entrusted the responsibility of Harre and Gree to her. Stacy had kept her two young brothers, day, night, evenings, weekends, and most of all, when Helen was out of town. Helen would never call Stacy like Victor; preferring only to give her the number where she could be reached. Helen encouraged Stacy to ask a question if she wanted to know how to do something; but never volunteered her method or interfered. When Stacy did things differently, Helen never complained.

Stacy had no fear of how to wash the boys clothes or what to feed them. Although Stacy performed a multitude of motherly functions, Harre and Gree knew she was their big sister. They played with her as such, but respected that change in the voice, at bedtime or when it was time to put up the toys. Responsibility helps all youth to mature, and for Stacy it hadn't been any different. Victor was pleased with how his sweet daughter was responding to her self-inflicted chores. She cared for her brothers as if they were her own.

Helen treated Stacy as an adult, while Samantha still pretty much treated her as mama's little girl. It's no wonder she rebelled; getting along with her mother only half the time. Never allowed to think for herself or enjoy those precious individual rights made Stacy, at times, hostile toward her mother. Stacy often displayed a coolness and expressions of resentment when Samantha told her to do something. Samantha still directed Stacy around like a colonel ordering a private. And of course, that's why Stacy had moved out; because it was obvious, she was never going to be allowed to grow up, as long as she remained in the domicile of her mother. When your hair is not worn in the right style or your clothes are not suited to mom's specification, it is time to move out.

After all Stacy was over twenty five, but Samantha failed to realize it. The fact that Stacy had failed to live up to her mother's expectations of graduating from college had probably stifled Stacy's growth in her view. No matter the conversation, Samantha always got around to conveying the message of going back to college or criticizing her for dropping out. As of late, to save an argument, Stacy pretended not to hear and just ignored her mother.

Samantha had, however, accomplished something without her knowing it; because Stacy had quizzed Helen, her idol, on the education subject. Helen merely said "make up your mind what you want to be, and enjoy it." "Some flowers bloom early and some bloom late", was Helen's answer to not readily working on a career. Helen was low-key when it came to Stacy, but had a magical effect on her. For sure, she could never be accused of not allowing Stacy to think for herself. And she never exerted any pressure on Stacy; which was unusual, because of her persistent persuasion on everyone else.

One of these days Stacy, no doubt, would escape from her shell; but for now she was in a hold pattern; still working those mediocre hourly jobs. Making enough money to pay rent, buy food, and not much of anything for herself. All of her other money was spent on Harre and Gree. She spared nothing when it came to her darling brothers. Helen wanted to give her money for keeping the boys, day in and day out; but Stacy refused, saying it was her duty to look out for her brothers. Stacy, nonetheless, did not refuse Victor's offer to replace her old car; but then, she never refused anything from her father, who respected her wishes. Victor also paid her utilities and her gasoline bill each month, because she had his gas card. Then there was the occasional rent payment.

Samantha was ecstatic about the make up, and as always, was trying to psychoanalyze Stacy; hoping her educational wake up call was fast approaching. Samantha's temperament was short, to say the least, when it came to Stacy. Her unwanted advice to Stacy, mostly fell on deaf ears. Every now and then, Stacy would be receptive and go along, but those were rare moments indeed. It's not that they did not love each other; and Stacy always bought presents at Christmas, birthday, and mother's day to display such. What went on between them was that constant tug of war between mother and daughter. Please do not get the impression they argued all the time, or did not ever get along; because it was not like that at all.

Stacy had not matured enough to assume a positive role for her own responsibility, thought Samantha. That in a nutshell, meant going to college and graduating. Samantha remembered her college days at Spelman on numerous occasions while talking to Stacy. The educational atmosphere and experience is like none other, she said. Samantha continued; stating how the rewards reaped, far exceeded the hard work necessary on being a successful student. She pointed out many of the schools alumna who had gone on to have prosperous careers in terms of satisfaction, accomplishments, and well-paying professions. Samantha would have sold the average young lady on attending her prestigious alma mater, and rightly so; but Stacy wasn't bulging.

Angela, could hardly wait to tell Victor, about today's event, but became resentful of Carolyn, for some unknown reason. She had cause to be resentful of Carolyn these days, who could make Victor spend a week with her anytime she wanted. And as this Monday rolled around, Carolyn was in Victor's office again, with sufficient reasons for him to do just that.

"Victor, I missed you so much when you left on Saturday morning; the weekends are so miserable without you; I need you to be with me again this week."

"Carolyn, you must understand I have other obligations, family obligations which have to be attended to."

"I do understand Victor; Helen and Angela deserve the attention you are giving them, but you deserve the loving attention I am willing to give you. Even you said so yourself, last week; and I am more than willing to give of myself again, this week."

"After loving you five nights last week Carolyn, my body deserves a rest, I'll be honest with you. Another week of the same and a back to back week, will truly sap me drier than the Sahara Desert."

"Victor, you are so funny; if you are so sapped, why are you always so ready?"

"Carolyn, you must understand, you make me ready; just looking at you makes me ready; even, thinking about you, makes me ready, but that does not mean, I should make love to you, just because I'm ready!"

"Well, that is hard for me to understand Victor. When you are ready and I am willing to give you what you deserve, you should be passionate with me."

"Passionate, yes; making love, no! Let me put it another way Carolyn; my body is tired and running down, because of all your loving."

"So you do not enjoy me anymore Victor?"

"Sure I enjoy you very much Carolyn; the point I am trying to get you to see is, I am enjoying you, too much."

"Well, what do you suggest Victor; are you saying I will have to give up more than the weekends!"

"Now, you are beginning to understand, what I have been saying for the last ten minutes, Carolyn! My body just needs more rest after a solid week with you."

"That sounds like too much of a sacrifice for me Victor; losing Sharonda was enough sacrifice for me. Now you are saying I must lose you too! I don't know if I'm going to be able to cope with that, Victor."

"Okay Carolyn—okay; I'll stay with you this week; see you after work."

"You should not be so good, big boy!"

"Yeah!"

"I will work something out Victor, that will make us both happy; see ya!"

"Uh huh."

"Goodbye Tiff, your boss is so nice!"

"Bye, bye Carolyn; you are wearing the hell, out of that outfit, today."

"Thank you girl! Winking at Tiffani, but never missing a stride in her stroll."

"Victor, I could not help, but hear Carolyn putting the squeeze on you; even playing on your sympathy with her daughter. She knows you to a T, and apparently will stop at nothing, to capitalize on your every weakness."

"Yeah Tiffani, she got my number all right."

"I followed everything Victor, but that big boy, stuff. I had not heard it in quite a while; what is that all about?"

"Oh, nothing Tiffani; a private joke."

"Though Carolyn needs your help Victor, you are still too nice to her. And speaking of help, Angela wants you to come by after work."

"Did she say what it was about, Tiffani?"

"No Victor, but she did say it was extremely important. I guess that shoots the first day of the week with Carolyn, huh."

"Yeah; and she's not going to like it very much, either. I'll call and explain to her, on my way to Angela's."

Victor was taking the light way out, not facing Carolyn with a denial. To be honest, he took the only way out; knowing he could not turn her down, in his sight. To his surprise though, Carolyn was nice about it, telling him she understood, and that he could make it up to her on Tuesday night. In Victor's drive to Angela's, he figured Ms. Lincoln was going out of town again, and Angela had bright ideas of her own.

"Victor, you will never guess what happened yesterday; I almost called you last night, but I wanted to tell you in person. I am so happy—"

"Well Angela, let me in on it, will you!"

"Brace yourself. Stacy invited me to visit with her, over to Samantha's house yesterday, we made up Victor. Isn't that wonderful?"

"Well, I suppose—made up from what Angela?"

"Oh, I can see you know nothing about it; I thought maybe Samantha or Stacy, might have told you of our feud."

"Feud! What kind of feud?"

"It is nothing to get alarmed about Victor, especially now, that it is all over. In order to cut a long story—but since you are spending the night—maybe I can take my time. Anyway, when we were in high school together, I beat her out for the last spot as a majorette, and Stacy accused my mother of buying me the spot; that is when and how the feud got started."

"Why didn't somebody tell me about this Angela, why didn't you tell me about this—this—feud?"

"Apparently, nobody wanted to bother you with such frivolous matters Victor. I did not know you then anyway; I was merely a little underaged, teenage girl."

"Well, how about later, Miss Teenage America; when did this surface again?"

"I intended on telling you Victor; but changed my mind, because I was in love with you; and I was not going to have her messing up my first and only love. It is true, I knew you were married, but somehow, I was going to pursue you and hope for the best. Then after I finally coerced you to bow down on your knees, before me, the thought of telling you was definitely out. Victor, I did not know I could feel that good, and you have been making me feel that good ever since. And what little chance there was of telling you about our feud, faded all together, when Stacy accused me of causing you and Samantha to get divorced. That news made me feel so terrible, until Stacy gave me the date of the occurrence; which exposed you as being alone, all the time. It dawned on me then, that Stacy could be a nice news-carrier on the Victor-express, so I sat back and let her."

"Oh, I see; well Angela, I can't blame you for that. Now, a lot of things are falling into place."

"Next week Victor, mother is spending spring break with Molly, in Galveston; so, could you please adjust your busy schedule for spending some quality time before me. By the way, you look awful Victor; those bags under your eyes are beginning to turn darker and darker. Get some rest tonight, you can thank me for it, next week, when Queen Angela sits on her throne."

Victor laughed with Angela, thanking her to himself, for being so kind. Between Carolyn and Angela, his body was getting no relief; it seemed as if they had teamed up on him, and was competing for his carcass. Spending time with Helen and the boys was really the only sexual relief he had, and he truly welcomed it. Victor found it interesting, that two women could now run his body raggedy. His appearance was again noted the next day at the office.

"You look rested this morning, Victor; got some sleep, huh?"

"I sure did Tiffani; mean you can tell the difference after only one night."

"You certainly can Victor, but you could really use the entire week to rest up; but I suppose, that is out, with Carolyn, huh?"

"Yeah, probably—she suppose to work something out—she says; can't imagine what though, knowing how horny she is every night, Tiffani."

"You can always go home and forget about Carolyn, Victor."

"I could, Tiffani, but I promised her, I would stay."

"Like I said, Victor, you are too nice to Carolyn."

Carolyn was not all bad, just selfish; she had come to understand Victor's confession of a tired body, and offered her gratifying solution. Victor listened attentively as Carolyn dries herself off; she knows how to get his attention and hold it. And as Victor says,

Carolyn knows how to get her point across.

"This week Victor, well what is left of it, I plan to take it easy on you; there will be no sapping or draining, or whatever it was that you said, I do to your body."

"It is still a full week Carolyn, its only Tuesday, you know; anyway, what is your plan?"

"As far as I am concerned Victor, you can save your bigness for another time, at least a week; me, myself, I do not mind being sapped or drained!"

Carolyn winks at Victor and crawls into bed, rubbing her fingers across her woolly center, lying there, looking sexy- innocently and smiling upward at him. Victor had thought of what Carolyn had in mind, but had not thought of doing it alone, for an entire week. What the hell, he thought, it might work; and he was promptly about the business of enjoying Carolyn's woolly center. Tuesday night, the first night, Victor had to admit was the most difficult; the thought of getting nothing in return disturbed him. That is until, he mentally accepted the challenge of enjoying what he made Carolyn produce. By the end of the week, Victor was quite proficient at enjoying Carolyn's abundance of sweetness. Each night, it seems to him that Carolyn produced more and more; he learned that skipping dinner helped tremendously. Carolyn apparently, knew what she was doing, thought Victor, because he found, holding her woolly center before him, so relaxing and filling; always putting him to sleep, as after any hearty meal. The effect upon Victor's body was dynamic, as both Tiffani and Angela noticed that those bags had completely disappeared. Victor thanked Carolyn with more of the same as opportunity presented itself; and there were many of such, with Carolyn. Victor never had a complaint from Carolyn, that her resources were running low or dry; he even teased Carolyn about what a tremendous supplement it was. This of course did nothing to solve Carolyn's real problem. Victor, after a short while, really forgot about why he was spending time with Carolyn; other than the fulfillment of his appetite; enjoying the sappy sweetness of her woolly center.

CHAPTER FORTY FOUR

BOARD MEETING

It was a sobering feeling to Angela to realize one of them was now in a position to help make a change. A change for the best that is. A change whereby the Corporate Executive Changes would no longer be like a snow blanket. Knowing that significant moves took place within these board walls, an eerie feeling propelled millions of tiny bumps upon her body. As Angela gazed upon them, each mound appeared to be representing ancestors of centuries ago. Her father, John Baron Tankerstroke was there, giving Angela the needed confidence; saying, "I know you won't let us down." Grandmother Matilda, sat urging her forward with her secrets still bottled up. Angela's uncles with clenched fist raised, saying, "do this one for us." The illiterate mama's and papa's and their kids who saw no future, chimed in with a victorious cry. And all the others laboring in the fields and working on the plantation singing that one last spiritual for Angela. Their eyes: Tired. Their expression: A comforting grin; all focused upon Angela this morning. This was their moment—their time to shine—their time to speak. This was their morning glory and all would be forgiven. They saw farther than Angela and Angela HAD to see them through. Angela could never let them down—Angela would not let them down. Her banner waved for all of them to see.

A neophyte, rookie, newcomer, a new beginning is what Angela was for the board. There was a number of important issues on today's agenda. However, none was more important to Angela than the corporate affirmative action program and a surprise entry; the sale of the corporation.

Angela had worked hard in preparing her presentation on the affirmative action program. Facts had been gathered and statistics formulated to show the discriminatory hiring and promotion practices of Black employees. Angela's statistics would show a negligible 2.5 percent of Black employees (851); and all of these with the exception of twenty one jobs, were either clerical or warehouse type jobs. Angela's facts would show where a nearly one hundred year old corporation had never promoted a Black employee into its management ranks, or for that matter, there had never been a Black in a supervisory position.

Angela would argue the benefits accruing to the corporation, both directly and indirectly, due to a diverse work force. More jobs and better jobs meant greater buying power, translating into additional sales of their products to their workers, their families, and the communities in which they lived. It meant gaining a good reputation within the communities, simply by treating people equal; letting them spread the corporation's positive image. It meant to no longer under-utilize the skills and abilities of the pool of talented Black employees. It meant opening employment doors for Black workers previously shut by the corporation. All of which would increase the operating efficiency and improve profits of the corporation.

Angela would challenge them to enforce their nepotism policy; to discontinue only hiring and promoting friends along with those relatives; and to forget about being color blind. She would explain how a corporation divided from within was not good business sense. Angela would insist on any manager or supervisor not following the affirmative action guidelines, be relieved of their duty immediately.

In a prepared statement, Angela would have read the following: "Gentleman, our corporation today is blessed with a Black woman on its board. I represent the locked out and powerless people, who sent me here. I am their voice and must speak for them. I am here to address their problems and their needs. Their problem is the corporation's insensitivity to the hiring and promotion of Black people. Their need is to get a corporate affirmative action program to solve their problem. So my job is to appeal to you for that program."

"An affirmative action program is a means of correcting injustices in the work place. It is a means of maintaining fairness in the work place. We are talking about justice and fairness to a people that make up twelve to fourteen percent of the population of this Country; but generally do not approach those numbers in our corporations. And when we do, we are all at the low end of the totem. We are hired there and we remain there, getting smaller wage increases on top of already lower wages."

"We as a corporation must address this unequitable situation. Don't do it only because of my appeal; but search your heart, and do it because it is right, just, and fair; savoir-faire if you please. Think of yourself; years ago when you came into the work place without prejudiced restrictions; and moved up without prejudiced restrictions. Think of your sons and daughters enjoying those same benefits without any prejudiced restrictions. And then, think of the many qualified Blacks who are denied jobs because of their color; and if hired, are denied promotions because of their color."

"Somewhere along the way, Ancestral Racism must stop. You must not follow in the footsteps of your grandfather; and must deviate from the racist path your father took. I ask you to think for a minute and search your conscience; ask yourself the question— do I want to continue ancestral racism and the status quo, or do I want to do what is fair and equitable. Be honest with yourself, because that's what an affirmative action program is all about. It is being honest with men and women of all races; it is being honest with our corporation; and, it is being honest with America. We are not talking about doing something because of pressure, or the threat of a legality; but because of a moral right."

Angela thought of her father—John Baron Tankerstroke; knowing that he would be very proud of her, trying to help correct the evils of the World. I'm sure he would have told her, "Get your heart right and follow it, wherever it goes." And Angela would try desperately to get that point across to the board.

"Gentlemen, the affirmative action program, I am speaking of today should propel our corporation into the twenty first- century. It will jetstream us pass our competitors. We are talking about using all of our human resources to its fullest. We are not merely talking about setting an example; but about being the leader. We want to exceed all goals and limitations in the arena of justice and equality in the work place. You can never feel bad doing the right thing; and you will never regret having an affirmative action program. You will not only have fulfilled an obligation and duty to the corporation; but will have satisfied a debt to mankind."

"I know, I might be asking you to sacrifice your diehard deep entrenched roots. I may be asking you to relax principals you have lived with for forty years, or for that matter, all of your life. But this might be that golden opportunity knocking at your door for the first and last time. To error during your generation is correctable and forgivable; to error against future generations is hell's travel on greased wheels, downhill. So let us pass a healthy torch, burning bright with good deeds, rather than a dimly lit one, inflicted with pain and suffering."

Angela would have discussed and read the above to support her position for the affirmative action program; but all items on today's agenda was postponed indefinite, except the sale of the corporation. A surprise indeed, but it set Angela's mind to thinking. There were two serious companies or should I say Countries in contention—Britain and Japan. Both offers had something in common; they were comparable and they were both substantial. Employees knew nothing of a sale yet; and the board members were asked to keep it like that for a while.

Angela thought; "every time we turned around these days, companies were being sold into foreign dominance. This, more than likely meant their group of management trainees starting all over again. It would also mean the loss of employees; meaning the last hired was sure to be dismissed. Angela could see their dynamic ten being reduced to a program that went the way of the dinosaur. They had worked too hard to rise to their current level and in one swoop, have a new hierarchy annihilate all those gains. Their position could become worse than climbing an ice covered hill."

Later, Angela discussed the sale with Victor, expressing her opinion that the timing was ripe for an African-American group to buy in.

"The minimum price sought, Victor, is 2.5 billion dollars; which is not bad."

"The only problem, Angela, is bids which could drive the price through the ceiling."

"Your help will be desperately needed Victor."

"I'm familiar with leveraged buyouts, Angela, so that's the chosen route. Two other main concerns is the investment group, and convincing the board to sell to us. How much time do we have to put a package together, Angela?"

"It is hard to say Victor, but we meet again next month, and at that time, I want to make a proposal and be in a position for an offer."

"What we need to do Angela is try and keep it friendly and non-competitive, because the lower the debt the better. Let's concentrate on the investment group first, Angela."

"How about the African-American Association at the company, Victor?"

"That will come into play later Angela. What we need is a smaller investment group; one that could put together about thirty five to fifty million dollars."

"You mean we would be in good shape with that amount, Victor?"

"Angela, if I'm calculating correctly, that's quite a sum of cash."

"Yes Victor, but I talked to mother about this; and she is willing to put up about seventy million, and I could add twenty million to that."

"Whoa, you're kidding, Angela."

"Nope; but we figured we would need more than that Victor."

"I tell you what Angela, I can muster up two million. Why don't we figure forty million—you two can split the remainder any way you want to. We are the investment group; I'll arrange the financing through a leveraged buyout specialist, I'm familiar with. They generally want about thirty percent equity in the venture if it's sound. You could own yourself a company in less than a year, if everything goes smoothly, Angela."

"A year!"

"Yes, Angela, these things are time consuming. Do you think they have any idea, you would try to purchase the company?

"I doubt it, Victor; we are not suppose to have that much money or be that smart."

"Angela, let me be the first to admit it; you're sharper and better still, more advanced than I ever imagined."

"All that credit goes to you Victor—you gave me a wake up call. You have been the greatest asset in my life, besides mother; and I love you for it."

There was little time or thought, in the absence of Ms. Lincoln, for Angela's famous sofa duty; she and Victor were too busy thinking and planning on how to become entrepreneurs on a very large scale. Angela had surprised Victor with her advanced interest of corporate ownership; and the excitement of this possible endeavor had made its way into his office.

"Victor, I am so excited about becoming, THE EXECUTIVE SECRETARY, the top of them all. I could hardly sleep last night, just thinking about it. The colors for my new bathroom will be royal blue and gold; those are kings colors, you know. And you will feel like the king that you are in this room, Victor, when I am through decorating it."

"Whoa—,hold on there Tiffani, it is not done yet, or even close to it, I merely mentioned it to you in private, to keep you abreast of me, and what might happen."

"You can save that reserved attitude for people like Angela, Victor. I know for myself, when you put your mind to accomplishing something, its as good as done. Please let me know when to pack Victor; I can be ready in about thirty minutes."

"Since you are so positive and sure about things, Tiffani, why is it going to take you so long to pack."

"Maybe I should clarify myself Victor; packing was really a bad usage of words. I really meant thirty minutes of clearing out my desk and discarding all this old junk; there will definitely be no place for it, in my new desk and office; and besides, Victor, it is not good ethics among our profession to leave the next executive secretary with a dirty and junky desk. You are aware that my rep. is among the highest in this town, and I want to keep it like that. The girls already envy me, you know; and I want to keep them chattering on something good about the sister."

"Oh, I see! Well Tiffani, I suppose, I should just inform you of the positive acquisition reports."

"There you go Victor!"

As the conversation evolved and they went about their respective duties, Tiffani sat at her desk, and thought of Ralph. She wondered about him and whether they would be able to continue their investment sessions in Victor's office. If he decided not to go with Victor, then there would have to be other arrangements made for their important meetings; especially now, that it seemed, he was responding halfway favorable. Tiffani was not about to even attempt, to fool herself; Ralph had become a big part of her life, in more ways than one. He knew about investing in the stock market and it had given her some good returns; her account was approaching one half million dollars. And there was the other important feature; her personal sacrifice of denying anyone else a chance of enjoying her furry furrow; not to mention the sacrifice of depriving herself of this pleasurable enjoyment. Having a man just for that purpose alone, however, never appealed to Tiffani, who always wanted her man to have a bit more substance than that; her girl friends had too many stories to tell of the guys who found them, f——them, and forgot them, seemingly in the same breath.

Anyway, Tiffani had made her mind up, to hang in there with Ralph, who she felt, after the other day to be getting real close to being the aggressor. He realized now, according to his own words, Tiffani was "real sweet and good." Tiffani thought, "I am not going to worry; Ralph is probably sitting in his office right now, thinking of a way to ease his taste-tester into my furry furrow." That, she thought, was a great possibility of happening on their very next meeting. Tiffani had ceased to wonder daily, what Ralph was all about, though the curiosity did cross her mind every now and then. She also ceased in being frustrated after their last session, in which she had manipulated his fingers to perfection upon her furry furrow; and if nothing more occurred, she thought, she at least had advanced to a stage, where Ralph got the feel and taste of things with her good assistance. Of course, it was with this same assistance, Tiffani felt good about her chances of Ralph putting his head and lip service to something that really paid good dividends. Tiffani reasoned, the best strategy, was to stick to Victor's "imagination theory"; mixed with a little hand twisting of her own. After all, Ralph had not objected in her being aggressive with her hands, to force him to be active; so, she thought, for their next session, she would manipulate another part of his body, placing it exactly where she wanted him to respond, and softly talk him into responding exactly the way she wanted him to. And for the second time this morning, Tiffani found excitement stirring within her body; suddenly, wishing for Ralph to call her!

"Tiffani——Tiffani——Tiffani——Tiffa"

"Oh excuse me Victor, I was doing a little daydreaming; what is it?"

"Sorry I interrupted you Tiffani, but we do have to work every now and then, you know. Could you please get me that report on the project you completed last week?"

"Sure Victor; it is here at my fingertips; there you are."

"Thanks Tiffani; you can go back to daydreaming, but first, get Ralph on the phone, and see if he can meet me for lunch; tell him it's extremely important."

While Tiffani was delivering Victor's message to Ralph about lunch, she wanted to inquire if he would like to have dinner on her. She wondered what his response would have been, if she had asked; and after telling Victor, Ralph was available, Tiffani was back to her daydreaming, also on Ralph's availability. It was a given, he would call her next week, when Victor was in New York with Helen, but those sensuous feelings arousing within, dictated his presence this moment.

CHAPTER FORTY FIVE

ON CALL

The word was getting around on Helen and her commitment to the AIDS cause. She wanted to please everyone, but had to delay seminars relating to prevention. Helen's stature had risen in the medical profession, and research was her number one priority. So when the call came for her to address the Governor's conference in New York; she started packing for the trip, more than two months away. Helen had been recommended to the convention by some of the Mayors who had heard her. She had been asked by the conference committee to do a similar video presentation, without limitations. Helen was delighted to know, AIDS was a major topic on their agenda. It's easier, she said, to talk to someone who is already receptive; someone who is willing to listen to the World's woe's.

Helen saw this journey as one of "maybes." Maybe times were changing and attitudes and minds were getting serious about AIDS. Maybe, pocketbooks would loosen and there would be more dollars for research. Maybe, just maybe, some huge body involving thousands of people would take up this enormous fight against this deadly disease. Maybe, she could proceed with her research on an uninterrupted basis. And the maybe of all "maybes;" she would emerge triumphantly within the decade, and before the turn of the century, with a cure. It was not unrealistic for Helen to have this kind of hope. She had come to believe that "a cure was only a dollar away."

This was Helen's first trip to the big apple, and she was all excited about that. At no time did Victor ask if she wanted him to go; he merely found out the dates and got ready. It had become understood; he would accompany her on any out of town trip. How they reached that conclusion is beyond him. Helen expected it and Victor expected to go. Call it Victor's love of travel if you will.

Also as expected, they did their share of sightseeing. The thing that fascinated Helen most was walking out atop the World Trade Center; which competed with the clouds for space. She stated, the winds smacked her lips with a heavenly kiss; "a breeze which whisked through my nostrils and watered my eyes upon its gracious journey."

A distortion of the World below, but the waterways glistened, as did the moisture in Helen's eyes. The magnificent bridges which they understood was in grave need of repair; yet looked from their view as the eighth wonder of the World. Yes, this was the city of all cities; with monuments, a statue of all statues, and skyscrapers to enhance its glory. A city so magnificent that it would take a volume of books to do it partial justice. A city with such diverse culture and over a billion stories to be told.

The story told during the time, however, was the one illuminated by Helen on the convention floor. Helen again was appealing for funds for AIDS research. There's no need to get into her speech this time, because of the effect it has. Helen's speeches always come to life or death, depending upon how it hits your imagination. There's never an in between. The audience again was captivated and again Dr. Helen was able to pry loose some necessary funds for research; and again in Helen's words, "it's just not enough." Helen left them with a thought which has impacted Victor until this day; "we are pinching pennies for research, while AIDS is pinching lives."

The one thing they weren't pinching pennies on were souvenirs. People were buying everything to take home to their love ones. Helen bought Stacy an—I love you New York bracelet. On the back was inscribed—I love you...signed Helen. They attended some plays and theaters for live performance while there. One can see why the city is so expensive; there's always something to do and somewhere to go. Helen was happy and needless to say, they were having a good time. Her bubbly smile warmed Victor's heart; that look of satisfaction and achievement was shining through.

Helen had reason to smile. She was doing what she enjoyed doing—converting people over to her way of thinking. Divesting of yourself and investing in a worthy cause was her motto. Plus, as she put it, "I have my number one fan with me." And she did have Victor. As they walked, Helen always locked both arms around Victor's bended elbow; undoubtedly, that's her way of showing possession. New York was full of those beautiful sisters; but Helen was not worried, because none would get a chance. Victor figured they'd want nothing of a one arm man.

They had taken four extra days to see and do things in the city; but it just wasn't enough. A promise to themselves to return at some point in time had to suffice. Of course, leisure time for Helen was always a premium, and with Victor's extended obligations, his too had become scarce. At one time Victor took vacations and forced Helen to do so; now it appeared all they were doing was a few days here and a weekend there. It mattered not to Helen, who focused her next trip to the Senior Sitizens Senter or to a local seminar. Helping out was her joy and satisfaction; and one can truly say, Helen was On Call.

ON CALL

To benefit the cause——she spoke
For research and prevention
To enlist the Doctor's help
AIDS was the word to mention

On seeing others suffer
What pain she must have had
Research money was needed
She wanted a cure——so bad

People would sit and listen
Funds for research——she cried
Most had a deaf ear
But a few took to her side

Nickels and dimes poured in
Funds for research, she'd holler
To conquer this dreadful disease
She had to have their dollar

Went anywhere, met anyone
She thought might do some good
Speaking for the worthy cause
As often as she could

Delayed an appointment or two
So she could make them all
She spoke to save the masses
The Doctor was definitely——On Call

But once on vacation, Helen was dynamite. The best description is; Helen enjoyed where she was; she accepted each moment and made the most of it, wherever it was. And this trip was no exception. While Victor had been to New York and had spent countless hours there; he had never been to Central Park. Strolling arm in hand with Helen over this vast area reminded him of years long ago, with Samantha. On a trip to London, Samantha and Victor walked, sprawled, and relaxed, for the greater portion of two days in Hyde Park.

These parks had their similarities, displaying an array of greenery—trees, shrubbery, flowers, vines, grass; crisscrossed with pathways to stampede the acreage. And people, there are always people; but a uniqueness existed—one could always find his own space, the cozy corner, a lover's lair; that serene setting where only your private world existed. A world in which you daydreamed and wished they'd never end. A world—for the moment—was paradise. Here, in this special and personal cove, there were no worries; there were no problems. There were no heartaches or pains, no sorrows to bemoan. Only pleasantries came to mind and you wanted them to last forever.

The movement of the squirrels were different as their bushy tails seemed to twirl in rhythm with the songs of the birds, that danced to their own music. The sun itself, which filtered and flickered through the branches was also in step with the birds harmonious sound. Helen and Victor looked at each other, trading stares that only two people in love could understand. No words were exchanged; their hearts were in sync, and their eyes upon each other told the story.

Although the convention went well, and they had a great time; Helen was only half of her bubbly self near the end of the trip; speaking softly into Victor's ear.

"I'm just not feeling very well Victor. Maybe my body needs some more rest and relaxation. I'm going to take a few days off when we return."

"It's about time you realize you're not a machine, Helen. The rest will do you good."

Anxiety must have been building in Ralph, the way it was in Tiffani, because early Monday morning, the first day of Victor's absence, he was there to visit with Tiffani. Suddenly, her normal and otherwise, routine day became vibrant. The not-too talkative Ralph, stayed only seconds though; only long enough to inquire if she was taking visitors that evening. Startled and a bit off guard at Ralph's inquisitive remarks, Tiffani recovered in time to nod a smiling approval. A strange occurrence for Ralph, but then, Tiffani had grown accustom to stranger and wilder occurrences from him. Still his presence set the tone of the day, causing a lot of mind wondering for Tiffani; for Ralph normally called a day or so in advance to discuss their investment portfolio. One wonder was; what would she wear or not wear, being more appropriate, on such short notice.

Tiffani remembered how she teased Ralph during this last session with a very short blue skirt and black pantyhose, which had been planned and which worked to a perfection on his imagination. Looking downward at her white blouse and long ankle length red skirt, gave no appearance of sexiness or teasing appeal; only enough material to cover the world, she thought. Tiffani, still feeling Ralph's fingers upon her furry furrow from the last session, said out loud, "I am not going to settle for anything less." She had heard that sometimes, one has to take a step backward to move forward, but Tiffani was fearful of losing ground or vital contact in this case, by not following through with some imaginative plan; just stripping had produced nothing but frustrations. And it seems, just thinking about a return to the old days was causing a slight frustration in Tiffani right now.

Tiffani's thoughts of going home to change, faded when she came to the realization, it was just too far away. Shopping at lunch—a brilliant idea—and her next brainstorm, fell by the way-side when she discovered her powerful buying resource—the checkbook—was also at home. Tiffani could only smile, thinking of her self imposed predicament of worrying about sexy-teasing-imaginative outfits to wear; and smiled harder, when she thought of the trying situation Ralph was in for this evening. Her ingenious idea filled her body with tingles and a desire to get loads of work done today. Tiffani knew the time would fly by if she was busy; and Ralph would be stepping tall coming through those doors—glancing in their direction.

Tiffani even managed to start throwing useless items out of her desk. She had told Victor, thirty minutes moving time was adequate, and it would be, but why not cut it to about five, Tiffani thought. Following Victor to another company was really a no-brainer; the pay scale was high and the boss was good to work for. Her tenure with this company had been extremely rewarding, because of Ralph and his financial nurturing. Thanks to Ralph, Tiffani had virtually no bills and even at her tender age, could afford to retire now and live comfortably, depending on her new type of lifestyle, of course. For Tiffani that time was getting close; her dream was to spend at least two years in Paris, after her investment portfolio reached that three-quarter million mark. Ralph had been a big help financially, but had also taught her, inadvertently, how to survive without a man. So the idea of getting married was not even a borderline thought. Ralph was all Tiffani cared for at this point, mainly she reasoned, he in essence told her no, which became invitational. In all of her limited relations of one guy and the many stories of her girlfriends, Ralph was by far the toughest nut to crack. Tiffani, however, hoped for the best this evening; then she would try and find out why.

Sure as Tiffani was busy, lunch came and went, and the evening clock told her it was time to freshen up, for her guest. She was confident her plan would work on Ralph, if imagination still meant as much as it did, when they last met. Shortly after five, punctual as usual, Ralph came through the doors, locking them as part of his ritual. Tiffani was patiently waiting on him, sitting in Victor's soft leather chair at his desk, looking like a top executive. She motioned for Ralph to come on in and pull up a chair on the opposite side. Ralph was only five minutes into his analysis, before the folded articles of clothing on the left front corner, were in his way. Tiffani smiled as Ralph sought more and more room, ultimately, pushing the garments to the floor. And as any normal person, he leaned to pick up the particulars, discovering the two pieces to be a long red skirt and a pair of gorgeous black panties. Victor calmly laid them back on the desk, but after a short while, they fell again.

Tiffani could see the change in Ralph's demeanor and knew immediately, his imagination was acting up. It did not take a genius to figure this one out; the top executive in front of him was bottomless. Sensing that Ralph was ready for the challenge, after about ten more hard grueling minutes, on his part, Tiffani slid him a familiar note which read; "you will try my goodness first hand——THIS MINUTE." Tiffani knew this was a bold move, but everything was in her favor; Ralph looked highly receptive and he knew what she had in store for him. Tiffani knew, however, not to wait on a response from Ralph too long, opting to spread before him on the desk. Close as his face was and as wholesome as Tiffani's furry furrow appeared, Ralph had little choice and even fewer options, when her hands quickly pulled him into her. For the first, four to five minutes, there was no reaction, but again, there was no resistance either. Tiffani did not want to embarrass Ralph by telling him what to do, when a position as such was self explanatory. Finally, there was a warm object slipping around and about on the surface of her furry furrow. She could tell Ralph was enjoying himself, because she was enjoying herself. For more than an hour, Tiffani felt these warm smooth delicate movements upon her, slashing at times with an occasional moan, here and there; sending her into a delirious state of mind, for this first time adventure.

Tiffani's body was sensationalized and bombarded with a series of orgasms, one after the other, after the other; revolutionary thrills were tearing inside her body, ripping up and down her spine, tightening her anus and widening her furry furrow, causing Tiffani to cry, from feeling so good. Then she began to scream as more burst and spurts streaked through; seemingly small cannonballs blasting the walls of her furry furrow where extreme heat syrupified the sweet abundance of fluids for Ralph's enjoyment pleasure. Tiffani cried and screamed as these continuous reactions occurred; never before had she felt so good.

Tiffani could feel Ralph flinch each time one of her cannonballs exploded; he was either too proud or too busy to make anything other than a gurgling sound as her hot streaming fire power rolled across his lips. Tiffani could also see a round puffiness within Ralph's jaws as each explosion occurred; each quickly disappearing with a corresponding gurgle and Ralph attempting vigorously to press even deeper into her wide-opened furry furrow. This exciting activity now had Tiffani fiercely crying and screaming, kicking her legs upward, but widening her thighs even further, careful not to interfere with Ralph's dividends, as more explosions occurred. Tiffani thought, "they both deserved everything they were getting at this moment; the time had been long in coming, but the wait was paying off. Suddenly Ralph's head disappeared from Tiffani's view, with her eyes closed, but she could still feel his presence as her hands were gripped even tighter against his cheeks, pulling him deeper and deeper into her flooding furry furrow.

Then seemingly Tiffani's cries and screams really took off. Cries and screams from the electrifying stings of Ralph's deeply penetrating-rotating tastetester inside her; cries and screams for solving her long frustrated dry spells; cries and screams for the sensational explosions bursting within her furry furrow continuously swelling Ralph's jaws before streaming onward; cries and screams for a first time terrific mind-body piercing she never ever wanted to end; cries and screams that pleaded with Ralph to never remove his tongue from her furry furrow. Tiffani thought, "I had heard, but never figured a tongue-twisting tantalization could produce such torrential liquidity, and watching Ralph is joyfully producing more and more. His tastetester is slashing upon, round and through my furry furrow with such smooth precision; his onslaught of me is masterful, just look at him slide that tongue to unimaginable spots, and look at his magnificent lip modulation, and what beautiful tongue-lip synchronization pulling my superfluous juices into his mouth. Oh my, he is devouring my furry furrow with a flurry of very powerful but gentle strokes—just look at those strokes—look at those strokes—look at those strokes—." Crying aloud, "oooooooe—look at—ooooooe—oooooe Ralph— Ralph..."

The explosions were diminishing but Tiffani's cries and screams grew louder as her legs slowly fell on each side of the desk creating a wider comfortable gap for Ralph to obtain the finest of her first multiple dividends, and hopefully in Tiffani's opinion, the first of many to come. Finally Tiffani's loud cries and screams ceased and she lay joyfully exhausted, hearing only pleasant swishing sounds of Ralph cleaning up the last of today's sweet lucrative dividends. Now only purrs and occasional climatic flinches came from Tiffani, but her palms were still clasped to Ralph's cheeks as he slowly and busily moved about her furry furrow. Tiffani thought, "I never want to ever let Ralph go." Those were her last thoughts before her arms gradually fell upon the desk and she commence snoring with the most pleasant smile upon her face.

And for the first time, Ralph did not run away; he had been too busy enjoying himself, but what more, he had received the corrective therapy he needed. He knew now, it would be only a matter of time before he completely recovered, saying silently, "Tiffani is definitely the answer for my impotency, I feel rejuvenated already. I am afraid to...."

CHAPTER FORTY SIX

NURSEMAID AND KEEPER

"Tiffani, I don't know whether you are aware of it, but you have been humming some tune all morning. Once I thought I recognized it, but you changed it, and then changed it again; sounds good, whatever it is. Probably one of those young people's songs, I suppose."

"Oh, I do not know about that Victor, no particular tune really; matter of fact I could not tell you what I was humming. All I can say is, it's a feeling inside of me."

"Like I said Tiffani, sounds good; so obviously this inside feeling is good, huh?"

"It is better than good Victor, let me tell you, I feel liberated——I mean, my body feels free of all obstructions. In other words, if there is anything higher than cloud nine, then that is what I am on right now."

"That sounds real good Tiffani, I hope it never ends."

"Me to Victor; if it does though, at least I know where I can get some more."

"Some of that kind of stuff, huh, Tiffani."

"Yeah Victor, that frigid man of mine is now sizzling; he had to have awakened every muscle and nerve in my body. For the first time in my life, I cried and screamed because of a joyful feeling.

In short, I never knew my body could vibrate all over, at the same time."

"Huh, sounds like the man is mean, Tiffani."

"Mean—would be something I could relate to Victor."

"This is the same frigid guy; what was his problem, Tiffani?"

"He is definitely the same guy Victor, and as to what his problem was, I do not know. Whenever I get the nerve, I am going to ask him, but definitely not now—I cannot take a chance on missing out on more good things for my body, and my pocket book. While I am talking Victor and please do not repeat this to anyone, but my man gave me fifty thousand dollars—for my action—I am a little reluctant to say because of the connotation, if you know what I mean."

"I understand Tiffani; highest total so far, but I suppose there have been other large amounts."

"Uh huh!"

"I see what you mean Tiffani, when you mentioned getting paid more than what you gave. Well, I hope you're not throwing the money away."

"There's not any problem with that whatsoever; matter of fact, he is investing it for me Victor."

"Uh huh—I see; well, it sounds to me like you're in good hands Tiffani."

"I hope so Victor. And for your information and my conscious, the feeling I have right now, has absolutely nothing to do with money. I would gladly give the money back to lie in his arms every night without feeling mystified."

"I know—I know, now that, I really understand Tiffani."

"Yeah, no doubt you would Victor, with that Carolyn around."

"Oh, speaking of Carolyn, I am so mad at that girl, but I should be mad at myself Tiffani."

"Now Victor, I would not go blaming myself for what Carolyn did to herself; you could not make her go to work."

"Yeah, I know Tiffani, but deep down, I feel, I gave up on helping Carolyn and started helping myself. I mean, it was so easy for me to take advantage of her body, when it was handed to me on a silver platter. It was convenient and selfish of me to do so; I started using Carolyn because I was not getting anything anywhere else."

"You are much too hard on yourself Victor; Carolyn started out using you, and in my opinion, is still using you. She deserves whatever she is getting. I just hope and pray that she realizes what's happening and put that alcohol aside."

"Easier said than done, sometimes, Tiffani. Anyway, I will be staying with Carolyn until she gets her act together. And this time, I will try and stay focused."

"Yeah, good luck in that department Victor."

Victor's time, as of lately had ceased to be that—all extra moments were spent with Carolyn, who now had lots of time for him and everything else for that matter.

"Victor, I cannot see why the company let me go; after all the hard work and dedicated service I gave them. Just like a damn company, to kick you when you're down. You would have thought my seven years of service meant something. Wouldn't you Victor—shouldn't that have counted for something?"

"Sure Carolyn, but what did you expect; you wouldn't even go to work. And when you went, you always left early."

"Victor, I do not think that is the point—I did my work when I was there. Anyway, I told them, I was going to start coming regular."

"Your promises ran out with them Carolyn—just look at all the times you promised me, you were going to quit drinking. They were more than fair with you—giving you a year's severance pay. And my guess is, you are probably still drinking. To be honest with you, my patience is wearing a little thin. You're suppose to be my friend Carolyn, but you're taking advantage of my sympathy. You're not the first person to lose someone. I'm getting fed up with you acting like an immature overgrown child."

"Well, I am not drinking now Victor, and I have not had a drink this week."

"Yeah, I know Carolyn, but that's because I'm here—I can't stay with you every week."

"I asked you to come over Victor, because I thought you were my friend, and I thought you understood. Anyway, it was you who volunteered for the long term assignment—nobody needs you hanging around all week; you are in my way. It's funny, I never hear you complaining Victor, when we are making love. I do not hear one mumbling word when you're screwing and having a good time. Now, at the end of the week when you're all screwed down, you voice your petty dissatisfaction. I might be turning into an alcoholic, but you're already a gynecomaniac. I have an excuse for being like I am, but you—you Victor, is just a greedy bastard. All the time, you pretend to be helping me and you are satisfying your own ego and sexual appetite."

"Sexually, I am the best thing that ever happened to you and I know it Victor. I am your nursemaid and keeper, and without me, you would have starved to death. That other pussy you are getting is a mere facsimile of what I have to offer. You know it's true, or you would not be sniffing around me for weeks at a time. And it's not that I do not enjoy it Victor, because you are great; but I do not want you to keep fooling yourself, as to why you are here. I do not mean to criticize you Victor, because I love everything about you; but you just rubbed me the wrong way." And she began to cry.

"Oh, that's okay Carolyn, I didn't mean to upset you.

Part of what Carolyn had said was the truth. It was something about the sister's body that turned Victor on. Her tall brown statue had a mesmerizing effect upon him. And sexually, Victor is starving, because Angela and Helen never want to do anything. Having those babies really brought about a sudden change in their fulfilling his desires. They are consumed with their careers by day and the children by night. Plus, Helen has been sickly as of late; so Victor's status is not bound to change anytime soon.

"But, you are right Victor, I have to get my life together. I am sinking further and further into a dismal state. It's not that I am not trying to lay off booze, because I am; but my mind keeps drifting back to things I did wrong. Sharonda would be alive today if I had not given in to her so easily. Victor, it's like something's haunting me, and the only outlet is alcohol. I cannot seem to cope any other way. When you are here I am okay, but that's because you are occupying my mind, not because it went away. Your presence has prevented the annihilation of countless bottles of liquor. I keep telling myself I can shake it, but my resistance is not strong enough. It's not that I am craving alcohol, but besides you Victor, it is the only thing that makes me forget my troubles."

"Something is going to have to give though; because my other daughter is begging me to come home. I have made her stay with her father since the ordeal. It worked out fine at first; he was terribly upset and wanted her company, and I just needed to be alone. Now she wants to return and resume her former life. I am afraid if I keep putting her off, our relationship could become strained. Victor, I could not afford to lose her precious love. But I cannot risk letting her see me in one of my drunken spells either."

"And now, Victor, I am afraid because of all the idle time on hand. Every moment I sit alone lures my mouth to a guzzling status."

"Getting another job would help temporarily but you'd only get fired once your drinking habits become known, Carolyn. Before reentering the labor force, you'll have to come to grips with yourself."

"Victor, I have tried so hard and it is no use; I can only hold out an hour or so when I know you are not going to be here. It's as if my non-drinking is directly related to your presence Victor."

Carolyn's days as a dipsomaniac were fast approaching. She talked sensibly, all to no avail. One problem of feeling guilty, had now led to a bigger problem; with many more on the way unless the stream of booze had a sudden drought.

CHAPTER FORTY SEVEN

ABOLITION OF THE CORPORATION

The leveraged buyout of the corporation was successful. Ms. Lincoln was named, Chairman of the Board. So all her business knowledge and new college degree would be utilized. Her first task was to see that Mr. Richard and Sarah Cooper had jobs with the company. It was this poor family, in that little house in Waco, which had taught her to be humble. It was this family and that prayer, which taught her, health was far more important than wealth. And it was through their daughter—Molly, where Ms. Lincoln had learned not to be selfish. It was the helping of Molly, who at this time was continuing her education, that had put a new meaning in her life. Ms. Lincoln had learned so much from them, she thought, and would always be in their debt.

These experiences put more joy and happiness in her life than all the millions from J.B. Tankerstroke. It wasn't that the wealth did not count, because it did. It bought her all the luxuries she wanted; but was never necessary for the joy and happiness she needed. Ms. Lincoln's next task was to set up a scholarship program to benefit employees and their family. The program was also extended to needy children within the corporate community. Ms. Lincoln sat on the board and exercised her "uh huh's" to perfection, as Victor ran the show.

Victor was the President and Chief Executive Officer, who had paid his dues with his former company. They hated to lose an officer of his caliber; but wished him well in his new company. They felt with his financial and leadership ability, his company would be successfully led into the twenty first century. This was a life long dream fulfilled for Victor, who was not only ready for the challenge but prepared for it.

Crashing the glass ceiling had never been a problem with Victor; because of the fairness in his former company, but he was well aware of the problems involved. He promised himself, he would bring that same fairness to his new corporation. Of course the bottom line for Victor was increased profitability for the company. His fiscal conservative views only meant one thing; and that was cutting overhead to help achieve those goals. However, Angela was far ahead of him in that category; though for a different reason.

Angela's first task was to dismiss her former boss, Trebor and Mr. Turley. She fired them because in her opinion; there was no room in the corporation for Ancestral Racism and the Trebor's and Turley's of the world. Her next task was the creation of a corporate affirmative action program. It's ironic, she had to implement her hard fought efforts on her own company; but it still gave her a thrill. Angela was able to use parts of the "would be statements." Especially the part about releasing anyone immediately who chose not to follow the affirmative action guidelines. She met with the managers and supervisors to make sure there was no mis-understanding.

Angela also addressed maternity rights to these managers; and, further stressed, there would be no bias among women pertaining to assignments or wages. She established a hotline to her office to report any ills caused by male chauvinistic bosses. Angela was serious and determined, there would be no sex discrimination among the female employees. She was also determined, there would be no race discrimination in the corporation. The affirmative action officer reported directly to Angela. And though, Angela was an integral part of the corporation, it was no surprise when she announced:

"Victor, I have been putting off doing some things that are

important to me."

"What's that Angela?"

"A school—a private school."

"I can see the need Angela, but what's the importance?"

"Well, take my case for example. I went to the finest schools in the Country; learned what I was suppose to learn, academic wise, that is; but I was not prepared to deal with the racial ills of society. Because in sixteen years of schooling, I was virtually sheltered or misled. If it had not been for you Victor, I would still be lost, so to speak, and still having problems coping. You taught me the need for cultural awareness and knowing about our Black heritage, and I want to pass that on. Before, I never knew of Black literature, and now, I realize its importance to today's Black youth. Many of them are lost like I was."

"We need all the help we can get to overcome Angela."

"We must overcome Victor. We as a race must overcome the obstacle of being Black. Too many times we feel or use the statement, "if I was white this would not happen to me or I would be in a better position." That is a barrier that stands in our way to the path of success. The first step of breaking out of that barrier is to admit who you are, and your race. The next step, done simultaneously, if you will, is to become proud of who you are and proud of your Black race. To do this and the only way to do this is to study our Black heritage."

"It really helped me Angela; what is your suggestion to others, if any?"

"I say, study the history of Black people prior to slavery; during slavery; and after slavery Victor. Read about the struggles and how we as a people survived and made it through. Then study specific cases of Black people who went on to achieve greatness. Greatness, might just mean graduating from high school or learning to read, because of the adversity. Also look at cases where Blacks went from a small somebody and out of obscurity to a big somebody; straight to the top of a particular profession,

"What then Angela?"

"Then we began to feel proud of us and yourself as a people. We will see at that time, where we have achieved and are still achieving against the odds; against all the racism and bigotry;

against all the unequal and unfair treatment; against all the injustices. When the Black youth know the truth of our heritage, they will realize—if countless others did it—they can do it. The artificial barrier will be broken down, and each Black youth and African-American can achieve the greatness, you and I know, they are capable of."

"And you feel Angela, a private school would assist in that regard huh?"

"It's a start Victor, my school would not only prepare and give the child a superior education, but would prepare them for the greatest social ill of America—Racism. The white man is not only talking about a color blind society, but doing so by eliminating college minority scholarships and affirmative action in the work place. Those types of actions serve to put Blacks further behind, so we must be prepared to overcome."

"It certainly isn't getting any easier Angela."

"You are so right, when progress for Blacks should be getting easier Victor, it is actually getting harder. Students of today and tomorrow must be prepared to deal with that type of hidden double standard. In other words, Victor, you are qualified for the job, but never get it. Or you get the job and be constantly passed over for promotions."

"There has been a lot of talk here lately on color blind Angela, what are your thoughts on that?"

"In a true color blind society Victor, we would get the job without problems and move on without problems. Or should I say without the racist problems that are stopping us today. And to think on it Victor, I would be the first to admit, my color has sheltered me somewhat."

"You might have been sheltered also Angela, because of your wealthy status."

"And that is part of the problem too, Victor. We have too many Blacks—middle class so to speak—who believe they have escaped racism because of the chump-change in their pockets. Whereas if the truth be told, the racism that exist has nothing to do with money permanently sheltering you. It always eventually goes back to one's race, and sooner or later, believe me, it will catch up with you. We snub each other and look down on our less fortunate brothers and sisters. Then reality sets in, and you both find your-self in the streets together; neither of you with a job, the educated and the uneducated."

"I believe you have the patience Angela for such a task, but what about the stamina?"

"I am tested tough, Victor, and believe that I must do it. Our company cannot hire all the qualified Black applicants; so they will need to know how to cope. The new day is upon us Victor. The question now becomes; are we going to continue the status quo or will we map out a new destiny into the twenty first century. The choice is ours. My father, John Baron Tankerstroke, did not want me to let him down. He sacrificed his happiness for his mother who knew of troubles of the world His mother, Matilda, sacrificed her dignity; while others sacrificed their lives. None of those sacrifices were easy, nor were they cheap. An unfair price to pay, I would say. However, the struggle, unfortunately contin-ues."

Darryl was now head of the advertising and publication depart-ment. He is in a far better mood now than his last article, prior to abolition of the corporation. His poem had expressed all of their sentiments.

MY COUNTRY TOO

Born in Chicago, Po parents I know
Still don't really, have nuthin to show
Makin low wages, struglin every day
It's My Country, I'm not goin away

I'm from Detroit things bout the same
Gotta job, gotta car, token political gain
In labor union, sweatin for what's right
Leave America sister; not without a fight

Big Apple, yes New York is my home
Understand yo problem, you're not alone
Wall Street, Manhattan trying to keep us out
We're gonna hang, and there is no doubt

Took over the Mayor's job; pressin for more
No mo rear; name now on the front door
Makin this place go; Cultural Center USA
Apollo's ours, we're not goin away

Inherited my home, from my Dallas family
Still denied our rights, each side of Trinity
High unemployment, high crime, all bad news
Can't leave though, got too much to lose

Started slow, but comin on fast
Here for the duration, can't forget the past
Sinned against yesterday, lied to today
Don't worry cuz, Houston will make a way

What about Boston, some say its okay
Not law school, our women Prof. still astray
Travelin to Martha's Vineyard, eatin hearty
Be right for sure, or another Tea Party

Looks better outside, than from within
Atlanta is no different, than next of kin
We're further along, than most of the rest
Each passin day, the man put us to the test

Washington DC; forefather laid out this town
No sense talkin leavin, we'll be around
Turnin back, Nah, that's no good
Watch closely, follow us into Statehood

Tried to be first, with Governor from LA
Congratulations Virginia, you're on your way
Things are hard, still lookin for the gold
We'll find it, or so I've been told

Brotherly love, is what we're cracked to be
Listen! As the bell ring expressin LIBERTY
This is my city; beautiful Philadelphia
And this is my Country: Good ole AMERICA

Fought in the Civil War, and World War I
World War II, Korea, also Vietnam
We're entrenched now, Ain't goin nowhere
We'll fight next warfare, for Soul Welfare

Racism, injustice, discrimination all around
Each community, city, state; yes every town
Tell me, why don't white folks, leave us be
We're in America to stay, FIGHTIN til free

This was a joyous occasion for the employees, who could now expect and receive fair treatment in the work place. It was doubly joyous for those who elected to get a piece of the rock. Everyone was happy, if for no other reason; all received a personal bonus from Ms. Lincoln, who was in an "uh huh" good mood these days.

And of course, the other two new faces at the corporation were none other than Tiffani Tafeel and Ralph Krendec, as its Treasurer. Tiffani had redecorated the bathroom in the king's colors, she promised Victor, and was currently musing herself over all the latest changes. Settling down with a morning's cup of coffee, she also wondered as she sipped, what all, Ralph and Victor were talking about in their closed door meeting.

"Now that we have concluded the business portion of our meeting Ralph, there is someone dear to my heart, we need to discuss; that is Tiffani."

"Sure Victor; well, I have been seeing Tiffani; I assumed she would probably tell you."

"No, she told me nothing. I mean, no names, just bits and pieces of some modeling and finance. She definitely would not give me a name, preferring secrecy, nor did I press her for one. But curiosity got the best of me and I figured it out; the key on top of everything else was when she said her man was investing for her. And for your information, Tiffani does not know of my discovery. If you don't mind Ralph, what is the story?"

"Well Victor, you already know of my impotency problem, and believe me man, it has been a real struggle since my operation. The only therapy that seems to be working, I accidentally discovered, was being in the presence of Tiffani. At first I would come by, and have her go through these stripping antics for me, so I could get up for my wife; but after much success with Tiffani, by the time I arrived home, the feeling and everything else was gone. Well you know Victor from your relationship with our friend Carolyn, that a woman must have good sex from her partner to be happy. My wife was no different, and after a while of performances or no performances, she simply walked out on me; and I am not bitter; I can understand. Tiffani, no doubt, told you of her frustrations of her man leaving at the height of a moment for pleasure; well, that was me getting ready and running home, hopefully to satisfy my wife, and obviously as I just mentioned, it did not work. Then after my wife left, I finally succumbed to Tiffani's advances, and you know the rest; she is happy."

"I know the rest Ralph, but Tiffani does not; she does not know of your being alone, nor does she know, why you pulled all of those frigid runaway shenanigans. My point Ralph, Tiffani is my heart and she deserves to know."

"I have wanted to tell her Victor, but is afraid when she found out about my impotency problem, she too will leave me; Tiffani is really good for me Victor."

"I understand Ralph; believe me, I understand."

Ralph and Victor were laughing and chatting tidbits when the door opened for Ralph's departure. Tiffani looked puzzled when Ralph asked her in a loud cheerful voice:

"Tiffani, how about lunch today?"

She glanced at Victor, as if to ask for an approval, giving a simultaneously smiling answer.

"Yes Ralph, I would love that very much; that would be wonderful."

The joy in Tiffani's facial expression had even made a similar countenance on Victor's face as he refilled his large coffee cup.

"I will return for you at noon Tiffani....see ya Victor!"

CHAPTER FORTY EIGHT

APPEAL TO GOD

"Victor, you know I have been feeling bad lately. The doctors confirmed my worst fears today—I tested positive for AIDS. We confirmed it happened during some of my research. You will have to get an examination and (crying furiously) you will have to have Angela and Carolyn get an examination." Helen was now crying uncontrollably. "I'm sorry, I'm sorry, I'm sorry, I'm sorry."

Helen must have said that a hundred times. Victor held her in his arms and they both cried. It was all they could do at the moment. They cried themselves to sleep. The next day Victor got an examination. An exercise that was so meaningless to him.

It was the first time ever that life did not mean anything to Victor. If Helen died, he wanted to die. Victor had so much to live for; to raise their two sons, Gree and Harre, who were so very young. But none of that seemed to matter. Helen had forced herself into his life, captured his heart, and now it was shattered. He was beginning to feel cheated. Cheated out of happiness and the smiles that accompany it. Cheated out of life. How could he go on.

APPEAL TO GOD

My appeal to God; lift my suffering
Take me out of this misery
My body, my soul, I'm offering
Spare Helen, my love so tenderly

Oh Master, please, take me instead
No more tomorrow's can I stand
My only dream is that I'm dead
With thee I go, please take my hand

You heard us cry, I now cry out
No more tears, have I to shed
Please Master, oh hear my shout
Take ne now, I'm not afraid

I care nothing else for tomorrow
It was always a dream away
So much gloom, so much sorrow
To look forward, to such decay

Today will be my only thought
Tomorrow's blessing may not come
Looking ahead, I will not get caught
Must linger, until today is done

Hear my appeal, take me along
If that is, your will to be
I'm weak, I'm no more strong
Please Master, please take me

I haven't strength, or the will
On earth, I be no more good
Please Master, Oh hear my appeal
Take me! Isn't that understood?

The President of the United States heard of Helen's misfortune and called her to Washington. She received a plaque which read: "To Dr. Helen Tafeel, A Champion of Humanities. Awarded to you for tireless and relentless service of a personal battle against a deadly enemy—AIDS." The President promised to continue her fight until the foe had been conquered.

Victor, Helen and Carolyn listened and only hoped he was telling the truth, rather than just saying, the right thing at the right time. Victor prayed that a cure was now. Too many times, he thought, has Helen given every moments rest to conquer this epidemic. Why, of all people, could she be asked to leave before the mission was over; before the war was done. Helen had waged many battles though, and won them all. The battles of caring and devotion to all those near her path; the battles of dedication to her profession. She had to be weary from the battles she fought, but it never showed. Even now, that bubbly smile was warming the hearts of those who looked on.

Carolyn, who had insisted upon coming, and Victor accompanied Helen on the trip. On the plane to Washington D.C., they did not say very much—just sort of smiled and held each other's hand. Victor sensed Helen was not feeling that well, but she never complained. However on the way back, Helen talked up a storm. She was the happiest that Victor had ever seen any person. She went on and on about how she was a celebrity and all. And indeed she was.

Upon their arrival home, Angela met them at the airport with the kids; to include Gree and Harre whom she had gotten from Stacy. That was good to see, because Angela had given Victor hell for not knowing about Helen. She had also given Helen hell from time to time, or every chance she got, would be more descriptive. So this must have been her way of saying to Helen; I forgive you, and to please forgive me. A gesture so eloquently spoken.

Everyone else had been given a clean bill of health, but Victor had lost twenty pounds due to worrying and not eating. Samantha was worried about Victor and called to express her concerns.

"Samantha, I'm doing okay and so is Helen—she has one last request; and that is to be Mrs. Helen Previtt. So we are going to be married at her bedside. You don't have to come; Carolyn and

Stacy will be here."

The wedding was lovely. Helen was weak, but she was strong in repeating her vows. She was so happy and the most beautiful bride ever.

Helen lived only a short time after that. She felt that she had accomplished something in life. She said, "I truly believe I have helped somebody." Helen's last words to Victor before she died were—I love you. Victor thought about his friend Joseph saying to himself: "They both died as they lived; but for Helen, it just did not seem fair. Life dealt her a losing hand, but she rose above it all and became a winner. There was only one way her epitaph could read—A CHAMPION...I gave it all I had."

Helen never told Victor to take care of the boys. It's apparent, there was no doubt in her mind, they would be all right.

Victor received tons of support during the funeral; Angela and Carolyn both walked with him. Stacy openly wept as she clung to the bracelet given her by Helen. Tiffani and Ralph, holding hands and looking very much in love. Everyone imaginable was there; most noticeable was Mrs. Edna Garley, Samantha, and Ms. Ehtyl Harre. Ms. Harre had a lot on her chest as she reminisced about Helen and how, she and her sister Hazel Gree came to rear her:

"We were asked to take Helen by Mrs. Hayes, a State Human Resource worker who attended our church. Mrs. Hayes must have known we could turn the child around. We took one look at the innocent little girl with that selfish look and said we'll take her. Those roving brown eyes just spelled trouble. She was so skinny and to be honest—a pitiful sight for sore eyes. But I saw something in the ugly little monster and Hazel thought she was so cute."

"I had raised five daughters and knew a mischievous look among girls when I saw one. Hazel had reared a son and saw this as an opportunity to have that daughter she always wanted. Mrs. Hayes explained to us that Helen had no known parents and had been in orphan or foster homes all of her ten years. They tried to get her adopted early, but she was either passed on because, she was too skinny or too dark."

"Mrs. Hayes said: As she grew older, she developed a bad attitude moving from orphan homes to foster homes and back. Helen became a problem child, either causing havoc with other children, foster parents or both. She is very intelligent and has no learning disabilities; but age has just caught up with her. It's no telling what she has been through in her short youthful life; so you'll have to take it easy on her, explained Mrs. Hayes."

"I could see right away, that one of her problems was—no discipline or a lack of respect for discipline. Of course the other problem was equally pronounced; the way Helen cuddled up to Hazel, the child needed love desperately. It was like they had known each other all of their lives. A match made for heaven, one could say. I applied all the discipline and Hazel applied only her love. For Hazel the child could do no wrong. As a result, Hazel saved her from some very good whippings."

"Helen knew I loved her, but she knew how far to go with me, in terms of doing things she had no business. We treated her like our own. One day, several months after Helen arrived; she crossed me by not washing the dishes as instructed; and Hazel was not there to rescue her. I think I whipped her for some of the other things, she had gotten away with. It was a whipping Helen would never forget. One of those old fashioned whippings like my mother use to give me. The difference was the usage of a belt instead of the switches that welted my back."

"It was also a whipping I'd never forget, because Helen ran away. Hazel had come home and no Helen to meet her. Helen always met her with hugs and kisses like a sweet little girl and critiqued Hazel's brain of the day's happenings, like a nosey old lady. They both discussed what all had gone on in their lives that day. Hazel looked forward to the evening gossip sessions. So when Helen didn't show up, upon her arrival, Hazel knew something was wrong."

"I told Hazel, I gave her a pretty good thrashing today, she's probably in her room. Hazel took a look, but there was no Helen to be found. So we naturally thought she was down the street with her girl friend; but this disturbed us because Helen never left home without permission. We looked all over the neighborhood and no Helen was anywhere to be found. Then we began to get worried, so we called the police. We gave them a description of Helen and what she had on."

"If she shows up, please give us a call, a police officer said as they left. It neared ten p.m. and still no Helen. We were both worried sick. Now Hazel was getting mad at me for whipping Helen, and I was feeling guilty for whipping her so hard. That only made matters worse as we continued to feel bad. At eleven twenty p.m. the phone rang. We both rushed and picked up an extension; "This is Captain Gooden; have you heard anything?" We both started crying in the Captain's ear. He tried to assure us that everything would be all right. We'll find her, now just don't you worry, he said."

"That was all right for him to say. Where could a small child be this time of night. We thought all kinds of things and cried some more. We couldn't console each other. We were feeling real saddened, thinking the worse. If ever there was a time for prayer, it was now; and we did a lots of that. We asked God to return our child to us safe and sound. About two a.m., the phone rang again; "Hello, this is Captain Gooden,"—we were fearful of saying anything— "is anybody there," he said! Er—yes, one of us managed. Then he said; "We found the child, we're bringing her home."

"I've never experienced relief like that in all my born days. Our prayers had been answered. To cut a longer story short, Helen had been found asleep on a bench at the bus station; some twenty five blocks away. I don't have to tell you, but that was the happiest day of our lives. Hazel and I were sixty one and fifty respectively, and we didn't need scares like this."

"The child was a real comfort to us. I never whipped Helen again. She saw how she had hurt us and promised to do her chores and never run away again. And for the most part, she was pretty good. She didn't know it, but she was going to have to do something pretty drastic before getting another lashing like the other one. I think we both had learned our lesson."

"Helen was no longer the skinny little girl with short nappy hair. She was eating like she had been starved. Hazel and I just looked at each other and smiled as she ate. I told Hazel the child loves my food, but Hazel says, the child is just hungry. It was a combination of both, because I've been told by people around and about that I was just about the best cook in these parts. Of course, I knew that cause I didn't raise no po chilluns. Anyway, Helen was healthy looking and that dimple in her left cheek, made her the most beautiful thing you'd ever laid eyes on."

"We were in love with that girl. She was our heart. We thought several times about trying to adopt her; but decided to leave well enough alone. We felt that at our ages, we would be turned down. You know, one of those bureaucracy cases, where you're okay to be used as foster parents, but not good enough as real parents. Anyway, Helen was an integral part of our household. She was happy and we were happy, and that's all that really mattered."

"As the years sailed by, and it seems like only yesterday; we tried to instill in Helen the values our parents endowed us with. You know, that good stuff like, respect and love yourself and your fellowman; Do unto others as you would have them do unto you; Standing up for what you believe in and demanding what you really want. She caught on pretty good; because at times, she'd use all of that to manipulate it in her behalf. It's like she was testing you to see if you practiced what you preached."

"Oh, I could go on and on about that gal and it would all be good. She was the valedictorian of her high school class; and we were there to hear her important speech. We had heard it a hundred times before as she had used us for her audience. But before the speech that day, in a surprising move, Helen had us stand. Helen said, this is my mama and papa, two sisters who cared enough to care; two sisters who prevented an orphan from falling through the cracks of society; two sisters who gave me love when needed and discipline when warranted; two sisters who made the difference; two sisters—my mama—my papa—my family—I love you."

"At that point the house was a thundering uproar, as they gave Helen a long standing ovation.I can still hear that clapping; it seemed like it would last forever; and needless to say, Hazel and I were crying. We had raised our own children and believe me, it was a job. For Helen, it was also a job, but it was something we enjoyed doing. She wasn't perfect, but she was pretty close to the mold we shaped."

"We were also there when she graduated from college. Helen graduated with honors, but thanks heaven for no speeches. It was no surprise when Helen chose nursing as a career. Both Hazel and

I had had our health problems and she was concerned, but it went deeper. Helen wanted to help other people and see immediate results. We were so proud of that child. It's a real tribute to us for her to have named those two boys after us, Gree and Harre. My only regret is that Hazel is not here to see them growing strong and handsome."

"Victor, you appear to be a fine young man, and I'm counting on you to take real good care of the boys. I'll miss Helen and what's more, I'll miss those yearly mother's and father's day cards. Helen was more than a child to me, she was Special."

Tears filled the wrinkles of Ethyl's ageless lined face; a face that resembled waves in a stormy sea; terrorizing a drenched handkerchief that set sail, but unable to calm the tidal assault.

CHAPTER FORTY NINE

DAYS TO COME

Samantha was so kind and warm during Victor's ordeal. Her support should not go unnoticed.She volunteered a plot for Helen in her family cemetery.

"Victor, my life will never be the same because of Helen. I plan on expanding my work to help Black orphans find loving families. My life is now complete; I no longer have that void feeling. Helen has also inspired Stacy to go to college. She is going to enroll this fall at my alma mater. Helen succeeded where we both failed."

And Carolyn had finally gotten herself together. These days she was hardly drinking water, and heavens forbid, no alcohol.

"Victor, I want you to be the first to know I'm leaving town. I have accepted a position in the Nations Capital, with a law firm founded by a former classmate. We have talked about it for some-time. Now with my daughter graduating from high school, the timing is just right."

"She wants to attend Howard University, so everything is work-ing out fine. I'll be near my parents and we need to work that situation out. I won't be back!"

"Why is that Carolyn?"

"Life is too short Victor, and too precious. I am not getting any younger and realize there is more to life than looking out for number one. I have valuable skills that can be put to work helping others as well as making a living. I have managed my earnings well as a corporate attorney, so money or security is no longer a factor. I am really looking forward to the move."

"I have already volunteered my services, to work on a committee to help Washington, D.C. obtain its Statehood. This is one of the most important issues facing our people, as we head into the twenty first century. Taxation without representation can no longer be tolerated. We must fight for that as well as all the other inequities oppressing us. Victor, the racial injustices of the day are too great for one to sit idly by and do nothing. Yet they are unsurmountable for one person to conquer. But each of us can make an impact if we fight racism where we find it."

"Well Carolyn, if it doesn't work out, you can return and work in our corporation. We could use a sharp legal mind like yours."

"Thanks, Victor, I will keep that in mind. But, do me a favor; save the job for my daughter; she is following in my footsteps. I am so proud of her."

"That's a deal Carolyn. I'll do one better; send her down each summer, so she can get a feel of the corporate world."

"Victor, you are wonderful."

"It makes a difference when you can call the shots Carolyn."

"Yeah, the only shots we called before were on my office sofa, Victor." (both smiling)

"If I can remember, those were not too bad, Carolyn."

"Man I'd say."

"Times have changed somewhat Victor, but the progress is much too slow. If Blacks just learn to help each other more; we would make faster progress."

"That's true Carolyn. Do you think the younger generation will be as strong, Carolyn?"

"That is a good question Victor; a lot of it is going to depend upon our teaching and preaching as parents. It could be tougher for them, because covert racism is getting worse. But if they learn to stick together, they will make it."

"I like the way you clarify things with IF, Carolyn. It does not sound too positive, does it."

"Oh, I don't know, Victor."

"Maybe, we'll get a drastic attitudinal change in white America during the twenty first century, Carolyn."

"It would not do any good Victor, because their heart is on the wrong side. And the two must work together. We cannot count on none of that happening Victor. Blacks are going to have to do for themselves. Because, when you are looking for handouts, you will get crumbs every time. We experience that now on a daily basis."

"For a lighter subject, Carolyn; what are you going to do about wearing those fine clothes?"

"I thought you would never ask Victor. Gerald is opening a shop in D.C. later this year. He proposed, and I said maybe."

"The ole maybe with a yes hum in it, I suppose, Carolyn."

"Well, I am not getting any younger. And if there is anybody that knows my body better than you, it's Gerald; although we are definitely talking about different things. I have never been happier Victor. I am also excited about opening the shop; so some of your entrepreneurial spirit is rubbing off on me. By the way I have already secured Angela, Tiffani and Samantha as exclusive customers."

"So many things have happened to me Victor since I have been here. Most of them have been good and all have been inspirational. You were good for me and to me Victor, when I needed it the most. A shoulder to cry on and a voice to tell me what I most wanted to hear during difficult times. Angela has inspired me to have the fortitude and tenacity to never give up—just hang tough and keep going. Never leave her Victor; please marry Angela; she not only needs you but she loves you."

"And Helen, may God bless Helen, she inspired me to conquer the World." Carolyn now had tears in her eyes. "Helen was my greatest friend. A piece of me will always remain in this city because of Sharonda and Helen; and a piece of you Victor, will always remain in my heart. Take care of yourself and take care of Angela and the kids."

As Victor watched the plane disappear into the clouds; he knew he had loved Carolyn for the last time but had made a friend forever.

FATE

Fate, Oh Fate
Endeared us all
Fate, Oh Fate
...way life fall

Fate, Oh Fate
Cut no deal
Fate, Oh Fate
Was God's will

CONCLUSION

"Victor, she was a special lady, I hope I can measure up."

"You already have Angela, in your own way. Helen served a need of the World. Just one in a million. Everyone she touched, she made them better; they became stronger."

Tonight, nestled upstairs in the Queen's suite of the mansion, Angela and Victor lay peacefully within the serene setting, over-looking Uncle Lonzo's tulip beds. Victor's head was lodged firmly between Angela's widely sprawled thighs as deeply and snugly fitted as a wedge into a mighty pine prior to "TIMBER" being yelled. And at the rate Victor was doing his job, with his smoldering tastetester, it would not be long before Angela too yelled "TIMBER". Victor sank his long moisturized tongue far into Angela's curly cavern touching all sides with smooth circular movements, gliding his large broad lips over her tender curly cavern as extremely warm juices commenced to flood into his mouth. This seemed like a new beginning, Victor thought, as the delicious outpouring of liquid was by far the sweetest he had ever tasted. Angela no longer needed to make Victor obey, but she held her palms upon his head maneuvering Victor slowly about her curly cavern anyway, until his tongue slide onto her clit, gently massaging it in a sensational titillating motion. Victor's slow-tongued-mouthwatering-revolutions upon this excitable swollen glowing-red sugar enriched object was extraordinarily mind boggling to Angela, sending nerve-stinging thrills throughout her excessively-overheated body. The gorgeous engorged clit manipulative adventure took its toll, enticing Victor's simultaneous tongue lashing, on around and through Angela's curly cavern.

This too seemed like a new beginning to Angela, (the beginning of the end no doubt) as she locked her powerful thighs around Victor's cheeks. Angela knew this obviously was her day for conquering all dreams and dreamers as their fiery entanglement escalated to her highest peak ever, and her screams began. Angela screamed for all the trials and tribulations along the way; she screamed for Victor and the expanded family; she screamed for joy as the abundant jubilant sweet juices flowed from her into Victor for his delight and enjoyment pleasure, to his total satisfaction, as he himself murmured between swallows: "I love you so much Angela, you are so sweet."

Angela was one woman who would fight for Victor and victory to the death. Not that life would ever oblige her with that decision; so she fought it her way. Victor felt comfortable with Angela in his corner. Life throws so many obstacles our way, that the path sometimes becomes rough and treacherous. If we have that extra something, we can tough it out and ride the waves to victory. Angela did.

ROBIN SINGS

Oh what a beautiful lullaby
...only a hungry robin could know
Grasshopper escapes not her eye
Hopping on the foliage below

Robin watches, waits and sing
Routine; yet efficient as a drill
Grasshopper; having fun of a king
Not knowing, he's her next meal

Robin sings, high in the tree
Patiently: Oh what a view
Grasshopper heard final melody
Off to her nest, they both flew

THE END